The sign ab[...] Team, USA. [...] ones he was down here to meet?

The driver pushed a handle forward and the door opened with a hydraulic swish.

"You guys got a few minutes? I gotta do a story on you."

A moment of awkward silence came and went. Finally the "coach" beckoned the reporter aboard.

He happily climbed up the steps. He saw two dozen dark eyes staring back at him. It was nearly pitch-black aboard the bus. This was not a typical Greyhound. There were actually two compartments onboard.

*Strange,* he thought.

"We got a real scoop for you," the coach said. "Some very interesting stuff."

Tired and clueless, the reporter cued up his photophone and walked toward the rear of the bus. One of the players opened the padlock and pushed the door ajar.

The walls were lined with . . . weapons, including some kind of missiles.

The reporter could only utter one word: "Wow!" The pistol was against the back of his head a second later. The trigger was pulled twice.

He was dead before he hit the floor.

"**Mack Maloney has created a team of realistic characters that pulse with patriotic fervor…Maloney hasn't just crafted a great war story, he has set a new standard for action-packed thrillers.**"

—Robert Doherty, bestselling author of the *AREA 51* series

# SUPERHAWKS

★ ★ ★

## STRIKE FORCE CHARLIE

**Mack Maloney**

St. Martin's Paperbacks

SUPERHAWKS: STRIKE FORCE CHARLIE

Copyright © 2004 by Mack Maloney.

ISBN: 0-312-98607-6
EAN: 80312-98607-0

Printed in the United States of America

St. Martin's Paperbacks edition / December 2004

St. Martin's Paperbacks are published by St. Martin's Press, 175 Fifth Avenue, New York, NY 10010.

10 9 8 7 6 5 4 3 2 1

*For Pat Tillman*
*True American Hero*

# SUPERHAWKS

★ ★ ★

## STRIKE FORCE CHARLIE

# PART ONE
## The Seven Dead Khamenis

# Chapter 1

### Somewhere in the Pacific

Diego Suarez had been lost at sea for three days.

He had little memory of his fishing boat sinking. One moment the ocean was calm; the next, a strange darkness had enveloped everything. The huge wave had come out of nowhere, blotting out the sky. He'd been belowdecks when it happened, making himself a cup of coffee. The *tsunami* hit with such ferocity, the trawler disintegrated around him. Pieces of wood, pieces of metal and glass, pieces of fish from their recent catch, flying in all directions. Then came the mighty crash of water. And then, nothing. . . .

When Diego woke up, the sun was reflecting off the ocean so brilliantly, it hurt his eyes. He was sure he'd died and gone to heaven. No one could have survived that catastrophe. But then he thought, *People do not feel pain in heaven.*

That's when he realized he was still alive.

But how? He'd been washed overboard when the wave hit. In the confusion that followed, he'd somehow climbed on top of a large wooden box. It looked like nothing less than a water logged coffin. He'd hung on to it so tightly that even when he was unconscious his fingernails dug deep into the soft pine. Where had the strange box come from? He had no idea. Certainly nothing like it had been aboard his cramped fishing boat. But it didn't matter. *He was alive. . . .*

But he was also alone. The rest of the crew was long gone; he could see no wreckage from the boat. And because these fishing grounds were so far off the charts, he was nowhere near any shipping lanes, big or small. Diego knew the only soul he would meet out here would be just as lost as he.

Three days passed. The sun was brutal and the nights cold. His hunger and thirst grew mightily. But then, at the end of the third day, salvation! It came just as the sun was setting. Off in the distance Diego spotted not one ship but two. Both gleaming in the fading light. Both stopped dead in the water.

One ship was a freighter, old and rusty. Two very strange items were lashed to its deck: a pair of large vehicles, gray, silver, and white, partially hidden under tarpaulins. They weren't trucks. They were a bit too sleek for that. Both had lots of windows and chrome.

They were buses. *Greyhound* buses. Diego knew this because as a boy he'd journeyed from his hometown in Mexico to Los Angeles and his fondest memory of the trip was riding on the bright shiny Greyhound bus. But why did this ship have two of them on its deck? In the middle of the Pacific?

Even stranger was the vessel tied up next to the freighter. It had huge fins, a stout conning tower, and antennae bristling all over. It was not a surface ship at all. It was a submarine, riding not unlike a huge black whale just above the waves.

Diego began paddling madly, laughing and crying at the same time. He could see sailors in smart black uniforms on the submarine lifting boxes up to people on the freighter's deck. They were working very quickly. Diego could even hear shouting from one vessel to the other, a disagreement on how best to move the boxes from the sub to the steamer.

He was just 50 feet away when one of the men on the submarine spotted him. Diego actually saw the look of bewilderment on this man's face. The last thing he'd expected to find out here was a man floating on a big pine box. The sailor waved to Diego tentatively, checking to see if he was alive or not. Diego wildly waved back.

Now everyone on both vessels saw him—but no one was

waving anymore. The transfer of boxes stopped. All attention became focused on Diego's approaching raft. He heard more shouting, more anger, on the wind. People on the freighter began scrambling about, but no one was making a move toward the ship's rescue boat. Instead, they were using searchlights to zero in on Diego.

And that's when he saw the guns.

Incredibly, the men on the freighter's deck started shooting at him. Rifles, pistols, even shotguns. Diego couldn't believe it. Why were these men doing this? Why didn't they want to rescue him? It didn't make any sense.

Bullets began ripping into the water all around him. Diego could hear them sizzle as they went by. He wet himself, he was so scared, so confused. The sailors in black uniforms were moving in great haste now, climbing down inside the conning tower. A whistle blew, three times. Then the submarine slowly began to sink into the choppy water, this even as the men on the freighter continued their fusillade.

Diego didn't want to drown out here or die of thirst or starvation or madness. But he didn't want to be shot to death, either. So he did the only thing he could do.

He stopped paddling.

And eventually, the men stopped shooting at him. Diego heard a great roar as the freighter's engines were engaged again and a telltale churning of water erupted from its stern. The ship lurched forward and began moving eastward, away from the setting sun.

Leaving Diego and his floating coffin behind.


## Port of Los Angeles
## Two nights later

Georgie Mann hated this part of LA.

The mechanical loading docks. The rotting wooden piers. The jumble of railroad tracks. Dirty harbor water running around and underneath it all. The Port of Los Angeles. It sounded exotic. It was anything but.

As for coming down here at night—forget about it. Venturing around some of these docks after dark was more dangerous than driving the freeways. Crackheads, *Latino* gangs, drunken longshoremen could be lurking about anywhere. Yet this was where Mann found himself. Stumbling around the old fishing wharves, tripping over the Alimeda tracks, hopelessly lost, looking for a phantom.

He'd been at it for more than two hours; it was now close to midnight. A thick mist had begun to fall. Everything became cold and dank. The bare orange glow of halogen lights perched high overhead only added to the creepy *noir*. Mann could hear voices arguing, radios blaring foreign music, the baleful moan of a foghorn. And was that gunfire off in the distance? He shivered once.

This was no place for a sportswriter.

It was stupid, the reason he was down here. An amateur soccer team from Indonesia was touring the United States this summer. They'd arranged for pickup games across the country, their goal being to improve relations with the United States through the common love of soccer. True, soccer was big in LA. But Mann hated this kind of touchy-feely bullshit. He didn't even know where the fuck Indonesia was. Yet because his boss didn't have the beans to come down to the docks himself at night, he'd told Mann to do it. His assignment: hook up with this team of foreigners, interview them, then follow them to a couple "local" games, in quotes because the nearest one was almost a hundred miles away.

At 42, Mann was way too old for this. He'd been breaking his ass as assistant sports reporter for the tiny *LA Weekly Sun* for nearly 10 years now. He hated his job. He hated his boss. Hated every high school soccer practice he'd ever covered, every dikey coach he'd ever interviewed, every snotty pampered kid he'd been forced to write about. But he had to make his rent and keep gas in his car, and there was nothing else he really knew how to do. So here he was.

The name of the ship he was looking for was the *Sea Conqueror,* or at least that was its name when it left Manila, 11 days before. According to his boss, the ship was not a passenger liner; it was more of a cargo vessel. And no, he didn't have a pier number or even a guess where the *Sea Conqueror* might tie up at the huge, spread-up port facility.

But don't worry, the boss had told him. How hard could it be to find an entire ship?

By the stroke of twelve, Mann had reached a line of warehouses close to the southern edge of the port. Across a narrow, putrid inlet, two immense loading cranes hovered over everything like frozen mechanical monsters. The rows of warehouses seemed to go on forever. Staying in the shadows, Mann set out between two of the buildings, walking down an alleyway so dark and dreary, even the bravest mugger wouldn't dare venture into it.

Reaching the end of the alley, Mann found himself looking at yet another dilapidated docking area. They could have used some halogen lighting down here. There was a single street lamp, fading and blue, struggling to illuminate just a small part of the pier. The rest was absolutely black. Mann pulled up the collar of his jacket. Seagulls cried off in the distance. A ship was tied up to the dock. A cargo vessel no doubt, but it looked like something from World War II, it seemed that old. It was so rusty, in fact, Mann couldn't read the name on its hull. He crept forward a few feet, shaking off another chill. He was not a muscular person; *roly-poly* was a better description. And suddenly he felt very exposed.

*I wish I was a smaller target,* he thought grimly.

Three more steps forward and finally Mann was able to make out the letters on the ship's hull. This was indeed the *Sea Conqueror*. What's more, there was evidence of a recent arrival. A worn and rickety gangplank was still in place. Steam was still hissing out of the ship's stacks. And there were definitely voices coming out of the fog surrounding the pier. Mann couldn't believe it. He'd actually found the damned thing!

He allowed himself a small moment of triumph, a *big* mistake, as suddenly there came a great crashing sound off to his right, an explosion of combustion, followed by the merciless grinding of gears. Mann turned to see a Greyhound bus heading right for him.

Strange what things go through one's mind when one is about to be run over. Snapshots of the last few seconds of life. This was a very clean bus about to kill him, Mann thought queerly. Clean and brand spanking new. And the sign above the front windshield read: *HELLO SOCCER TEAM, USA*. The words seemed out of order. But it was the look on the driver's face that burned its way onto Mann's retinas. It was a grimace of absolute fear, not so much that Mann had suddenly stepped in his way but that he was driving such a huge vehicle in the first place.

Luckily, Mann was just able to get his head around the notion that a Greyhound bus traveling at high speed down these rotting wharves was about to flatten him if he didn't act quickly. So he jumped. Longer, higher, and faster than he ever had before. The bus went by him a second later, nipping the heel of his sneaker and dislodging it from his foot. Mann hit the ground hard, just avoiding what could have been a fatal dose of exhaust fumes pouring out of the rear of the bus. Even in midair, he'd seen a wall of dark faces staring out the dirty windows at him. Again, a strange thought: not one of them looked like a soccer player to him.

He picked himself up, his knees scratched and bloody. His knapsack, containing his cell phone and his notebook, had flown some twenty-five feet away from him. His sneaker had gone just about the same distance in the other direction.

Dazed and confused, he stumbled off to retrieve the sneaker first. He found it lodged between two railroad ties. He bent to pick it up. That's when he saw a second Greyhound bearing down on him.

Well, he was a pro at this now. He dived with the grace of an Olympian, landing back in the alley just before this bus, just as new, just as shiny, went by in a whoosh of night and fog. He hit hard again but was quick enough to turn around and see more very unlikely faces staring out of the dark bus windows at him. Older faces. Astonished faces. Strangely, angry faces, too.

Mann pushed himself to his feet, caught his breath, then stuck his head out of the alley just long enough to see the second bus leaving, as had the first, through a nearby side gate.

Only then did something dawn on him: *HELLO SOCCER TEAM, USA?* The people on those buses—were they the ones he was down here to meet? They *had* to be. He grew so mad so quickly, he thought every vein in his head was going to pop. Here he was, trying to do these assholes a favor by writing about their shitty little team, and they nearly killed him!

He collapsed to the ground, injuring his butt on a stray piece of rail.

*I've got to get another job,* he thought, shaking his head. *This sports stuff is getting too dangerous.*

## Mojave Desert
## The next day

There was no shade in Shade Hill. No trees, no awnings, nothing to deflect the brutal heat of the day. The small town, 95 miles northeast of Los Angeles, was hot 24/7/365. Its residents, all 82 of them, usually stayed indoors during late morning and early afternoon; the combined whine of all those air conditioners could sometimes be heard a mile away. In fact, the only thing worse than the heat in Shade Hill was the duststorms.

It was now almost 11:30 A.M., beginning the hottest part of the day. The temperature was expected to top 104 degrees by noon, with no clouds and no wind.

Not the best weather for soccer.

The only playing field in Shade Hill was on the east end of town, next to the tiny Apache Regional High School. Built as a football field, neglect and the unrelenting heat had so hardened the surface, playing football on it was almost as crazy as playing, well . . . soccer. The field was more dirt than grass, and what grass there was had long ago turned brown. There were two sets of bleachers, one on each side of the field. They were made of aluminum, another poor choice for the desert climate. In the past, people had fried turkey eggs on the metal seats to snack on during games.

There were about two dozen people sitting in the bleachers at the moment, a real crowd for Shade Hill. Most were parents of the eleven teenagers currently doing wind sprints up and down the field, torture by another word. The boys constituted the Apache School District Class C soccer team. This was their last day of school before the summer break. Many had already started working jobs as cattle feeders and wranglers. None of them wanted to be out here.

It was all their coach's fault. About two months ago, he'd accepted an invitation from a foreign soccer team to arrange this late-season match. The foreigners were barnstorming their way across the United States, playing local teams and spreading the good word about their native country of Malaysia. Or was it Indonesia? In any case, this was supposed to be a big deal for Shade Hill. The townspeople had been gabbing about it for weeks.

Jim Cook was Shade Hill's sheriff. His brother, Clancy, was the high school soccer coach. Jim was sitting in the top row of the white-hot bleachers now, looking down onto the blazing field. Things were not going well. The game was supposed to have started at 10:30. The opposing team was nearly an hour late. The Apache players were almost dead from their wind sprints, and the crowd, such as it was, had started growing restless. Cook wiped the sweat from his brow. He was beginning to think the foreigners weren't going to show up at all.

The original invitation from the barnstorming team had come by fax—and all along Cook had suspected it was actually sent by someone in town as a joke. The locals were always pulling Clancy's leg; such things served as entertainment in the sun-baked town. Plus Jim knew his brother hadn't heard from the opposing team since that one and only message two months before. He chuckled to himself now. If this *was* a gag, it would go down in Shade Hill history as one of the best ever. And his brother, Clancy? He would be remembered as the town's biggest goat.

But then a surprise. An engine noise, coming from the west. The top of the bleachers had the best view in town of Route 14A, the only way to get in and out of Shade Hill. Cook stood on the back bench and looked out on the highway. He was the first to see what was causing the commotion.

It was a bus. A *Greyhound* bus, new and sparkling—and approaching the town at approximately a hundred miles an hour. It was traveling so fast, while weaving all over the road, Cook thought it was a runaway, with a dead driver at the wheel. Yet it entered the town seconds later and, remarkably, slowed down, a little anyway, to make the turn at Elsie's Chicken Shack and onto Arrow Drive, at the end of which sat Apache Stadium.

Cook relaxed a bit; the bus was under control at least. But why was it here? There had not been a Greyhound bus—or any other kind of bus—through Shade Hill in decades. If anyone wanted to travel far out of town, he would have to get himself over to Sand Lizard Creek, 12 miles away. Trailways went through there once a week.

It wasn't until the bus screeched to a stop and a gang of very well dressed soccer players bounded off of it that Cook realized this was the visiting team. The foreigners. It hadn't been a gag after all.

Activity on the scorched field came to a halt as the dozen or so dark-skinned men streamed onto the playing surface. A smattering of applause came up from the small crowd. The newcomers began kicking soccer balls around, this in between having hushed conversations with one another in some indefinable language. Their uniforms looked brand-new and were vivid blue and red. Their sneakers were bright, *bright* white. Cook took off his hat and wiped the sweat from his brow a second time. He was as surprised as anybody.

So there *would* be a game here today. . . .

The match began with very little ceremony.

Eli Port, the town banker, served as the lone official. He was almost as big as Sheriff Cook; Eli's referee's striped shirt gave no illusion of a thinner physique. He would not be running up and down the field today. As was his practice, when doing the work of several men, he stood at center field and watched the play as best he could by using a tiny pair of binoculars.

It didn't make much difference, though. What followed hardly could have been called a game. Spiffy as they were, the visitors seemed lacking even the basic skills needed to play soccer. They couldn't kick, couldn't carry the ball with their feet, couldn't hit it with their heads. Indeed, more than once they went to great lengths moving the ball toward their *own* goal. It was only the laughter from the stands that turned the visitors around and heading in the right direction. No passing, no defense, no strategy at all on the part of the foreigners. They were simply terrible.

It lasted for less than a half hour. The heat was so overwhelming, Eli finally called the match. Apache wound up winning by a very un-soccerlike score of 22–0.

The players on both teams were relieved to hear the final whistle. The Apache schoolkids quickly shook hands with their hapless opponents, then headed for the rear door of the nearby school gym. There was a shower room there. They would dive into it, en masse, still wearing their sweaty clothes.

The visitors meanwhile simply turned as one and hurried back onto the bus. Sheriff Cook saw his brother chase after them; a postmatch handshake between coaches would have been the proper thing to do. But the foreign coaches jumped onto the bus, practically closing the big silver door in Clancy's face. Cook saw his brother begin to pull madly on his chin whiskers, a sure sign that he was very, very confused.

Cook wiped his brow a third time. The brand-new bus. The gaudy uniforms. The atrocious play. The whole thing was one of the strangest things he'd ever seen.

*Where are those guys from again?* he wondered.

It wasn't much cooler aboard the bus. The men inside were used to the heat, but running up and down the hard, hot field for 30 minutes had taken its toll. There was no conversation among them now as they slumped into the cloth seats and began whispering prayers. Outside the dark-tinted windows they could see the small crowd of spectators drift past the bus. Some looked confused. Others were pointing and laughing.

The plan was to stay here, parked in Shade Hill, for the afternoon, moving to a KOA truck stop/campground 60 miles to the east as soon as darkness fell. It was a risk, but the people on the bus, including its very inexperienced driver, were in dire need of rest. No one onboard had slept in the past 48 hours. It was very important then that they all get as much sleep as possible in these next few hours, parked in plain view, on the edge of Shade Hill. There was no way of knowing when they'd get an opportunity like this again.

The group of men (they were not boys) finally settled down, some closing the shades on their scenic-outlook windows. Those who didn't were mildly shocked to see a huge cloud of dust heading in the direction of the town. One minute, everything was clear, deep blue, and hot. The next, a tidal wave of sand swept over them, turning day to dusk. The bus began rocking; the wind became fierce and noisy. But those onboard actually welcomed the dirty blizzard. The more cover they had, the better.

That's why it was such a surprise when they heard a loud pounding at the bus door. Nervous glances went all around. One of the men who'd impersonated a coach signaled for everyone to remain calm. Then he nodded to the driver, possibly the most anxious person on the bus. The driver pushed a handle forward and the door opened with a hydraulic swish.

Standing on the bottom step, sunburned, sweaty, and covered with a thin layer of dust, was Georgie Mann, assistant sports reporter for the *LA Weekly Sun*.

"You guys got a few minutes?" he yelled up to no one in particular, waving his very puny press badge. "I gotta do a story on you!"

A moment of awkward silence came and went. Finally, the "coach" beckoned Mann aboard.

Mann happily climbed up the steps and collapsed into the first empty passenger seat. He saw at least two dozen dark eyes staring back at him. It was nearly pitch-black aboard the bus, and not just because of the shuttered windows and the ongoing sandstorm. This was not a typical Greyhound bus, at least not inside. There were actually two compartments onboard. The partition was located about halfway down the aisle. A small door, closed and padlocked, led to the second, unseen section.

*Strange,* Mann thought.

The coach stood across the aisle opposite Mann's seat, a clipboard pressed tightly against his chest.

"I speak just a little English," he told Mann nervously. "And we don't have much time."

"That's OK," Mann replied. "This will be real down and dirty. . . ."

Mann took out his cell phone and dialed his number back in LA. His home computer accepted the call, making the connection with an annoying chorus of blips and bleeps. Using his phone's keypad, Mann opened a new audio file in his computer, then entered a command for the PC to start recording the phone call. This done, he entered another command, which would allow him to transmit one image from his photophone every five seconds to be put into his PC's JPEG file. Words and pictures, just like that. This was the lazy man's way of reporting sports, and Mann had become very good at it. His hosts had no idea what he was doing, though. For some reason, they thought he was calling his mother.

For the next five minutes Mann asked questions from a prepared list, using his phone like a long-distance microphone. Where *was* the team from? What did they hope to accomplish during their tour of the United States? What international soccer stars did they hold in high esteem?

The coach's answers were murky at best, each one either too short or too evasive or just plain dumb. The team was from "the South Asian Pacific." They hoped to bring "peace and understanding" to anyone they met in the United States. They didn't know or care about any international soccer stars. They knew very little about the World Soccer League.

They'd never heard of Pele or Ubu. They had no opinion on the movie *Bend It like Beckham.*

"How about your schedule?" Mann finally asked in exasperation. "Can you at least tell me how many places you're playing?"

The coach shook his head no, pointing to his ears as if he didn't understand. Yet the clipboard he was holding had the word "Schedule" written right across it.

Mann already knew the story was a stinker. This coach was a moron, and the only pictures Mann got so far were of the gloomy, weird cut-off interior of the bus. But no story, no paycheck. Maybe he could fill up some page space with a simple map showing where the foreign team would be visiting during its tour.

So Mann gently took the clipboard from the coach. Flipping it around, he showed the man the word "Schedule" on it, saying, "This . . . this is what I need." Indeed, the schedule was a map, with arrows pointing to the various places Mann assumed the team was expected to play. There were no dates, though, just the names of some cities and towns, numbered 1 through 9, and located mostly in the American South and Midwest. He snapped a bunch of phone-photos of it, hoping by now he'd transmitted enough data back to his home computer to scrape some kind of column together.

He handed the clipboard back to the coach. All Mann wanted now was to get off the bus, get back into his car, and drive like hell so he could be in LA before dark.

But he had one more question. He'd almost been mowed down not once but twice the night before, back on the docks.

"Where's your other bus?" he asked.

Now a real jolt of tension went through the compartment. Those players pretending to be dozing sat straight up in their seats and began looking anxiously this way and that. A stern nod from the coach settled them down. He turned back to Mann and smiled.

"Well, I guess you've uncovered our little secret," he said in his best English of the day.

"What do you mean?" Mann asked him.

The coach stood up and with a hand gesture motioned Mann toward the padlocked room divider.

"We've got a real scoop for you," the coach said. "Some very interesting stuff."

Tired and clueless, Mann cued up his photophone and walked toward the rear of the bus. One of the players undid the padlock and pushed the door open.

Mann walked in—but suddenly stopped. This second compartment looked nothing like the first. It was well lit and, he noticed, heavily soundproofed. On the floor were boxes and boxes of cell phones. And camping supplies, like tents and Coleman lanterns.

But most astonishing, the walls were lined with . . . weapons, including some kind of missiles. Fifteen of them at least. *Are those Stingers?* he thought.

Mann could only utter one word: "Wow!" The pistol was against the back of his head a second later. The trigger was pulled twice.

He was dead before he hit the floor.

# Chapter 2

## Guantánamo Bay, Cuba

The storm had blown in just after sunset. The rain was coming down in sheets; lightning was crashing. The thunder rolling across the bay was horrendous. With visibility down to zero for most of the mid-Caribbean, it was no weather for flying. Yet an unusual cargo plane was sitting on Gitmo runway number two, hard on the edge of the U.S. Navy base, its propellers redirecting the fierce downpour into a violent, driving spray.

Though all of the cargo plane's insignia had been painted over, this aircraft belonged to the Iranian Air Force, an unlikely visitor to this American facility hanging by its fingernails off the eastern end of Communist Cuba. The plane, a two-engine French-built Transall-2, was here as a result of top-secret negotiations between the United States and Iran, part of a very hush-hush diplomatic arrangement. The United States kept several hundred Taliban fighters at Guantánamo Bay, illegal combatants captured during the war in Afghanistan. Many of these people were not Afghanis; in fact, terrorists from more than two dozen countries were being held in prisons here. Seven of them were citizens of Iran—*highly placed* citizens. In fact, all seven were related to someone on the governing board of mullahs that ran the

troublesome Persian country, a place where family trees
could spread for miles.

The aim of the secret negotiations was simple. Iran was
holding seven top-echelon Al Qaeda fighters, none of whom
was Iranian. The seven Iranian citizens the United States
was holding were foot soldiers, with friends in high places.
The United States wanted the Al Qaeda lieutenants for
questioning and prosecution; the mullahs wanted their relatives back. It was a prisoner exchange then. Seven-for-seven.
An even swap.

The howling storm was a complication no one had fore-
seen, though. The two sides had argued each other right
down to the last comma on the exchange document, which
was so classified, it would be burned and its ashes scattered
after the transfer was made. Timing was the most important
element. The Al Qaeda prisoners were being held at an Iranian border crossing, ready to be pushed across into U.S.-held
Iraq as soon as word of the plane's departure from Guantánamo was confirmed. Any delay, be it weather or mechanical, would be a deal breaker, the distrust between the two
sides ran so deep.

That's why the Transall-2 had to be loaded, had to get
into the air, and had to make the all-important confirmation
call back to Tehran.

So, hurricane or not, it *had* to take off.

Things had to go right on the ground, too. The isolated section of the air base was surrounded by no fewer than a hundred Marines, backed up by at least two squads of SEALs
watching the waterfront nearby. (There would later be some
dispute about the number of SEALs present.) There was also
a Delta Force sniper team stationed in the hills above. This
small combination army had been in place for hours, sweat-
ing out the brutal heat of the waning day, only to be soaked
through now by the driving rains of night.

A stretch van would be transporting the seven Iranian
prisoners from Camp X-Rray, the main Gitmo holding facility,

to runway number two. The van would be escorted by two Marine LAVs, small, heavily armored tanklike vehicles. A U.S. State Department representative would also be accompanying the van, traveling in a separate car. His name was John Apple. His counterpart, a general in the Iranian Air Force, was serving as the copilot for the transfer plane.

Once the van reached the runway, Apple and the Iranian general would individually count each of the seven prisoners as they got out of the van and again as they climbed aboard the plane, this last bit of diplomatic nonsense insisted on by the Iranians. Only after both men were certain that the seven prisoners were safely aboard the plane would it be cleared for takeoff.

It was just one of many complicating factors in this anxious exchange that all seven of the Iranian detainees were named Khameni. In fact, five of them had the exact same name: Rasef Rasanjani Khameni. To avoid confusion, it was agreed early in the negotiations that the detainees would simply be known as K-1 through K-7.

The plane's first destination would be Mexico, but only by necessity. When it touched down at Guantánamo, the Transall-2's fuel tanks were nearly empty. It needed gas to get home. The United States had steadfastly refused to refuel the plane, though, just as the Iranians had steadfastly refused to allow U.S. fuel in its tanks. So, with a nudge from the United States, the Mexican government agreed to allow the plane to refuel, no questions asked, at a tiny military base in the Yucatán before starting its long flight westward. With another fuel stop in Fiji and a final one in Beijing, the plane was expected to arrive in Tehran 32 hours later.

A huge celebration would be waiting for it in the Iranian capital, timed to lead off the government's national nightly news.

The seven fighters were expected to be greeted as heroes.

The prisoners' van arrived a few minutes late, this as the rain grew more torrential and the winds picked up to 40 knots.

The van pulled up to the back of the waiting airplane, along with Apple's car. Conversation was nearly impossible around the loading ramp, thanks to the gusting wind, whipped up further by the gyrating turboprops. The Iranian general was waiting impatiently at the bottom of this ramp. He, too, was soaked. He'd been nervously watching the line of Marines standing close by. Both sides wanted to get this over with quickly.

Apple and the Iranian general met at the ramp, but there were no handshakes. They simply stood side by side, ready to count aloud as each detainee stepped off the small bus. Per the agreement, each prisoner was still shackled by hands and feet and had a black mask pulled down over his head. Each was wearing a bright orange jumpsuit adorned with his ID—K-1, K-2, and so on—painted in large black letters on the back.

The process began. Apple and the Iranian general sounded off as each man emerged from the van. Then, as two Marines escorted each detainee to the bottom of the ramp, the general would check off a number corresponding to the back of the prisoner's uniform. The detainee would then be allowed to climb up into the plane and be seated. At U.S. insistence, the shackles and hoods would not be removed until the Transall-2 was airborne.

The loading process took longer than expected because the detainees came off the van out of order. They were re-arranged in their seating by the plane's pilot, and only then did Apple and the Iranian general agree that the exchange was complete.

Again, there were no handshakes. The Iranian general simply climbed up the ramp and closed it himself with a push of a button. Not 30 seconds later, the plane's engines revved up and it began pulling away. The Marines slowly withdrew from the runway. The Transall-2's pilots added more power, their props now screeching in the tempest. There was no conversation with the base's air traffic control tower. The plane immediately went into its takeoff roll.

It needed the entire length of the 6,000-foot runway, but

somehow, someway, the plane finally went wheels up and, in an explosion of spray and exhaust, climbed into the very stormy night.

Apple returned to his living quarters just outside Camp X-Ray, went directly to his kitchen cabinet, and broke out a bottle of cheap Cuban whiskey. He poured some over a few melting ice cubes and, with the thunder still crashing outside, drained the contents of his glass in one noisy gulp.

He was three weeks away from retirement. Full pension, house on Chesapeake Bay. The works. That this pain-in-the-ass deal was finally over made him very happy. All he had to do was phone in a report to his boss in Washington; then he would go to sleep for about a week. After that, he could start thinking about packing his government bags for good.

He poured himself another healthy drink, then padded into the living room of his glorified hut. He picked up the secure scramble phone to Washington, but before he could punch in the first number he heard a commotion outside. He could see through his picture window that a Humvee had screeched to a halt on his sandy front lawn. Six Marines fell out of it; two immediately ran up to his front door. They did not knock, didn't bother to ring his doorbell. They simply burst in, soaking wet, M16s pointing everywhere. They looked scary.

"What's happened?" Apple demanded of them.

The Marines just grabbed him by the shoulders and carried him out of his hut.

"You've got to come with us!" one of them yelled at him.

The ride up to the detainee compound was the most hair-raising event of Apple's life. The Humvee driver was a kid no more than 18, and the other Marines were screaming at him to go faster . . . faster! . . . *faster!* The kid followed orders and drove the winding, muddy, very slippery road like a madman, nearly sending the Humvee hurtling over the cliff many times.

Somehow they made it to the main compound gate. This

barrier was open—never a good sign. The Humvee roared right through, drove the length of the barbed-wire encirclement and down another series of hills to an isolated plywood barracks. This was where the seven guys named Khameni had been kept during their incarceration.

There was another gaggle of Marines here, and a few SEALs, too. All of them were excited and soaked. Conversation had been hopeless in the swift ride here; the wind and torrential rain did not help it now. The Marines yanked Apple out of the Hummer and into the isolated prisoner barracks.

The interior was dark; only the beams from several flashlights broke through the fog that had seeped in here. The State Department rep, not used to all this excitement, nearly slipped three steps in. The floor was coated with something very sticky. A young Marine beside him directed his flashlight at the floor.

"Be careful, sir," he told Apple.

That's when Apple realized they were both standing in a pool of blood.

More flashlights appeared and now they lit up the entire room. On the floor in front of him Apple saw the bodies of seven men lined up in a row. Clad only in their underwear, each had had his throat cut.

Apple's first thought was that these people were Marine guards—but actually the opposite was true. They were detainees, more specifically, the seven Iranian prisoners named Khameni. It took several long moments for this to sink into Apple's brain. Then, through the blood and rain and wind and chaos around him, it hit like a lightning bolt. He grabbed the young Marine next to him.

"Are these really K-One through -Seven?" he asked in astonishment.

The man nodded blankly. "We've already ID'd them through photographs," he said. "Those are them, sir."

Apple nearly slumped to the floor. He felt like he was suddenly living inside a ghastly dream. What his eyes were telling him simply seemed inconceivable. *How? Why?*

Then another thought struck. This one even more troubling than the seven murdered prisoners.

"But if these are the Iranians," he mumbled, "then who the hell . . . ?"

"Got on that plane, sir?" the Marine finished his question for him. He just shrugged. "We have no idea."

# Chapter 3

The MCI Arena was packed. Rock music was blasting. Strobe lights were flashing. The gigantic scoreboard was pumping out waves of virtual excitement. For the first time in a very long time the Washington Wizards pro basketball team was in the play-offs, the Finals no less. This was a *very* big deal in D.C., and the MCI was filled to the rafters for the occasion. When the home team ran onto the court, the crowd's response was deafening.

But Mary Li Cho was already bored. She knew nothing about basketball, didn't know if the ball was filled with air or stuffed with feathers. She was here on a date—or she was supposed to be anyway. A guy she'd been seeing had called earlier in the week asking if she wanted to see the Wizzies play. She'd quickly accepted. He was all military, a captain at Army Special Operations Command, GI Joe handsome, and very unattached. He even had a soldierly name: Pershing Nash. Li got her fill of midlevel Army jerks at work, but she actually liked this one. Or at least, she had.

So here she was, way, *way* up in the cheap seats, after picking up her ticket at the will-call window. But Nash was nowhere in sight. She'd been scanning the place for the last half hour, looking for him. She saw many military types walking around and politicians everywhere and lobbyists cluttering up the expensive boxes below. But so far, no Captain Nash.

The people around her were the loudest and the drunkest in the arena. She was becoming uneasier by the minute. This would be the third time that Nash had stood her up. She realized he had a high-level job—he was attached to the National Security Council. He never missed a chance to tell her *that*. But she had an important job, too. And he knew all about it. And after two months she felt she deserved better from him than stranding her here in the Jerry Springer section.

Li was Asian-American and very attractive. Nice hair, nice face. Nice *everything*. Even dressed in simple jeans and a bland top, she could feel many of her boozy neighbors locking in on her. It was not a pleasant feeling, though. She'd always been uncertain about her looks, never seeing what others saw. One of her ex-boyfriends once told her, *You're too good-looking; that's the problem*. She'd even been approached by *Playboy* to pose for a pictorial, "Secretaries of the Pentagon." The offer both amused and horrified her. Even in her best moments, she tried not to think about it.

Appearing in *Playboy* was something Li could never do even if she wanted to. She worked at the Pentagon; that much was true. And she went to the typing pool every morning and picked up piles of documents to be word-processed. But she was not a secretary. That was her cover. Actually, she worked for one of the most secret operations within the U.S. government. It was called the Defense Security Agency.

Created after September 11th, the DSA's mission was deceptively simple: "Maintain security within the ranks of the U.S. military." Truth was, the cryptic agency played many roles. It sniffed out members of the U.S. military who might be terrorist agents in disguise—it had caught several in the past three years. It investigated unresolved disappearances of U.S. military weapons, from bullets to bombers. It watched over the Pentagon's online security systems and its communications networks, another line of defense against would-be terro-hackers. It even monitored the Pentagon's bank accounts, looking for any irregularities.

The DSA was so classified, it was all but unknown to the other U.S. intelligence services. Even the Vice President was said to be unaware of its existence, as were 99.9 percent of the people who worked in the Pentagon. It was a secret unit hiding in plain sight.

It was also a very small operation. Three people assigned here in D.C., just a half-dozen more serving overseas. Modest though it was, the DSA could throw some weight around. Not only did it have unfettered access to all intelligence gathered by every other U.S. spy agency, but it could also call on any number of U.S. special ops units to do its dirty work. It took its orders directly from the NSC and no one else. These days that was like getting the Word directly from God.

As she was the daughter of a career military man—her father was a colonel in the Marines—and just eight months out of grad school at Georgetown, working for the DSA would have seemed the ideal job for Li. Though she was also a talented artist, her real talents lay in the newly birthed science of counterterrorism, and the DSA was certainly on the front lines for that. But lately, she felt more like the lookout on the *Titanic,* with the iceberg dead ahead. Many things were out of control in D.C. these days security-wise. Things she wished she knew nothing about.

This was another reason she was feeling unsettled tonight. The terrorist chatter lately was not good; she knew this because she had access to every byte of information coming into the Pentagon about every known terrorist group around the world. Despite some recent setbacks, the lines in and out of Al Qaeda had been burning especially bright for the last month. Many of their key sleeper cells were being activated, a very bad sign. Their illegal money-laundering operations were also spiking, a sure indication funds were being passed down to their foot soldiers. The results so far: car bombings all across Europe, suicide bombings in Afghanistan and Israel. Plutonium missing in Pakistan. Smallpox found in Kenya. And everywhere rumors of nukes and dirty bombs about to go off.

These things were a thumbprint strategy for Al Qaeda: start a lot of small actions and get U.S. intelligence people running this way and that, all as a diversion from the big hit to come. *Something* bad was going to happen soon. Li could feel it in her shoes, and she wasn't the only one. The problem was, there were so many potential targets, it was impossible for anyone to even guess what might be hit and when. The FBI and the CIA were useless, the Department of Homeland Security a sad joke. So that iceberg kept getting closer every day.

Yes, these were *very* strange times at work—but not just because of the uptick in terrorist activity. It was more personal than that. The small, secret DSA unit housed inside the Pentagon was now down to just one person: *her*. Why? Because her boss and his second-in-command had left on assignments two months before and neither had been heard from since. Officially, they were TWA, as in Temporarily Without Assignment. But Li knew this was just spy talk for missing in action. Or worse.

It was too bad. She really liked Ozzi and Fox. Ozzi was a Navy jg, midtwenties, a top graduate of Annapolis. Major Fox was a tall, handsome, dreamy but very married guy from Alabama, a retired CIA veteran lured back after September 11th. They'd made a great team, the three of them. Ozzi was the cyberspace guy, Fox was the CO, and Li fit nicely in between. As the system intelligence officer, she traffic-copped everything that came through the door. They were all easygoing, good at keeping secrets, and genuinely liked one another. Even now, her eyes misted over thinking about them. She missed them both terribly.

This also meant she'd been without a boss for eight weeks. What does one do in such a case? The next level of command was the NSC itself, and she wasn't about to go to them looking for help. She'd even asked Nash for advice. Again, because he was attached to the NSC, he was one of the few people in town who knew what she did, sort of. And they were both at the same security clearance level, so they could talk about such things. Sit tight, Nash had told her.

That was the *only* thing to do when dealing with the military high command. Carry on as best as you can until someone tells you otherwise.

Carrying on, to Li's mind, was fulfilling the last assignment Fox had given her before he and Ozzi disappeared. But this was weird, too: check out every Defense Department employee named "Bobby Murphy." She had no idea why, but in his last memo to her Fox asked that she cyberstalk anyone in the DoD by that name, even though there were no indications that any of them were criminals or moles or anything other than simple worker bees. Strange. The DoD was a big place. Li had already checked out several dozen people by that name, without finding anything unusual.

So this whole Bobby Murphy thing was just another mystery to her.

The Wizards finished their shootarounds. The lights inside the MCI began to dim.

Li checked her watch again. The only empty seat in the arena was the one next to her. How long should she wait for this human Ken doll? Why hadn't he called her? Should she call him? Suddenly her cell phone began vibrating. She retrieved it from her ankle holster. A text message had blinked onto the screen. It was from Nash.

It read: "Call me ASAP." But he had added: "MTSL first." Li was surprised to see this. MTSL was spy talk for "Move To Secure Location," a code used when sensitive or classified information was to be discussed. Why would Nash want her to take this unusual step if just to tell her why he wasn't here?

*Whatever,* she thought. At least she would not have to sit through a basketball game. She got up to leave.

But then the lights in the arena dimmed even further, until there was just a single spotlight shining on center court. According to the PA announcer, "America the Beautiful" was about to be sung. Li couldn't leave now. The way things were in D.C. these days, she'd probably be called a Taliban.

So she sat back down but stayed poised on the edge of her seat. What happened next would stay with her for a very long time.

Two young children walked onto the court. A boy and a girl, no more than eight years old, both dressed in their Sunday best. Both kids were holding microphones as big as they were. Both looked nervous. A recorded piece of music began to play, the opening notes to "America the Beautiful."

The kids started singing. Off-key but cute. The crowd warmed to them immediately. Even Li had to admit it was precious—for the first few seconds, anyway. Because when the part about the "fruited plain" came along, both kids froze solid. They'd forgotten the words.

The music played on; the crowd became hushed. The kids began to cry, tears falling onto their microphones. The spotlight seemed to be burning holes in them now. No one knew what to do. Finally someone stopped the music and the lights came back on. Li just shook her head. What was happening to this country? *We can't even sing our favorite song anymore.* . . .

Suddenly, from across the court, a small, wiry man appeared. He was sixtyish and dressed plainly in slacks and a golf shirt. He was certainly not part of either team; nor was he wearing the red blazer sported by all arena employees. He had to be one of the spectators.

The crowd went silent as this tiny man walked across the floor, approaching the children with a smile. The two kids stopped crying, looking up at him more curious than anything. He patted each one on the head, then took the boy's microphone. Everyone in the arena heard him say, "OK, let's try it again. . . ."

A few uncomfortable seconds passed, but then the music recued and resumed playing. Very softly, the little man started singing the first verse to them. The kids got the idea. He would tell them the words, and the kids would sing them, somehow keeping pace with the recorded music. It became very awkward, though. The crowd began hooting; some were even mocking the unlikely trio. But the little man persisted, and so did the kids. They sang on, getting a bit louder, a bit more confident, with each note.

And slowly . . . everything began to change. The crowd went quiet again as the three voices rose, shaky but oddly in tune. Li began to listen to the words of the song. They actually *sounded* beautiful, so much better than the screechy "Star Spangled Banner." By the third line, the kids were really into it, the little stranger easing them along with every measure.

Then came the chorus . . . and very unexpectedly *other* voices began to rise. First from the balconies. Then the loge. Then from the fat-cat seats way down front. Just like that, the entire MCI arena was singing. Li felt pins and needles from head to toe. What was happening here? She stole a glance at the father and young son beside her. The father was holding a cup of beer in one hand and hugging his son with the other. Tears were in the man's eyes.

Li spied other people around her. Many of them were crying, too. Crying and singing. The overhead scoreboard came to life: a moving digital image of the American flag, blowing in the wind above the wreckage of the World Trade Center. It was so sad yet beautiful at the same time. Li felt something wet fall on her own cheek. She thought it was beer. It wasn't. . . .

The kids, the little man, and the crowd soared into the big finish: *"From sea to shining . . . sea!"* Then, complete silence—for about two seconds. Then the cheering began. It washed through the arena like a giant wave. Louder and louder. Feet stomping, hands clapping, seats smashing. The building's foundation began to shake. The crowd was delirious and the delirium seemed like it would never end. Finally, the little man drawled into the microphone, *"Now,* let's play some *ball. . . ."*

The crowd erupted again. Twice as long, twice as loud. The players took to the court. Someone secured the microphones and the kids were escorted off, waving and laughing and taking happy bows.

As for the little man, he disappeared back into the crowd, leaving as quickly as he came.

Li drove to the most secure location she could find in a hurry, the top floor of a parking garage three blocks from the MCI Arena. Hers was the only car up here, and the other six levels below were practically empty. She was sure no one would intrude on her. She parked in the farthest corner and shut off her lights. The garage was so high, she could see almost all of Washington from here. The White House. The Lincoln Memorial. The Pentagon. The Potomac. All of them sparkling in the warm evening air.

She speed-dialed Nash's number more than 50 times in the next 10 minutes, and each time his phone was busy. She was quickly growing annoyed. What kind of game was he playing here? Why all the mystery and intrigue? She got enough of that at work.

It was now 8:45. She tried Nash five more times. Still busy. This was bullshit. Seat back, she opened her moonroof and looked up to the stars. But instead, she saw the silhouettes of two fighter jets pass silently overhead. They were F-15s. . . . This was strange. Fighter overflights had not been seen in D.C. since the days immediately after 9/11. Yet these two were clearly circling the capital. Why?

She tried Nash again. Finally, she heard ringing. He picked up right away.

"It's me," she said sourly. "Your date. . . ."

"I'm sorry," he began in a hushed voice. "I'm still at work. And work just got nuts. Are you alone?"

"You're not here," she shot back. "So I must be, right?"

A short pause.

"I'll make it up to you," he said. "It's just . . ."

But Li had already heard enough. He had to work late. OK. No big deal. Certainly no need for a song and dance.

"Just call me then," she told him coolly. "When you're *certain* you can get away."

She started to hang up but then heard him say, *"Wait. . . ."*

"Yes?"

"I have something else I have to tell you," he said. "And it's disturbing news, I'm afraid. Some things that we just got in here at the office I think you should know about."

Li felt a chill go through her. *This* was unexpected.

She asked, "What kind of 'things'?"

"Absolutely top-secret things," he replied, his voice low. "*NSC* things. Are you sure you're in a safe place?"

"I am," she insisted. "And frankly, you're scaring me."

"Well, get used to it," he said. "Because there's some scary shit going on." Another pause. Then he said, "What do you know about Hormuz and Singapore?"

Li was speechless for a moment. This was not a geography question. Nash was referring to a pair of highly classified, highly mysterious incidents that had happened in the past few months.

First, Hormuz. As in the Strait of Hormuz. What occurred there was nothing less than Al Qaeda trying to pull off an attack to rival 9/11 or anything since. They hijacked ten airliners and two military planes and attempted to crash them into the U.S. Navy aircraft carrier *Abraham Lincoln* as it was moving through the narrow Persian Gulf waterway. The attack failed because every airliner was either forced to land before it reached the *Lincoln* or shot down by the Navy. The carrier made it through untouched. The 5,500 U.S. sailors aboard were saved.

The Navy had been heaped in glory for its defense of the *Lincoln*, but there was more to the story than that. A last-minute piece of intelligence, delivered to them in a very unconventional way, allowed the Navy to know exactly where the hijacked airliners were coming from, what their flight paths were, and their estimated time of arrival over the carrier. The advance warning came from a deeply secret special ops team that had been skulking around the Persian Gulf for weeks—or at least that was the rumor. At first, the U.S. intelligence community scoffed at the idea that a bunch of "ghosts" had prevented another 9/11. Yet the Navy was hard-pressed to deny it. In any case, the American public knew very little about the details of the secret assistance. Rumors and whisperings mostly. Few people in the U.S. government or the military knew much about it, either.

The Singapore Incident was even murkier. The city's Tonka Tower was the tallest building in the world. Six weeks before, Al Qaeda–led terrorists managed to take over its top-floor function room, trapping several hundred American women and children inside. The terrorists wired the building's glass-enclosed summit with nearly 60 pounds of plastic explosive, knowing the blast would likely topple the entire building and kill another two thousand people caught in the floors below.

The terrorists had alerted the world's media to what was going on, and indeed the whole drama played out live on America's nightly news. Just as the terrorists were about to detonate their explosives, though, one of the dozen TV news helicopters circling the building suddenly landed on its top-floor balcony. Someone inside the chopper shot four of the terrorists dead. Other men from the copter and leaping in from the roof killed the three others and defused the bombs with seconds to spare. As soon as the crisis was over, the rescuers, who were dressed in U.S. military special ops uniforms, briefly displayed an American flag, then got back on their TV news helicopter and promptly disappeared.

The Pentagon spin on the matter was both deceitful and marvelous: The rescuers were part of an elite special ops group, so secret, neither their names nor anything about them could be revealed. Truth was, no one with any power inside the Pentagon, the White House, or anywhere else in the U.S. government had the slightest idea who these mysterious soldiers were, only that they were probably the same group who had saved the day at Hormuz.

So the ghosts were not ghosts after all. The problem was, they were not under anyone's control. They were a rogue team operating on their own, without oversight from higher authority. This type of thing sent shivers down the spines of the top brass. Heroes or not, whoever they were, the rogues had to be reeled in, and quick.

Li had seen reports indicating the group was at one time

thought to be hiding out in the extreme southern portion of Vietnam, using a camouflaged containership as cover. There were also whispers that a SEAL team had been dispatched by the NSC to the Mekong to disarm and return the rogue unit. But the SEALs never came back. And, as it was later rumored, when a team of crack State Department security men was sent after the SEALs they vanished, too.

The whole Hormuz-Singapore thing hit particularly close to home for Li. She'd always suspected that her colleagues Fox and Ozzi had gone off to look for the mysterious unit as well, either with the SEALs or in separate, parallel operations. She even had some evidence of this. Li had been receiving strange e-mail for Fox and Ozzi for weeks, the same two attachments sent over and over again. She couldn't open them, at least not all the way. But she'd been able to get a few lines to print out from the first one, which was titled "Fast Ball." Though it was mostly blurred and blacked out, she was able to make out a few words like "Hormuz," "Singapore," "Vietnam," "Philippines," and "SEALs," along with mentions of the Abu Sayeef terrorist group and some missing U.S. weapons. Oddly, the format of the attachment did not seem to be a text document but rather a transcript, possibly of an interrogation. As for the second document, labeled "Slow Curve," she couldn't open it at all. But she was able to discern part of its origin title. It read: *"Notes. G. Mann, LA Weekly Sun."*

The weird thing was that these same files kept getting sent to them and, just lately, to her as well. At least once a day and sometimes as many as a dozen times they would show up in her computer. It was almost as if someone *wanted* her to open them fully, to somehow read them, yet wasn't telling her how.

So when Nash asked about Hormuz and Singapore, she replied, "I know what happened at both places, more or less. . . ."

"OK—well, now there's a third side to the triangle," Nash said. "Something that ties in Hormuz and Singapore, and here it is: There's been a jail break at the detainee compound at Guantánamo. It occurred while a prisoner exchange was taking place with, of all people, the Iranians. We were releasing seven of their citizens, Taliban types we'd caught in Afghanistan, while they were giving us seven Al Qaeda *capos* they'd grabbed up recently. The Iranians flew an unmarked cargo plane into Gitmo to pick up their people, and these seven characters were put aboard, still in hoods and shackles. The plane took off, but about ten minutes later the seven Iranians who were *supposed* to be on the plane were actually found back in their detainee hut—with their throats cut. They were all laying on the floor, lined up in a row."

Li almost burst out laughing. "This is a joke," she told him. "And a really pathetic way to get out of our date. . . ."

*"It's no joke,"* Nash replied harshly. "And I could get shot telling you all this. So just listen. This is where Hormuz and Singapore come in. Besides the Al Qaeda and Taliban types at Gitmo, there's also a number of so-called 'special prisoners' being held down there—and that's also highly classified, by the way. These 'special prisoners' are all Americans. There's a bunch of them. They've been deemed threats to national security and have been locked up down there, without trial, without access to attorneys, some of them for months."

Li couldn't believe this. "Are you saying these are American citizens who were helping the terrorists?"

"No," Nash replied. "What I'm saying is that these 'special prisoners' and the guys who showed up at Hormuz and Singapore are one and the same."

Li was astonished, almost speechless. "These heroes everyone has been looking for are *in jail*? Who the hell is responsible for that?"

"That's a question for another time," Nash said hurriedly. "The important thing is that the way it looks now, seven of these 'special prisoners' somehow managed to take the place of the seven Iranian POWs who got their throats slit. How? No one has a clue. But even *that* doesn't matter anymore— in fact, it's a very moot point."

"Why?"

"Because," Nash said deliberately, "shortly after takeoff, this transfer plane blew up in midair. One second it was on the radar; the next it was gone. It went right into the sea, taking everyone with it."

She gasped. "My God . . . what happened?"

"The Iranians themselves most likely planted a bomb onboard," he told her. "You know, set to go off as soon as the plane left Gitmo? The brain trust here think the Iranian bigwigs never intended for the plane to get back home. Their POWs were all related to high government officials in Tehran, and the mullahs probably didn't want a bunch of Taliban heroes, with connections inside the government, to be running around loose. Iran's a pretty volatile situation these days.

"Now, you'll probably never hear word one about this ever again. We got our Al Qaeda guys as promised at a checkpoint in Iraq, and the Iranians got rid of seven troublesome relatives, one way or another. A good day all around. Everyone should be happy."

"Except for the 'special prisoners' on the plane," she said. "Who were they really?"

"Well, that's the bad news," Nash answered slowly. "That's why I felt it was important to tell you all this. That you heard it from me first—and not someone else."

A much longer pause. "They've ID'd at least two of the people who were aboard that plane."

A troubled breath.

"And it was your bosses, Li," he said. "Those guys Fox and Ozzi. We just got the official word from Gitmo. Both are confirmed deceased."

# Chapter 4

Li drove around Washington for the next hour, aimless, confused. Crying.

Very unlike her.

From the Potomac Parkway to Independence Avenue, along Constitution, and back on the Parkway again, she'd tried to hold it in. But the tears finally came near 26th Street. There was a box of tissues in her car, just for such rare occasions. It was nearly empty by the time she reached the Whitehurst turnoff.

*Fox and Ozzi . . .*

After they'd first gone missing, she eventually came round to thinking they'd simply be missing forever. Never to be heard from again. Now this freaky plane crash. Their last moments a violent death in the Caribbean. That the Iranians would blow up their own plane was most certainly true. Li knew the mullahs had done it before to get rid of troublesome expatriates. *But Fox and Ozzi?* How did *they* get on that plane? And why? And what the hell were they doing in Cuba as prisoners in the first place?

More tears. More tissues. Maybe this was a grieving period she couldn't have anticipated. Maybe this was closure. But what really hurt, and it was selfish, she knew, was that all that time she'd been missing them, and thinking about them, the two had actually been alive, until just a few hours ago.

*Fox and Ozzi.*

*The bastards . . .*

They'd never even bothered to give her a call.

A light flickered to life on her dashboard. She was running low on gas. She found herself back on the Parkway, in third gear, going 20 miles under the speed limit. The fuel-warning light got brighter. She didn't want to, but finally she put the pedal down. It was time to go home.

Windows open now, she looked around her and realized she was the only one on the road. The *only* one. This was odd. . . . It was not yet ten o'clock. It was a spring evening. A Friday night, and the weather was perfect. The Parkway traffic was usually brisk at this hour. Instead, it was empty.

Foolishly she tried calling Nash again. Their conversation on the garage roof had ended with her hanging up on him just as he was saying: *When can I see you again . . . ?* But now his cell was turned off and she was being routed to his office voice mail. She was sure that was being tapped, so she didn't leave a message. What was the point? They were through, probably, her and Nash. And maybe that was a good thing. This was hardly a time for spies to fall in love.

She got off the Parkway and eventually reached 17th Street, not far from the White House. Again, the prospect of returning home was not a great one, but she needed some tea and then some sleep. She pulled onto Pennsylvania Avenue, heading west. The streets were empty here, too. Strange again. It wasn't *that* late. She passed New Hampshire Avenue and then 26th Street again. Still no traffic, no cars at all. Suddenly panic rose in her chest. *Oh God. . . .* She snapped on her radio, expecting to hear that a major catastrophe had taken place, an Al Qaeda attack or something. But her favorite station was playing soft rock as usual. So were her second favorite and her third. She flipped around. She heard news, weather, sports, commercials. But no Emergency Broadcast

System. Nothing out of the ordinary. The iceberg hadn't hit . . . yet.

She turned onto M Street—and was suddenly blinded for a moment. A line of very bright headlights was coming right at her, and not at a slow pace.

What was this? A parade? A funeral?

It was neither. It was a convoy of Army vehicles. Humvees and small troop trucks painted a very dark green. They went by her like she was standing still, two dozen in all, heading back toward Pennsylvania Avenue. She felt another chill go through her but fought the temptation to turn around and follow them.

Instead, she just kept going straight, heading for home.

It wasn't quite House on Haunted Hill, but it was close.

It sat behind a row of empty warehouses at the end of a dead-end street, near the Potomac Reservoir extension road, just over the line in Virginia. The Navy had built this place back in the twenties as an auxiliary weather station, but the sailors back then were better at sailing ships than constructing houses. This one was ugly from the first nail, and eighty years of rain and heat had only compounded the error. It had a strange miniature Kremlin look to it, with a skin of faded green shingles and two creaky turrets rising from the back. A black brick chimney, leaning 70 degrees, sprouted atop the sagging roof. Add the rickety fence, the dirty brown lawn, and the two dead apple trees out front and what was once homely was now just plain creepy.

This was what Li called home. She lived here for one reason only: the rent was very, *very* low. In fact, when she first came to D.C., she nearly had to turn around and go back home, so scarce were safe living spaces for young women just starting out on the government payroll. After weeks of searching and living out of a bag, this place became available. It was convenient and it was affordable. So, creepy or not, she took it.

She parked out back now, in the small turnaround. Li had lived here for almost a year, but she'd yet to go into the

garage, never mind park in it. It was chilly up here as usual.
A fog had lifted off the smallish reservoir and was pouring
through the old chain-link fence into her backyard. She
made sure her car was close as it could be to her back door,
then grabbed her briefcase, her phone, and her unused
overnight bag. Because this place was so isolated, she made
it a habit to always hurry inside.

She climbed the back steps to the porch. From here, over
several neighborhoods and the winding Potomac beyond, the
lights of the Lincoln Memorial burned dully in the mist. The
normal bustle of the city was lacking; she could tell even way
up here. Li paused for a moment, trying to make some sense
of it. Everything was *so quiet*. Even the wind was still. But
then a muted rumbling from the south. What was that? Not a
truck on the highway nearby. Not thunder, in the clear sky.

She looked out from under the porch's roof.

Two more F-15s flew overhead.

She fumbled a bit with her keys, finally letting herself in.
But she stopped two steps over the threshold. Her place was
dark. *Completely* dark. This was not right. She always kept
two lights on during the day, one in the hallway and another
in the living room, just so she wouldn't come back to a dark
house at night. But both were off now.

She thought a moment, frozen in the doorway. Did she
forget to leave them on that morning? No—she had painted
her nails during breakfast and had a definite memory of
pushing the living-room switch up with her elbow and fi-
nessing the hall light on as well. Maybe then there'd been a
power outage?

She dropped her things and waited for her eyes to adjust
to the dark. But even after a half-minute or so, she was still
blind as a bat. She heard something creak up on the second
floor, an area of the house she avoided at all times. *Might be
the wind,* she thought uncomfortably. If there was any wind.
She took a deep breath and let it out slowly. *Can this night
get any weirder?* she wondered. A voice deep inside her
replied, *Don't ask. . . .*

She began creeping down the hallway. The lamp was located on a table to her left. By touch and feel she made it without stubbing her toes. She found the light and tried to switch it on. Nothing. She tried again. Still nothing. Her power outage theory was gaining support. But then she reached up inside the shade . . . and discovered the lamp's lightbulb was not there. The socket was empty.

Her hand instantly went to her ankle holster. Her cell phone wasn't the only thing she carried here. She came up with a Magnum 440H Specter, a powerful handgun with not an ounce of metal in it. Composite fibers and plain old plastic, it was the first Stealth gun. And Li knew how to use it. That was a requirement for her graduate degree.

She continued down the hall, a bit flush now with the confidence that comes from a gun. The living-room door was shut tight. She *never* shut this door. She twisted the knob and toed the door open. The living room was dark inside. The wall switch was to her right. She reached up and pushed it on. Nothing. She reached down to the lamp itself, not bothering to try the switch. She just felt where the lightbulb was supposed to be. It was gone.

Now her gun was up in front of her, pointing this way and that, just like in the movies. She slipped through the living room, carefully, leading with her weapon as she'd been taught to do at Quantico. Into the bathroom now. No lightbulbs in the ceiling lamp. None in the fixtures over the sink. A huge bar of Ivory soap she always kept here was also gone. She turned, slowly, and opened the shower curtain. The stall was empty, but another bar of soap was missing from here, too.

She moved out of the bathroom and edged her way through the kitchen. It was even darker here, and she did her best to avoid walking into the breakfast table. She went into the pantry backward, her gun pointing in front of her. She felt around on the top shelf with her free hand. Brushing aside some oatmeal and aluminum foil, she found a bag she always kept up here. Within was her one and only spare lightbulb.

Back across the kitchen, back through the living room, to

the lamp beside the door. She screwed the bulb into the fixture and tried the switch again. The light came on.

This startled her. A movement off to her left turned out to be her own reflection in the coatrack mirror. She almost blew it to bits. She caught her breath and looked back at the dimly burning bulb. This was no power outage. Someone was messing with her. But taking her lightbulbs? And her soap?

Then she looked around the room and noticed something *else*. The place was clean. Vacuumed. Newspapers picked up. Dinner tray put away. Not a dirty dish in sight. Even her original pencil drawings were stacked neatly. Everything was in order. Everything was in its place. Li was not the best of housekeepers. And this was *definitely* not the way she'd left it. . . .

She killed the light and retreated quickly. Down the hallway. Back to the foyer. Whoever had done this might still be in the house. But she could not simply call the police. Not with her job. This could be some crackheads or vagrants—but it could be something else, too. And the local cops weren't exactly Scotland Yard. She didn't want them stumbling into places they shouldn't go.

She composed herself, knowing she had to stay calm and be strong. But how exactly?

Another noise from upstairs. A door closing, maybe. Outside, she heard the fighter jets go overhead again. The fog was growing so thick around the old house, she could barely see her car anymore.

Lightbulbs? Soap?

Finally, she just slumped to the floor.

*Iceberg, hell,* she thought.

The whole world was going crazy.

# Chapter 5

The waiters rolled three carts of champagne into the reception hall to polite applause. There were about fifty guests on hand, the usual crowd for the Portuguese embassy's weekly Friday night cocktail party. The *raison d'être* this evening was the announcement of a new EU trade agreement between Portugal and France. It was expected to garner both countries upward of $50 million, mostly in the exchange of costly dinner wines and perfumes.

Or that was the excuse for the gathering, anyway. Most of these events, especially those held here at Portuguese Hall, were just a cover for various European operatives to exchange intelligence. Trade secrets, military assessments, weapons sales. Most people here were interested in things other than Beaujolais and *Paree Sourie*. The place was crawling with spies.

Among them was an agent of the DGSE, the General Directorate for External Security, France's equivalent to the CIA. This man, sometimes known by the code name Palm Tree, lived in a world made up of weapons that shot down aircraft. Stingers, Rolands, Hawks—surface-to-air missiles of all shapes and sizes. He bought and sold them like some people bought and sold Merlots. The difference was, he made sure these weapons, purchased either on the black market or in third-party deals, secretly went to organizations that saw eye-to-eye with French foreign policy, even in its most subtle forms.

The French agent mingled, ate frogs' legs, did a little business, but then left the reception early, meaning before midnight. He had a flight back to Paris tomorrow morning that he *had* to make. He had to get back to his hotel and check his cables, his faxes, his e-mails. Then he had to pack and get to JFK before 4:00 A.M., for the 5:30 plane out.

He walked out the front door, looking for the embassy's street captain; he needed his rental car brought around. But the doorman was not in sight; neither were any of his assistants. *"Lazy asses,"* Palm Tree cursed under his breath. Though his home station was actually in Paris, he'd spent enough time in Washington to dislike just about everyone who lived here. Blacks and foreigners mostly, crude and undependable. He would have to retrieve the car himself.

He walked two blocks, then turned right down a side alley. His car was parked in a private lot one more block away. His mind was on his Air France ticket upgrade . . . when suddenly two men stepped out of the shadows in front of him. They startled him. Palm Tree wasn't just DGSE; he was also ex–French Special Forces, a veteran of Chad and Bosnia. Even though Embassy Row was not the safest place in town, he was surprised the two men had come upon him so quickly. Usually his senses were better than that.

But now here they were, blocking his way in the dark alley, dressed all in black, including ski masks.

Palm Tree decided to attack with good humor. He buried his French accent and took on that of a typical D.C. citizen.

"Have you guys seen my car?" he asked them.

A switchblade was up to his throat a second later.

"Hand it over," the man with the knife growled.

"Hand *what* over?"

Suddenly a straightedge razor was also at his throat.

"Everything you got," the second man told him.

Yes, Palm Tree knew the rabble of D.C.—and these two needed to get everything he could give them, as quickly as possible. He pulled out his wallet and his billfold. He took off his gold wedding band—a fake, as he was not married—and finally his Rolex King watch.

He gave it all to the switchblade man. But an insolence that creeps up on robbery victims during the act began to rise to the surface. "Are you happy now?" he asked them bitterly.

"No, we're *not* happy," the first man hissed at him, the switchblade now pricking Palm Tree's skin.

"What else could you possibly want?" he asked them, authentically puzzled.

They never replied. Instead, the man with the switchblade shoved him to the ground while the other mugger tore the lapel from his suit coat. This uncovered a secret pocket. Palm Tree's most valuable asset—his personal data assistant—fell out to the pavement.

Palm Tree went to grab for it, but one man's boot landed squarely on his hand. The other man retrieved the cell phone–size device instead, and both muggers examined it for a second, keeping Palm Tree pinned to the ground. Then they nodded to each other and displayed two thumbs-up. Almost as an afterthought, the first man looked in Palm Tree's billfold and discovered 300 American dollars, all in fifties, and a similar amount in euros. He crumpled the bills and threw them in Palm Tree's face. Then he tossed Palm Tree's other valuables into a trash barrel nearby. Both muggers then spit on him and left, vanishing back into the shadows.

Palm Tree picked himself up, his entire body shaking, especially his hands. He turned for one foolish moment to gather up his money and retrieve his things from the trash can. He stopped himself, though, knowing he had to get out of the area *tout de suite,* before the muggers realized they'd left most of their booty behind.

He turned up the alley, intent on going back to the embassy for help. But this, too, was foolish. A man in his position did not go looking for help. And certainly not from the local police.

He had to get to his car, leave quickly, and figure out what to do from there. So he ran down the alley, soon reaching the relative safety of the dimly lit parking lot. The muggers had not taken his car keys; still, he had trouble getting them into the lock, his hands were shaking so much. Somehow the key went in, though. The door popped open and he leaped inside, starting the engine and hastily locking all the doors.

He left the lot with a squeal of tires, screeching down the alley to West Avenue. But it was blocked by a construction detour, so he was forced to continue over West and down another alley. At the end of this side street, a white delivery van was parked half on the sidewalk, half on the pavement. There was only a thin space for him to squeeze through.

He slowed to a crawl and began the tight navigation. As he was halfway past the van, he noticed something strange propped up on its dashboard. A car battery . . . surrounded by a web of electrical wires.

*Damn. . . .*

The van exploded an instant later. The bomb, hidden under the passenger seat, was made up of two pounds of gunpowder and such curious items as thumbtacks, lightbulbs, gelatin, and soap. The tacks provided the outer core of the blast. Three dozen in all, they vaporized the rental car's windshield and driver's side window. The soap and gelatin, fused by the explosion, transformed into hundreds of tiny blobs of quasi napalm, igniting everything they touched. The lightbulbs, or what was left of them, came last. Six of them had been embedded deep in the gunpowder. Superheated by the blast, their outer shells evaporated into a cloud of minuscule glass particles that moved with such velocity, they easily cut through exposed skin and bone. This deadly combination tore Palm Tree's head off in less than a second, leaving his upper torso a burning, bloody mass.

In that eternal second between mortal injury and death, though, the French spy had one last thought: *Those crazy bastards . . . they finally got me. . . .*

# Chapter 6

**Three hours later**

Beethoven's Fifth . . .

Digital notes, more annoying than dramatic, woke Li from her deep sleep. It took a few seconds for her to realize where she was, what was happening. But suddenly she was sitting straight up, eyes wide with terror.

She couldn't believe it! She'd fallen asleep on her hallway couch—a *very* scary thought considering what she'd come home to a few hours before. She was still wrapped in her sleeping bag, still in her street clothes, pistol still in hand. But the couch itself had moved. It was no longer next to the back door where she had positioned it, intending to sit guard, with a clear means of escape, until morning. Instead, it was up against the wall, clear across the hallway. *How did that happen?*

She froze now, truly realizing what a dangerous thing she'd done. Falling asleep while an intruder might still be in the house? As a highly-trained intelligence operative, she should have known better, should have at least retreated to her car. But then again, she *was* fairly new to all this, with exhaustion and the weirdness working against her. To make things worse, though, she'd left the back door open and the fog that had rolled into her yard had rolled right into her hallway as well, leaving everything covered with a sticky dew.

Beethoven's Fifth started playing again. . . . *What was that?* She reached down to her ankle holster. Her cell phone was ringing with a newly programmed tune. She looked at the screen and groaned. It was a text message. From Nash. A glance outside told her it was still at least 90 minutes before dawn. What the hell was he doing buzzing her at this hour?

She tried to read his message through bleary eyes: "DGSE op term'd ex prej this PM west ave improv car bmb. Sht hits fan. Call me ths AM plz."

Li collapsed back on the couch. The long message was in text-speak, a language she could barely understand when she was wide awake, never mind half-asleep. She had begun to attempt a translation when . . . she heard a noise. It came from upstairs. A definite thud. A footstep, maybe. Or a window closing. Her gun was up, pointing toward the top of the staircase nearby. But then another noise came, this one from the front of the house. She looked down the hallway. A light was coming from her living room. . . .

She'd always been prone to vivid dreams, especially ones about haunted houses, but Li had never sleepwalked before. That's what this felt like now, though. Everything—from her troubles at work, to the troubles in the country, to what had happened earlier this night—all seemed part of a bad dream that wouldn't go away. She stood up uneasily and felt as if she were floating on clouds, where it was really just the fog. Safety off, her gun ready, she glided down the hall to the living-room door. It was wide open this time. She took a half-step into the room. The lamp was still off, as she had left it; the light was actually coming from her kitchen.

She pinched herself to see if she really was awake. What was going on here? Was this old place haunted after all?

She took two more steps in. The light from the kitchen was flickering crazily. She could hear dull clinking noises. Glasses? No—cups. And the sound of water boiling, the mild whistle of steam. Two more steps. Shadows, moving against her kitchen wall. A candle—she could smell the burnt wax.

Two more steps. At the edge of the kitchen now. Her breath caught in her throat and stayed there. Two figures were sitting at her breakfast table, their backs to her.

She lifted the pistol up to eye level. Two more steps and she was suddenly right behind them. They were drinking tea. *Her* tea.

"*Don't . . . move . . .*" she said with as much gumption as she could muster. *Can a bullet kill a ghost?* she found herself thinking.

The figures went rigid at the sound of her voice. The fog from outside had somehow surrounded them, too, and Li half-expected them to disappear into it—and then finally she could wake up.

But the figures did not vanish. Instead, they turned around and smiled at her.

And they *were* ghosts.

It was Fox and Ozzi.

The next thing she knew, Li was flat out on her back, a wet facecloth draped across her brow.

She'd never fainted before, and judging from the size of the bump on her head, she never wanted to again. Only slowly were her surroundings coming into focus, illuminated by the light of another candle. She was no longer in her kitchen. The walls around her now were painted cruddy green, the ceiling a hideous navy blue. There were two open windows off to her left, bare light and fog streaming through both. To her right, a painting of somebody's steamboat paddling its way up the Potomac. Spiderwebs covered the vessel's name.

That's when she realized she was still in her house. But she was upstairs, on the second floor, the place she always feared to tread.

And finally, she was aware of two worried faces looking down at her.

*Fox and Ozzi . . .*

They really *were* alive. . . .

She pulled them both down to her, as if she were going to smother them with kisses. That would have been very unlike her, though. She was glad, if totally flabbergasted, to see them but shocked that they were actually here. In *her* house. Going through *her* stuff.

*The bastards. . . .*

She didn't kiss them—she knocked their heads together instead, eliciting a painful *crack!* Both fell backward, stunned. Li started kicking at them, furious that they had scared her half to death. And these were not wild kicks, either. She'd dabbled in Tae Kwon Do. And she knew how to hurt a guy.

Both men tried to disentangle themselves from her, abandoning their effort to lift her up from the floor. Li tried to get to her feet . . . but suddenly *many* hands were on her, grabbing her wrists and ankles, trying to hold her down. There were *more* people in the room besides these two—at least three more. Li saw gloved hands, boots, black uniforms, face masks. Self-preservation took over now, her training really kicking in. She began to fight them viciously even though Fox and Ozzi were pleading with her not to. Somehow she knocked the candle over, causing the room to go black. She never stopped throwing punches, though, connecting with jaws, stomachs, knees, crotches. She was almost on the verge of winning the brawl when two *more* figures appeared, inexplicably climbing in through one of the open windows, inexplicably soaking wet. They quickly joined the fray. Only with their extra help was Li finally wrestled back to the floor.

"We are not going to hurt you!" Fox kept shouting at her. "Just let us talk to you. . . ."

Finally, Li stopped struggling. She was on her back again, looking up this time at a sea of faces illuminated by the beams of two powerful flashlights. Her eyes darted around the room; she could see more of it now. In one corner, two M15A2 rifles, the civilian clone of the military M16, were leaning against the wall. Both had bayonets attached to their muzzles with thick rubber bands. Next to them was a large hunting rifle, complete with an electronic gun sight. Next to the rifle, a jumble of laptops sitting atop a spaghetti pile of modem wires. More M15s were hanging off the coat stand beneath the big painting. And everywhere on the floor were junk food wrappers, soda cans, blankets, empty ammunition boxes, newspapers, and cigarette butts. Li was shocked. The room was a freaking mess, far worse than anything downstairs.

"Jesuzz!" she finally gasped. "How long have you people been up here?"

The embarrassed reply from Fox was: "Three days, going on four. . . ."

Then she spotted another pile of refuse down near her feet. Empty packages of Jell-O gelatin. Bright red shotgun shells emptied of their gunpowder. A box of thumbtacks. An empty package of Ivory soap. . . . Her mind went into overdrive. Suddenly Nash's text message was back in her head: *DGSE op term'd ex prej this PM west ave improv car bmb.* Translation? A French intelligence agent had been killed in D.C. last night by an improvised car bomb.

Li began fighting again. This time she was just plain scared. She knew what was needed to make an improvised car bomb—and most of the ingredients were on the floor in front of her. The intruders held her down firmly, though, while Fox kept imploring her to take a deep breath and *just listen.* . . .

It took more than a minute, but she finally settled down a third time, exhausted and out of breath. Her mind was racing now, her heart beating right out of her chest. Ghosts in her house? A French agent killed? Was any of this real?

But then, for some reason, she started counting faces. Fox and Ozzi. And now five others. *Seven in all.* . . . Something was beginning to come together here. Seven Americans killed in the supposed plane crash over the Caribbean, including Fox and Ozzi. Seven people now standing over her . . . including Fox and Ozzi.

"How?" was all she could ask them. "How come you weren't all killed, like they said you were?"

Fox just shook his head wearily.

"Sorry, Li," he said. "But that's top-secret. . . ."

They finally let her up. One of the masked men went downstairs to make her a cup of tea; another helped dust her off. Then Fox and Ozzi brought her into the next room, closing the door behind them. Outside, it had begun to rain.

They were in the master bedroom. Li had been here only once before, the day she first moved in. With its ancient four-poster bed, decaying lace curtains, and cobwebs everywhere, the place was just too creepy for her. Ozzi lit another candle as Fox led her to an old dilapidated divan, sitting her down with a plop. Then he and Ozzi pulled up chairs in front of her. For a long moment, the three friends just stared at one another in disbelief.

"I just can't accept this, Major," Li finally said. "I mean, I *know* what's going on. You faked your own deaths somehow, and came up here to kill this Frenchman? *Why?*"

"Because he deserved to go," Fox responded coldly. Ozzi grunted in agreement.

"But you're *already* escaped prisoners," she shot back at them. "Am I right? Now you've become murderers, too?"

"It's not like that," Ozzi told her, adding. "not exactly, anyway."

"You just ran a car-bomb attack *inside our own country,* for Christ's sake!" she cried. "How does that make you any different from a bunch of terrorists?"

Fox took her hands in his. She was on the verge of tears, and maybe so was he.

"I know it will be hard for you to get your head around this," he said. "I have a hard time believing it myself—and I lived it. But OK, yes, we managed to get out of Gitmo. And yes, we whacked the French guy. And he *did* deserve it. But that's *all* we can tell you. Not because we don't want you to know everything—but because if you *did* know, it would mean serious trouble for you down the line, guaranteed."

"But Major," she said soberly. "This can't be part of any

DSA operation. You've broken some serious laws and certainly some national security edicts. . . ."

Fox just shook his head sadly. "We can't be concerned about those sorts of things, Li," he said. "Not anymore. It's gone way beyond the DSA. . . ."

Silence . . . except for the rain thumping on the roof of the old house.

"You won't tell me how you got out of Guantánamo?" she asked them.

"We can't . . ." Fox replied.

"Or how you got mixed up with the 'special prisoners' down there?"

"I'm sorry, Li. . . ."

She took her hands back from Fox and folded her arms across her chest. "OK, then—were you planning on living in my attic forever?"

Both men rolled their eyes.

"We knew we'd have to tell you eventually," Ozzi tried to explain to her. "We just stayed quiet while you were here, and waited for you to go to work in the morning. But, I have to tell you, we didn't think you'd be coming back tonight. I mean, of all nights . . ."

Li took another moment trying to make some sense of this. Then it hit: they knew about her and Nash, and about her unused overnight bag.

"Damn! You've been *tapping my phone,* too?"

Neither man replied. They just hung their heads. *Guilty.* . . . A very uncomfortable moment ensued. Li studied them by the dancing light of the candle. They looked so different, especially Fox. Unshaven, tired, eyes sunken in, he wasn't the sunny person who'd left on his last mission just a few weeks ago.

"Have you called your wife?" she asked him coolly.

It was like Li plunged a knife into his chest. Fox's face dropped a mile.

"No . . . I haven't," he replied softly. "I can't. Just like with you, this is simply too dangerous to involve her."

There was a tap on the door. Li's tea was here. Fox got up to retrieve it, disappearing for a moment into the shadows.

"Well, *that* should show you how serious this is," Ozzi told her now, his voice low. They both knew how much Fox adored his wife. "And like the major said, we *can't* tell you everything, because then you'll wind up in front of a firing squad, just like we're going to. We're doing this to *protect* you."

He lowered his voice even further. "But *I* can tell you this: Someone in Higher Authority made the Major a real fall guy while we were away. He cleaned up a big mess for them—and then they cut him off completely. Iced him, right out in the cold. And *then* they arrested him. So before you rip his heart out, just realize that of all of us, he got screwed the most."

Now Li studied Ozzi. He was a different person, too. He'd always looked like nothing more than a nice, slightly overage college student to her. The person sitting here now seemed old before his time. He'd seen terrible things, done terrible things. Li could tell.

Fox returned from the dark and very gently placed the warm cup of Morning Madness in Li's hands. Rain was now splattering against the bedroom windows.

"But why did you come here at all then?" she asked them. "Especially if you're so afraid of involving me in anything. I mean, once they figure out you're not dead, this will be the first place they'll look. . . ."

Fox and Ozzi nervously glanced at each other. "Well, we're not staying that long," Fox told her. "And besides, you have something of ours. Something we need. . . ."

"Something of yours? What?"

Fox held up his other hand to reveal he was carrying Li's laptop.

"Can you get on-line up here?" he asked her. "Because we have to get into your e-mail right away."

They set up her laptop on the creaky vanity near the window, running a long modem wire to a telephone port on the first floor. Li opened her e-mail as instructed, more confused than ever. And just like every day for the last three weeks, the first entry contained two files: *"Fast Ball"* and *"Slow Curve."*

"That's what we need," Fox told her simply.

*"These* files?" she exclaimed. "I *thought* they had something to do with you two. Someone's been trying to send them to me for weeks. But I was never able to open them . . . at least not all the way."

Fox and Ozzi froze. "What do you mean?" Fox asked. "'Not all the way?'"

"I mean I was able to get in through a few cracks," she replied. "I know one file seems to be an interrogation and the other has something to do with a sportswriter."

Then she turned and looked directly at Ozzi. "You weren't the only hacker in the office."

"Someone we're working with has been sending these files to your address," Fox told her, his tired voice now betraying some aggravation. "So when this day came we'd be able to finally get to them. But you weren't supposed to see any part of them."

Li just shrugged. "I had time on my hands. Once you two were gone . . ."

Outside came the rumble of two more fighter jets flying high overhead. Fox and Ozzi just looked at each other again, as if to say, *Now what?*

Here Li saw her opening. Exactly who *were* these people hiding in her house? And what were they really here for? She had to get to the bottom of it, one way or another, because that's just the way she was.

"You see, I know a lot," she told them boldly. "And that means you'll either have to tell me everything . . . or you'll have to kill me. Because if you don't, as soon as you leave I'm heading right for Pentagon CID."

Fox and Ozzi put Li in another bedroom, this one at the other end of the second-floor hallway. They would just have to deal with her later. A member of the shadow group had retreated to this room in hopes of getting some sleep. Failing that, he agreed to keep an eye on her.

The two DSA officers then hurried back to the master suite, calling the remainder of the team in with them. On cue, the storm outside doubled in intensity. Lightning flashes could be seen coming from every direction, with thunder booming off in the distance. Or was that the fighter jets circling over D.C. again?

The group gathered anxiously around Li's laptop. They were, in fact, the infamous "ghosts," the people who had pulled off the miracle at Hormuz and the rescue at Singapore. Or a handful of them, anyway. The actual rogue team numbered more than 50. Marines, Delta guys, SEALs, Navy sailors, Air Force pilots, State Department bodyguards—the rest of them were still back in Gitmo, still behind bars. The individuals here had been handpicked to escape, selected because each had a skill requisite for the very nasty business they knew lay ahead. Fox and Ozzi, for instance, were plugged into the military's internal security apparatus; that's where their talents lay. Two Delta Force guys, Dave Hunn and Sal Puglisi, were also at hand. At six-three, 240 pounds, Hunn provided the muscle. Nearly as big, Puglisi was the bomb maker. It was these two who'd taken out Palm Tree and then swum across the Potomac Reservoir to evade any pursuit. That's why both were still soaking wet.

Ron Gallant, a USAF pilot and dead ringer for Clark Kent, right down to the goofy eyewear, was here as well. He'd flown one of the team's Blackhawk helicopters back before the Hormuz Incident when the ghosts were prowling around the Persian Gulf using an undercover containership as their floating base. Though he cut his teeth on helos, Gallant could fly just about anything these days. That's why he was here.

The youngest of the small group was Gil Bates. Tall, thin, goateed, with punked hair, and barely 22 years old, Bates had been an employee of the super-secret National Security Agency for almost four years before getting involved with the rogue team. A graduate of MIT at 17—in Advanced Military C(3) Theory, no less—he was a superhacker, someone who could break into just about any computer and any computer file, no matter how many security barriers had been placed around it. When he was on, it was almost magical what he could do.

He was sitting in front of Li's laptop now. He'd downloaded her most recent e-mails, they being the mysterious *"Fast Ball"* and *"Slow Curve"* files. Both were important to every man here, in more ways than one. They believed one contained information that would prove there had been no legitimate reason for locking them up in Gitmo. More important, though, the other might hold evidence of a very grave threat against the United States—one that nobody seemed to be doing anything about.

But how did they know this? How did the team have any more than a guess as to what might be on the two files? And who was sending them in the first place? In all cases, the answer was: "Top-secret. . . ."

Bates opened the file called *"Fast Ball"* first. Breaking into it was child's play for him, quickly solving the security code that had prevented Li or anyone else from reading all of it. And, just as she'd suspected, it was a transcript of an interrogation, one carried out by "senior U.S. military officials," aboard an unnamed U.S. warship in the South Pacific just a few weeks before. Its entire contents were marked: AUTHORIZED EYES ONLY.

The men gathered around the computer laughed at seeing this. Why? Because *they* were the people being grilled in the interrogation, they and their still-incarcerated ghostly colleagues down in Gitmo. Their grand inquisition had been conducted a few weeks after the Singapore Incident, and after the team had been rounded up by the U.S. military in the Philippines and whisked aboard the aircraft carrier *Abraham Lincoln,* ironically the same warship they'd saved weeks before at Hormuz. This would be the first time the team members would see the official document produced as a result of that interrogation. They all read it silently now, looking over Bates's shoulder.

In an odd, roundabout way, the transcript chronicled just about everything the rogue team had been doing in the last six months. Their heroics, their secret battles, their over-the-top derring-do. Within the endless pages of Q&As was the true story of Hormuz, how the original team, assembled nearly a year before to track down those responsible for 9/11, had stalked the Al Qaeda hijackers the morning of the planned attack, finally breaking their code and alerting the Navy that trouble was coming. So, too, the rescue at Singapore, where on prime-time TV the team saved thousands of innocent people before disappearing just as quickly as they came.

The document read like the stuff of movies and best sellers, but far from *braggadocio,* the team members' tales were told in terms of bravery and sacrifice, especially by their comrades who'd died during the Hormuz operation.

And while it might have seemed to the world's eye that the rogue team had vanished after the incident in Singapore, the interrogation document showed, in their own words, that just the opposite was true. They'd never stopped their secret war against Al Qaeda. In fact, shortly after the Tonka Tower rescue the ghosts began not one but two operations against the terrorist organization. One involved a handful of ghosts hunting down and brutally assassinating Abdul Kazeel, the man who'd helped mastermind both 9/11 and the Hormuz attack. The second mission had other team members looking for a wayward shipment of American-made Stinger missiles, surface-to-air weapons highly prized by the Islamic terrorists. The ghosts eventually tracked the missiles to an Al Qaeda–linked cell in Manila, but that's when the U.S. military finally caught up with them, arresting the team *en masse* just minutes before they could seize the weapons cache. After that, the transcript clearly showed all of the team members insisting not only that the missiles, 36 in all, had been paid for and delivered to Al Qaeda by none other than the DGSE agent Palm Tree but also that the weapons were heading to America, to be used by other terrorists to shoot down U.S. airliners.

And therein lay the first problem. Certainly three dozen Stinger missiles on the loose inside the United States could wreck havoc in the skies above the homeland. But instead of pursuing crucial leads given to them by the team members, their inquisitors went in the other direction: they tried mightily to get the ghosts to *change* their stories, to turn on one another, and, most important, to tell the military authorities just who put the team together in the first place.

This was someone's ploy to dissolve the team once and for all. But it didn't work. None of the ghosts fell for it. While those questioned gave explicit answers, no one spilled his guts. No one gave details about *who* organized them or *who* managed to get them a containership filled with the latest in combat gear and snooping systems or *who* had the guts to gather together such an elite group of war fighters in the first place, all of whom had lost loved ones to Islamic terrorism in the recent past. In other words, the team members had no problem telling their inquisitors what they had done at Hormuz and Singapore. They just didn't tell them how.

So, too, did every man stay true to the group. Their interrogators even went so far as to suggest that the team was actually involved in moving illegal drugs when they were caught in Manila and *not* trying to find the Stinger missiles. It was total bullshit, of course, but if just one team member agreed to change his story and follow this script, then, it was promised, he would be set free and given a million dollars in cold cash, not a bad payoff for about an hour's work.

But again, not one of them took the bait. *Not one* of them even remotely flipped on his friends. These guys weren't just patriots. They were *loyal,* too.

By the end of it, their inquisitors were stumped as to what to do.

So they threw them *all* in jail.

Where were the Stinger missiles now? No one knew. But there were some clues. And they were contained in the second cryptic e-mail, the one called *"Slow Curve."*

Once again, Bates worked his magic and opened it in a snap. But unlike the first attachment, *"Slow Curve"* was not all text. Rather, it also contained images caught by a photophone, along with some audio downloads. Together they told the strange story of a sports reporter from Los Angeles named George Mann and what had happened to him shortly before his body was found, with two bullets in the head, dumped in a ditch in the desert northeast of Los Angeles.

Stitched together from smaller files Mann had sent by phone to his home computer, the file presented a morbidly disjointed picture of the last hours of the reporter's life. He'd been assigned to cover a Southeast Asian soccer team that had traveled, by boat, to LA and was barnstorming the United States. Mann apparently met their ship at the port of LA but was nearly run down by the team's pair of Greyhound buses, purely by accident, it seems. Mann later caught up with one of those buses in a small California desert town, where his picturephone transmitted images of at least some of the soccer team riding in one of the Greyhound coaches. As it turned out, this bus was also carrying an arsenal of weapons in a secret storage area—an arsenal that included at least 18 Stinger missiles. The file ended abruptly just as a fleeting phone image of the missiles was sent back to Mann's home computer.

As sketchy as the *"Slow Curve"* attachment was, anyone viewing it could only reach one, rather incredible conclusion: These soccer players weren't soccer players at all. They were Al Qaeda terrorists. And they were now inside the United States, carrying at least 18 Stinger missiles with them.

*Scary. . . .*

A qualifying paragraph inserted at the end of the file indicated that the bombshell info was *not* obtained by a physical break-in. Rather, an ultrasecret NSA eavesdropping satellite known only as *Keypad* had been used to access Mann's information. This system could zero in on, listen, and secretly record any cell-phone call made by anyone, anywhere in the world, including the United States.

*Very scary. . . .*

Whoever it was who intercepted Mann's phone images had also done an analysis of them. They were able to determine at least 18 men were aboard the bus, all of Middle Eastern descent, all between the ages of 21 and 30. The lone image taken inside the weapons compartment was a blurred shot of the 18 Stinger missiles, attached to their launching mechanisms, hanging on both sides of the storage-room wall. A trail of smoke could also be seen, in shadow, against one of the walls, the result, the analysis said, of two bullets being fired into Mann's head. The sports reporter's cell phone ceased sending data shortly after that.

Who secured the *"Slow Curve"* file? Why was the NSA's *Keypad* satellite intercepting Mann's phone transmissions or was the system routinely monitoring *everyone's* cell phones? How was it that *"Slow Curve,"* as well as *"Fast Ball,"* wound up in Li's e-mail box? And, most important, why hadn't this information raised alarms within the Homeland Security department?

The file did not provide any answers to these questions. But it did contain one last tantalizing piece of information. Shortly before he was killed, Mann had taken a phone-picture of the *faux* soccer team's schedule, a cross-country map of the American South and Midwest showing where they were supposed to play their goodwill games. Was it possible that these sites, Numbered 1 through 9, were the places where the terrorists intended to use the missiles to shoot down U.S. airliners?

The answer was: yes. The analyst confirmed each site was within 12 miles of a major airport and each had ample higher elevations around it, providing the terrorists with perfect hiding places from which to do their murderous work. And there were 9 game sites in all. Eighteen missiles. Two missiles per airport? It seemed logical—and no doubt the first bus was heading to one of those locations right now.

*Very, very scary. . . .*

But as unsettling as this information was, it also left one last, very disturbing question: Mann was able to track down one of the buses—and he saw 18 of the missiles aboard it. Yet the ghost team members knew there were at least 36 missiles on the loose and *two* buses involved.

So where were the other missiles?

And where was the other bus?

Li Cho was not a patient person.

She remained in the small bedroom far down the hall, her nose pressed against the dirty windowpane, confused, tired, and wishing the rain would stop and the sun would come up and some reason and sanity would arrive to save the day.

But while the first 15 minutes passed with her barely moving a muscle, she couldn't take it anymore after that. She turned to the man stretched out on the bed, the seventh team member. Her unofficial guard. He hadn't said a word since she'd come into the room. She could hardly see him, in fact. As he lay atop the old, ratty mattress, the sooty canopy cut off all but a blurry shadow of him. He might have even been asleep.

But thanks to her cup of Morning Madness, Li was wide awake.

"So, holding someone prisoner in her own home . . ." she finally said to him. "Is that usually how you guys operate?"

"I'm sleeping," came the reply, though he sounded totally awake, as if he'd just been lying there all this time, thinking deeply about something.

"Well, can't I talk to you?" she asked. "About all this, I mean. Or do I have to just sit here quietly?"

"Sit. Quietly. Please?"

But there was no chance of that.

"Why you?" she persisted. "Why are *you* the one watching me? Why aren't you with the others?"

"Because I'm not a computer freak," he answered wearily, his words raspy from cigarettes. "And the legitimate brains have to figure out some information that just came our way."

"Oh, really?" she asked. It was rough, but she actually liked the sound of his voice. "And what if what you're looking for isn't there?"

A sigh. Was he growing annoyed with her already?

"If it isn't there," he replied, "then we should all just head back down to Gitmo, so they can lock us up again. . . ."

Li laughed, wishing she could see his face better.

"What is it that you do, then?" she asked him. "If computers aren't your thing?"

"I fly airplanes."

"Oh . . . were you flying the plane that supposedly crashed off Cuba?"

A pause. "For someone who is supposed to be sitting quietly, you're asking a lot of questions. . . ."

"That used to be my job," she said. "But never mind that. How did you do it? Fake the plane crash, I mean. . . ."

He yawned. A flash of lightning outside.

"Sorry," he said. "Top-secret."

She stamped her foot. "*Everyone* keeps saying that around here. . . ."

"Well, *that* should tell you something," he replied. "It's just another way of saying 'please shut up.' "

Li was hurt, a little. She kept probing, though. "I understand now why all my lightbulbs were missing," she said. "And my soap and thumbtacks. And all my Jell-O, I guess. You used them to build the bomb that killed that French guy, right?"

"He deserved a lot worse than just getting his head blown off," he answered.

"So I've heard," she whispered coyly. "But I have to ask you: why did you clean my place, too? I've never seen it so tidy. That scared me more than anything."

She thought she saw his shoulders shrug.

"One of my colleagues spilled a box of Jell-O all over your floor," he told her. "Yellow Jell-O—and it went everywhere. We knew we had to clean it up, at least a little bit. But once we started . . . well, let's just say it turned into a project."

Li almost laughed again. There was a hint of good-natured humor oozing out of him.

She switched gears. "So, how'd a pilot get caught up in

all this? I thought you flyboys were supposed to be smart."

"Top-secret," he moaned.

"But I'm level eight security," she said. "You can tell me just about anything."

"Can—but won't," he replied in shorthand.

She thought another moment. "These files your friends out there are opening. I know one's an interrogation. It names names, I assume?"

"Probably. . . ."

"And might you be one of those names?"

A pause. Then: "Top-secret."

"Oh, so your name *is* in there then?"

Silence.

"Because when I read that file I'll want to know which one is you," she added awkwardly. "You know, just to keep everybody straight."

"Who says you're ever going to read it?" he shot back.

She didn't reply. Another silence in the room, this one for about fifteen seconds.

Then he surprised her by saying, "I'm the only Air Force three-star in there. Ryder Long."

"A colonel?" she asked. "Really?"

"Really—or at least I used to be. It's a little hard to tell these days."

She smiled again. This guy had shown more personality in these two minutes than Nash had in two months.

"My father's a colonel—in the Marines," she said. "But I'll bet he's not quite as old as you."

He might have chuckled for a moment. "Thanks for nothing," he said.

Another silence. More rain on the window. Another flash of lightning outside.

"And are you married, Colonel?" she asked, her words floating up into the dark.

She saw him shift uneasily on the bed.

"Used to be . . ." he replied.

"And were you happy?"

"Used to be . . ." he said again.

Silence—at least 30 seconds of it.
"And do you miss her?" Li finally whispered.
The shadow on the bed let out a long, sad breath.
"Sorry," he said. "Top-secret. . . ."

# Chapter 7

When dawn finally came, the rain had stopped and the fog had gone away. But all was still not right with the world. Ryder Long could feel it in his bones.

He hadn't slept a wink, not unusual, as he rarely slept anymore. Sleeping meant dreams, and his dreams were haunted by memories. They could be so painful, sometimes it was just better to stay awake.

He eased himself off the bed now, just as the first bit of sunlight peeked through the dirty window. His boots made only a minimum of noise when they touched the creaky floor. He'd spent a lot of time in this room off and on in the past few nights; he was getting good at working the planks by now. He was, after all, a ghost. He glanced out the window and groaned. The sky above was bright, bright red. ·

*"I knew it,"* he whispered.

Red skies in the morning were never a good sign.

He moved across the floor to the other, much larger, much dirtier window. Here he found Li, head down on the massive sill, finally sound asleep. He leaned over for no better reason than to get a good look at her up close, his first, really, since coming here.

*"Wow! . . ."* he exclaimed, much too loudly. She really *was* gorgeous.

Ryder was tempted to lift her head and put a pillow under it—others in the team had moved her before without waking her. But it wasn't in him to disturb such a sleeping beauty. He moved silently across the room instead, going out the door with the skill of a cat burglar.

He stepped out into the hallway, wondering if there was any semblance of breakfast in the offing. One sniff of the same old musty air told him no. He wandered down the hall and stuck his head into the master bedroom. Here he found the rest of the team. They were no longer gathered around the computer like a den of Cub Scouts on steroids, though. Just the opposite. The place looked like a bomb had hit it, with bodies scattered everywhere.

Ozzi was lying half off the bed, just staring up at the ceiling. Fox was slumped in a corner, head down on his knees. Gallant was beside him, hands together, as if in prayer. Even Hunn and Puglisi looked wiped out. Their wet clothes still drying in front of a dangerously old-looking space heater, they were sitting close by the window, in their underwear, their M15 weapons at ready, should anyone come down the reservoir extension road.

But it was Bates who looked the worst. Eyes red, jaw clenched. Punked hair more out of control than usual. Still sitting in front of the computer, only he turned around to look at Ryder.

"What's the matter with you guys?" the pilot asked the whiz kid.

Bates just shook his head. "You missed a long night. That and the fact that we just found out we might have bitten off more than we can chew in this whole thing."

"Just give me the highlights," Ryder told him.

Bates ran his hands through his hair and took a deep breath, trying to stay awake. "You know that personal organizer Hunn and Pugs took off the French guy?" he asked Ryder.

"Yeah, sure, the PDA," Ryder said back. "Aren't you supposed to be trying to break into it? I mean, that's one of the reasons we're up here. . . ."

Bates just nodded. "Well, I cracked it, all right," he said. "It took me four freaking hours. But what we saw when I did . . ."

Ryder studied the kid for a moment. He'd known him since way before the Hormuz Incident. Like Ryder, Bates was one of the original members of the rogue team. And despite their varied backgrounds and ages, because of all they'd gone through together the original guys were as tight as brothers by now.

But Ryder had never seen Bates look like this. What could he have seen inside the PDA that would twist him up so?

"Show me," Ryder finally told him. "Show me what you found."

Bates sat Ryder down in front of Li's laptop and pointed to the *"Fast Ball"* and *"Slow Curve"* files.

"Get a load of these first," Bates told him. "You'll need the info to appreciate what comes next."

Ryder read the files quickly. The interrogations. The top-secret classifications. The story of Georgie Mann. At the end of them, though, Ryder actually felt relieved, especially by what he'd seen on *"Fast Ball."*

"Well, at least we've got something on record that says *we* warned those assholes about the missiles being smuggled into the U.S.," he said. "It's just too bad this poor bastard Mann had to take two in the hat to prove we were right."

Bates almost laughed. "All that's just the beginning, Colonel," he said. "The water gets a lot deeper from here on in."

Using his own laptop now, Bates showed Ryder how he had hooked up Palm Tree's PDA to what he called a drain line. It was a gadget that was able to literally suck information out of the DGSE agent's device.

Bates went on: "The problem was, his little PDA turned out to be loaded with memory chips. Hundreds of them. They added up to almost a gig. And they were able to hold tons of stuff."

"Seems like overkill," Ryder said, as if he knew what Bates was talking about, which he didn't.

"It was," Bates replied. "But that was the whole idea. He filled most of his memory up with totally useless crap. Stuff like the entire French dictionary. And the four phone books of Paris. The individual results of every person ever to race in the Tour de France. On and on and on. . . ."

"All this was camouflage?" Ryder asked.

"Exactly," Bates replied. "Hiding the real stuff by putting tons of nonsense in front of it. On top of it. All around it. And then he set up so many security codes protecting these files, even the most hopped-up cyberfreak would give up trying to break through."

"But you succeeded, right?" Ryder asked.

"It was like peeling back the layers of the mother of all onions," Bates replied. "That and lots of typing. And retyping. But yeah, I finally got through, to the stuff that asshole was hiding in there. And this is what I found. . . ."

He showed Ryder the first attachment he'd come upon after getting through all the security diversions. It was marked, in English, "Travel Plans."

"I was immediately suspicious of this," Bates explained, "because it contains nearly a hundred megs of data. That's much more than a normal person would have in a file labeled 'Travel Plans.'"

And Bates was right. The file didn't contain travel plans. In fact, all Ryder saw was reams of numbers with names beside them.

"The numbers represent payments going in and out of a bunch of Swiss bank accounts," Bates explained. "The names are the beneficiaries of these transactions. Look at this one: 'Monsieur A. L. Zeke.'"

Ryder laughed out loud. Even he knew this was a very lame anagram for *Kazeel,* as in Abdul Kazeel, top Al Qaeda mook and a victim of the rogue team's brutal justice not long ago.

Bates ran down the length of the file. More numbers, more fake names, more transaction confirmations. It was all moving too fast for Ryder. But Bates explained that by connecting all the dots he was able to determine that Palm Tree and, by association, the French government not only transferred funds to Al Qaeda for the Stinger missile purchases but also had arranged for the missiles' shipment out of the Philippines, as well as their smuggling into the United States, including an inspection-free port of entry in LA.

It was dramatic stuff, but truthfully, Ryder wasn't surprised by any of it. They'd all come to know that Palm Tree had blood on his hands. That's why the team had popped him.

Bates then showed Ryder another file, one that traced another money trail that proved Palm Tree and Kazeel had paid for the Stinger missiles first and then their launchers. This confirmed another suspicion held by the ghosts, that the weapons had actually been bought in two separate purchases. The launchers they knew came from an Iraqi arms dealer named Bahzi; he, too, was later whacked by the ghost team. But where did the missiles themselves come from? Or more important, how was such a large number procured for the terrorists, via Palm Tree?

"Remember now, these are American-made weapons," Bates told Ryder. "And I might be wrong, but I think that while the launchers can last awhile, the missiles only work well if they are up-to-date. Those missiles in the Mann photo look to be the latest model. And believe me, the Pentagon keeps close tabs on where they all are. Am I right, Major Fox?"

Still slumped in the corner, Fox replied in a mumble, "That was one of our main jobs at DSA: keep track of all weapons, big or small. For thirty-six brand-new Stingers to suddenly go missing, without a trace, means that French asshole must have had some help inside the U.S. military. *Deep* inside."

Ryder just shook his head. They had all discussed such a possibility before, so again, it was no surprise. "But who?" he asked now. "Who in Higher Authority would have gotten in bed with these guys?"

"You really want to know?" Bates asked him cryptically.

Before Ryder could reply, the whiz kid began banging on his keyboard again, retrieving yet another bonanza: a list of Palm Tree's phone calls for the past two months.

Ryder was surprised. "What were they doing in his personal organizer? I thought these spy types didn't like to leave evidence of who they've been talking to. . . ."

Bates smiled grimly. "Usually they don't," he said. "And for sure, I just assumed this guy would be like the mooks. You know, shedding cell phones on an hourly basis? But believe it or not, he used the PDA to dial for him."

Ryder was stumped. "Why?"

Bates just shrugged. "Too lazy to dial it himself, I guess," he said. "Or maybe he *wanted* to keep track of who he was calling, thinking that no one would ever get into his pants like this. But it was an amazingly stupid thing to do, because no matter how many cell phones he used, the PDA kept track of all his calls."

Bates showed Ryder the long list he'd recovered. It looked just like a phone bill, details of who was called and for how long they talked. There were lots of phone calls to car rental agencies and restaurants.

"But look at this number," Bates told him, pointing to the screen. "This is where it gets really weird."

There was indeed a certain number—011-333-0001—that had been dialed several times over the past few weeks but had been cut off before it ever made a connection, almost as if every time the caller thought better of what he was doing. Or was sending some kind of signal.

That the number had the area exchange 011 was the surprising thing. Bates explained that when he worked at the NSA, before he joined the rogue team, he was told many tip-top-secret things. Like that area code 011 was a secret phone exchange used exclusively by the White House. And that the next three numbers—333—were used for secure phones in the White House offices reserved for the National Security Council. And that the last four numbers—0001—indicated that this particular phone was the first in a line of many.

"So, ponder this," Bates concluded. "Why would a French intelligence agent, one with a very dirty past, and obviously out to fuck over the U.S., have the number for someone in the NSC office at the White House?"

Ryder just shrugged. "These numbers have to be closely held secrets, right?"

Bates replied, "Are they ever. My boss at the NSA used to keep them in a nuclear blast–proof safe. *That's* how secret they were. No one I know would have been stupid enough to let one out in such an unsecured location as a cell phone or a personal organizer. In fact, you're supposed to keep them in your head."

"Well, then who the hell was this French asshole calling at the White House?" Ryder asked.

Bates smiled grimly again. Then he handed Ryder a clean cell phone and said, "See for yourself."

Ryder understood right away. They had done this type of thing before. He punched in the number.

A woman answered.

She said, "General Rushton's office."

That was it.

The smoking gun . . .

General James Trimble Rushton.

Special Assistant to the President on military special ops. Longtime senior adviser to the NSC. One of the few people in Washington with access to the Oval Office day and night, 24/7.

He was also a disturbingly incompetent human being, who knew almost nothing about the military or special ops yet frequently ran roughshod over both. Arrogant, effete, and patently dishonest, Rushton nevertheless held great sway inside the Beltway and especially on the NSC. When he spoke, he was usually speaking in *bono vox* on the NSC's behalf.

What was his connection to all this?

Plenty. . . .

It was Rushton who'd sent Fox on his last mission, which was to track down the rogue team right after their dramatic rescue in Singapore. He'd dispatched Fox not to bring the rogues back to justice, however, but to enlist their aid in locating a downed B-2 bomber that, they would all come to suspect, was somehow tied up in the Stinger missile deal, too. In fact, the Stealth plane might have been carrying the missiles themselves, a frightening prospect that would mean the Stingers had come *directly* from America and then been handed to the terrorists. At the very least the weapons might have spent some time in the cargo bay of the specially adapted B-2F bomber.

And indeed, the rogue team found the missing B-2 crashed on a very isolated island off the northern coast of the Philippines. But when they did, Rushton first ordered Fox to inspect its bomb bay and, after finding it empty, told him to pinpoint the billion-dollar bomber's exact location—so it could be destroyed by a massive cruise missile attack. Tellingly, after this was done Rushton cut off all communication with Fox, leaving him stranded with most of the rogue team on the very small practically prehistoric Filipino island. Very unusual behavior, for sure.

But that was not the end of Rushton's involvement. Hardly. It was Rushton and a jackboot unit of Green Berets who stopped the rogue team in their tracks just before they were able to catch up with the shipment of Stingers leaving Manila. It was Rushton who took the team into custody, whisking them aboard the USS *Abraham Lincoln* and locking them up in separate brigs like a bunch of convicted felons. It was Rushton who led the interrogations spelled out in the file called *"Fast Ball."* It was Rushton who tried so hard to get the members of the team to flip. And failing that, it was Rushton who sent them all to Gitmo, vowing that none of them would ever set foot in the United States again.

After all that, the team couldn't help but suspect him of somehow being mixed up in the Stinger affair. But now they had a definite link between him and the agent Palm Tree. This smoking gun was still red-hot.

And again, Ryder thought this was a good thing. Certainly it was clear from everything he'd seen that the terrorists had managed to buy the missiles and get them into the U.S. with some high-level help. But if the terrorists and their missiles were riding around in Greyhound buses, well, all the government had to do was put out an APB for law enforcement everywhere to simply stop and search every Greyhound bus, wherever they may be. Or better yet, the government could order the Greyhound company to simply freeze all its buses in place, just as all airline flights were frozen in the hours and days after 9/11. All it would take was a few calls from the NSC, via the Homeland Security department, and the terrorists' buses could be found in no time. Heroes again, the ghosts could then explain their own outlaw situation to someone higher up and stop this life on the run before it even started.

Simple, right?

"Wrong," Bates told him, even before Ryder could blurt it all out. "Take a look at this. . . ."

Going even deeper into Palm Tree's hidden files, Bates retrieved a very top-secret NSC operations memo, something that Rushton had obviously turned over to the French spy. In this memo Rushton stated that "only cognizant threats to homeland security identified by me will be given priority for any follow-up discussion or investigation." His rationale was that the country's intelligence services were barraged with rumors and tips about pending terrorist actions in the country every day, many of which were dead ends. This was a massive case of overload, and Rushton had taken it upon himself to sort it out by determining which threats were real and which were not. Only he would decide which threats were important enough to be looked into. Only he would direct the response if a terrorist attack should happen inside the United States. And in fact, these orders were written under a so-called national security directive, something that was just one step below an executive order from the President himself.

As if to prove the point, Rushton ended the top-secret memo by saying: "All threats involving ground transport vehicles, including cars, trucks, and buses, will be given low priority for the time being."

"This is fucking treason!" Ryder roared. "This guy is setting it up so the mooks can do just about anything they want."

"Exactly," Bates replied soberly.

Ryder looked around the room again. The rest of the team had stayed nearly silent the entire time he'd been here. Now he knew why. Rushton was in this thing up to his beady eyeballs. Not only had he laid out the perfect conditions for the terrorists to move about the country freely, at least for a few days, to do their dirty work, but he'd also rigged it so even when airliners started getting shot down he would be in a position to steer any investigations in other directions, away from what the terrorists were really up to.

"This guy has suddenly become a very powerful person," Bates said. "And in doing so he's covered all the angles. And his actions are so outrageous, it would take days, weeks, or even longer for us, or anyone, to convince people that all of this is real. And by that time, it will be too late. I mean, who is going to believe one of the top military officers in the country is in league with the terrorists? Especially if it's us—outlaws ourselves—who are the first to blow the whistle on him? They'll lock us up again and it will be months before we could even get a peep out. Just the fact that *we* have this information irreversibly taints it."

He paused. The room suddenly grew dark. Outside, the sky had turned deep bloodred.

"You know, something like this could never have happened in this country ten years ago," Bates said, his voice low. "Or even five years. But with 9/11, and everything's that's happened since, abuses of the Patriot Act, the CIA and the FBI running around with their heads cut off, Iraq . . . shit, a guy like Rushton was able to come out of nowhere and fill a vacuum. And this is the result."

Ryder just shook his head. What a fucking mess. . . .

"But *why* is he doing it?" he asked. "*Why* is he committing such high treason against the country?"

Bates just shrugged. "It's usually money, Colonel," he said. "Though, for some reason, I think this guy has motives even deeper than that. He's not just powerful. He's arrogant. And downright evil. But he's not a fool. How we could wish he was. If he was willing to do all this back and forth with the asshole Frenchman, that tells me he'll stop at nothing to see his agenda through, whatever it may be. And that will include finding us once he realizes we're not all dead. God, he could send the entire 82nd Airborne after us and no one would blink an eye."

"In other words," Ozzi moaned, suddenly coming to life nearby, "we're screwed."

Fox, too, was suddenly back among the living. He got to his feet, walked over to the computer, and, without asking, took a cigarette from Ryder's dwindling pack.

"Now show him the really bad news," Fox told Bates.

Ryder slumped farther into his seat. "There's more?" he moaned.

Fox lit his purloined butt and let out a long stream of smoke.

"Oh yeah," he said drily. "*A lot* more. . . ."

The rest of the team grudgingly revived themselves at this point. Gallant retreated downstairs to the kitchen and made a pot of coffee from the last of Li's Maxwell House. There weren't enough clean cups, though. So they had to drink the coffee out of milk glasses.

Bates meanwhile never stopped typing, noisily slurping his liquid caffeine as he retrieved yet another of Palm Tree's hidden files. This one, particularly large, was titled "Family Photos."

"Here's our next very real screwy thing," Bates announced.

It, too, was chock-full of what seemed to be useless data taking up space. Still sitting beside Bates, sipping his own glass of coffee, Ryder watched a parade of Palm Tree's "family" pass by in the form of JPEG photos. *Mum-mère. Pa-pa. Mon frère. Mon sœur.* Dozens of kids and aunts and uncles, big noses, dirty faces, rotten teeth, most likely none of them even remotely related to the DGSE agent. But why was Bates forcing Ryder to endure this gallery of Gauls, flipping by at a rate of about five a second? He was about to ask when

Bates alerted him to a series of photos coming up that depicted an old lady visiting the island of Capri. Dozens of these images were soon flipping by, moving faster than a slide projector on speed.

"What is this?" Ryder finally demanded to know. "He took pictures of someone's grandma at the beach. What's the big deal?"

"Just watch," Bates told him, manipulating the keyboard to get the images to move even faster. Suddenly one white blotch appeared among the flipping photos. It went by so quickly, Ryder hardly noticed it. But Bates had caught it. Now he isolated it.

"Check it out," he told Ryder.

It was not a photo, but what was it? Ryder had to study the image for a few seconds before he realized he was looking at a photo of a napkin, one with a very crude drawing scribbled on it. The napkin had a large brown coffee stain in its upper right-hand corner, along with, oddly enough, the impression of two coins, embedded beneath the stain.

With all the artistry of a six-year-old, the drawing appeared to show a collection of things in flight, both big and small, traveling over what might have been hundreds, if not thousands, of people but, tellingly, no buildings. Because of the large stain and the imprint of the coins, though, it was difficult to count just how many of these flying things were being depicted. There may have been at least a dozen. But what were they flying over?

Groggy from his night of nonsleep, Ryder still failed to see the relevance of the image. "OK, so when he took Grandma's picture at the beach in Capri, he bought her something, an expensive espresso, no doubt. This is her napkin. And she scribbled on it. So what?"

But Bates just shook his head. "No," he insisted. "This is a very special thing. Think about it. It *has* to be. That French bastard wouldn't have stuck it in the middle of this humongous file and then surrounded it with a galaxy of security stuff if it wasn't important, right? I mean, he was hiding it in a place that if anyone actually got in, they'd get so sick of looking at two hundred images of toothless Granny there, they'd probably give up and move on."

Ryder thought about all that for a moment, then nodded. He had to agree.

"Now, see that logo on the napkin?" Bates asked him. "It's in English. It's from a place called Drive, Shop 'n Go."

He began pounding on a second laptop nearby doing a Google search under that name. The information that popped up indicated that "Drive, Shop 'n Go" was a chain of 7-Eleven-type stores located throughout the eastern part of New Jersey.

"And those two coins?" Bates asked, manipulating the screen to zoom in on that part of the napkin. "They're nickels, see?"

Again Ryder had to agree. Clearly the coinage was American.

"OK, so first of all, we know this napkin isn't from Capri but from somewhere in Jersey," Bates said.

Ryder nodded again. He tried to study the drawing in this new light, but it was hard to do. The most primitive caveman art put this thing to shame.

"Well, if those winged things in the air are supposed to be airplanes," Ryder said, "then it's a drawing of an extra-busy airport."

But again Bates was shaking his head. "There isn't an airport in the world that would have *that* many airplanes in the air over it at the same time," he said. "Plus look: they're all going in the same direction."

"Well, maybe it's a bunch of crude time lapses, you know?" Ryder said. "Showing a bunch of airplanes in the process of taking off and landing, but at different time intervals."

But Bates wasn't buying that. Neither were the rest of the team now gathered back around them.

The disturbing thing was, in the lowest part of the right-hand corner, below the worst of the coffee smudge, there was another crude drawing that, when Bates was able to zoom in on it, showed what appeared to be a Greyhound coach with a series of more or less straight lines coming up from it, heading toward the overcrowded sky.

"That's *got* to be a bus," Bates said, pointing to its boxy appearance and its three wheels per side. It also showed many windows and a big windshield, as well as a hole in its roof. No one could disagree with him. Though still childlike, this drawing was the most identifiable scribble on the napkin. Bates also showed him that there was some writing in the upper right-hand corner of the napkin, but that it was almost totally obscured by the massive coffee stain and the imprint of the two nickels.

Ryder just shook his head. "Well, it's *got* to be a mass attack on a busy airport," he said. "O'Hare or someplace. What else could it be?"

"But assuming this might be the second bus," Bates said, "why stage a mass attack at one airport while your mook brothers are driving around the country setting up *separate* attacks on as many as nine different airports?"

He was right. It didn't make sense—and it left them all scratching their heads. Everyone present was fairly sure that the drawing had something to do with the mysterious second bus.

But the images in the air remained very puzzling.

They drained the rest of the coffee and sat there in near silence, trying to comprehend all that Bates had uncovered.

Finally Hunn began to speak.

"We've got to start talking about this," he said. "The more we avoid it, the more time we lose. . . ."

"So talk about it then," Gallant told him testily.

"OK," Hunn began again. "Look at all the shit this Rushton guy's been doing. There's no freaking way those missiles *accidentally* fell into the hands of the mooks. Rushton was behind it—all these files prove it. And that means he *had* to be paid off, somehow, someway. Or he's got something else up his sleeve. . . ."

Hunn was a good soldier. Brave, loyal, and smart. But he also had anger issues. They all did. He had already done a number on many of the Al Qaeda operatives they'd been able to track down, a small hatchet being his weapon of choice. At this point, though, he was ready to invade France.

"And don't forget," he went on. "This asshole general went to *great* lengths to prevent us from stopping those missiles from getting into the U.S.—and he had us locked away indefinitely to boot. He's not just some stupid ass trying to get out of his own way. He's in thick with the French *and* the mooks, one way or another."

Everyone nodded solemnly. They knew what was coming next.

"So, are we going to do what we said we were going to do when we got up here?" Hunn asked.

A long silence. The team had given up a long time ago on the niceties of conflict. Rules of war, Geneva Convention—all that crap. They moved in a new world, a place where things happened as fast as the bings and bangs of the Internet or the speed at which a picture could be flashed around the world. Close to the speed of light. Instantaneous. That's what their world was—and that's what they had to be, too. They didn't have time for long-drawn-out investigations, or trying to explain themselves, or committees being formed, or going the standard route and allowing the FBI to fuck things up.

They had come up here for many reasons, but two of them stood out: The elimination of Palm Tree, ending his little dance once and for all. And now Rushton. . . .

"But we've got several problems going here," Fox reminded them. "Sure, we've probably got the goods on Rushton. But all that means is that no one in the government is going to start looking for those buses anytime soon. And, even if we could, there's *no way* we could show all this to someone higher up and convince him that it's all true in time before those assholes out there start shooting down airliners. That shit might start happening less than a day from now."

"It's just like at Hormuz," Gallant groaned; he'd been there, so he knew of what he spoke. "Once again, we're the only ones who know what's *really* going on. We're the only ones that are in a position to stop it."

They all hung their heads. They'd been expecting this—or something like it. But that didn't make it any easier.

The buses were out there; they had missiles in them. And if the government wasn't going to stop them, then it was up to the ghost team to. Again, they had planned for this eventuality. But it still took a while for it to finally sink in.

"But not only do we have to find the two buses," Ozzi said, "*and* deal with Rushton. We have to figure out that *other* thing."

Ryder looked at the rest of them. They were staring back at him with sunken, tired eyes. They all looked miserable—and, he supposed, so did he.

"What 'other thing'?" he asked. "Are you telling me, *there's more*?"

No one said a word. So Ryder just turned back to Bates, who nodded grimly.

"There is," he finally revealed. "And this one is almost impossible to figure out, more so than the napkin."

Once again, he started banging on his keyboard.

"I went as deep as I could go into Palm Tree's memory banks," he went on. "And just when I thought I was at the end, I got stopped at one last file Rushton sent him. It has the absolutely tightest security regime I've ever encountered surrounding it."

Ryder saw the file icon pop up on Bates's screen.

"This file was given even higher priority and therefore more protection than even his most obvious correspondence with Palm Tree," Bates went on. "And notice how it's marked: 'For Immediate Action.' Yet it's labeled 'May 1 through 7.'"

Sure enough, the icon's label seemed to indicate something having to do with the first seven days in May.

Ryder shook his head wearily. "But it's June," he said.

Bates just shrugged. "I know," he said. "Makes it even more screwy, doesn't it?"

"Can't you get *anything* out of them?" Ryder asked,

looking at the frozen screen that represented the dead end
Bates had run into.

"Very, very little," he replied. "But the trace I was able to
suck out looked like orders for troop movements, moving air
assets around, things like that. But that's all I can see right
now."

"What could he be hiding *more* than the fact that he's
working with the French and Al Qaeda to shoot down a bunch
of planes in his own country?" Ryder asked incredulously.

It was a good question. But no one had a clue as to what
the answer might be. Another long silence. The world was
back on their shoulders.

"So, what *are* we going to do?" Hunn asked again. "The
clock is ticking here, and suddenly it looks like there isn't
enough minutes in a day for us. . . ."

Fox finally spoke up: "I say we proceed like we were going to anyway. This added complication with Rushton isn't
that big of a surprise, though personally I never thought he'd
go so far as to *actively aid* the mooks with that low-grade-
threat order on ground transport.

"But we'll just have to deal with it while we are on the
move. Getting an ID on those buses, figuring out what's on
that napkin, and stopping the mooks from shooting down
airplanes is what we have to fix first. If not, we let a lot of
people down. The whole country, in fact. And a lot of people
will die, too. So, let's get our stuff together, and whoever is
leaving, let's get to it."

More silence. They were all tired, hungry, and miserable.
No one wanted to move.

Then Ozzi said to Fox, "But what about Li?"

Fox thought for a very long time. He looked over at Ryder, the senior man, who just shrugged.

Finally Fox said, "Bring her in here and let her read
everything, including those first two e-mail files. We're going to need her help more than we thought. And we can't
keep her in the dark, not if she's going to put herself at
risk."

Then he looked back at the two files *"Fast Ball"* and *"Slow Curve,"* which Bates had brought back onto the screen.

"And tell her she can stop looking for Bobby Murphy, too," Fox added. "Because I think we just found him."

# PART TWO
## The Sky Horse

# Chapter 8

*There's a full moon up there, somewhere,* thought Master Chief Eddie Finch (Ret.), watching the low clouds blowing over his head. *At least I think there is. . . .*

He was on his knees, a large flashlight in one hand and a pair of hedge clippers in the other. A small hatchet was close by, too, but he was woefully unprepared for the job that lay ahead of him. He was cutting down weeds, hundreds of them, poking through the cracks in the old CG airstrip. Some were the size of small trees, thus the hatchet. But he'd been at it for nearly four hours now and he was still only a third of the way up the 3,600-foot runway. A very strange way to spend a Saturday evening.

It was almost midnight. Finch was cold, and it was dark without the moon, and, at 62 years old, he knew this was going to leave his knees in agony for weeks. Still he kept pulling and chopping. The job had to be done, because an old friend had asked him to do it.

An old friend named Bobby Murphy.

Cape Lonely Air Station was the most isolated CG base on the Atlantic seaboard. It was built on a cliff nearly 300 feet above the ocean. Six hundred acres, held in by a rusty chain-link fence, the road to get here ran two miles through a thick pine forest. A wildlife preserve bordered the station on the north; a 20-mile stretch of empty sand dunes and beach lay to its south. The closest highway, old U.S. Route 3, was more than 35 miles away.

There was a time, though, when Cape Lonely was the *busiest* Coast Guard station on the East Coast. CG aircraft from all over came here for engine change-outs and maintenance checks. New pilots endlessly practiced touch-and-go landings on its extra-wide runway. But that was back when the Coast Guard not only rescued people in peril but also searched for Russian submarines. Ten years ago, the base had been downsized to the point of nonexistence. It was like a ghost town now.

The only two things of value left at Cape Lonely were a small lighthouse and a Loran radio navigation positioning hut. Both ran automatically. An administration building, some support huts, and four dilapidated aircraft hangars were the only other structures remaining of the once-bustling air station. Behind the hangars was an aeronautical junkyard, a place where old CG aircraft had come to die. Airframes, big and small, wings, tail sections, landing gear assemblies, all rotting away, many leaking nasty fluids into the soil. No surprise, Cape Lonely was a hazardous waste site, too.

The wind was really starting to blow now and Eddie Finch knew rain might not be far away. He yanked up a milkweed that was the size of a small conifer. He was amazed at the size of some of the plant life up here. *Must be all that chemical crap in the ground,* he'd thought more than once.

He finally stopped for a much-needed breather; he hadn't worked this hard since he'd retired 10 years ago. He checked his watch. It was a few minutes past twelve. He looked down the remaining length of runway and groaned. God, did he still have a long haul ahead of him!

He was not up here alone at least. Not exactly anyway. Way down in Hangar 4A, he could see a very dull light peeking out from beneath the huge rusty door. *You'd think a couple of those guys would come out here and help me pull weeds,* he thought. But then again, they had their jobs to do as well.

Finch put his head down and got back to work. But suddenly from behind him came a strange sound. Even though he was alone on the old runway moments before, five armed men had materialized out of nowhere and were now standing over him. They were clad in weird black suits and ski masks and carrying rifles. Each man was also wearing a black rain poncho, all five blowing mightily in the wind. They seemed frightening, dangerous even, if a little frayed around the edges. Like a SWAT team that had lost its way.

Finch just looked up at them, though, and said, "Oh, it's only you guys. . . ."

It was the ghost team minus Hunn and Ozzi—Fox, Puglisi, Bates, Gallant, and Ryder—and all five were still miserable. It had been a long, hot trip down here in Li's very small car, with all their gear. They hadn't eaten anything of substance really and were down to rationing cigarettes. Except for a few interrupted naps, none of them had slept much since busting out of Gitmo seven days ago. Add in the headful of stuff they'd just learned up in D.C., the result was they were all feeling punchy.

They trooped inside the admin building now. It was a four-story cement block structure, its white paint all but chipped away, located on the other side of the landing strip from the cliff. Finch led them down to the large mess hall, a reminder of the former glory of this place. The interior looked like something from a time capsule, though, right down to the yellowed recruiting posters falling off the walls. An old Coleman lantern provided the only light these days. Finch produced a pot of coffee and five paper cups but then said, "Sorry, we're outta cream and sugar."

The five men collapsed into metal folding chairs set up around a cafeteria-style table. "Just as long as it's hot," Fox mumbled.

They'd just taken their first tentative sips of the coffee when, far at the other end of the mess hall, another door opened and eight very elderly men, dressed as if they had just come off the golf course, filed in and sat down. This was strange. . . . The old guys exchanged glances with the team members, but there was no formal greeting.

Finch finished pouring coffee for the team, then walked across the mess hall and had a brief conversation with the group of elderly men. When he returned, he had a bag of doughnuts with him. He passed them out to the ghosts.

"Those old boys hate to see anyone go hungry," Finch told them.

Finch himself looked like a trim Santa Claus. White hair, white beard, Saint Nick after a year on Atkins. An NCO in the Coast Guard Reserves, he'd been stationed here at Cape Lonely, off and on, from 1964 until it went nonstatus a decade ago. A bit stooped over, with very thick glasses, he could have been mistaken for a retired grocer or a banker.

But he'd been a godsend to the ghost team. And not just for the coffee and doughnuts.

If not for him, they would all probably be back in prison.

"I won't ask you how it went up in D.C.," he said to Fox now. "I'm just glad you made it back in one piece."

"We're not staying very long this time, either, I hope," Fox replied, checking his watch. It was almost twelve-fifteen. By his reckoning, they were already three hours behind schedule. "We've got to get moving as soon as possible."

Finch just nodded toward the elderly men at the other end of the mess. "We're ready on this end," he said. "All of us. . . ."

Fox took a huge bite of a doughnut and washed it down with a gulp of coffee.

"Why were you out there pulling weeds on the runway?" Fox asked. "It's a little late for that, isn't it?"

Finch rubbed his aching knees. " 'Our mutual friend' said that we might be needing the airstrip again soon. Not for you guys. But maybe for something else. That would make it twice in about twenty years."

Fox thought about this for a moment—*why would they be needing the runway again?* he wondered. But then he just went back to his doughnut. He already had enough weirdness floating around his head; he didn't need to be thinking about something else.

The others ate and drank their coffee, too, but their respite would indeed be brief. Between bites, Puglisi checked over the team's small cache of weapons, now minus the hunting rifle. Gallant meanwhile had been carrying most of their ammunition in a backpack. He now laid it all out on a nearby table, making sure none of the rounds had come apart or got wet. Right beside him, Bates unwrapped his laptop, plugged it into an ancient phone jack, and was soon on-line. As for Ryder, he had other things to do. He drained his coffee quickly, lit one of his last cigarettes, then grabbed a flashlight and headed back outside.

The clouds above were still heavy, and fast moving, but the moon was finally poking through in a few places. He walked to the edge of the cliff, for a moment looking down at the sea crashing against the rocks below. Finch had told them earlier that when the government finally closed this place sometime in the coming year it was going to be developed for luxury condominiums. Three levels, ocean views, very private location.

*Nice place to live,* Ryder thought. *If I had a million bucks . . .*

He power-dragged the cigarette to its end, then flicked the expended butt over the side of the cliff, watching the tiny orange glow all the way down. Then he started across the wide, broken runway.

The four old hangars were all the same size, and all four were in the same state of disrepair. Ryder walked up to the first hangar and examined its padlock. He took a key from his pocket and tried to put it in, but the lock would not cooperate. He tried again—still no luck. The lock was rusty even though it had been placed here just a week before. The salt air had already corroded it.

*Maybe not such a good place to live,* Ryder thought.

The key finally slipped in and the lock popped open. It was so suddenly unleashed, though, the door abruptly swung out a foot, nearly knocking Ryder on his ass. He managed to push it back in place and roll it open. Then he turned on the flashlight and pointed it into the hangar.

That's when he saw the airplane again. The Transall-2

turboprop special. The cargo plane from hell. Former owner: the Iranian Air Force.

The plane was a mess. There were small trees still wrapped around its wings, clumps of weeds still stuck in its engines. It was covered with sea salt, some of it thick as mud. All of the wing-mounted landing lights had been shattered, as were two of the eight cockpit windows. Of the 16 tires on the craft's landing gear, a half-dozen were flat.

It looked like a shitbox on wings, but it had carried them here, somehow, from Cuba, so from that point of view it wasn't a shitbox at all. In fact, it had played a very crucial role in their escape. Busting out of Guantánamo was one story. It was getting *here* that had been the really hard part.

Using purloined weapons and shackle keys they'd hidden in the crotches of their prison uniforms, the ghosts had taken control of the transfer plane as soon as it lifted off from Gitmo. The three Iranians onboard took a swim for Allah— considering their no-win situation, it would have happened to them sooner or later. With Ryder and Gallant flying the plane, they'd climbed to 7,200 feet but not any higher, a wise choice, as it turned out. The Transall-2 was not *that* difficult a plane to fly, in good weather, that is. But at night, in the middle of a small hurricane, it proved a bitch. The fierce storm had been their one and only cover, though, and it topped out at 7,500 feet. As bumpy as it was, they'd been forced to stay in the thick of it if their escape plan had any chance of succeeding.

Just seconds after they'd reached 7,200 feet, Bates plugged a small handheld device called a signal diverter (slipped to him by one of the Marine guards) into the plane's flight computer. With just a few buttons pushed, Bates was soon manipulating every primary control on the airplane except steering and throttles. He then began punching commands directly into the flight computer itself, intentionally over-loading it. It actually made a sizzling sound before it finally went *kaput*. At this point Ryder and Gallant had to start fly-ing the plane manually, no hydraulic assists, no autopilot, just muscles and wires. Then Bates pushed one last button, sending a barrage of false signals to the plane's safety control systems: its environmental suite, its temperature sensors, and most especially its flight data recorder. These bogus signals were designed to do one thing: mimic a sudden explosive fire aboard the aircraft.

At that moment, Ryder and Gallant put the plane into a gut-wrenching dive, this while the others onboard held on for their lives. Ten seconds into this plunge, Bates administered the *coup de grâce*, blacking out all communications, both electronic and radio, from the plane. To anyone monitoring the flight, like the air traffic controllers at Guantánamo, it appeared the Transall had suffered a massive short-circuit, then a fire, then an explosion that literally blew it out of the sky. Even the air safety computers in the Gitmo control tower had been fooled. Automatically clicking into a search and rescue program, one studied the last signals from the plane and concluded that not only would nothing bigger than a seat cushion be found at the crash site but also the storm would scatter the wreckage for miles.

It was only because Ryder and Gallant were able to pull the plane out of its death dive at 500 feet that some kind of crash *didn't* occur. The plunge had rattled every nut and bolt onboard and had shattered most of the interior lights as well. Once level, though, they'd brought the plane down even *lower,* right to the wave tops, below any radar net they knew of, U.S., Cuban, or otherwise.

Only then did they turn north. Toward America. If they remained at this altitude, they thought, and the weather stayed awful, they just might be able to sneak up the East Coast and reach their destination in just a couple hours. At least that was the plan.

It was brutally turbulent, though, and the plane had sounded like it would come apart at any moment. But the escapees breathed a sigh of relief once they left Cuban airspace. It appeared their ruse had worked. They'd even relaxed a little, hoping to maybe see the dull lights of the Florida coastline through the storm. Up to that point, it had been so far, so good.

Then they found the bomb.

. . .

It had been taped to the roof of the tiny modular commode squeezed in behind the flight deck's engineering station. Placed there days before, no doubt, by a member of Iran's notorious secret police, it was discovered when Puglisi went into the Porta Potti to take a leak and smelled the distinctly sweet odor of plastique. He'd quickly informed the others, and it didn't take much brainpower to realize the Iranian mullahs had intended to blow up the transfer plane all along.

Luckily, Puglisi knew about bombs, including ones like this. Hooked to a primitive altimeter assembly, it had been set to go off once the plane reached 7,500 feet. That's why it had been wise, if not totally dumb luck, that Ryder and Gallant had leveled off at 7,200. They'd come within 300 feet of blowing themselves to Kingdom Come.

Disarming the bomb was another matter. It was very crude and unstable. The altimeter-trigger assembly was held together by nothing more than an elastic band. Rather than defusing it and taking the chance of something going wrong, Puglisi strongly suggested that they stay as low as possible and take care of the bomb once they were on the ground. Of course, flying low had been part of the plan all along. Ryder and Gallant had already been busting arm and ass just keeping the damn plane a few feet above the minitsunamis kicked up by the Atlantic gale. One wrong move and it would have been all over for them very, very quickly.

The anxiety of the bomb, the shitty overall condition of the airplane, the fact that despite all their deceptions, they still might be picked up on U.S. radar, and that would mean facing at least a couple all-weather-equipped F-15s or F-16s whose pilots would be working under the post-9/11 rules of shoot first and ask questions later—all these things had made the dash up the stormy Atlantic seaboard a bit uncomfortable, to say the least.

"We might wind up in the drink yet," Gallant had said more than once during the trip.

So it was almost a surprise when, 122 minutes later,

they'd found themselves approaching the tiny isthmus called Cape Lonely.

The storm had been almost as bad here as down at Gitmo, which was a good thing, because it had indeed helped mask their flight up. But at that point, they needed to get some air under them to rise above the cliff, turn around, and land. Though loath to go up even an inch, Ryder and Gallant had eased the balky craft to a hair-raising 3,000 feet. They didn't linger there for very long, though. Putting the plane into a wide bank, they lined the nose up with the northern end of the runway and started back down. They'd had no contact with anyone on the ground, of course. This was strictly a seat-of-the-pants landing. No lights. No wind direction. So it wasn't until the very last instant that they realized the airstrip was badly in need of a haircut. They came down in a small forest of ragweed and nettle, hitting hard and fast. Ryder and Gallant had to stand on the brakes with such force, three tires blew out—*Pop! Pop! Pop!*—one right after another, each one sounding, yes, just like a small bomb going off.

They'd needed every inch of the overgrown runway to get the Persian beast to finally grind itself to a halt, accompanied by a cloud of sand and dust and muck and pieces of weeds being shredded up by the big, wet propellers. It seemed like the screeching would never stop, even when they nosed down into the ditch at the far end of the strip. The front wheel finally collapsed, though—and so did Ryder and Gallant, right over the controls, both exhausted. To their utter dismay, they'd discovered their fellow escapees had dozed during most of the trip. Only the less than gentle landing woke them up.

Recovering from their ordeal, both pilots had looked back at their groggy colleagues in the cargo compartment, yawning and stretching like they'd just got off the couch from a nap.

"They'll pay for this," Gallant had grumbled.

All this happened a week ago, and this was Ryder's first look at the plane since. They'd headed north for D.C. not 30 minutes after landing. (That ironic trip was made mostly by

Greyhound bus, a nightmare of cramped conditions and broken air-conditioning that made them all yearn for the Transall.) He'd left something behind on the plane that night, though. He was here now to get it back.

He climbed inside the airplane; the cargo hold smelled of low tide and oil. The flight deck itself was as messy as Li's house. Finch and his cohorts had been up here trying to steer the beast while pulling it out of the ditch and into the hangar with their small fleet of jeeps and SUVs—all this after first disposing of the bomb. Ryder was glad he missed that little adventure.

He sat down at the controls and looked over the flight panel. He threw a few switches, but nothing would even turn on. He tried the engines, just for the hell of it, but there was little power left inside the plane. There was no way anything was going to start. The Transall appeared dead for good.

Enough of that. He reached up to the sun flap above the pilot's side window, and there it was: the photograph he'd hidden here. It showed a beautiful woman, in her garden, just turning to smile after being caught unawares by the camera.

It was his wife, Maureen.

The only true love of his life.

Gone now almost four years. . . .

She'd been aboard Flight 175, the second plane to go into the World Trade Towers. Ryder had taken this picture a few months before that dark day and had carried it with him ever since. Yet he'd left it here, inside the Transall, after landing seven days ago. For some reason, he'd decided not to bring it up to D.C. with him. Perhaps he'd been afraid that if he got caught doing what he was doing they would take it away from him after he was arrested and he'd never see it again. Or maybe it had been something else.

But at last he had it back again—a great relief. He looked at it now, and as always, her eyes looked right back out at him. Blond. Sexy. Sweet. Deep blue beauty with a big smile.

*Damn. . . .*

The flap where he'd stashed the picture fell back down

suddenly, startling him. Its hinge had been shaken loose in the landing just like everything else aboard the airplane. But there was a small mirror attached to it, and now Ryder was looking right into it. From forehead to chin he didn't recognize the person in the reflection. Skin burned and creased, hair not cut in months. Nose looking broken, though it wasn't. Lips cracked, beard erupting. Chin quivering. But it was his eyes—they scared him the most. Red and watery, they looked absolutely insane.

He flipped the mirror back up in its place and pushed it in so it stayed there, cursing the cosmos for this unneeded piece of synchronicity. He already had enough reminders that he was spiraling downward. He didn't need any more.

He returned to Maureen's picture, gleaming in the flashlight. If he'd ever had any doubts about what he and the others were about to do, those misgivings were gone now. She'd been his life, and the mass murderers of Al Qaeda had killed her—and in doing so had killed him as well. He was not the same guy he was before her death. Back then, he was a highly paid test pilot for Boeing and the Air Force, this after many years of flying black ops. He was a normal person, or as normal as a test pilot could be. Then, in a blink, she was gone and he knew he would never be normal again. At the bottom of the blackest pit on the blackest days that followed, he'd never got through the last stage of grief: acceptance. *Just couldn't.* Instead, he'd jumped right over it to the next emotion: revenge. Get mad; *then* get even. That's what he was doing in the secret outfit.

That's what they were all doing here.

He put the picture in his pocket and wiped his crazy eyes. Someone was approaching.

It was Gallant. He stuck his head in the flight compartment, half a doughnut still hanging out of his mouth.

"You think flying this pig was a lot of fun?" he asked Ryder. "Wait 'til you see what we're riding in next. . . ."

The rest of the team were already standing at the entrance to the fourth hangar when Ryder and Gallant approached.

Refueled by the half-gallon of coffee they'd just split between them, the ghosts were jumpy now, anxious to get to the next step.

Master Chief Finch had prepared himself well for this moment. He had a regulation three-ring binder with him and was reading it by flashlight. He was calling out numbers, weights, speed, things like that. But as the two pilots drew near, Ryder heard Fox say to Finch, "You gotta convince these two guys first. They're the ones who'll have to fly this thing." The other team members were staring into the air barn with shared looks of amusement and horror. This was not what any pilot wanted to hear or see.

Ryder and Gallant reached the door of the hangar and finally saw what the others were looking at.

It was a helicopter. A very *old* helicopter.

"What *the fuck* is that?" Ryder just moaned.

Finch went back to his three-ring binder again, returning to the first page.

"This is a Sikorsky Super S-58," he announced. "They used to call it the 'Sky Horse.' Big engine. Lots of power. Lots of range. New tires. Ain't it a beauty?"

Well, *that* was in the eye of the beholder, Ryder thought. This thing looked like something from a bad fifties war movie. It *was* big—nearly 55 feet long. And bulky—at least 15 feet off the ground, probably more. And Sky Horse? It looked more like a huge insect. The nose was bulbous and thick, the cockpit stuck on top of it almost as an afterthought. It had a gigantic four-bladed rotor, the tips of which drooped so much, they nearly touched the hangar floor. This made the thing look not only ancient but very sad as well. And it got worse. Most advanced choppers these days needed little or no tail rotor for stabilization. Microprocessors did much of the work. The tail rotor on this craft, however, was about the size of one of the propellers on the Transall-2. This meant the copter would be very hard to keep stabilized in the air, and that would make for very bumpy riding.

"We can't go in this thing," Gallant said now; he was the

team's lead copter pilot, so he would know. "It's too big, too ugly. Too old."

Finch just shrugged. "It's also all we got."

Gallant went up and touched the helicopter on its nose, as if he had to convince himself that it was real. "But . . . when was the last time its engines were even turned over?"

"Last night," Finch told him simply. "Those old boys who shared their doughnuts with you? They put this thing together in six days. From scraps out back, and stuff they stole, and stuff they've had here in storage since I was a recruit, and, of course, stuff from Radio Shack."

Everyone's jaw dropped.

"*Those* old guys built this for us—from *Radio Shack* parts?"

"*Re*built it, yes," Finch replied. "Mostly in the cockpit."

Gallant was almost speechless. They all were.

"But have they *flown* it?" Gallant pressed him.

Finch just shook his head. "If they say it will fly . . . then believe me, it will fly."

Exasperation now filled the air. Gallant just looked at Fox and then walked away. On cue, the rest of the team members left, too. It would be up to the DSA officer to explain the situation to Finch.

"Look, Eddie," Fox began. "We realize these are difficult times. And we're all taking a great amount of risk here, with what we are doing, especially you. But my friends and I have a long way to go, and a lot of things to do when we get there. We were expecting something a little more . . . well, *up-to-date*."

Finch just shrugged again. "Besides finding you a place to land, 'our mutual friend' also asked me to provide you with something to get you where you needed to go." he said. "Something untraceable. Something with long range and power. And he gave me exactly two weeks to get it done. *This* is what I came up with."

Fox shifted nervously. "Well, I appreciate that," he began again, stumbling a bit. "But it's just that *your* friends look, well, *very retired,* let's say. And *my* friends here are used to having real sharp tacks working on their things."

Finch just looked back at him—and then laughed. He handed Fox the three-ring binder.

"Believe me, Major," he said. "If those guys say it will fly, it *will* fly."

With that, he walked away.

The team reassembled and discussed the situation amid a storm of windblown cigarette smoke.

They were under the gun. They had to get moving. They had a timetable to meet, and if they were just a few minutes late, it might mean disaster. As unappealing as the Sky Horse seemed, it was obviously the only ride in town. Where they were going they couldn't walk. Or take a bus. Or Li's little Toyota. The S-58 would have to do.

Ryder and Gallant climbed up into the old chopper's cockpit. At first it seemed to have so many levers and dials, it was like they were seeing double. It made the Transall-2 look like the space shuttle. But while everything original was very old, they were surprised to see the control panel had three laptops connected to it by cable wires and modem strips—a shoestring adaptation of a modern flight computer. There was also a GPS device hooked up for navigation, a heads-up display for both pilots, and a bank of TV monitors carrying video transmissions from small cameras placed strategically around the old copter. It looked ancient, but some very high-tech additions had been made inside the S-58.

But still there was the question of flying it. Finch's three-ring binder helped them locate most of the crucial controls: the power systems, steering, and so on. They'd both learned how to fly an enormous Kai seaplane during their last operation in the Philippines. But the Kai was a relatively new design. The Sky Horse had been built approximately the same year Gallant had been born. It would take the best of pilots days, if not weeks, to learn how to fly the copter properly.

Trouble was, Ryder and Gallant had less than a half hour to accomplish the same thing.

· · ·

Meanwhile, down below, Fox, Puglisi, and Bates were helping install some even more unusual additions to the old copter. Finch had wheeled in a large wooden box wrapped in red metal strapping. His weed clippers broke this binding to reveal three .50-caliber M-2 machine guns inside, huge weapons still used by many militaries around the world today.

The three team members helped Finch set up one of these guns in the helicopter's nose, bolting it to a rigid brace set in a hole cored out right below the elevated flight deck. The two other enormous guns were then put on swivel mounts attached to either end of the left-side cargo door. The swivels gave both guns nearly 180-degree fields of fire, but they could be taken off quickly, for hand-held use too. Their attached ammo belts seemed to go on for miles.

Fox asked, "Where did you ever get these?"

Finch smiled slyly. "Let's just say 'our mutual friend' told me they might smell like shamrocks."

They finished bolting the third gun to its movable stand. "This is a lot of firepower," Finch told them. "No one will expect you to have anything more than a squirt gun aboard this chopper, if that. You'll surprise a lot of people, if you have to."

Fox examined the M-2s and just shook his head. "If they catch us, we'll get life in prison just for these guns alone. . . ."

No one disagreed with him.

It was about 1:00 A.M. when they finally pushed the old chopper out onto the cracked, weed-strewn airstrip. Things had moved quickly. The copter was fueled up. The machine guns were cleaned and readied. What little gear the team had of their own was stored onboard. But they were still at least two hours behind schedule.

After a few false starts, Ryder and Gallant finally managed to get the aircraft's prestart systems running. Fuel pressure up. Engine oil heated to proper temperature. Batteries holding even. Gyro in place and balanced.

Gallant pushed the starter—and the engine behind them burst to life. No rattle, no roll. Barely a noise. Both pilots watched in amazement as the control indicator needles all climbed in unison, almost like an orchestra timed to the engine's increasing RPMs. Once engaged, those four droopy blades straightened right out and started spinning with a controlled frenzy. Incredibly, they were almost silent, too.

The attached laptops lit up with a myriad of colors now, showing them readouts on just about everything onboard. These visual displays helped identify more newly added equipment around them. A high-powered radio receiver promised to let the pilots monitor all sorts of communications from miles away. A FLIR set would allow them to see very far in the dark. The onboard video monitors would allow them to see above, below, in front of, and behind the copter. They had a weapons panel that would allow the pilots to fire the .50-caliber gun in the nose. They had flare dispensers, hard-points to attach bombs, even large inflatable pontoons attached to the landing gear struts that would allow them to set down on water if they had to.

Ryder and Gallant were simply amazed. But even bigger surprises were about to come.

The computers automatically raised the power up to takeoff speed. Their improvised flight computer screen flashed a message indicating that one push of the key enter button would lift them off. Ryder and Gallant just shrugged and Gallant hit the magic button.

Suddenly they were airborne.

To those on the ground, it was an astonishing sight.

One moment, the big chopper was idling quietly, the huge rotor blades creating a mighty downwash. In the next, the aircraft literally jumped into the air. The power was startling, yet the helicopter itself remained amazingly quiet.

They watched as the copter translated to forward flight. Suddenly it shot forward almost as if it were jet powered. It went over their heads, turned right, and soared way out over the ocean in just a matter of seconds. It continued a wide bank, circling back over the base once before streaking out toward the water again.

Then the helicopter began a very steep, very fast climb. It went up not unlike a Harrier jet, all power and exhaust. It climbed so high, so fast, those on the ground quickly lost sight of it as it disappeared into the clouds. They waited. Five seconds, ten seconds, twenty . . .

Suddenly they were besieged by a great whoosh of wind and spray. An instant later the huge chopper went right over their heads no more than 30 feet off the ground. It had come at them from behind, but they hadn't seen it or heard it until it was practically on top of them. The ghosts hit the deck; that's how sudden the copter's appearance had been.

The aircraft then banked sharp left, back out over the ocean, and, incredibly, nearly went completely over, showing an agility matched only by the latest supercopters of the day, like the Apache, the Commanche, or the Euro-copter Tiger. It soon righted itself, turning the corner sharply, and began to climb again.

This time, though, it swooped up to about two thousand feet and then went into a sudden hover. It turned 360 degrees on its axis, displaying amazing agility, before coming back down again and pointing its nose out toward the open sea. Suddenly there was a huge flash of light. For an anxious moment or two, those on the ground thought something had gone wrong. But no—Ryder and Gallant had simply engaged the big .50-caliber machine gun in the nose. The resulting pyrotechnics lit up the sky like fireworks.

It went on like this for the next ten minutes. It was almost dreamlike, the big chopper flashing all over the sky like some futuristic flying machine. Finally, it came in for a landing, touching down in front of the small crowd of observers with barely a thump, the only noise being the remaining weeds getting stirred up by the huge rotors.

The pilots shut everything down and climbed out to meet the small contingent of elderly men—now forever known as the "Doughnut Boys"—who'd been watching along with the ghosts.

"Who *are* you guys?" Gallant exclaimed to them.

Finch was also there. He replied for the group. "They are simply good Americans," he said. "Just like we were told you were."

Gallant was still shocked, though. "But how were you able to get that piece of—"

"Running like a top?" one of the men finished Gallant's sentence for him. The others just laughed. The joke certainly was on the two pilots.

Finally one of the group stepped forward, took a picture from his wallet, and showed it to the pilots. It was a photograph of an X-15. One of the most advanced aircraft ever built, it was a rocket plane that could actually fly to the edge of space.

"I just helped rebuild one of these," the old guy told him. "For NASA. They're going to start flying it again to test parts for the new shuttle design. But that's just a hobby. I worked for Lockheed Special Projects for years."

He turned to his colleagues and started pointing. "And this guy helped design the F-117 Stealth plane. This guy worked on the F-22 Raptor. This guy helped design the *Apollo* capsule. This guy worked on the Osprey."

On and on: This guy retired from advanced designs at Boeing. This guy from the Jet Propulsion Lab. This guy former Air America.

Then the spokesman patted Gallant on the shoulder.

"So don't worry, my friend," he said. "We did a good job on your chopper. In fact, 'our mutual friend' thought you'd appreciate the concept."

*The concept?* Ryder thought. Yes—something *was* beginning to sink in between his ears. When the ghost team was first assembled, they'd been given a very plain-looking, very rusty containership as their ride to war. But the floating hulk actually had billions of dollars of high-tech, top-secret combat and eavesdropping equipment hidden onboard.

Now they had this old helicopter. It looked ancient, harmless even, on the outside. But inside it was packing a punch.

And it could fly fast and quiet. And it could see and hear for miles and do many other things as well.

"How?" was all Ryder could say now.

"You really don't have to know 'how,'" the elderly man told him. "The real question is 'why?'"

Again, the ghosts were puzzled for a moment.

"We have something for you," the old guy said. "Might explain some of it."

The Doughnut Boys gathered around the ghosts. This was the first time the team members really got a good look at them. They were big and short, tall and skinny. Bald, glasses, red noses. But they were clearly not just mechanics but rather aeronautical geniuses with résumés listing employers from NASA to the Lockheed Skunkworks.

"We really shouldn't go into too much detail with each other," the head Doughnut said. "True, we're all from deep security environments. But once you've 'gone underground' it's best not to know too much about what your friends are doing. But we can tell you this: we know where you are going and what you have to do.

"And we just wanted to say thank you. For what you've done before. At Hormuz. At Singapore. In the Philippines. We wanted you to know we appreciate it."

He had something in his hands. It was in a simple paper bag. He reached in and came out with a crude but crisply folded flag, at least six feet long. It had 13 red and white stripes like a typical American flag, but instead of the field of stars there was a picture of a coiled snake, with the words "Don't Tread On Me—Ever Again" embroidered underneath it.

"My only son was killed in the Pentagon on September Eleventh," the old guy went on. "He was helping rescue his office mates when he died. The wife of a man he saved sewed this together for me, stayed up for two days and two nights doing it, for his memorial service. I know it's not the prettiest flag in creation, but it meant a lot to us then, and it means a lot to me now."

He retrieved a handkerchief, wiped his eyes once, and then blew his nose.

"This is a great country," he went on. "But only because its people are great. It's a brave and fair and moral and honest country, too—but only because a great majority of its people are. This country is not about its politicians or its corporate presidents or its movie stars or its nutty generals. It's about the guys fighting in Iraq because they feel it's the right thing to do. It's about the guys dying in Afghanistan trying to find the rest of those pukes. It's those cops and firemen who died that day in New York City. It's about those people who crashed that plane in Pennsylvania so it wouldn't hit the White House. The world *has* gone crazy, but that doesn't mean this country has to be pulled down with it. At times like this, it's up to us to step up to the plate and try to fix things."

He looked back down at the flag.

"I've been holding on to this for a special occasion," he went on, fighting off another sniff. "And now that I know about you guys, and what you've done and who you really are, well . . . will you take it with you?"

Ryder and Gallant were speechless. All the ghosts were. Their sad, miserable, aching backs suddenly straightened a bit. The wind had come back to their sails. Ryder shook the guy's hand.

"Sure we will, pops," he said softly, taking possession of the flag and handling it with reverence. "It will be our honor. . . ."

It was time to go.

It seemed to Ryder that between their two visits to Cape Lonely he'd been living atop the cliff for weeks. Added up, though, they'd only been at the base a few hours combined.

There were a few more items Finch had for them that were loaded aboard. A cardboard box full of uniforms to replace the ones Finch had given them when they first landed. These opened the box and saw that these were newer, even darker versions of the uniforms the original team members had worn during their heyday in the Persian Gulf. They even had the unit's patch sewn into the right-hand shoulder. It showed an image of the World Trade Center towers, with the Stars and Stripes behind it, the letters *NYPD* and *FDNY* floating above it, and the group's motto, *We Will Never Forget,* floating below.

They also loaded aboard a box containing several dozen MREs—Meals Ready to Eat, the contemporary version of the old GI C rations. Finch handed them another paper bag, this one containing nine standard American flags, each one about three feet long. "You'll be needing these types of flags as well," Finch told them with a wink.

Then came aboard the strangest piece of cargo of all: a huge battery-powered freezer. Inside were three dozen tiny dead pigs, flash frozen to the point that they almost looked like cuddly toys. There was also several packages of bacon in the cooler.

"Now, don't go eating any of that stuff," Finch joked with them again. "That wouldn't be *kosher*. . . ."

As they were loading on a half-dozen more laptops for Bates to use, Ryder climbed back up to the copter's flight deck and spent about five minutes alone, checking on the aircraft's primary systems. Their improvised flight computer was keeping everything up and on-line. All of his cockpit lights were green. All of his power modes were in the red. They could leave at any time now.

But when Ryder looked back down into the cargo bay he was surprised to find everyone was gone. He climbed out of the copter but again found the area around the Sky Horse deserted. He was just starting to wonder what other weird thing could possibly happen when he heard a voice coming from the air station's Loran building. Loran was a worldwide communication net that was maintained for the U.S. military by the Coast Guard in many locations around the world. Like one big electromagnetic antenna, the building itself seemed to be crackling with energy. Ryder could see flashlight beams inside.

He walked over to the igloo-shaped building, opened the door, and found the rest of the team huddled within. Finch was with them, as were the Doughnut Boys. They were all smiling, ear to ear.

*What was going on here?*

As soon as he appeared, Fox said to him, "I know we're in a hurry. But man, we *had* to see this. Check it out."

Everyone extinguished their flashlights and now all Ryder could see was Eddie Finch. He was holding a halogen lightbulb in his hand—but it was not attached to anything. He was simply holding it. Yet it was glowing, very brightly.

"Can you believe it?" someone asked Ryder. "These Loran places have so much juice running through them, you don't even have to screw the lightbulbs in. . . ."

Ryder just stared at Finch as the retired Coast Guardsman held the lit bulb under his bearded chin like a Halloween prank. He looked like something from a horror flick.

"Damn," was all Ryder could say.

It was one of the strangest things he'd ever seen.

# Chapter 9

The mysterious noise came just after midnight.

It wasn't an explosion exactly, even though it was loud enough to wake dozens of people in and around the small town of Campo, Kentucky. Some would later say it sounded more like fireworks or old Civil War cannons going off. Some even thought it was an earthquake. The rumbling was so intense, a few people were thrown from their beds.

The one thing everyone agreed on was that the disturbance had originated from the top of Mount Winslow, the 2,500-foot peak that dominated Campo's skyline to the north.

Campo had no full-time police force. There were only 250 people in the town, and the state police barracks was just 22 miles away, down nearby Route 41. In cases like this, unexpected emergencies and such, the town's plumber, a man named Bo Tuttle, became the temporary sheriff. His brother Zoomer and his cousin Hep became his deputies.

All three men lived near the base of the mountain. They, too, were roused by the strange commotion. Their homes were barraged with phone calls, neighbors wanting to know what was going on. The men didn't bother to answer their phones, though. Within minutes of being shaken from bed, the three men were in Tuttle's improvised patrol car, actually

his Chevy Tahoe, and climbing up the south face of Mount
Winslow.

There were only three things of any value at the top of the
mountain: a cell-phone tower erected a year before by Southern Bell, an amateur weather station operated by the local 4-H
group, and an automated radar relay dish used by the control
tower at Louisville International Airport, 18 miles away.

The road up to the summit was gravel mixed with oil to
harden it. It had rained fiercely the day before though, and
the gravel was still loose. Still the 10-minute ride to the top
went smoothly; in fact, all three men were able to gulp down
a cup of coffee from a thermos Hep's wife had prepared before his hasty departure.

The three men were fairly sure they knew what had happened up on Winslow. The Southern Bell tower had collapsed. The wind had been blowing hard all day, along with
the heavy rains, and more than once people in town claimed
they could see the cell-phone tower swaying mightily in the
strong breeze.

"That's why my cell phone ain't working," Zoomer had
reasoned during their ascent.

But when they arrived at the peak, the cell tower was still
standing. So, too, the 4-H weather station and the airport
radar dish.

What they found next to the radar dish, though, would
haunt the three men for a very long time.

There were four bodies in all.

Two had been shot, at close range, through the head—and
not by a peashooter, either. Two others had been chopped to
pieces. Arms, legs, pieces of fingers and toes. Cousin Hep
was a butcher, but at first sight of this he vomited up everything he'd eaten in the past 24 hours. Bo and Zoomer, too,
nearly went into shock. The sight was incomprehensible.

The grisly discovery was even more baffling as the four
dead men were already lying in a grave. A shallow pit, 10 feet
by 10 feet, had been dug close to the radar station. All four
had been dumped into it.

But still, this was not the strangest thing. Because also thrown into the pit were four tiny pigs, their throats cut, their blood dripping all over the corpses and mixing with their own.

The three temporary lawmen tried to make some sense of it all, but none was forthcoming. Four dead bodies, already in a grave, with pigs' guts splashed all over them? It just didn't seem real. The wind was really howling up here, too, adding greatly to the weirdness around them. For years the townspeople thought the top of the mountain was haunted. Maybe they were right.

All three men wanted to jump in the Tahoe and get the hell off the peak, but to their credit, they stood their ground. They would have to rely on their basic police training to get them through. Tuttle told the other two to search the rest of the summit; it was a flattened top no more than 1,000 square feet in all. Zoomer found some camping equipment and four bloodstained sleeping bags. Meanwhile Hep was able to snag a couple of pieces of paper that had blown into some bramble bushes on the southern side of the big hill.

And it got even weirder here: Two of the pieces of paper had notes scribbled on them—but they weren't written in English. Hep had done almost a year at nearby Clarksburg Community College; he was the most educated of the three. He guessed the writing was Hindu or something from the subcontinent. He was close. It was actually Arabic, written in code.

From what the three men could make out, the sheet with the most writing contained instructions of some kind, the words being accompanied by crude drawings. But the drawings made as little sense as the words. They seemed to be showing the user how to fly something. But what? Their best guess was something along the lines of a radio-controlled model airplane or maybe a large amateur rocket.

They returned to the bodies. Bo was the senior man. It was up to him to climb down into the grave to look for any identification, this as Hep tried again and again to get his cell phone working. Bo gingerly eased himself into the pit.

The smell down here was putrid, the gore overwhelming. He vowed never to watch another horror movie again. The dead men looked like foreigners, and there was no doubt at least two had been killed in a ritualistic way. But where did the pigs come in? And what had caused the loud noise in the first place?

Bo knew it wouldn't be wise to contaminate the crime scene and, on that excuse, decided that he would check for ID on only one of the bodies. He selected one of the gunshot victims, a small dark man wearing only his underwear and a torn suit coat. In the inside right-hand coat pocket Bo found not a wallet but two Immigration Department green cards. Both gave the name "Abdul Moisi." One identified him as a "soccer player" from Bali.

"Didn't a bunch of foreigners play a soccer game over in Oxville yesterday?" Bo yelled up to Hep and Zoomer. "I thought someone said they saw their bus pass through town."

But neither man heard him. The wind was blowing too hard.

The other green card identified the dead man as a "student." Bo looked at the card and then at the body. Bo was 30. The dead man looked at least five years older than him, maybe more.

"What the hell kind of student were you?" he said out loud.

Hep helped Bo out of the pit just as he finally got his cell phone to work. He'd reached Bob's Gas Station in town— Bob was a notorious insomniac and Hep knew he would answer his phone. Bo told Bob what had happened, and he promised to drive out to the highway and flag down the state trooper who would be coming by in the next 10 minutes or so. Then Bo instructed Bob to call over to Clarksburg and ask one of the doctors at the poor people's clinic to somehow get out to the top of Mount Winslow. Bo then said all three of them would wait at the murder scene until the state trooper arrived.

Bo was about to hang up when Bob stopped him. The station owner had a piece of news for him.

As he was probably the only person awake in Campo when the big noise was first heard, Bob told Tuttle he'd run outside his station within seconds and was astonished to see a helicopter coming down the side of the mountain, heading right for him. It was making very little noise, but it went right by the gas station, flying very low. So low, in fact, Bob was able to read the words painted on its fuselage: *United States Coast Guard*.

"Coast Guard?" Bo bellowed. "We're about a thousand miles away from the nearest ocean."

But Bob insisted that's what he saw. What's more, he said he had observed several men riding in the back of the copter. They were dressed like soldiers and looking out the side window as the aircraft zoomed by. Two of them waved to him. One gave the two-finger V-for-Victory sign.

Then they were gone.

Bo finally hung up, wondering if Bob was drinking again. If not, his information only added to the gruesome puzzle they'd just found at the top of the formerly peaceful mountain.

That's when Hep came up beside Bo and tugged on his sleeve. He didn't say anything. Between the wind and the gore, all three of them were having trouble talking now. Hep simply pointed, straight up, to the top of the Southern Bell cell tower, rising 250 feet above the peak.

Bo had to squint to see what Hep was pointing at. But then, yes—he saw it, too. A small flag was flying from the top of the cell tower. All stars and stripes, it was an American flag.

Bo scratched his head.

"I don't recall ever seeing that up there before," he said.


## Chicago that night

The first thing Chicago police detective Mike Robinson saw when he pulled up in front of the North Street mosque was small American flag up on its roof, flapping mightily in the breeze.

This was very odd.

"What's that doing up there?" he wondered aloud as he squealed to a stop in front of the alleged holy place. This part of Chicago was close to some particularly notorious housing projects and hard by the approach path to O'Hare Airport. It was a neighborhood filled with crack dens and flophouses. There was at least a couple murders here every night.

Strange place for a flag. . . .

The mosque had opened here about two years before, in a building given free of charge to a Muslim group by the city in return for a promise to renovate it, as part of an overall neighborhood beautification project. No renovation happened, of course, but the mosque remained.

And it was a mosque in name only. The structure was far from the magnificent architecture of Muslim holy places found in the Middle East. This was a building in a slum, made of rotten wood and crumbling brick, with burned-out shells of buildings on either side of it.

Robinson ran this district's anticrime unit. His six detectives were called to the mosque on a weekly, if not daily, basis, mostly looking for merchandise stolen from a shopping mall nearby. At any given time, between six and eight people were known to be living in the building. The size of the actual congregation was unknown.

Robinson was here checking a report of shots fired inside the mosque. Two patrol cars roared up behind him. Four uniformed cops jumped out, already wearing their SWAT helmets and body armor and carrying M16s, adapted police rifles.

Robinson put on his own bulletproof vest and had a quick conversation with the four cops. There was no one else on the sidewalks or anywhere within sight of the mosque. This, too, was strange. True, this block was a free-fire zone on most nights. But there were always a few people out on the streets, on the corners or in the alleys, even on the warmest of nights, which this was. But right now, the streets around them were empty.

"Two out back?" Robinson suggested to the four cops. A pair of them wordlessly broke off from the pack and ran around to the rear of the decrepit building. Robinson gave them a minute to get in position; then he and the other two walked up to the front door. They had a battering ram with them, but they didn't need it. The door was not locked. Robinson easily pushed it open with his foot.

It was dark inside the entryway. Dark and very quiet. Robinson looked back at the cops with some trepidation. They would all have rather come in with a bang—forced entries tended to scare the bad guys inside. Being sucked in quietly was not the best way to enter a trouble zone.

But enter they did. It was their job.

The hallway smelled awful—and it was not just the garbage piled up to the ceiling. The stink of burnt gunpowder and cordite was also in the air. Robinson and the cops inched their way through the foyer and into the first room. It was dark, filled with smoke, but empty. Down the hallway another six feet to the second room. Here the cordite was especially thick, but this room was empty, too.

Next came a set of stairs that led up to the second floor. Robinson could see a candle flickering up there, somewhere. He went up first, his Glock out, front and center. The two uniforms had their M16s up, too. They were vets at this sort of thing, though this sort of thing rarely went the same way twice.

They reached the second floor and were naturally drawn to the bare light of the candle. It was in a bedroom to their left. This was where they found the first two bodies.

Both had been shot multiple times—lots of bullet wounds in the arms, shoulders, kneecaps, and groin, with one massive wound in the stomach. The candle had been positioned at the feet of the victims. Whoever did the killing wanted the two victims to suffer first. And they did, greatly. A message was being sent here; that was obvious. But it got stranger. Both dead men had something very odd stuffed into their mouths. At first, Robinson thought it was entrails, as repulsive as that sounded. Only by bending down and looking closely did he see what it really was: handfuls of raw, bloody bacon.

He looked up at the two cops who just shook their heads, baffled. "What's up with that shit?" one asked in astonishment.

The two dead men were mosque members. Despite their gross wounds, Robinson recognized them both from his previous visits here. They were of Middle Eastern descent. Both were named Abu.

Robinson and the two cops moved on. Several other rooms were thick with gun smoke but empty. Instinct told Robinson that more bodies were to be found. There was a ladder leading up through the ceiling to the roof. Ladders were not a preferred means of movement among cops, especially in a situation like this. But again, duty called.

Robinson went up first, chunky in his suit coat and tie, waddling in his heavy vest. It made for hard climbing. Three steps up, Robinson lost his balance. Without ceremony, one of the cops behind gave him a mighty push on the rump, propelling him up through the open trapdoor and onto the roof itself.

He found two more bodies up here.

They, too, had been shot. They, too, had had their mouths stuffed with bacon.

The two cops followed him up the ladder. Jets landing and arriving at nearby O'Hare made it hard to talk, hard to think. But they were as baffled by the scene as he. Next to one of the bodies was a suitcase—or at least what appeared to be a suitcase. Closer inspection by Robinson proved it was not something clothes would be packed in. It appeared to be more of a carrying case for some kind of computer tool or electronic device.

The case had to be dusted for fingerprints, so Robinson placed a small yellow marker next to it letting the CIS team know his intentions.

Meanwhile, one of the other cops noticed something else unusual. The roof was flat and covered with tar, a typical cap for buildings in this area. Playing his flashlight along the widest part of the roof, the cop had discovered a long, thin indentation that appeared to be newly made.

He called Robinson over, and they both inspected the strange imprint. Incredibly, it looked like tire tracks.

*"On a roof?"* Robinson said out loud.

They found another, similar indentation about eight feet away and very close to the edge of the building. *Two* tire tracks, made by something heavy, embedded deep in the tar.

This made no sense.

At this point, the two cops watching the back arrived on the roof. As it turned out, one of them was ex–Army aviation. He studied the tire marks and just shook his head. He recognized the mark of a helicopter wheel when he saw one.

"A good-size chopper was up here," he told Robinson. "You can bet on it."

To reinforce his theory, he pointed to a series of strange scrapes along one side of the building's metal-pipe chimney.

"See? This is where the tips of the copter blades hit," the cop said, also noting an ancient clothesline rope was ripped to shreds nearby. "But it was a very tight fit. Whoever was flying this thing knew what they were doing. Or they might just be crazy."

The ex-Army cop took one long look around and concluded: "Whoever iced these guys came and left in a helicopter."

Robinson was more baffled than before. Dead mutts with bacon stuffed in their mouths? Helicopters landing on top of tenement buildings? An American flag, left behind, rippling in the wind?

Robinson just shook his head as a jet screamed overhead on its way to landing at O'Hare.

"Whatever happened to drive-by shootings?" he asked.

## Near Danson, Nebraska
## The next morning

Donny Eliot had just sat down to breakfast at the All-Star Diner when his walkie-talkie crackled to life.

"That's about ten minutes too early," the waitress joked, pouring him a cup of coffee. "They must be on to you."

Eliot was the head ranger at nearby Great Mesa State Park. It was a natural preserve, more than 50 square miles in area, perfectly square, flat prairie, most of it, and as such practically indistinguishable from the rest of Nebraska. Except for two things, that is: The park featured one of the state's few mountains—or sort of a mountain, anyway. It also had an airport, a big one, right in the middle of it.

It was not a commercial airport, but one that primarily serviced cargo planes, bringing in farm supplies, feed, fertilizer, and sometimes even moving livestock out. Cargo that was the lifeblood of this farming area, things that for whatever reason had to be here quicker than a truck could bring them in. A former SAC base, these days the airport was called Lee Field.

The walkie-talkie buzzed again. Eliot knew it was his boss, the park supervisor. He called Eliot every morning, just to make sure he was on the job. But the boss was definitely early today.

Eliot took one long slurp of his coffee, then hit the respond button. The supervisor didn't say hello. He was already in the middle of a sentence. But his words were breaking up. ". . . something weird . . . people up near . . . Lee Field . . . do you copy?"

"I'm here, boss," Eliot replied. "But I only copy half of what you said. Say again, please?"

"Goddammit!" The supervisor was yelling now, but the reception had got worse. "Something . . . Big Rock . . . Lee Field . . . hurry!"

Eliot yelled into the walkie-talkie, "Boss, I can't hear you. You're breaking up!"

But only a storm of static came back to him.

Then the walkie-talkie went dead.

Five minutes later, Eliot was in his truck, roaring up Route 213. Before him was Great Mesa, the 700-foot formation of rocks and ledges that gave the park its name. But strangely, the mesa wasn't really a mesa at all. Not in this part of the country. It was simply an extraordinarily large stacking of huge rocks that rose up from the otherwise flattened plain. Most people just called it the Big Rock.

Lee Field was just beyond, about a quarter-mile away, down inside a natural bowl that gave the huge rocky formation an even further illusion of size and height. Anytime he saw it, Eliot always thought the same thing: *Flat as hell for hundreds of miles and they build an airport next to the only mountain in the state.*

Eliot was at the foot of the Big Rock a minute later. He leaped from his truck, ran to the first wall of boulders, and looked up. The highest point of the mesa was a flattened outcrop that stuck up about 150 feet above the northern face. This must have been why the boss had called him. A group of people was up there—four young men, Eliot could see them clearly. They had a telescope with them, or at least they were looking through some kind of tube. Each man had a beard and a great tan.

"Christ," Eliot breathed. "Hippies, again?"

It was the bane of his existence that a local group of pot-smoking, weed-hugging kids had decided the Grand Mesa was actually a holy place. A place of harmonic convergence. A place that UFOs visited. Take your pick. It was high, and usually so were they. Eliot was forever shooing them off the summit.

He was about to try his walkie-talkie again, to raise his boss and report in, when he heard the rumbling of a large jet taking off from Lee Field. It distracted him for a moment, because when the wind was blowing right the big jets took off directly over the *faux* mesa. This plane was definitely heading in his direction.

He turned back to the rocks. Up on the peak, the hippies were raising their telescope, or whatever it was. One had it up on his shoulder now. And that's when Eliot realized that these people were not wearing the ripped jeans and dirty T-shirts the hippies usually wore. In fact, two looked like they were wearing suit coats. And the two others were dressed like soccer players. Strange. . . .

The jet flew over a moment later. It was a FedEx plane, its red, white, and blue color scheme making it hard to miss. It went over the highway and climbed steadily toward the peak. Suddenly Eliot saw something that made no sense: a helicopter, a big white one, had come out of nowhere, and soldiers in black camouflage uniforms were jumping out of it and on top of the four young men on the mesa's summit. Then, even over the roar of the big cargo jet, Eliot heard the unmistakable sound of gunfire.

That's when he saw an explosion of red and yellow flame erupt from the top of the peak.

"God damn!" Eliot screamed. *What the hell is going on here?*

Before he could take another breath, he saw a fiery trail rise up from the peak but then suddenly change direction, as if one of the men jumping from the helicopter had knocked it off-course at the last possible instant. The FedEx jet went over the mesa a moment later. Two seconds after that, something corkscrewed its way through the air and impacted in a wheat field back down near Lee Field's main runway.

Eliot was stunned. He just couldn't comprehend what was happening simply because it was all happening so fast. Were those fireworks? The Fourth of July was but a week away. He'd had the wisdom to bring his binoculars with him. He trained them on the peak and saw a huge fight was now in progress. The people from the helicopter were absolutely pummeling the young bearded men. Even amid the chaos, Eliot could hear them shouting, screaming, crying. Above it all, the helicopter had not landed but was hovering just a few feet above the summit.

Eliot wasn't sure what to do. For some reason, the soldiers didn't look like real soldiers, and the helicopter certainly wasn't brand-new. And he couldn't get out of his head that the people on the peak of Big Rock were just local kids, just fooling around, maybe with bottle rockets or something. But one thing was certain: all these people were on State Park property. And for some crazy reason, Eliot felt compelled to find out what was really going on. So, he ran down the highway embankment and, reaching the bottom of the rocky formation, began to climb.

"What am I doing?" he yelled to himself. The peak was 700 feet nearly straight up, and Eliot was not a tiny man. He was instantly bathed in sweat. He was screaming at the top of his lungs for the people above him to stop. *"Stop fighting!"* But of course, they couldn't hear him.

He surprised himself, though, by how fast he climbed. He'd never done anything like this before. The Big Rock's southern face was a much easier approach, but every place he found his feet now was a solid stepping-stone to the next foothold. His hands, too, were gripping all the right places. In seconds, he was going up the side of the formation like he was Spiderman.

During his quick ascent, he managed to look back toward Lee Field. He could see vehicles with flashing red lights rushing toward the near end of the runway. They'd obviously seen the fiery impact, but that was as close as they could get. Eliot was really the only one who could see the strange goings-on at the top of the mountain.

How long did it take him to climb the peak? A minute? Or five? He wasn't sure. All he knew was by the time he was two-thirds of the way up, the fight up on the summit had reached its climax. He could see the soldiers in the camos still viciously beating the young men, the helicopter still hovering in perfect position above. Eliot could read the lettering on its fuselage now—but this just added to the mystery.

"United States Coast Guard?" he yelled to no one. "What the hell are they doing here?"

Only a long slope of rocks separated him from the summit at this point. He started running up this slope, still astonished at his strength and surefootedness. The soldiers on the peak spotted him. As he shouted at them to stop, he saw them pick up one of the four young men they'd been beating, throw him into the helicopter, and then climb in themselves. Then the chopper started moving. It dipped slightly, then gunned its engine and rocketed away, at amazing speed. Strangely enough, Eliot could barely hear its engines.

*That's pretty quiet, for a helicopter,* he would recall thinking.

By the time he reached the peak, the copter was nearly out of sight, heading north. He found all three of the men up here dead, obviously beaten to death. That's when he realized for sure these were not local kids. These three men were very dark and not as young as he'd thought. Two were wearing suit coats. One was in a soccer uniform. Eliot pegged them right away as being of Middle Eastern descent.

That's when it all came together for him.

*Terrorists . . .* he thought. *Up here?*

It was the only explanation that made sense.

He examined the bodies closer, not wanting to touch them, of course. All three looked like they'd been flattened with a sledgehammer. Bones and skulls, fractured and bleeding. And what was that in their mouths? He looked closer. *Was that bacon?*

And flapping in the breeze nearby? A small American flag, hastily adhered to a small bush, the only vegetation of any kind at the top of the Big Rock.

At that moment, his walkie-talkie crackled to life, scaring the hell out of him. It was his boss again—and this time, he was coming through loud and clear.

"Donny! What the crap is going on up there?"

Eliot pushed the respond button but then just collapsed to the seat of his pants.

"Boss," he said, finally out of breath. "You won't frigging believe it. . . ."

## Saint Helena, Nebraska
## Two hours later

The only bar in Saint Helena was packed. This meant just about thirty people were jammed inside the Eastside Tavern, and just about all of them were drunk. This meant nearly half the population of Saint Helena was currently intoxicated.

It was early Monday afternoon. Summer school had been

dismissed and most people had taken the afternoon off from work. A special occasion had been planned for this date; that was the reason for the unofficial holiday.

A foreign soccer team was scheduled to come to town and play a goodwill game against the county's youth soccer club. The match had been in the works for about two months. As the county seat, Saint Helena had the only regulation soccer field this side of Danson, Nebraska, which was 100 miles to the south. Downtown Saint Helena, which consisted of the tavern, a drugstore, and Casey's Cafe, had even been adorned with red, white, and blue bunting, small American flags, and hundreds of balloons for the occasion.

The problem was, the foreign soccer team never showed up. Practically the entire town had turned out at the nearby soccer field, dozens of people in folding chairs and umbrellas, picnic lunches at hand, kids running, playing, adults swatting the cow flies away. It was the end of June. It was hot. And the town had been looking forward to this for some time.

But the foreigners were supposed to be here at 10:00 A.M. By noon, the crowd had begun to wilt. By twelve-thirty, the kids had scattered, and the women had left, leaving the menfolk to their own devices. The Eastside Tavern was packed shortly before one.

Darts was the game of choice these days in the Eastside, this ever since the mechanical bull fell into disrepair. Fueled by cheap Larry's Home Brew on tap and the occasional drag of some skunkweed out back, a huge match began. With a lot of money on the table and people making side bets everywhere, the darts really started flying. The match grew so intense, no one even blinked when a huge thunderstorm rolled over about two, dousing the town and its balloons and bunting with two inches of rain in less than 15 minutes.

The match neared its peak by 3:00 P.M. Ten teams had been whittled down to just two—and there was $500 on the table. That's why everyone was so shocked when Charlie Ray, the town's 95-year-old minister, burst into the tavern and announced "Someone just told me the foreigners are here!"

Everything froze inside the bar. *They were here?*

"Actually," Reverend Ray corrected himself, "Joey, the janitor, called me and said all of us better get back over to the soccer field darn quick."

The field was behind the four-room Saint Helena's elementary school, about a quarter-mile down the road from downtown.

The rain had let up considerably by now, but the sky was still very dark. Almost as dark as night. This was real tornado weather, but the revelers piled into their pickup trucks and old Fords anyway and proceeded back down to the grade school.

They met Joey the janitor in the small parking lot. Joey was not a very bright bulb, but he seemed very agitated when the townspeople arrived. They had expected to see the bus that had carried the foreign soccer players here parked in the lot, but no such vehicle was there. Only Joey. And he was almost crying.

He just pointed out to the field; the crowd—now about twenty people, most very drunk—couldn't get much out of him. So they all walked out to the rain-soaked field, this as lightning began flashing off to the west.

But there was nothing there. The field was empty; the trees that lined it on one side—and just about the only trees of any height in the county—were blowing mightily in the wind. There certainly was no soccer team out here, foreign or not.

Just as the men were beginning to think this was a prank played on them by the wives, for surely they had all gathered at someone's house to drink and talk as well, Joey led them to one of the trees about halfway down the field. He pointed up.

The crowd looked—and saw a dead body caught in the branches. Or at least it looked like a body.

At this point some of the drunker men believed this was still a joke. The figure in the tree, high up at about twenty feet, was wearing a soccer uniform and was covered in blood. But it looked more like a dummy that some of the schoolkids had stuffed earlier, as a way to taunt the foreigners.

But two men, sober ones, climbed the tree and they confirmed the ghastly truth: this *was* a body, and it was indeed wearing a soccer uniform. The man appeared to have been beaten to death, at the very least. But most bizarre, there was what looked to be a handful of bacon—yes, *bacon*—stuffed down the crotch of his shorts. A small American flag was stuffed into his mouth.

Still, many in the crowd below didn't believe it was real.

On their lips was the same question, asked over and over: "How the hell did he get up there?"

# Chapter 10

## Minnesota

It was called Lost View Lake and the name was appropriate. It was two miles long and a half mile wide, and an underground spring pumping warm water from its bottom almost always gave it a dense layer of fog on its top. This was especially true near the lake's center, where the fog was frequently its thickest.

The strange mist was present in the morning hours, sometimes not burning off until noon, even in the warmest days of summer. It would return at dusk and linger again until the next day. For this reason, local boaters and fishermen avoided the rectangular lake, preferring to use one of the hundreds of others in the region for their recreation. There were no cottages on the lake, no hunting lodges, no tour boats. No people around at all. It was the perfect place to hide.

This is where the Sky Horse found itself this morning. Floating on its inflatable pontoons, all systems shut down, the five members of the ghost team trying to get some much-needed sleep but failing miserably at it, especially Ryder.

He was uncomfortably jammed in between the two pilots' seats up on the flight deck. The others were flopped about in the cargo bay below. All the access doors and windows were shut tight. But still, some of Lost View Lake's mysterious mist was seeping in.

"Are you sure *none* of those mooks we whacked had any cigarettes on them?" Ryder called down to the others now.

Only Puglisi stirred. "They did and we smoked them already," he called back up to Ryder sleepily.

Ryder checked his own dilapidated pack of Marlboros. He had exactly two whole and three partially smoked cigarettes left. Under normal circumstances, that would have lasted him about an hour this early in the morning. That is, if he'd had a couple cups of coffee available to him. Which he didn't.

He tried to stretch out his legs; with the light of morning, it would be impossible to keep trying for any substantial sleep. He knew it was unhealthy and that lack of winks would catch up with him sooner or later. But he wasn't totally unhappy that he hadn't caught any more than a nap or two since the team left Cape Lonely. With his psyche turned inside out, going to sleep risked an even greater possibility of unwanted dreams these past few days. It was bad enough that his late wife haunted just about every moment of his sleep time; when he closed his eyes now, he saw flashes of hatchets and huge .50-caliber rounds tearing into dark flesh, and tiny dead pigs, having their throats cut. He could hear the pleas of those soccer players who were about to have their bodies filleted, the choking sounds of their comrades having their mouths stuffed with bacon. For a Muslim to be buried with a pig was the ultimate disgrace. It would prevent said Muslim from ever entering heaven. So far, the tiny flash-frozen pigs had suited that purpose for the victims the team had been able to throw into a grave. Those they couldn't bury, well, stuffing their mouths full of bacon would have to do.

Yes, this was a nasty business he was engaged in. He knew it. They *all* knew it, coming in. But it was nasty because it had to be. Brutal and nasty and painful and disgusting was the only language the Muslim fanatics understood, because that's exactly the way *they* conducted themselves. This was what the ghost team was all about. Eye for eye, tooth for tooth, American style. Their mission out here in Middle

America was long-winded but apt: If the terrorists believed that killing Americans and dying in the act would get them a ticket into heaven, with 77 virgins waiting for them—if they died without disgrace, that is—then it was up to the ghosts to at least make sure that, in addition to stopping them before they fired their Stinger missiles, they indeed must die in disgrace, as a warning to future terrorists that if the ghosts caught you, there would be no virgins waiting for you at the Pearly Gates. There would be no Pearly Gates. That's why all the pork products. That's why all the new fodder for his frequently disturbing dreams.

"And just for the record," Ryder moaned now, "we don't have anything that could be called 'extra' coffee?"

"One cup a day," Puglisi replied rotely. He'd been given the job of lording over their scant provisions. "You can have it now, or tonight."

Ryder yawned. Coffee would be better later in the day, when he really needed it. Master Chief Eddie Finch's Care packages had been well intentioned. They were indeed stuffed with MRE field rations. (Food was not a problem—and if it ever was, well, they could always eat the frozen pigs, right?) But giving them just one jar of instant coffee was an astronomical miscalculation. With this crew, it was gone the first night.

And no cigarettes at all? That was almost inhuman with this group of smokestacks. Even Bates was smoking now.

Ryder surprised himself by actually dozing off—but only for a minute or so.

He was woken again by the sound of the William Tell Overture—in digital burps and bleats. In other words, a cell phone was ringing.

All five team members were up, awake, and alert in a second. Ryder jumped down to the cargo bay. Gallant started the copter's generators running. Fox and Puglisi unsheathed their weapons and ammo. Bates, though, was especially animated. One side of the copter's interior wall suddenly lit up with a barrage of colors. Green, yellow, blue, red. Laptops were hanging all over the wall, their screens flashing madly, keyboards dropping as if on cue, modem wires going everywhere. This was Bates's monster. He called it his Eyeball Machine. Built with giddy determination from a care package full of Radio Shack components and, as it turned out, some stolen NSA software, no one else on the copter had a prayer of understanding what it was exactly. They weren't sure Bates understood it himself. But they all knew what it could do. It could find the Al Qaeda missile teams up to an hour before they were ready to strike.

It had taken Bates about two hours to put it together, maybe another three or four to get it working right. It was the stolen NSA software that did all the work. Very top-secret stuff that Bates didn't even realize was inside the care package until he opened it. Who put it in there? Who would have been in a position to steal it in the first place? No one even asked the question. The team had stopped thinking about such things long ago.

Ryder had asked Bates how the Eyeball worked right after the Campo Raid. Bates had looked back at him like he was from the Stone Age.

"Do you really want to know?" Bates had asked him back.

"Sure," Ryder told him, reminding him he'd flown X-planes for twenty years; he wasn't such a rube to new technology.

"OK, do you know what a Tee-Voh is?" Bates then asked him. When Ryder shook his head no, Bates just let out a sigh.

He knew this was going to take a while.


As Bates explained it then, the popular TIVO device had the ability to continuously search for TV programs on its owner's cable system, pulling in shows that its memory chips knew the owner had a preference for. Bates's machine worked on the same concept, except his preferences were to track down the Al Qaeda missile teams, and instead of scanning a TV cable system, his rig was continuously scanning all of the information-gathering computers belonging to the

CIA, the FBI, the NRO, just about every U.S. intelligence agency in the alphabet soup of acronyms, including the NSA itself—and doing so quietly, of course. Again, the top-secret software did most of the work, worming its way into those agencies' systems, revealing everything and leaving no tracks behind. And because much of the data flowing into those systems was in real time—satellite photos, wiretaps, intercepted Net communications—the information bouncing back to the 50-year-old chopper, floating in the middle of the foggy lake, was pretty much instantaneous. For many hours of the day, the ghosts were more plugged in than 99 percent of the intelligence officials in Washington.

As such, Bates's monster could do many things. But it was most effective in intercepting and then tracking cellphone calls. Of course, this was relatively easy to do if you happened to hold the cell phone the call was being made to. That's why above the monster included a gallery of just that: cell phones. All different shapes, all different colors and sizes. Two dozen in all, with 24 different "rings," these had belonged to the 12 terrorists they'd iced in the past 72 hours. Each mook had been carrying two cell phones on his person when the ghosts attacked. It was the first thing the ghosts looked for, before dispatching their unfortunate adversaries. The more cell phones they had, the closer they got to sniffing out the other "soccer players."

The ghosts also knew how the underground Stinger cell worked; it worked the same as *all* Al Qaeda cells worked. The individual missile teams were broken down into subcells. They had no contact with one another once they'd been dropped off by the team bus at the place they were supposed to shoot down their target airliner. Only when they were in place in their snipers' nest would they make a call to another subcell, not talking, simply letting it ring. A call coming in on that particular phone meant the team was established and ready to proceed. It was the twenty-first century version of simple tom-tom communication.

As they had taken all these phones from the terrorists, when one of them rang it meant another terrorist missile team was slithering into position. Simple as that. Hearing that noise inside the Sky Horse, though, was the equivalent of hearing an air-raid siren going off.

And this was where the NSA software *really* came in handy. It could tap into the ultrasecret *Keypad* satellite. This was the spy system in the sky that could trace any cell-phone call in the world and put a location to it. So, once the missile team made the establishing call, it was like they were putting a target on their backs. And as the ghosts had the team's schedule taken from the George Mann file, with each site marked 1 through 9, they knew approximately where the terrorists were going to strike next.

(Bates's machine could do many other things as well, which meant that he was getting even less sleep than Ryder. When Bates wasn't trying to track down the different missile squads, he was on the Internet nonstop, tapping into all kinds of things, in an effort to find the buses themselves. He routinely hacked into the Greyhound company's corporate computers, trying to pick up a clue on the missing vehicles. He also monitored state police computers, highway department computers, even those set up in tollbooths along the highways of the Midwest, hoping to catch any stray report of a Greyhound bus "acting funny." But the mooks had the advantage here. They could move day or night and not attract any undue attention. On the other hand the ghosts had to be very judicious in when and how they flew. They couldn't give up precious flying in the dead of night to try to look for either bus; the time they used for that would probably allow one of the missile teams to get a clear shot at an airliner. So while they'd be able to catch the missile teams before they had a chance to act, they'd yet to catch up with the bus that was dropping the teams off. They were always just about a day behind.)

The team members crowded around the display of cell phones now.

Bates got the monster working. Jamming a pair of headphones down over his head, he started pounding on his keyboard like a madman, all while the cell phone continued to ring. The others heard a storm of bleeps and clicks; then Bates reached over and finally turned the blinking cell phone to talk, in effect answering it. The other team members froze. The person on the other end quickly hung up, as he was supposed to. Bates typed some more, assaulting the keys at near light speed. Not two seconds later, he went thumbs-up. A colorful graph suddenly appeared on his main laptop screen. The others knew what this meant: Bates had been able to trace the call. They clenched their fists in silent triumph.

He began typing again. Now his main laptop graphic split in two—one was registering the residue of the call's electrical pattern. Each one was unique. The other side of the graphic was showing a GPS screen. A flashing "pong" circle began moving down from the upper left-hand corner. It got smaller and smaller. They watched this screen closely until the circle stopped flashing. Only then did Bates reach over and finally push the phone to off.

Then he turned to the others and said, "Just as we thought. They're close by. . . ."

They'd hit a home run with Campo. The flight over to Kentucky had been swift, low, and adventure-free. It was hard for the team members to think this way, because they were around it all the time, but the typical person on the ground, looking up, was not an expert on aircraft types. People saw a jet airliner—not a Boeing 737. They saw a military jet—not an F-15 or an F-16. They saw a helicopter—not a UH-60 or a CH-56. Or a half-century-old S-58 Sky Horse.

So the team members were able to make the initial trip with little ruckus. According to the Mann schedule, Campo was stop number 1 for the Hello Soccer club. It was rough terrain and because it was not far from Louisville Airport, planes flying in the area were either descending for landings or still climbing in their takeoffs. In either configuration, they were slow, their pilots were distracted, and the planes were without much maneuverability at all—in other words, extremely vulnerable to a hit by a Stinger missile. So, thinking that the terrorists would head for the highest point in the

Campo area had the ghosts locked in on Mount Winslow from the beginning.

Chicago had been a different matter. It was the second site on the soccer team's schedule, yet it called for the Sky Horse to fly into the heart of a vast urban area without anyone knowing exactly who they were. While seeing a Coast Guard helicopter in the skies above the Windy City was not all that unusual, the team had to contend with the fact that they would have to pass in and out of three major radar nets, essentially as an unidentified aircraft. They got around this just as they used to get around various checkpoints when sailing in the containership during their first undercover mission: they simply and boldly lied to any air traffic control person who contacted them, claiming they were a training flight from the nearby military facility on the Great Lakes and while identifying themselves as Coast Guard never mentioning exactly what kind of CG craft they were riding in.

The overworked air traffic control guys at O'Hare, their hands full with the busiest airport in the world, let the team fly because they knew what to say and how to say it. Fox did the talking, as his authoritative yet smooth southern voice seemed to be the most convincing.

And apparently a helicopter landing atop a crack house disguised as a mosque was not much of an event in that part of the toddling town. The team members could clearly see people in their tenements or hanging in alleys as they flashed overhead. Because there were no graves this time, they'd resorted to the bacon instead. In all, the operation took less than 10 minutes, including the 2 minutes it took for them to find a place to set up the flag. It had been smooth all the way.

Nebraska, though, had been a mess. They rode in fine, everyone in position. But due to bad weather starting out, they'd arrived a little late. That's why it turned into such a tussle with the mooks at the peak of the Big Rock.

Taking one of the terrorists with them had been a last-minute decision. They thought he would give them some information on where the team bus was heading next and how it was getting there. But either the mook was particularly clever or he misunderstood their demands. He took them up to Saint Helena, where the team was *supposed* to play its next match. But the bus wasn't there. The terrorist went out the door at 5,000 feet, courtesy of Puglisi. The team could still hear his screams all the way down.

Messy—but in the end, the result of the Nebraska action was the same as the two previous ones. Four dead mooks, another two missiles confiscated and destroyed. Another bloody message left for anyone who cared to look for it.

Now it was the next morning—and they were at it again.

Two minutes after they zeroed in on the latest cell-phone signal, the helicopter's engines were started and its rotor was spinning. Ryder was behind the aircraft's main controls; Gallant was turning on its makeshift laptop weapons system. Fox and Puglisi were sitting at the two cargo door guns. Bates was still glued in front of the cell-phone display.

They were getting good at this now.

Minneapolis Airport was 22 miles south of Lost View Lake. Bates's information said that the person who had dialed the cell phone was inside a quarter-mile area about a mile north of the airport. But a topographic map called up on one of the flight-control laptops showed no naturally elevated locations around the airport, places the terrorists would be drawn to. However, there was an amusement park in the general vicinity. The locator ring was practically burning a hole in it on the GPS map.

Once airborne, they raced down the length of the foggy lake using its cover for as long at they could. Then they rose and turned due south, going right over the heavily populated Litchfield area, no doubt attracting attention from below. The air traffic control people at Minneapolis Airport tried to raise them; they'd been picked up by the airport's radar when they were forced to go up and over some particularly hilly neighborhoods. But there was nothing they could do about that now. They simply shut off the radio, dipped back down to 200 feet, and went full throttle toward the amusement park.

Called the Great American Adventure Land, it was a huge

complex with everything from modern roller-coaster type rides to old-fashioned Ferris wheels. There was also a large water park, a concert arena, and many food concessions. One mile out, Ryder and Gallant clicked on their FLIR device. It gave them a heat register of the area. The first thing that jumped out at them was the hundreds of people lined up at the park's main gate, waiting for the waterslide attraction to open.

"Damn," Gallant cursed. "This isn't going to be clean as we hoped."

"Let's make it quick then," Ryder replied.

They did a scan of the interior of the park. It took a few moments, but then they found two heat signatures at the top of the tallest hill of the park's roller-coaster-type attraction, something called Space Ride.

"Could be maintenance men," Gallant said, compressing the image on the screen. "They have to check those things every day before they let anyone on them."

"Could be our mooks, too," Ryder replied. "It's the highest point this side of the Rockies."

"Let's buzz them," Gallant suggested.

And buzz them they did. Ryder put the copter into a quick, sharp bank, pulling a tight 180 degrees. This put their nose pointing directly at the top of the Space Ride's highest hill. Then he pushed them to full throttle.

They roared over the metallic peak a second later. What they saw was two men in soccer-style clothing, sitting very casually atop the roller-coaster hill. They watched the chopper as it went by, playing it cool, even waving in a bid to seem friendly.

But then Gallant saw something else: On the ground, 200 feet below the structure, clear as day, were two bodies. They were wearing bright yellow and blue shirts and caps. The overall color scheme of the Space Ride and the park itself was the same shades of yellow and blue.

The three men riding in the back saw the bodies, too.

"Those are mooks up there!" Puglisi screamed up to the pilots. "They threw those two poor bastards right off the top!"

"That seems to be the case . . ." Fox agreed.

They turned sharply again and went back over the big hill. This time the two men weren't waving at them. Everyone on the helicopter could see the telltale suitcase and tube assembly that was used to transport Stinger missiles. The two soccer players were sitting on it.

Ryder looked over at Gallant. "That's enough for me," he said.

Gallant just nodded. It was *that* time again.

He pushed a series of keys on one of the connected laptops. Its screen burst to life with an icon representing the large .50-caliber machine gun mounted in the chopper's nose. The word *READY* flashed on the screen. Gallant hit the enter key. The huge nose gun burst to life. Two seconds was all it took. The two terrorists, their launcher, and about fifteen feet of the top of the Space Ride's hill exploded into a cloud of fire and metallic dust. No sooner had this happened than a Northwest 747 airliner passed over the amusement park no more than 2,000 feet high and still climbing.

Ryder yanked back on the throttles as they passed over the remains of the big hill. There was no sign of the terrorists' bodies. They'd been vaporized.

"We won't have to waste a couple pigs on them," Gallant said drily.

Ryder clicked the FLIR back on. The soccer cells always traveled together, four to a cell. This meant two more mooks were still down there somewhere. There was no way the team was going to let them go.

"There!" Gallant called out. He was pointing at the expanded FLIR screen that showed two figures running through the park's concert arena, heading toward the food court. "The other two—I knew I could smell them all the way up here. . . ."

Fox was already disconnecting one of the side door fifties from its swivel mount. They would have to do an insertion to take care of this. Bates started gathering up ammunition. Puglisi was checking his knives. Ryder and Gallant just looked at each other. One of them would have to go, too.

"My turn," Ryder said. Gallant had done the Campo Raid and the Nebraska job.

But Gallant just shook his head.

"I'll go," he said.

Ryder swung the Sky Horse down toward the center of the park. There was an open area to the left of the waterslide, hard by the food courts.

Puglisi threw out the access ladder and started down almost immediately. Fox was close behind, holding the big fifty by its strap below him. Bates went next, his skinny post–hippie dude frame weighed down by two bandoliers of ammo. Gallant went down last, carrying Bates's gun as well as his own. And like Puglisi, Gallant was carrying a hatchet.

All four made it to the ground next to a huge attraction, a kind of high-tech fun house called the Angry Alien. Gallant gave Ryder the wave-off; Ryder immediately put some air under the chopper. He could see twice as many people pressed up against the park gate now. They were all looking in with great curiosity. Some were shouting; some were laughing. Some thinking it was perhaps a simulated battle being put on by the amusement park or maybe an antiterrorist security drill. Many were taking pictures and even videotaping the action. Ryder tried to keep his head together. It wouldn't be the first time the team had performed before an audience. During the Hormuz adventure, they'd made headlines on CNN more than once.

But that didn't mean he liked it.

The two remaining terrorists *were* hiding close by the waterslide, as it turned out. They'd scrambled behind the sparse cover of an overturned picnic table. On their right was the food court. On their left, the entrance to the Angry Alien. To their rear was the huge wave tank, which was the size of a small ocean. In front of them, the four heavily armed, and armored, American soldiers were advancing on them.

The Islamic gunmen hadn't anticipated any of this. Why would they? They'd been led to believe that they would not have to worry about getting caught or aggressively tracked down, at least not at first. They had been told that it had all been *fixed*. That when each four-man team was dropped off at their firing location there would be little to worry about concerning law enforcement agencies, that they'd be able to operate freely. They all had safe houses in Canada where they were to go once their individual missions were completed. As they understood it, someone high up in the U.S. government had even arranged it so they wouldn't have to stop for a search at the border.

So who then were these strange soldiers in their very strange helicopter? So suddenly they had blown away their two colleagues at the top of the roller coaster's big hill. This was not how the typical U.S. soldier acted. The terrorists knew this because each had fought Americans in either Afghanistan or Iraq. These days American soldiers did not shoot first and ask questions later but actually did the exact opposite. So sensitive were they to inflicting unwanted collateral damage, many gave up their own lives rather than harm an innocent civilian.

But not these soldiers. They'd turned their two colleagues into windblown gristle and now were making their way toward them. And they were trapped. There was nowhere inside the park for them to hide. The main gate was filled with hundreds of people—innocents true—but the terrorists didn't have any firepower to shoot their way through them. The rest of the park was surrounded by a security fence that was simply too high for them to even consider climbing over—it had been erected to discouraged troublemakers from sneaking in. Plus they were armed only with pistols. . . .

But that wasn't what drove all the fear into them. For now the soldiers were near enough for the terrorists to see them up close. The huge oversize helmets, the black combat suits, the gray body armor, the M16 lookalikes with trademark bayonets attached. But it was the patch the soldiers wore on their right shoulder that burned into their terrorists' eyes. The Islamic gunmen knew it well. It showed a billowing American flag with the silhouette of the Twin Towers on it. The initials

*NYPD* and *FDNY* floating above. And below, a motto: *We Will Never Forget.*

Seeing the patch told them who these bloody Americans from the sky were. Who they had to be.

They were the Crazy Americans.

The scourge of their comrades back in Hormuz and at Singapore and almost in Manila. The men who'd killed their sheikh, Abdul Kazeel.

Now they were *here,* in America, to get *them.*

Foolishly, in sheer terror, the terrorists began shooting at the Americans with their popguns. The badly aimed fire only served to pinpoint their position. Bates and Gallant opened up with their M15s immediately. The mooks were firing at them from behind nothing more than a wooden bench. Puglisi added fire, and the three streams of bullets pounded into the table, shredding it. One terrorist was blown away in the fusillade. The other scrambled away, fleeing into the entrance to the Angry Alien.

Ryder was watching all this from above, at least as best he could from a stationary hover. But then he was distracted from the one-sided gunfight by a flash of light off to his left. He looked out past the crowd at the main gate, out into the parking lot. That's when he saw the one thing he didn't want to see.

A police car. . . .

Lights flashing, siren wailing, it was screaming right through the middle of the huge empty parking lot, heading for the main admission gate.

"Son of a bitch . . ." Ryder breathed. "This ain't good. . . ."

The ghost team didn't mind people seeing what they were doing—or at least having no misconceptions as to what they were up to. But they didn't want to get *caught* in the act. Not by the police, not by anyone. That would put an end to this flying circus way too soon.

So, Ryder knew he had to do something—but what?

He raised the copter up and over the water park, over the remains of the smoldering roller-coaster hill, and headed toward the parking lot.

The police car had a lot of ground to cover—the parking lot was almost a quarter-mile long. Ryder brought the copter down to just 20 feet off the asphalt, perpendicular to the police car. He booted throttle and went rocketing over the top of the unsuspecting patrol car, carrying a storm of dust and noise along with him. The massive downdraft hit the vehicle full force, nearly tipping it over. There was a mighty screech of brakes; the two cops hadn't seen him until the very last moment. The concussion was so severe, it caused both airbags to burst open.

Ryder turned the copter over and was soon pointing back at the police car again. No doubt, the cops inside were stunned—and baffled as well. He could see them wrestling with the airbags, trying to look out their front window at the same time. They'd been called here for a report of shots fired. Why would a Coast Guard helicopter begin buzzing them?

Ryder turned up and over again. The police car, its occupants recovered, started creeping forward once more. Lower and faster, Ryder came at them head-on. The downwash slammed into the roof of the car, forcing it almost down to its axles. It screeched to a halt again. Ryder turned, hoping he'd popped least a couple of its tires.

No such luck, though. In fact, the cruiser started rolling forward yet again. Ryder could see one cop on the radio. The other was unhitching a shotgun from his dashboard.

*Not good. . . .*

He went around again, lost as to what to do next. Ryder could still see the cruiser's driver, steering the car with one hand while on the radio with the other. The second cop was pumping his shotgun and getting ready to aim it out the window. Ryder's mind was racing, weighing the circumstances. Then, reluctantly, he armed the copter's forward gun.

He booted throttles and came at the police car head-on again. Making sure he was well out in front, he let loose a barrage from the big fifty. As always, it was blinding, noisy, and violent. The stream of tracer shells smashed into the parking lot 500 feet in front of the police cruiser, tearing up a huge portion of asphalt. Still the police car kept coming.

Ryder came back around yet again and repeated the maneuver, this time laying down a barrage just 250 feet away from the patrol car. The police car kept on coming.

Ryder swore again, whipping the copter around tail first. These cops were fearless. Plus they were now halfway across the huge parking lot and getting near a cluster of parked cars. He bore down on them, not 20 feet off the ground, and put a surgically placed, noisy barrage right over the top of their roof. The concussion of the fussilade alone took out the flashing-light assembly on top of the cruiser, exploding it in hundreds of multicolored pieces.

That was all it took. The cops finally slammed on their brakes, put their car in reverse, and retreated.

Ryder breathed a sigh of relief. His hands were shaking.

"*That* was too fucking close," he whispered.

Meanwhile, back in the park, Gallant was looking everywhere for the Sky Horse.

"Where the hell did he go?" he yelled to Puglisi.

The Delta soldier just shook his head. "I don't know," he yelled back to Gallant. "I just hope he doesn't forget us down here."

They both turned their attention back to the matter at hand. They had the last terrorist cornered in the Angry Alien fun house. But how could they get him out? They could hear the siren in the distance and maybe the clatter of gunfire—and maybe that's where Ryder was. They could also hear the crowd at the main gate, yelling, shouting, screaming. It all added up to a shortage of time.

Puglisi and Gallant ran forward now, taking up positions near the ride's entryway. It was a large building, not one of the newest attractions at the theme park but elaborate nevertheless. Bates had scrambled around to the back and confirmed there were no rear exits that he could see. So the last mook was indeed trapped. Trouble was, the ghosts didn't have time to go in and flush him out.

Gallant and Puglisi just looked back at Fox, who had set up the big fifty near an ice-cream stand. All three just shrugged. Then Fox yelled, "Get Brainiac back out here!"

Gallant yelled for Bates; he soon came running back to the main midway, knowing what would happen next. Joining Gallant and Puglisi, they all retreated to Fox's position. Bates immediately fed a belt of ammunition into the .50-caliber. Fox cocked the gun and then let loose a fierce barrage at the front of the fun house. He never let off the trigger. The stream of tracer bullets was frightening as the huge rounds perforated the saucer-shaped building. Pieces of wood and metal went flying, some sparkling with sudden heat. Fox just kept spraying back and forth, taking the building apart seemingly one board, one piece, at a time.

It took almost a half-minute, so long the barrel of the huge gun was nearly red-hot. But the building finally collapsed on itself; then it caught on fire.

"Who the fuck is going to pay for that!" Gallant yelled wildly.

The terrorist staggered out, burned and bloody. Puglisi ran forward, hatchet in hand. Bates had a small video camera he'd found in his care package. He recorded the mayhem that followed. The screams were horrible. Gallant and Fox had to look away. When it was over, though, they saw Puglisi stuffing hot dogs into the dead terrorist's mouth.

"God damn," Gallant said. "That's freaking nasty."

At that moment, they heard a great roar above them.

The Sky Horse had returned.

Ryder had picked up the action on the ground.

He saw the fifty take apart the fun house. He saw Puglisi first riddle the terrorist with bullets, then chop off his hands. And Puglisi was now stuffing frankfurters into the man's mouth.

*Are hot dogs made out of pork?* Ryder found himself thinking.

Then he snapped back to reality. They were through here. It was time to go.

"Jesus, c'mon!" Ryder was yelling at his comrades on the ground now. Fox was already on the still-dangling ladder. Gallant was holding the bottom for Puglisi to start climbing. But where was Bates?

Ryder was straining his neck looking for the wayward computer whiz, this as he was doing his best to keep the old chopper steady as the others tried to ascend.

Fox reached the cargo bay and scrambled aboard.

"Where's the Brain?" he yelled back to the DSA officer.

"Jesuzz, he was right behind me!" came the reply.

Now Puglisi fell into the cargo bay. He was carrying the dead terrorists' weapons plus their cell phones. He didn't know where Bates was, either. Ryder could just about see through a hole in the roller coaster, out through the main gate. He saw a small army of police cars now approaching the park.

"Damn!" he cried again.

He looked below and saw Gallant, still holding the bottom of the ladder, looking up at him and pointing to a spot deeper into the food court. Ryder turned to where Gallant was pointing, and that's when he saw Bates. He was kicking the crap out of one of the concession vending machines and picking up its contents from the ground.

"Is he insane?" Fox roared. "We gotta get out of here!"

But then Ryder turned the chopper slightly, and this gave him a better view of Bates.

And he saw Bates wasn't busting up a candy vendor or a Coke dispenser. He was robbing a cigarette machine.

Ryder let out a whoop.

"Atta boy!" he yelled. "*Now* you're using your head!"

# Chapter 11

Ozzi heard a phone ringing just as they were entering the Holland tunnel.

Hunn was driving their van, a six-panel delivery type. They'd rented it earlier that day, maxxing out Li's Visa card, this after treating themselves to new duds at her local Kmart. They'd made the drive from D.C. to Jersey in about six hours, Hunn doing his best to behave, and keep their speed somewhere below 80 miles an hour. Only guilty people go the speed limit, he'd told Ozzi. But did the New Jersey State Police know that? Ozzi had to wonder.

The phone rang again. Ozzi took the brown paper bag out from under his seat and opened it. There were more than 20 different cell phones inside.

"Damn, I can't tell which one it is," he said as Hunn paid the toll.

"We're getting as bad as the mooks," Hunn replied. "With the cell phones, I mean. Between us and them, I'm surprised there are any left for other people to buy."

Hunn's complaints weren't helping, but Ozzi knew what he meant. The collection of cell phones was a necessary evil. Despite their brilliant escape from Gitmo, they knew the government would eventually realize they weren't all dead. When that happened, the Feds would start looking very hard for them, if they weren't already. The ghosts still had to communicate with one another, though, even if it meant using codes and having only brief conversations. So just like the Islamic terrorists, they'd gobbled up a bunch of cell phones—again, courtesy of Li's Visa card—got the phone numbers to their colleagues out west and now would use them for only one conversation at a time.

Ozzi heard the ring again, a very annoying digital symphony. He reached into the bag and took out a handful of the cell phones. None were lit up or vibrating. They entered the tunnel. Now Ozzi could hardly see—but that was good. When the phone rang again, he spotted the glow from its screen light at the bottom of the bag. He fished it out and finally answered it.

It was Bates. Calling from somewhere in Minnesota.

"I think the car you sold me is a lemon," Bates said cryptically.

"How come?" Ozzi replied.

"Because I've already changed the oil in it four times—"

"*Four times?* Wow—is that the only problem you're having with it?"

"We spilled a lot of fluid the last time. Almost got a speeding ticket, too. But yes, everything else is running OK. We will probably do a fifth oil change in the next couple days, or maybe sooner. What are you up to?"

"We're on our way to get some help to look for that cup of spilled coffee."

"You've gone Apple picking, you mean?"

"Yes, we will be able to do just that in about three minutes, I'd say. . . ."

"OK—let us know how that goes. And have you read the newspaper this morning?"

"Just the comics. There was nothing else I was interested in."

"OK—talk to you. . . ."

Ozzi hung up, put the phone on the floor, and crushed it with his boot. Then he threw the remains out the window and put the rest of the phones away.

"That's encouraging, I guess," he said to Hunn, translating the coded conversation now. "They've already found four of the missile teams and greased them."

"Four—nice!" Hunn whooped, illegally switching lanes inside the tunnel. "I *knew* those guys would wind up having all the fun."

"Be careful what you wish for, Sergeant," Ozzi reminded him. "Sometimes they comes true."

"Tell you the truth, Lieutenant," Hunn replied soberly, "I don't like it when things go *so* easy. Nothing stays smooth forever. It's almost like bad luck to have too much good luck, all at once."

"I hear you," Ozzi said. "The mooks will *have* to figure out at some point that we're on to them. We know they don't talk to each other at all, beyond ringing their phones when they're about to do something. But I'm sure they monitor all the important newspapers and watch the TV news. I mean, they expected four planes to be *shot down* by now. They must know *something* is wrong."

"Those assholes can really adapt, though," Hunn grumbled. "They're like a virus. They'll speed up their timetable, or they'll start skipping around. Or they'll have their ringmaster dream up something new. If they have a ringmaster, that is—and I'm sure they do. But they'll do something. That's why it would be so much easier just to hit the first bus."

"If only the copter guys could find it," Ozzi said.

Hunn wildly switched lanes again, not once, but twice, viciously cutting off several different cars.

"Four teams *kaput*!" he said excitedly again. "Well, this is going to hit the newspapers soon enough. About us and the mooks. I know when we were in the Middle East, Murphy was able to keep some things under wraps in the media, until we got a little crazy, that is. But it might be hard to keep all this out of the public eye for very long."

Ozzi was surprised. He rarely heard any of the original ghost team members invoke the name of the very mysterious Bobby Murphy.

Hunn went on: "I mean, eventually, people are going to freak out when they realize there's a little war going on, right inside our own country."

Ozzi just looked out the window at the dirty tunnel walls. "Yes," he said. "Freak out they will. . . ."

They emerged from the tunnel to see Manhattan standing before them like a large gray Oz. Hunn headed across the island, doing battle with the early-evening traffic. He began running red lights and driving very fast through the dense, pedestrian-packed streets of midtown. Ozzi just sat back and said nothing. He knew what Hunn knew: a van *not* driving like this—that is, like a typical New York City driver—would probably raise more suspicion than one that was.

*When in Rome* . . . he thought.

Speeding over bridges, along crowded expressways and parkways, around detours and traffic jams, they somehow got to Queens in one piece.

It was dark by now. Ozzi had never been in this part of New York City. He was surprised to see trees here and blocks of houses that almost looked like suburbia. There were many people out and about, enjoying a warm early evening. Ozzi had grown up in an exclusive part of Maryland. At the moment, he might as well have been on Mars.

Hunn wound them through the streets as if on autopilot. The huge Delta soldier got more animated with each intersection, each set of traffic lights they passed through. He was getting close to his old neighborhood, Ozzi could tell. He could only imagine the emotions building inside his oversize colleague.

Another set of traffic lights, a few more turns, left and right, then suddenly Hunn slowed down. On the next corner was a storefront with frosted-over windows making it impossible to see all but one dim light inside. The name on the door read: GREATER QUEENS SOCIAL CLUB. They rolled past the building; then Hunn went around the block again. When they drove by this time, the light behind the frosted windows had been turned out.

Hunn went around the block again, but this time he pulled into the dark alley next to the storefront. There was a small garage back here. Its door was open, and a guy almost as big as Hunn was standing beside it. Hunn eased the van into the garage and the man quickly closed the door behind it.

Hunn shut off the engine, then turned to Ozzi.

"If you don't mind, Lieutenant, let me do the talking, OK?" Hunn asked Ozzi.

Ozzi almost laughed. "Be my guest," he said.

They got out of the van to find the man waiting for them. He was holding a flashlight up to his face. His features were hard: deep black eyes, very red nose, and oddly, his eyebrows had been recently singed. He smelled of burning wood. He and Hunn just stared at each other for a very long time—so long, Ozzi had a sudden terrible thought: Was this the wrong thing to do? Had they been set up?

But then Hunn and the guy shook hands and even embraced. The awkward moment passed. "Good to see you again, Davey," the guy said to Hunn. "It's not the same around here since you've been . . . well, other places."

Hunn thanked the man, then asked, "Is everything set up?"

The guy just nodded. "Set up and waiting. . . ."

Then Hunn introduced Ozzi this way: "This guy's an officer. Everything we say, he has to be in on."

The huge man studied Ozzi up and down. Ozzi felt like he was looking up a side of a mountain. This guy might have been the whitest person he'd ever met. Ozzi finally shook his hand.

"Sean O'Flaherty," the man said. "Welcome to Queens."

O'Flaherty led them out of the garage, down half the length of the very dark alley, between two abandoned buildings, and back toward the street again. This roundabout route got them to the rear door of the social club.

O'Flaherty knocked three times, waited a moment, then knocked twice more. The door opened immediately; on the other side was an individual almost as large as O'Flaherty. Hunn and Ozzi hustled inside. They found themselves in a small wood-paneled room. Very dark interior, with a few low lights over a pair of card tables and a Budweiser sign on the wall. It took a moment for Ozzi's eyes to adjust.

The man who let them in nodded quickly, then disappeared outside. "Keep a good watch out," O'Flaherty told him as they passed. "We don't want any surprises tonight."

There was a small bar in the corner of the wood-paneled room. O'Flaherty headed right for it. "You guys want a beer?" he asked Hunn and Ozzi, even as he went behind the bar and got them two bottles of Bud. Ozzi accepted his without hesitation and drank it greedily. He'd been needing a drink for some time now. They moved to the rear of the first floor, through a kitchen, and down a set of stairs. Now in the basement, they came to a huge padded door. Again O'Flaherty knocked three times, then twice more. This door opened and inside was another room. This one had no windows; it was all cement blocks.

*An old fallout shelter,* Ozzi thought correctly.

There was a table set up at one end, with a bunch of folding chairs lined up in front of it. About two dozen individuals were milling about, all as white and huge as Hunn and O'Flaherty. Some of them were dressed casually, but others were wearing denim shirts and yellow utility pants and boots. Most had mustaches or beards. Many wore Fu Manchu facial hair and had heads shaved clean. They looked Irish and Italian mostly, hard-nosed, hard-drinking. Not unlike the cast of a Road Warrior movie.

Which was close.

Actually, they were members of the FDNY—the Fire Department of New York.

Ozzi would come to think of what transpired in the next two hours as historical, like signing the Declaration of Independence or drafting the Bill of Rights.

It should be said, though, he would drain six more Buds in that time and that may have altered his perceptions a bit. But not by much. What happened in the tiny cement block room in the middle of Queens went beyond civil disobedience, beyond simple defiance of authority. It bordered on sedition. Not quite insurrection—though you never knew how these things would turn out. But it was, no argument, an example of pure, unadulterated American anger and true-blue patriotism.

Strange.

*Historical* . . .

In a boozy sort of way.

Hunn knew everyone in the room. He was from a long line of firefighters—his father, uncles, cousins. They immediately fell silent and sat down when Hunn entered. It was obvious they knew he'd come here for a very important reason. And Hunn did not disappoint.

It was outrageous right from the start, for as soon as Hunn took his place at the front of the room he commenced to tell the firefighters *everything*. About the secret unit. About what they had done at Hormuz and Singapore. About what they'd tried to do in the Philippines. Hunn spoke with amazing eloquence yet in a language his audience could understand. They hardly moved, so rapt were they at his words. Ozzi found himself transfixed as well. Working on his second Bud now, he was hearing parts of the story for the first time, too.

Hunn told the jakes about the Stinger missiles, the two buses, about George Mann and what the reporter had found out before he was murdered. He told them about Palm Tree and about the split-off ghost team that was now in the American Midwest, trying to stop the terrorists before they could knock down any airliners. He told them the ghost team had proof that highly placed people inside the U.S. government knew the Stinger missiles were in the country yet were doing nothing to prevent the chaos the missiles could cause. He told them there was a good chance that TWA Flight 800, which had crashed off Long Island years before, as well as the more recent Flight 587 crash in Queens, not far away from this very neighborhood, were both brought down by Al Qaeda and that the government was covering it up. His point was: the terrorists were back and the threat was much, much greater this time.

It was strange for Ozzi to hear it all, laid out by someone who was there for most of it. He couldn't imagine the multitude of national security violations they were racking up here. But like Fox said, breaking the law and violating national security were things the team couldn't worry about. Not anymore.

The firefighters began to ask questions, and it didn't take long for their mood to turn angry. To a man the jakes agreed the government had not gone after Al Qaeda as hard as it should have. Everyone in the room knew someone who'd been killed on September 11th, friends, relatives, and neighbors. While the U.S. armed forces were fighting in Iraq, it seemed like the real enemy—the terrorists—had been allowed to run wild, expand their numbers, expand their terror. The jakes were also very pissed off at how the government had handled the whole investigation of 9/11. How were dozens of bin Laden's family members living in America allowed to fly home to Saudi Arabia in the dark days after the attack when every plane in the United States was supposed to be grounded? Why wouldn't the United States give the families of the 9/11 victims everything they wanted and more? The government was more interested in covering its own ass; that was the consensus.

"Which is why we're here," Hunn told the firefighters, finally pausing to take a long swig of beer. "We need your help to fight these Muslim assholes ourselves."

Hunn cued Ozzi, who was now on his third Bud—or was it his fourth? He staggered to the table and set up his laptop. The wall behind him was painted white. He began flashing images from his computer onto it.

The first one showed the mysterious soiled napkin. Hunn explained that this was their only clue as to what they thought the terrorists' Big Plan might be—that is, what the second bus was up to. He told them the ghosts had no idea what the drawing meant. They *did* know it came from a "Drive, Shop 'n Go" store located somewhere in New Jersey, though. The ghost team suspected the drawing was made in one of these places, the coffee stain being the clue, and the imprint of the nickels, as if they were part of the change. The problem was, Hunn explained, that according to a Google search, there were more than 150 "DSG" stores throughout Jersey.

The ghosts suspected that some people helping the terrorists' missile teams might be connected to these places. They were looking for one individual in particular who might be either working in one of these stores or visiting one frequently.

Hunn nodded and Ozzi put up the next image.

"In other words, we're looking for this guy," Hunn said.

The image filled the entire wall. It showed a man in a pen drawing—done by Li—with bad hair, bad skin, an ugly face, and very criminal eyes.

"His name is Ramosa. . . ."

Captain Ramosa.

Yeah, Ozzi knew *him*.

He was the guy whom the ghost team chased all over the Philippines and who got the drop on them not once but twice during the search for the Stinger missiles. He was connected not just to Al Qaeda but, no doubt, to French Intelligence as well. Ramosa's cover as a terrorist for hire, bloodthirsty and efficient, was a good one: he was a highly placed officer in the Philippine national police.

The ghosts had always suspected that if the missiles ever made their way to the United States, then Ramosa would come here, too. There *had* to be a key man inside the country, a ringmaster pulling the strings for Al Qaeda's airliner shoot-down scheme to work. No doubt, Palm Tree had provided support on this side of the Atlantic, too, but he was running back to Paris when the team settled their score with him. But like every good intelligence operative, he had "cutouts," spy talk for middlemen, the people who did the heavy lifting in the espionage business. Ramosa was already thick into the missile plot. He was up to speed on who and what was involved. He was the natural person to take the reins, to oversee the plan. The one with whom the others—most likely sleeper agents inside the United States, as well as the "soccer players"—would "get their hands dirty together," as the Muslim saying went. Besides, the ghosts knew Ramosa had found a secret phone number in Manila that would activate these sleepers once the missiles arrived in America. Obviously someone had already used it to awake this small army of fifth columnists.

So, if Ramosa *was* in the United States, then catching him might give the ghosts a solid lead as to what the napkin drawing was all about, if anything, and perhaps what the second bus was up to. But Ramosa was a very slippery fellow, Hunn explained again. With what they were up against, even if they tipped off the FBI or the New Jersey State Police and somehow convinced them that Ramosa was a dangerous person, there was a chance that the Philippine cutout would get word beforehand and disappear before law enforcement moved in. They couldn't take that chance.

That's why the team needed to find Ramosa quickly and quietly. But how could he be found? The ghosts didn't know exactly. But they had a good guess where to start: at one of Jersey's 155 "Drive, Shop 'n Go" shops.

"And that's where you guys come in," Hunn told them.

The meeting broke up 30 minutes later. A group of firefighters escorted Hunn and Ozzi upstairs.

As Ozzi was walking back into the dimly lit card room, one of the jakes pulled him over to the bar and bought him one last beer.

"They might be ducks," the firefighter said, handing him the bottle of Bud.

"Excuse me?" Ozzi was confused.

"That drawing, on the napkin," the jake said. "They look like ducks to me. You know, flying in formation, just some higher than others."

Ozzi thought a moment. It seemed to be an amateurish guess at best.

"But how about what looks like the bus in the lower corner?" he asked. "Are you saying the terrorists are going duck hunting?"

The guy looked at him like he wanted to take his beer back.

"No, but maybe the duck thing is a code or something," he said. "Or did you ever hear about that place down in Louisiana, it's a floating barge that's got a house on it? All these bigwigs shoot ducks from it. The Vice President, the Chief Justices. It's a very exclusive club. Maybe the terrorists are going to attack it when they know a lot of bigwigs are going to be there or flying in or something."

Meanwhile, on the other side of the bar, Hunn was power-drinking one last beer as well. Suddenly a man approached him from out of the shadows. He was older than all of the firefighters downstairs. Gray hair, same ruddy face, but softer eyes. He was a priest, the chaplain for one of New York's fire districts. He was also Hunn's cousin.

Hunn was stunned to see him. They embraced warmly, but then Hunn said to him, "You can't tell my folks I was here."

"I won't, you have my word," the chaplain replied. "And I wasn't even going to come here myself when I heard what was happening. But then I felt I had to."

Hunn eased up a little. "Is my family OK?"

The priest nodded, but with a little hesitation. "Everyone is healthy," he replied. "But they worry about you. About where you are. What you are doing. They get by knowing you're in these special operations, but . . ."

"I'm fighting for the people of this country, padre," Hunn told him. "I'm fighting for them. For my sister. For everyone who was killed on 9/11. This is just something I have to do—but if they knew anything about it, it could really be trouble someday."

"I understand," the chaplain said. "Just be careful, Davey. If your parents ever lost you, too, after your sister, well, I don't know if they could handle it."

The chaplain touched his shoulder, then said, "And if you must do this, then take this with you. If you ever have a vision, something that seems odd yet connected, trust your instinct. Such things are meant to happen. God bless you . . . and please be safe."

With that, he walked back into the shadows.

At that moment, Ozzi reappeared. He'd drained the last of his beer.

"We've got to get going," he told Hunn. "We've got a long ride back to D.C."

There were handshakes all round. O'Flaherty reassured Hunn that whatever was said downstairs would stay secret. He was dead serious about that.

They walked to the rear of the building, to the back door again. Just as they arrived there, the door opened and two more jakes walked in. They looked like they'd just stepped off their fire engine. They were in complete firefighting gear—hats, utility coats, boots. They were carrying a copy of the *New York Post*. They seemed to know who Hunn and Ozzi were.

"Have you guys seen the headlines?" one asked them.

Hunn and Ozzi just shook their heads no.

The firefighter held up the paper, and there it was, in bold type: **"Secret Army Battling Terrorists in U.S.? Sources link mystery team to Hormuz, Singapore Tower."**

Hunn and Ozzi just froze.

"I hope this isn't a joke." Ozzi said.

The firemen laughed.

"Joke, hell!" one said. "You guys just became famous."

Hunn asked if he could take the paper and the firefighter compiled. Then the ghosts said another round of hasty good-byes and left.

They climbed back into the van, exited the garage, and headed back toward Manhattan. Hunn sped past the street where his family lived but gave it only a passing glance, and it was gone. The Whitestone Bridge lay ahead.

Ozzi speed-read the newspaper, using the light of the glove compartment for illumination. Though the headline was a real screamer, the story itself, somewhat buried on page 12, was rather small. Basically it said that in the past few days a series of mysterious killings had taken place in the Midwest, the victims being undocumented aliens of

Middle Eastern descent who might be somehow mixed up in terrorism. One of these incidents took place inside a theme park and was witnessed by several hundred people, including a number of police officers. But details were sketchy as the paper went to print, just that the acts seemed similar, by boldness alone, to those attributed to the rumored secret unit who saved the carrier *Abraham Lincoln* and pulled off the rescue in Singapore. Tellingly, the story had been generated by a news service used by police departments across the country and not by the government or the FBI or anyone else in Washington.

Ozzi read the story aloud to Hunn, then said, "I don't know if this is a good thing or a bad thing. I mean, like you said, what the copter guys are doing was bound to hit the papers eventually. But if the government didn't know it before, they sure as hell must think we're still alive now. And when more details do come out, well, we might see our friends on CNN yet. . . ."

Hunn just shrugged. "Well, again, it won't be the first time."

They drove for a dozen blocks or so, but then suddenly Hunn screeched to a stop in front of an especially busy stretch of businesses: a grocery store, a hardware store, an OTB shop, and a liquor store. Hunn wordlessly bounded out of the van and ran into the liquor store. Ozzi could see him buying something with the last of his spare change. He ran back out and jumped into the van. He had a bottle of wine with him. Ozzi pulled it out of the paper bag and read the label.

*"Thunderbird?"* he asked incredulously. "Isn't this what the winos drink?"

"That's right," Hunn answered. "I used to love this stuff when I was a kid."

Hunn put the van in gear and quickly turned back into the traffic. They were under way again.

"Was that OK, sir?" he asked Ozzi. "Me picking this up, I mean?"

But Ozzi was already sitting way back in his seat; he wasn't really listening or even thinking about the news story anymore. Instead he was looking at the approaching skyline of Manhattan.

With a laugh, he just said, *"Ducks?"*

# Chapter 12

From the looks of it, the old refueling station hadn't been used in years. It was located on a tiny tree-covered island 100 feet off the shore of Minnebago Lake, a large body of water 50 miles south of Green Bay. There was an old log shack located on the bank of the half-acre island, though it was barely standing, battered by too many long winters and hot summers. There were two gas pumps next to its dilapidated dock. They looked to be vintage 1950s; they even had an old Cities Service green emblem on them. The place had once serviced floatplanes, as well as recreational boats. The cabin itself looked more like a hunting lodge than a gas station, though. Make that a very old, very small hunting lodge.

The Minnebago water was high now, which worked out well for the ghost team. They avoided having to land the Sky Horse in the middle of the lake. Instead they were able to put down next to the island and float the big copter right up to the dock. Incredibly—or not—the old pump's tank was full of fresh aviation gas, just the drink the copter needed.

This refueling stop began with a message from Finch back at Cape Lonely. He'd continued to be the copter team's intermediary for this mission, their "cutout," if you will. Via a quick coded phone conversation, he'd told them where and when they could find the precious gas. After hiding out most of the day back at the foggy Minnesota lake, they flew here, landing just after 5:00 A.M, their fuel tanks dropping below reserve, never a good thing. Before they activated the gas pump, though, Ryder and Fox stepped onto the island and checked it out thoroughly with their M15s. It was a wise move, a necessary caution, but not really needed. It appeared no one had been on the island for decades.

But then, appearances could be deceiving.

They soon had the gas pump's extra-long hose stretched out to the floating copter. Their tanks were so dry, they could hear the fuel gushing down into them. Though the team was now in possession of at least a dozen packs of cigarettes, thanks to Bates's quick thinking while on the ground at the theme park, they had to remind themselves not to light up while the refueling operation was going on.

Plus, they all had jobs to do. Puglisi watched the lake via the chopper's FLIR device. Gallant oversaw the fueling on the copter's end. And, as always, Bates stayed glued to his Eyeball Machine. Meanwhile Ryder and Fox checked out the interior of the cabin, as suggested by Finch. It was just one room, maybe 20 feet by 15, a combination kitchen, bunkhouse, and business operation. The floors were covered with soot; the ceiling was a canopy of cobwebs. The windows had indoor moss growing on them.

"I know those pumps look like they come from the fifties," Fox said. "But this place? I'm thinking more like Roaring Twenties."

Ryder scrapped some of the grime off the service desk. It was about a half-inch thick.

"Yeah, the *eighteen*-twenties maybe . . ." he said drily. "That looks like the last time anyone was in here."

But no sooner were the words out of his mouth than he knew he was wrong. Sitting in a wooden box on the service desk, partially covered by an ancient yellowed newspaper, were a bunch of MREs, the field rations they'd been subsisting on since leaving Cape Lonely. Beside them a dusty box containing eight one-gallon jugs of spring water, plus essentials like toothpaste and deodorant.

"Check it out," Ryder breathed, realizing the lengths some-one had gone through to leave these supplies for them. Who-ever had done it was fanatical in making sure it looked like no one had set foot in this place for years. Just like the gas still pumping into their fuel tanks, someone had bravely pro-vided them the necessities of continuing the mission, clev-erly disguising these necessities so they could hide in plain sight, so to speak.

The two men just stood there, astonished by the handi-work. The floor was so thick with dirt, they were making dozens of footprints, yet none were here when they'd ar-rived. The service counter was dirty and greasy, too, as if no one had touched it in a very long time. Yet it had been made just to look this way, for obviously whoever put all this stuff here had to have moved some of the dust and grime around.

"I don't think a special effects crew for a big-budget movie could have done a camo job this good," Fox said. "Unless . . ."

"Unless what?" Ryder asked him.

"Unless our friends have some kind of a top-secret tele-port device and they just beamed these things in here," Fox replied with a half-smile.

Ryder just shook his head. "Don't even joke about that," he said.

They continued exploring the kitchen area. They found more MREs and things like flashlight batteries, extra mo-dem cords, more "safe" cell phones, and a small combina-tion TV and AM/FM radio set.

"This will come in handy," Fox said wryly. They had heard from both Finch and Ozzi, in very hasty phone calls, about how the copter team had made the headlines. It came as no surprise, especially after the theme park episode.

But Ryder brushed past all these things to explore the last box on the counter. It was his nose that led him to it. Inside he discovered a family-size jar of instant Chase & Sandborn coffee. It was like finding a pot of gold. Now that he had coffee *and* cigarettes, what else did he need?

But then it suddenly went through Ryder's mind that this really *was* like the Roaring Twenties—or maybe more like the Depression years. Leaving this larder for them out here, so cleverly hidden, was not unlike the help provided by some people to the gangsters of the thirties, the Dillingers and Pretty Boy Floyds, bank robbers who became folk heroes and were aided and abetted in their efforts to evade the police by ordinary citizens. Strange times back then, indeed. But this wasn't a romantic notion now for Ryder. It was a scary one. *Is this what the country has come to . . . again?* he wondered. That ordinary people were so disillusioned with the nonsense in Washington that they were willing to help outlaws? *Federal* outlaws?

That's exactly what was happening—that and the person who did this for them, they could only assume, somehow knew the ghost team's guardian angel, Bobby Murphy.

Fox was thinking the same thing.

"He sure has a lot of friends," he said. "For someone hardly anyone knows."

Just then, they heard a commotion on the back porch. It was Gallant.

"Get back aboard quick," he told Ryder and Fox. "Bates just got a lead on another missile."

They were soon back on the floating chopper, gathered around the Eyeball Machine.

One of the mook phones was ringing. Bates had all his tracking gear already turned on; all he had to do was pick the phone up and answer it to get a location. He did so, and all they heard was dead air as usual. But again, it didn't matter. It wasn't important that anything be said during the call, only that the call was being made in the first place.

Bates got his laptops working and in just a few seconds had his pong blinking on a GPS screen, indicating where the call was coming from.

But there was a problem here. Although the circle highlighted a point on the map that was very close to the Milwaukee airport, the pong wasn't flashing over land. Rather, it was pointing to a spot over Lake Michigan.

This had never happened before. Usually they were looking for mountain peaks, the tops of buildings.

"Could that thing be wrong?" someone asked Bates.

"It hasn't been before," he replied. "I mean everything matches up. It's near a place where the soccer team was set to play. It's near an airport, and it's a 'real' phone call, just like all the others. It's just that the location is wacky. So, is my gear broken? Maybe?"

Ryder thought a moment. "Unless," he said, "the mooks got themselves a boat. . . ."

Matt Ring was an unusual type of fisherman. He was trained to catch gilltails and cold perch, his gear configured to haul up these fish that tended to stay down near the bottom of Lake Michigan. This meant his 35-foot boat carried extra-large nets, long poles, and a deep holding pool full of ice water for his catch.

But truth was, Matt Ring hadn't caught a fish in years. This had to do with underground economics and the fact that Lake Michigan was an unusual body of water. A few hundred miles up from Milwaukee, through the Mackinac Straits, the lake just touched the edge of Canada, only for 50 miles or so, around the Manitoulin Island region. This toe step into another country was significant, though. Things were so much cheaper up there. Liquor. Cuban cigars. Cigarettes. But mostly prescription drugs—the newest "hot" commodity of the twenty-first century. Ring could pack his boat with more than 50,000 dollars' worth of eproximin, dicodin, and lobrutrin and still haul another 10,000 dollars' worth of cigars and booze and *still* not give a hint to an unsuspecting observer that he was catching anything more than fish.

Again halfway down the western shore of Lake Michigan was Milwaukee. Not far inland was Mitchell Field, the beer city's airport. This proximity worked greatly to Ring's advantage, too. Many of the people who would eventually buy his contraband lived nowhere near Milwaukee. He had a deal with the manager of an overnight air delivery service based at Mitchell Field though. Ring would get his stash from his Canadian associates, make the journey 350 miles down to Milwaukee, and unload said stash into air shipping boxes waiting for him at the nearby marina. The boxes would then be flown out—without inspection—to places all over the United States, to people Ring did not know, who would split up the pharmaceutical booty from there. For every trip he made Ring earned himself $20,000, paid to him by the owner of the airfreight service. Ring made one trip every two weeks. He lived the good life of a smuggler. At 55 he'd once smuggled pot. But the way the drug companies were gouging Americans these days, moving pharmaceuticals was a lot more profitable.

Still, it was a risky business. There was always a chance the law might stumble upon you.

That's why Ring was so concerned this particular morning to wake up and find a Coast Guard helicopter coming right across the water at him.

He'd spent the night anchored here, just off the marina, close to the shores of Milwaukee itself.

He was waiting for his air-shipping contacts to show up at 8:00 A.M. It was now 7:30. The airport nearby was rumbling with flights ready to take off, a typically noisy start to its busy day. Nearby, the expressways were starting to fill up with commuters trying to get a leg up on the early-morning traffic. There were even people beginning to stir in the marina itself. None of them knew Ring was sitting on top of fifty thousand dollars' worth of cheap prescription drugs just a stone's throw from the dock.

But what the hell was the Coast Guard doing here?

He'd slept up on deck, as he usually did on warm nights, and woke up just in time to see the huge white helicopter coming, flying so low to the water, it was actually leaving a wake behind.

Before Ring could even think about it, the big copter went right over his boat—and, thankfully, kept right on going.

He let out a gasp of relief. But what he saw next bordered on the inconceivable and made him wonder if he was still asleep and just dreaming.

The copter was not interested in him. But it was interested

in the next boat over, a beaten-up yacht, with very dirty windows, moored about two hundred feet off Ring's port side. This boat had reached the marina's confines about an hour after Ring had, meaning about 3:00 A.M. He recalled hearing many voices talking at once over on the other boat, this as he was falling back to sleep. *Foreigners,* he remembered thinking.

Now this copter was circling the yacht like a bird of prey. He watched as it quickly pulled up into a hover. The aircraft wasn't making much noise, which struck Ring as being strange, too. But its engines were so powerful, the air itself around Ring's boat seemed to be shaking. His ears began to hurt immediately.

As this was happening, he saw a rope ladder fall out of the cargo bay of the chopper, and suddenly heavily armed men were coming down it. Ring was not just sleepy but also a bit hungover. He was trying to figure out if this was a real thing he was looking at, happening so fast, and in the bright early-morning daylight. Was this the Coast Guard's way of showing *him* what they could do—a kind of real-life, in-your-face warning? Or were they shooting an episode of *Cops* nearby? Or was this part of some reality show?

These were the thoughts going through his head as the first two men from the copter landed on the yacht's rear deck. Both were dressed in black camo and rigged up like SWAT team members. Big helmets, face masks, body armor. From Ring's point of view, they looked more like cops than Coast Guard guys.

The people on the yacht were now just coming to life. Two burst from the cabin door. The two armed men shot them down like dogs. Ring was stunned. Two other men appeared from the front of the yacht at just about the same time. They were armed with pistols. A gunfight broke out, and suddenly bullets were flying. Ricochets, glowing rounds zinging into the water, some even perforating Ring's boat.

Ring hit the deck. He happened to fall right next to a docking hole, so he still had a good view of what was happening not 200 feet away.

The gunfight went on unabated. The guys in the black uniforms were using tracer ammunition. It looked like a fireworks display gone wrong. When one of the people on the boat started moving toward the rear deck, a man in the copter's cargo bay opened up with a huge gun. The noise from it was so loud, Ring involuntarily put his hands to his ears.

The gun on the helicopter began tearing the boat in half. One of the boat's crew foolishly turned his pistol toward the hovering helicopter. That's when another person in the cargo bay opened up with another big gun. In the blink of an eye, the man was shredded to pieces.

Now there appeared to be only one person left among the boat's passengers. The two men from the helicopter advanced on him, this while the copter came down even lower. The man didn't know what to do. It appeared the guys in black were trying to converse with him. Put up your hands, they were telling them. Throw away your gun and we won't hurt you. The man finally compiled.

At this point, Ring could see the commotion had caused so much attention, people had stopped their cars on the expressway and were witnessing the unexplainable event. The same with the marina, people running out to its docks to see what all the ruckus was about.

Ring turned back to the yacht. The man was now having an animated conversation with the guys in black. They were asking something—this as the boat was starting to burn fiercely around them. Another man jumped down from the copter and went directly below. He emerged just a few seconds later, with a weapon that Ring was almost sure was a missile launcher. This man went back up the ladder as quickly as he'd come down. He was a strange-looking soldier, though, rail thin and wearing a goatee. He looked very weird in the SWAT-type combat suit.

This done, his colleagues turned their attention back to the lone remaining passenger. They were asking him for something else. He reached in his shirt, reluctantly at first, but then came up with two cell phones. He gingerly passed them over to the gunmen in black, then raised his hands above his head, smiling now that he'd done everything his attackers asked and had saved his own life.

But no sooner were the cell phones in their possession than the men raised their weapons and shot the man, six times, right in the throat. He stood there for one surreal moment, his face screwed up in disbelief that the men had lied to him. Then he toppled right off the side of the burning boat.

That was it. The two armed men climbed back up to the copter. It started to move away even before they were safely inside. The aircraft turned a 180; then someone onboard hit the gas—and off it went, in a burst of exhaust and power.

Just like that, it was gone.

In all, the entire incident had lasted less than two minutes.

Ryder and Gallant pushed the big copter up and to the left. Their escape plan was all set. They would pass over South Milwaukee and then back around to the north, to the Rock River beyond. They'd already scoped out its banks for some good hiding places, of which it had many, as it turned out. The most ideal was a grove of willow trees overhanging an isolated portion of its banks. With the pontoons inflated, the crew could maneuver the Sky Horse under the covering flora, where they would wait until dark or until they heard someone coming and had to leave in a hurry.

And everything was going well toward that aim. They went up and over the expressways and over the working-class neighborhoods of South Milwaukee. The more wooded areas lay just over the horizon. Milwaukee air traffic controllers were frantically trying to contact them, but they ignored these calls. This looked like it was going to be another clean escape.

Until . . .

"Shiiiiiit . . ." Gallant said slowly.

Ryder didn't like the sound of that.

"What's up?" he asked Gallant, quickly glancing at the control panel. Everything was green. Their power plant was OK.

But Gallant wasn't looking at the control panel. He was

looking at the bank of TV monitors for the handful of video cameras placed around the Sky Horse. There was nothing directly in front of the helicopter. Nor was there anything off to their sides or above them, looking down. But the monitor showing the view behind them was not so empty.

In fact, it was turning a very bright blue.

"Damn," Ryder whispered.

A TV news copter was coming right up behind them.

It was a Bell Textron, a very fast, very modern, very nimble, if smallish, helicopter. It was really bright blue with the logo *TV3 Sky Eye* painted on it so large, it could be seen from a mile away. Even before the pilots noticed the other copter on the TV monitor, the swift little aircraft was moving up on their left side.

"Get rid of the guns!" Ryder hastily yelled back to the three men in the cargo bay. But Fox had already taken care of that, just in time, too, as the news copter was now right beside them, matching their speed. A man belted into its open bay was catching everything on a video camera.

"First the newspapers, now TV," Ryder said. It was happening so fast, neither he nor Gallant had taken any evasive action.

"Hang on!" Gallant yelled as he was about to kick the S-58's engine into overdrive.

"Wait!" Fox yelled though from the cargo bay. "Now that they're here, it's not a bad thing if they see us! Just for a few seconds. . . ."

Ryder looked over his shoulder to see the three men in black had lowered their ski masks over their faces and were holding their large Revolutionary War flag, the one given to them by the Doughnut Boys back at Cape Lonely. The three of them were waving and giving the camera the V-for-Victory sign.

Puglisi went halfway out the hatch so the cameraman could get a good shot of his shoulder patch, the unit's talisman, the drawing of the World Trade Towers with the initials *NYPD* and the *FDNY* and their motto, *We Will Never Forget.*

"Get a good shot of that baby!" Puglisi was yelling at the cameraman now. "Remember 9/11!"

Then Fox cried out, "OK—time to go!"

Gallant pushed the copter's throttle forward and the over-size engine kicked in. It was like hitting the afterburner in a fighter jet. Suddenly they were pulling away from the news chopper at very high speed, literally leaving it in a cloud of exhaust.

It was the first time the pilots had really put the S-58 into high gear, simply because it used so much gas. But now both were very impressed.

"Those doughnut heads really knew what they were doing," Gallant said.

Ryder was watching the news chopper fade in their rearview monitor. He could barely move his head, though; the Gs were that high in the suddenly accelerating copter.

"You got that right," he replied.

They were quickly a couple miles ahead of the news copter when they finally laid off the throttles. They could see the other aircraft, now just a bright blue smudge in the sky turning away, heading back toward the city. No doubt the Sky Horse's unexpected acceleration had served as a fitting end to what was probably a dramatic piece of news footage, ensuring all of America would finally know about the team by the time the evening news aired that night—if they didn't know about them already.

"No such thing as bad publicity," Gallant said. "Now maybe someone in Washington will wake up."

Ryder just shook his head. "That's what I'm afraid of. . . ."

Now all the team members had to do was make good their escape, heading for the next hiding point, without any interference.

But that was not to be, either.

Because just seconds after the TV copter turned away, Ryder heard another commotion back in the cargo bay. Instinctively he knew something else was wrong.

He looked up from the GPS map he and Gallant were

reading, trying to find the coordinates of the next hideout, and turned to see that all three of the guys in the back had their noses pressed up against the cargo door window. They were shouting and swearing. Instead of yelling down to them or checking the TV monitor, Ryder simply turned and looked out his window.

That's when he saw the two fighter jets coming right at him. This was not good. . . .

It was strange, because the jets were flying so fast and so dead on, all Ryder could really see was the two trails of exhaust pouring out behind them. They went over the copter just a second later, one clearing the top of the rotor by no more than 50 feet. The other plane went right by the nose of the Sky Horse, and for the first time Ryder could see exactly what type of plane they were: A-10 Thunderbolts . . . More attack planes than fighters, they were essentially flying cannons, the weapon being the fierce GAU-8 gun. One of these babies could tear up a tank or an APC in about three seconds. While they were not really dog-fighters, the two A-10s would certainly have no trouble blowing the Sky Horse out of the sky.

"We're screwed now . . ." someone moaned from the back.

"Just make sure all those goddamn guns are out of sight!" Gallant yelled.

Luckily, Bates had the presence of mind to yank in the forward gun before the two A-10s went over. There was no way they wanted these guys to see them carrying those big fifties.

The Thunderbolts went way out and turned, slowly, almost as if the two pilots were talking about what their next move may be.

"The most they can do is force us to land!" Bates yelled.

"Don't be so sure," Fox replied. Again, they had to realize the pilots were operating under rules written after 9/11. Shoot first, ask questions later.

The two jets approached them again. This time much slower, as if in attack mode.

"Shit!" Bates yelled. "They're going to pop us!"

But at the last moment the jets split off, did a wide half-loop, and were soon riding off the right side of the copter.

Everyone aboard the copter breathed a sigh of relief. At least for a second or two.

"If they blink their lights we're going to have to follow them," Gallant said dejectedly. Blinking one's navigation lights was the universal aeronautical sign for Follow Me. Implied in the message was that the nonresponding party would get shot to pieces if they didn't comply. "And that *will* be the end of this little party. . . ."

But the A-10s didn't blink their lights. The two planes simply pulled a little closer to the copter, and on cue, both pilots saluted.

Then they gave the team members a thumbs-up.

Then they banked sharply and disappeared.

# PART THREE
### The Last of Gallant

# Chapter 13

The traffic in D.C. was a nightmare.

It was late morning, a Thursday, and every intersection within four blocks of the White House was gridlocked.

This was bad news for the person driving the heavily armored limousine code-named for this occasion *Lollipop*. He had to get to the White House or, more accurately, the Executive Office Building, which was right across the street from the presidential residence. But why all the traffic? Or better asked: why more than the usual traffic snarl?

It was the damn military vehicles. Hummers and troop trucks. They seemed to be everywhere lately. Washington was already overflowing with Lincolns, Cadillacs, SUVs, and tourists' cars. The crowded streets didn't need an endless parade of Army trucks, driving around and around, making a bad situation worse. But that's exactly what was happening.

The limo driver finally fought his way through the jam-up, reaching his destination only five minutes late. But considering who he was working for, those five minutes might cost him his job. Or worse.

He pulled up to the side entrance of the EOB, hidden in a U-shaped turnaround driveway. The two Chevy Suburban escort vehicles that had been following the limousine screeched to a halt right behind him. This was a stretch limo he was driving, big and black without an ounce of ornamentation on it. It was a tough car to drive, too. It was so heavily armored, it could take a direct hit from a 20mm cannon and still not get much more than a dent. But it was *so* heavy, it was a bitch to maneuver into the small oval parking area.

There were no fewer than two dozen security people waiting at this entryway to the EOB. Six Secret Service agents in plainclothes surrounded the limo even before it stopped rolling. Beyond them a phalanx of uniformed White House guards lined either side of the entryway's red carpet. Up on the roof, a squad of armed snipers watched the street in front. Inside the lobby was yet another small army of Secret Service agents.

The limo driver just shook his head at all the security. The person he was working for was getting more paranoid every day. Of course, that was fast becoming the worst-kept secret in Washington. That and a few other things.

The limo driver got out, ran around to the back of the car, and opened the passenger-side rear door. A 4-year-old girl stepped out. Behind her, twin 10-year old boys. Then a girl, 11, a boy 13, and another set of twins, two girls, age 15. A pretty but haggard woman came out next. She was holding an infant.

She nodded brusquely to the driver. Behind him, he heard a Secret Service agent speak into his wrist-mounted microphone.

"Tell General Rushton his family is here," he said.

The family was escorted through the lobby, onto an elevator, and up to the second floor. They trooped into a large office that had been filled with flowers, pink roses mostly. A photography team was also inside: cameraman, lighting person, and makeup artist. About a dozen members of the press were here, too. This room was known as the Presidential Service Office, a place where small ceremonies were held occasionally, minor legislation signed, and so on. But today the room would be used as a backdrop for the Rushton family photo.

The family members were put in their positions for the

portrait, and the makeup people went to work on them. The younger children were bratty; the older ones, sullen. All were uncooperative, including Mrs. Rushton.

After ten minutes of primping and much pancake powder, the family was set. The photo-lights were warmed and tested; the camera was loaded. But then everyone involved just sat down to wait, including the press.

The most important person for the occasion, General Rushton himself, was not here.

Up two more floors from the service room was a particularly dark and gloomy hallway.

It served as an outer office, but the secretary's desk here was covered not with paper clips and staplers but with ammunition for weapons: M16s, Glock 9s, Uzis. Yet another squad of security men was on hand here. Dressed in dark green combat suits, they were private hires from a firm called Global Security Inc., a company with blatant CIA ties. They'd been on guard here, around-the-clock, for the past five days.

Two were standing ramrod straight against the far wall of the hallway. Two were stationed on either side of the elevator doors. Two more were standing in front of the huge oak door that was the focal point of the outer office. There was no name on the door, no indication as to who might be on the other side of it. This was no big deal. Much of Washington's business these days was done behind doors such as this. No name on the door meant no accountability. All kinds of secrets could be kept within.

The elevator door opened and two Army lieutenants walked out. They were Rushton's military administrative aides. Six guns were on them in a heartbeat. Both men quickly began waving their security badges over their heads.

"God damn it, you guys," one of the officers grumbled as the lead security man checked his ID. "Don't you recognize us by now?"

The security man just scowled. "You're cleared," he said gruffly. "Proceed. . . ."

The two aides approached the pair of guards standing watch outside the office door. They'd learned over the last week that these two were a little less hard-ass than their boss.

"Have you heard anything from inside lately?" one of the officers asked them cautiously.

Both guards shook their heads.

"Nothing," one replied. "Except for the sound of the TV, I'm not even sure he's in there."

The military aides looked at each other in horror. "He'd *better* be in there," one said under his breath.

This man put his ear to the door. "I can hear a TV," he reported. "Or is that him talking on the phone? Or both?"

The other officer checked the time. "We've got exactly two minutes to get him downstairs. He's got his family and the press in one room, and he's got, well . . . *his guests* in the other."

Again, a very cautious use of words.

"Someone's got to go in and get him," the other officer said. They both looked at the private guard. But his sneer answered the question for them. No way was he going in there.

"I'll have to do it," the first lieutenant said.

The other officer laughed darkly. "Yeah, well, leave a trail of bread crumbs behind you . . . and a list of your next of kin."

The aide tried the door. It was unlocked, maybe a good sign, maybe not. He held his breath, bit his lip—and then let himself in.

Old Spice. Oak. Cigar smoke. These three odors hit his nose first. Not a big surprise. He'd been in this room many times before. The place always reeked of them.

It was also very dark in here, but he was used to that as well. The room was huge. It looked more like a prestigious university library than the secret office of a military man. But again the aide knew that while there might be several hundred books in the expansive office, some by the classic writers, its occupant hadn't cracked more than a couple of them, if that.

He was standing in the far corner of the room. Short,

bulbous, with soft, fleshy skin, and a very red face, General Rushton did not exactly have the cut of a military man. And his TV was indeed on. But the general was standing in front of it, preventing the lieutenant from seeing what was on. The aide could tell Rushton was absolutely riveted to it, though, and not in a pleasant way. His body was shaking, his right hand clenched. He was also talking on the phone. Not his desk phone—a cell phone.

As soon as Rushton realized he was not alone, he discontinued his conversation, then, with absolutely no grace, dropped the cell phone to the floor and crushed it with his foot.

"I'm sorry, General," the aide finally spoke up. "But we have to get you downstairs. Your family is waiting. The press is here. And people are arriving in the function room."

Rushton tried unsuccessfully to kick the remains of the cell phone under his desk. "How many guards were out in the hallway when you arrived?" he asked the aide harshly while turning off the TV.

"Six, sir," the lieutenant replied.

"How many teams escorted my limo over here?"

"Two teams in two trucks, sir. . . ."

"And downstairs?"

"Two teams of Secret Service, plus White House police. All the roofs are covered as well."

"Did it seem like enough people to you, Lieutenant?"

The young officer hesitated a moment. "Yes, sir," he finally spit out. "For the time being—for this occasion."

Rushton's red face went to a deeper shade of crimson. " 'For the time being?' " he asked icily. "Why don't you realize I need these people around-the-clock? Those fanatics are doing everything they can to get to me. To my family. That's why I need so much security. Why do you have problems with that?"

The officer gulped once—he really wasn't sure just what fanatics Rushton was talking about. Islamic ones or someone else? But he'd been down this road before. "The only problem I have, General," he said, "is that you'll miss your family photo, your opportunity with the press—and that the guests in the function room will get restless. So, sir, may I suggest we get going?"

Rushton stood still as a statue for a moment, a bit dazed.

"Did your people leak that memo?" he asked sternly.

This was another unsettling thing. Rushton was scheduled to sit down at 2:00 P.M. for an extensive interview with the *Washington Times,* a very conservative newspaper. Earlier this day, he'd arranged for a leak that indicated that during this interview Rushton was planning on laying a bombshell on the country: that there was a better than 50-50 chance that terrorists would set off a nuclear explosive of some kind inside the United States in the next week—and that there was really nothing anyone could do about it.

The leak was particularly cynical, as it was actually a *denial* of what the general intended to say. This was an old Washington tactic. Rushton's hero of fifty years before, Douglas MacArthur, would dispatch aides all the way from the wartime South Pacific to Washington simply to *deny* that the general was going to run for President. In this way, you were able to say what you wanted to say while at the same time denying that you ever said it. Rushton played by this set of rules.

But it was the last thing the country needed right now. From sea to shining sea, it was a continent of jitters. Yet because of his high, almost czarlike position, only Rushton, and maybe a handful of other people, knew whether the nuke bomb scenario was true or not. Even his closest aides never knew when to believe him. The capital had been rife with these kinds of stories for weeks, but so far, that's all there were: stories. In other words, it was a case of missing WMD—real or not—this time right inside the country.

"That 'message' was put out, yes," the lieutenant finally replied. "That's why we have so many press at the family portrait. They're expecting you to comment on it. . . ."

This did not seem to cheer up Rushton any.

"And what about the search for that Iranian airplane?" he asked.

The aide felt his shoulders slump again. This was another

bugaboo with Rushton—his new obsession with finding the wreckage of an Iranian cargo plane that had crashed off the coast of Cuba the week before. The aide had no idea what the Iranian plane was doing in Cuba or why Rushton was so interested in it, but only that he had diverted valuable Homeland Security assets to look for it, both Coast Guard and Navy search planes, and asked about it on an hourly basis.

"Nothing on that yet," the aide replied quickly.

Rushton did not like the reply and glowered at the aide for a moment. Finally, though, the general just said, "OK, let's get going."

With much relief, the lieutenant walked to the door, opened it, and gave a signal to the private security guards. They went into action. Two secured the hallway; two more cleared the first elevator that arrived. Then all six arranged themselves around Rushton, covering him from all sides.

They left quickly, onto the elevator and down to the second floor. Only then did the two lieutenants return to Rushton's office and turn the TV back on. What had Rushton been watching that seemed to upset him so? It was a repeat-loop videotape of the TV news footage shot two days before over South Milwaukee showing the mysterious white helicopter, with the men inside brandishing the old Revolutionary War flag. This video, of course, had been playing nonstop around the country for the past 48 hours.

But for the general to be watching it, over and over again?

One of the lieutenants just shook his head and said to the other, "Now, *this* is disturbing. . . ."

Down on the second floor, in the Presidential Service Room, one of the advance security men took a message in his earphone. He signaled the photographer.

"OK, he's on his way," the photographer announced. "Places, everybody."

The door opened a moment later and Rushton walked in. He did not look like the same man who'd left his office just a minute before. He was smiling, jovial. With press cameras flashing, he embraced the photographer warmly, though he

hardly knew the man. Then Rushton hugged his wife for far
too long, smearing her makeup and leaving her embarrassed
and confused. Then each of his children received a kiss,
whether they liked it or not—and the older ones certainly
did not. On cue, the small crowd of Rushton's civilian aides
on hand gave him a round of applause.

Again, there were about a dozen members of the press in
the room. They'd been given the opportunity to photograph
the general while he was being photographed. But they'd all
heard the whispers of what was coming up in his interview
with the *Washington Times* and that the quixotic NSC officer
had become somewhat of a loose cannon lately. These were
the reasons they were here.

They began shouting questions at him, but Rushton, never
losing his smile, held up his hands to his ears, pretending he
could not hear them. Then he took his seat in the middle of
the photo set, plopping down with a smile. At last, the photographer was ready to begin snapping. But then he hesitated.
A presidential seal about the size of a dinner plate was hanging on the wall behind the family. It was showing up in the
frame. The photographer signaled one of the security men
and through pantomime indicated the problem.

The security man crept forward and whispered in Rushton's ear. The general turned, looked at the seal—but then
thought for a very long moment. Finally he nodded and the
security man quickly removed the seal. But for those who
witnessed it, it was that long hesitation on Rushton's part
that stood out in their minds.

The photographer urged the family to relax and look
pleasant, a very tall order for Rushton's older children, who
looked like they would have preferred to be anywhere else
but here. Finally, everyone appeared as relaxed as they were
going to get. The photographer snapped the first picture, just
one of many, as he knew it would be wise to take at least a
few dozen.

But that's not what Rushton had in mind. No sooner had
everyone's eyes adjusted to the first strobe flash, than the
general quickly got to his feet and smoothed the wrinkles

out of his uniform. His smile long gone, he signaled his security men. One opened a side door. The others took up their positions around the rotund officer.

Then, with the press shouting more questions to him and without so much as a nod to his family, Rushton hastily left the room.

With more security men clearing the way for him, Rushton took another elevator to the top floor of the building.

Here he met the two Army lieutenants again. They were standing at the door to the building's elaborate, if somewhat cloistered, function room. From the looks of it, no one had gone in or out of the main door for a while.

But looks could be deceiving. The general was throwing a private affair here today; indeed, the aides had referred to it for weeks as the "secret lunch."

They knew that the guests had been coming in not by the front door but clandestinely through a rear basement entrance to the EOB, this while most of the Washington early-morning press corps were down on the second floor watching Rushton's kids compete to see who could be the brattiest. Up a service elevator, cleaned and made spiffy for the occasion, the guests filed into the function room through the kitchen, which had been cleared of all help before they arrived.

So, on the other side of the door now were no fewer than a dozen senators, from both parties, a number of influential higher-ups from several government agencies, including the FBI and Homeland Security, three Supreme Court judges and their clerks, as well as the base commanders of just about every military installation within 50 miles of Washington, D.C.

The general approached the two lieutenants, whose job now was to keep anyone from going through the function room's main door.

"Can you two handle this?" Rushton asked them as he was being whisked by.

The two junior officers assured him that they could. Rushton stopped and said to them, "Make sure of it. If there are any screwups, you will not want to know what will happen to you."

With that, Rushton's security people got him on the move again. He went down the hall, turned right, into the kitchen. Ten seconds later, the two lieutenants heard the function room behind them erupt into spirited applause. Rushton had just entered the room.

Both men relaxed, but only a little. They had no idea just how long they would be out here, guarding this door, while looking as if they weren't guarding it.

"All those heavy hitters in there," one said. "How he was able to keep something like this under wraps in this town for so long I'll never know."

The other lieutenant just shook his head.

"I don't *want* to know," he said.

# Chapter 14

New York firefighters Mike Santoro and Mark Kelly had both been injured on 9/11. They'd just come on duty that horrible day when word reached their firehouse in midtown Manhattan that the first plane had hit the towers. Fifteen minutes later, both men were on the scene. They saw the horror firsthand. The flames, the smoke, people jumping to their deaths rather than be burned alive. Twenty firefighters in their company, including Santoro, Kelly, and their lieutenant, started walking up the stairs, heading for the top of the first tower. They met the initial wave of injured coming down around the thirty-third floor. With the stairwells filling with smoke and the electricity starting to fail, the lieutenant told Santoro and Kelly to lead the most seriously injured out to ambulances. Santoro carried one man down the three dozen sets of stairs.

Then the second plane hit the second tower. Now back out on the street, both Santoro and Kelly were struck by falling debris and wound up riding in the same ambulance as the people they'd just rescued. They never saw anyone else in their fire company again. Eighteen close friends killed, trying to save others.

Santoro and Kelly were now sitting in Kelly's Ford Ranger, drinking coffee and eating junk food. They were parked in a

Drive, Shop 'n Go store in East Newark, New Jersey, not far from the Garden State Parkway. Though this was a very run-down neighborhood, the area surrounding the store was somewhat wooded, trees planted to shield those traveling the Parkway from having to see the likes of East Newark.

Santoro and Kelly been sitting here almost all day; it was now 8:00 P.M. Just like several dozen other firefighters, parked at other DSGs throughout upper Jersey, this was how they'd chosen to spend one of their well-deserved days off. Defending the homeland. Helping again. To their wives and friends, though, they were off fishing.

But it had been a long day, especially listening to news radio, which was reporting that a high administration official was now expecting a terrorist nuke to go off just about anytime and because of bureaucratic bungling, Pentagon infighting, and, most surprising, inaction from the White House there was really nothing anyone could do about it.

It was getting dark. They'd just drained their fifth coffee each when a white Chevy pulled into the store's parking lot. The car looked innocuous. It was beat up, dented, with a faded inspection sticker and a temporary license plate hanging off the back. Typical transportation in this part of the Garden State.

A man climbed out. He was slight, dark-skinned, wearing a T-shirt and baggy jeans. A ball cap was pulled low over his brow. The driver walked right by their big Ford, and both firefighters saw him close up. He had an oily face, with bad skin and eyes right out of a cell block. They secretly snapped a picture of him with their photophone, then compared it with the sketch of Ramosa given to them by the ghosts.

"I'll give that one an 'eight,'" Santoro said wearily. "And that will make six 'eights,' two 'nines,' two 'sevens,' and thirteen 'fives.'"

Kelly groaned and opened another package of Ring-Dings.

Their spirit was willing, and they were proud to help the ghost team. And at the meeting that night at the Queens Social Club the massive surveillance plan proposed by the outlaws seemed to have made sense: many eyes looking for one person believed to frequent at least one of the DSG stores.

The problem was, in this section of Jersey, a description of someone with dark skin, a bad complexion, oily hair, and penitentiary eyes matched just about every male walking into one of the convenience stores.

And a few of the women as well.

Sean O'Flaherty also had faith in the system he'd helped the ghost team set up. True, it was all based on a hunch, not unknown in intelligence work, that this character Ramosa was somehow connected to the DSG napkin. As Hunn and Ozzi explained to O'Flaherty, while hunches were based on intuition, there was also some reality to the situation. They wouldn't have linked Ramosa with the mysterious drawing had it been scribbled on a doily from Tiffany's or the back of a menu from a famous Manhattan eatery. While maybe not so in his native Philippines, Ramosa would stand out like a sore thumb in one of those places. But in a DSG along the Parkway in East Newark? He'd fit right in.

Couple this with the common knowledge that many Al Qaeda sleeper agents had been caught or tracked to Jersey since 9/11 and even before and that at least some of these stores were operated by people born not in the United States but in the Middle East . . . well, the search for Ramosa at the Drive, Shop 'n Gos seemed to make sense.

The firefighters from Queens were the key, though—the manpower they needed to pull it off. The plan was for pairs of jakes to stake out as many DSG stores as they could and simply take pictures with picturephones of anyone who might look like Ramosa.

But what they never expected was that in East Newark *many* people fit the cutout's description. This particular day, the jakes had three dozen DSG stores covered. Unexpectedly, instead of stumbling upon one mark, he being Ramosa, they came up with more than a hundred possible suspects, each one captured on the firefighters' photophones.

As per the plan, they'd been sending these photos to O'Flaherty since early that afternoon. And O'Flaherty, sitting at his young daughter's computer, was soon overloaded with pictures of people who looked a lot like Ramosa but not one that perfectly hit the mark. So many were coming in, at the rate his daughter's memory files were filling up with the phonephotos O'Flaherty was concerned the computer would freeze up—and they'd be sunk.

It went on like this for hours. O'Flaherty sitting in a toosmall chair in a bedroom overwhelming in pink and blue, posters of pop singers and movie stars staring back at him. By 9:00 P.M., they'd still yet to score. He was ready to hang it up and call the troops home. They'd given it a shot, they'd tried their best to help the ghosts, but had come up empty.

Then . . . a stroke of intuition. Or brilliance. Or just plain luck. But suddenly O'Flaherty hit upon a way to sort out this digital Tower of Babel.

More than 140 photos had popped onto his daughter's computer. And indeed, many of these people could somewhat match the description of the guy they were looking for.

That's when it hit O'Flaherty. Sure they all looked alike, but out of the 140, could 2 or 3 pictures or more be of the *same* guy?

It took O'Flaherty a while to separate and categorize just who sent which picture from what DSG—but then bingo! He spotted one character, sloppy dress, bad skin, Mets cap pulled down low over his eyes, going into the Parkway DSG. He looked pretty much like the illustration. The same guy also showed up at the DSG on Park Street around 8:10 P.M. Then, 15 minutes later, he was at another Drive, Shop 'n Go on Wooster Boulevard. Then, another team caught him walking into the Drive, Shop 'n Go near what used to be the Green Hill projects. Fifteen minutes after that, there he was again, at a store near the center of Newark itself.

O'Flaherty had been in a Drive, Shop 'n Go before. As their name implied, they were little more than junk food heavens and a place to gas up. Why would one person visit five in less than an hour?

Especially someone who fit the description of the guy they were looking for best?

O'Flaherty checked it, rechecked, and checked it still again. But each time he came to the same conclusion: same guy going into a handful of DSG stores in less than an hour.

That's when he made the call.

"We think we've tagged him," he said into the disposable cell phone. "How quick can you guys get back up here?"

Ahmeen Dujabi had worked at the Drive, Shop 'n Go in East Newark for nearly a year.

An emigrant from Lebanon, he had no valid passport, no visa, no green card, nor any other kind of legal immigration documentation. Nevertheless, Dujabi had been promoted to night manager at the Drive, Shop 'n Go just three months into his tenure. He was making nearly $50,000 a year in salary now. With another $25,000 in overtime, a lot of money for someone who didn't have to pay taxes, he was wealthier than 90 percent of the people who walked through the front door.

There were risks, though. Dujabi had been robbed 14 times in those 10 months, shot at twice, hit once, and he'd also been stabbed. It got to the point where he could spot a robber as soon as one came in. They had that certain look about them.

However, he never expected to see two soldiers in ski masks walk through the door.

It was just after midnight. Both men were heavily armed. Dujabi saw one M16 clone and a large-caliber rifle, a gun that could literally blow him away. The two men were also wearing body armor and strange, somewhat dated helmets. And one of them was gigantic.

They strolled in very casually, but their guns were up in Dujabi's face in an instant. He knew these were no ordinary criminals.

"You speak English?" the large masked man asked Dujabi.

The clerk was so stunned at their strange appearance, he couldn't talk.

"You speak the language?" the large one screamed at him again, putting the barrel of his gun right between Dujabi's eyes.

Again Dujabi tried to say something but couldn't. He began nodding furiously instead.

"Are you . . . *Immigration?*" Dujabi heard words finally spill out of his mouth.

Suddenly the big man's gun was making a dent in his brow.

"Why? You got a problem there, *sa-hib?*"

Dujabi clamped his mouth shut and opened the cash register drawer. He took out several hundred dollars in small bills and pushed them across the counter at the two armed men.

But the gun muzzle just went deeper into his forehead.

"We don't want your filthy money," the large man said, throwing it back into Dujabi's face.

In a flash Dujabi was looking at a crude pencil drawing of a man with bad hair, bad skin, and very criminal eyes.

His own eyes went wide open. . . .

"So?" the large man said. "He's a friend of yours?"

Dujabi tried pushing the money on the two men again. But this was an act of desperation; he suddenly knew who these two men were. News traveled faster on the Al Qaeda network than on the U.S. media sometimes. Dujabi had already heard about what was happening out west. Could these people be the Crazy Americans, too?

"You *know* him?" the big man thundered at Dujabi again.

But Dujabi was now too petrified to move.

At this point, the smaller of the two masked men vaulted over the counter and, bypassing the cash register and the money safe, went directly to the small bank of video monitors, the heart of the store's TV surveillance system. It was hooked up to an elderly but still-functioning videotaping machine that handled huge cassettes good for 24 hours or more. The masked man unplugged the player, grinding its megatape to a halt. He then took two previously filled tapes from the bottom shelf and, with the machine under his arm, went over the counter again.

Still the large man had his gun on Dujabi's brow.

"Where's your green card?" he screamed at Dujabi again. *"Where the fuck are you from?"*

Now the smaller of the two armed men tried to tug the larger one away. "Let's go," he said calmly.

But the large man would not move. "He knows this guy!" he was screaming now, shoving the drawing of Ramosa into the clerk's mouth. "He probably knows a lot of things!"

"We got what we want," the smaller man said. "Time to go."

But the large man would not budge. "One bullet and we've got one less asshole in this country," the man said. "*Our* country. . . ."

Meanwhile the smaller man's attention had been sidetracked by a case full of cell phones just below the cash register. He broke the glass with the butt of his rifle and took a dozen of the disposable phones stuffing them into his pockets.

Dujabi was distracted by this for a moment. When he looked back at the large man, he saw him pulling his rifle's trigger.

The blast was so bright, it burned right through the retina in Dujabi's left eye. He was rendered half-blind in an instant. The bullet, not fired into his skull but beside his ear, made him half-deaf as well, the concussion bursting his eardrum. Then the butt of the huge rifle hit him in the jaw, breaking it. He went down like a sack of bricks, fracturing his elbow on the hard cement floor. Then the large man picked up the cash register and threw it at Dujabi's head, cracking two vertebrae in his upper back. He began losing consciousness.

But still the large man's voice was ringing in his good ear. "Consider yourself the luckiest mook in the world," he said.

The last thing Dujabi heard before he passed out, though, was a strangely reassuring sound: that of a police siren, pulling into the store's parking lot.

Police sergeant Ernie Capp was the district supervisor for the East Newark neighborhoods near the Parkway.

He was about to go out on a 6-13—a lunch break—when he got the call from his anticrime unit. They, too, had just called in a lunch break and had pulled into the local Drive,

Shop 'n Go to get coffee. In the process, they'd interrupted an armed robbery.

Banks turned his patrol car 180 degrees and started driving very fast toward the convenience store. He was about five minutes away.

He asked the reporting officer for details. It sounded weird from the start. Two men, heavily armed, were exiting the building when the anticrime cruiser pulled into the parking lot. They let loose their siren immediately, but the men calmly walked to their van, stashing their rifles and booty behind the front seat. The two anticrime cops immediately went for their firearms—but then a strange thing happened.

"They were the ghosts, Sarge," the officer reported, this as the supervisor was still traveling at high speed to get to the scene. "You know, the guys in that secret war against the Muslims."

"You can't be serious," the supervisor replied.

"They told us everything," was the explanation. "Whomped the Arab clerk a bit, too. But—"

The supervisor had had enough. "Just hold the suspects until I get there," he told the officer.

But then came the very unusual reply: "Well, we can't do that sir. . . ."

"Why not?"

"Because we let them go," the officer said. "They had places they had to be. That's what they told us."

The supervisor couldn't believe what he was hearing. "Are you *crazy?*" he screamed into his microphone.

"Sarge—these guys are heroes!" the officer came back. "We can't arrest them. They're trying to save us from the terrorists. . . ."

And then he added: "But don't worry, Sarge. We got an autograph for you, too. . . ."

Ten miles down the auxiliary road off the Parkway was a place called Jack & Jill's Truck Stop.

It was comprised of a diner, a gas station, a diesel pump, a small lounge, and a 13-unit motel. Open all night, like most of its clientele, it was badly frayed around the edges. Jerry Shakes was sitting at the bar, waiting for a friend. He'd downed two beers an hour since arriving here earlier this evening from Portland, Maine. He had to set out for Pensacola in the morning, but because he was a trucker, night was frequently his awake hours. He always tried to work his schedule so he would make it to Jack & Jill's around this time, when he knew his friend would be available.

Shakes and the bartender had watched TV most of the night. It was nothing but news all over the box, so they wound up staring at the footage of the strange helicopter above Milwaukee over and over again, interspersed with breathless breaking-news reports on rumors of terrorists exploding nukes in as many as five major cities.

Secret war? Terrorists running amok? Dirty bombs about to go off somewhere in the United States? It seemed pretty crazy to Shakes, watching it all in this hole in the wall, with the commerce of America speeding by out on the Parkway, at approximately 70 miles per hour.

"Here she comes!" the bartender finally announced. The door to the bar opened and a fiftyish woman walked in. Her name was Tiffany. She was still attractive for her age, in a truck-stop-at-one-in-the-morning sort of way. She and Shakes had been meeting like this, twice a month, for three years.

He greeted her warmly. She thanked him for waiting— she'd been out visiting with her "other friends."

That didn't bother Shakes. He'd got over being fussy years ago.

"Drink first?" he asked her.

She smiled and grabbed him by the shirt collar instead. "I'm fine. Are you?"

That was that. Shakes paid the bartender, giving him a hefty tip. The bartender threw a room key to Tiffany. Shakes followed her out the back door.

Stepping into the parking lot, Shakes took in a deep breath. Exhaust fumes, marsh air, and spilled diesel—that's what he was used to here. He almost thought to talk to Tiffany about the crazy stuff on TV but stopped himself on their short walk to her room. *Why fuck up a good evening?* he asked himself. *Might not be many more left.*

They got to her room, a very small space at the end of the row. A bed, a TV, and a bathroom were just about all that could fit inside. She tried the key—but strangely, the door would not open. She tried again. Still no luck.

Shakes put his ear to the door. He heard noises inside. The TV was definitely on, but he could hear voices as well.

"You sure this is your room tonight?" he asked her.

She checked her key number against the door. Both were 13.

"This is my place," she confirmed. "My lucky Thirteen. *My stuff* is in there."

Shakes was just drunk enough to hit the door with his shoulder. It didn't budge. He hit it again and was as surprised as anyone that it burst open.

He'd expected to see some dude like him banging some broad like Tiffany. But he was in for a surprise.

What he saw was two guys in black uniforms, ski masks pulled up over their heads. They were wearing body armor and carrying very large weapons.

And strangely, they were watching TV. . . .

Their rifles were pointing at him and Tiffany in a flash. But somehow Shakes knew the men weren't going to shoot them. These guys seemed more intent on watching something on the TV screen. And the screen itself was segmented into eight different little screens, like a bunch of security cameras.

"What are you guys doing in here?" Shakes asked them. "You cops? You on a stakeout or something?"

"Just don't move," one of them said. "We're just using your TV for a minute."

That's when the other guy pointed at the screen. "There!" he shouted. "See it? There he is again. There's his car again."

"Bingo!" the other one yelled, writing down what appeared to be a license plate number from whatever they were watching on the screen.

Then they turned back to Shakes and Tiffany.

One just put his finger to his lips. "Don't tell anyone you ever saw us," he said.

With that, they fired their weapons into the machine they'd hooked up to the TV, blowing it to pieces. Then they climbed out the window, the same way they'd come in, and were gone, just like that.

Tiffany just looked at Shakes, pale but relieved. She began yanking on his shirt collar again.

"On second thought, darling," she said, "let's go get that drink. . . ."

The brothel was located in South Baltimore, not a part of the city tourists usually flocked to. There was a time when this place catered to the most powerful people in the state of Maryland: politicians, police officials, businessmen. These days it was a refuge for small-time hoods, Mafia wannabes, and the locals. It had downsized, in both prestige and prices.

It was located in a three-story brownstone, admittedly the nicest building on a deteriorating block. Neighbors were used to seeing activity in front of the building. Taxicabs and the occasional limousine showing up all hours of the day but especially at night, discharging passengers, who always hurried into the building, heads down, collars up.

This night was no different. It had rained earlier, so the street looked somewhat clean. The house was full; all 12 rooms were in use. The waiting area was also crowded, even though it was almost 2:00 A.M. Soft jazz music wafted out of the sound system. Somewhere, a TV was on. Occasionally laughter or even a groan of delight could be heard coming from an upper room.

All this was suddenly shattered by a scream.

It came from the top floor, and it was a cry not of passion but of fright. In years past, the house would have had two bouncers on hand for things like this. But tonight there was no security.

The scream came again—and then gunshots, fired into the ceiling, as it turned out. Now came a stampede of feet. Hitting the floor, hitting the door, customers barreling down the stairs. Gunshots were bad for business. No one wanted to be caught here, not if bullets were flying somewhere in the building.

In Room 5, on the third floor, a man was sleeping alone. Or at least he was trying to. He'd been living here for several weeks, a convenient halfway point between matters that had to be attended to up in New Jersey and those in Washington D.C.

He was woken by the gunshots, not the scream. He felt the floor under his bed rumble as the exodus of customers *en masse* began. He rolled off the mattress and made for the crappy dresser in the corner. He had a pistol hidden in the bottom drawer. The commotion outside his door was reaching deafening proportions. The man could not tell where the gunshots had come from, but the panic they'd set off in the building would surely bring the authorities to this place.

And that would not be good for him. Even though, technically, he was a cop himself, the last thing the man in Room 5 wanted at this moment was to have to speak to a local law enforcement person.

Make that the *second*-to-the-last thing.

For when he reached down to get his gun he was suddenly aware of someone standing next to his only window. How strange this was—no one was there a moment before. Now a huge shadow, in full body armor, including a helmet had appeared—carrying a gun the size of a howitzer.

Captain Ramosa looked up just as the heel of the boot came down on his temple. He was thrown across the room. Somehow the light got turned on and he was astonished to see in its very bare glow not just one but two men in military gear in the room with him.

Suddenly one of them was right in Ramosa's face. He lifted up his ski mask and at that moment Ramosa knew he was finished. He recognized this man, his angry features, his gigantic stature. They had met before—back in Manila. The man was from New York, a place called Queens. And of all the Crazy Americans, he was, hands down, the *craziest*.

*"Remember me?"* Hunn hissed in his face.

. . .

It had taken them just seven hours to track down Ramosa.

First came the lead from the jakes, then the taking of the surveillance tapes. Then they needed a place to watch them—the crappy motel room had to do. Seeing Ramosa on the tape interacting with the clerk Jubadi told the tale: they'd had a whispered conversation and the clerk gave Ramosa a set of cell phones. It also confirmed the ghosts' suspicions that the employees of at least five DSG stores—and probably many more—were Al Qaeda operatives. No doubt, Ramosa and Palm Tree had shared a coffee at one and that's where the mysterious napkin drawing had come from, something so precious Palm Tree had decided to hide it inside his PDA. The surveillance tape also picked up Ramosa's license plate number from a previous visit to East Newark two days before. With this information in hand, Hunn made a call to a special number that he didn't let Ozzi see him dial. But the DSA officer knew it was probably to the mysterious Bobby Murphy or one of his associates. Turned out Ramosa's car was a rental and all cars let out by this rental company had transponders in them. Like black boxes in airplanes, the transponders tracked the rental cars anywhere they went. In less than five minutes, the person on the other end of the phone call tracked the rental to South Baltimore, parked right in back of the brothel. From there, it was just a matter of Hunn and Ozzi getting to Baltimore, finding the cathouse, getting to the top of the building, and firing shots into the roof. Their aim was to see who came running out of what rooms and who didn't.

And that's how they caught Ramosa—and in that amazingly short amount of time, considering the fragility of the system they'd set up in the first place. But everyone had done their job, had gone the extra mile, and had paid attention. As a result, Hunn and Ozzi had managed to track down one of the most dangerous Al Qaeda operatives in the world— something the government might take months or, more likely, years to do . . . if ever.

So, now they had him. But what would they do with him?

Hunn put his boot on Ramosa's throat as Ozzi tossed the room. There was still a lot of tumult going on out in the hallway and downstairs, masking any noise they were making. But that didn't mean they were here to linger.

The room was filthy. The toilet had syringes and used needles scattered all over the floor. In the closet Ozzi found a full set of whips, chains, and various other S and M gear. He wondered if all this was Ramosa's gig or it just happened to be the room they'd let him use, in return for big bucks, no doubt. Hiding in a whorehouse was an old gangster trick; it was a place that some police departments would never think to look. But frankly, there were better places to go underground.

Ozzi searched under the bed—another graveyard for used hypodermics. But he also found a duffel bag full of the necessities of a terrorist these days: inside were 20 new cell phones, about two thousand dollars in small bills, and a collection of credit cards with different names, all stolen or probably counterfeited by Al Qaeda's ID masterminds. But there were other treasures underneath here as well. . . .

Hunn still had his foot on Ramosa's throat. Crumpled up against the wall, the Filipino henchman was now having trouble breathing. His eyes were red, indicating that some of the needles here might indeed belong to him. Not that long ago, back in Manila, Ramosa had ordered his henchmen to kill most of the ghost team, Hunn and Ozzi included, this after they'd unwittingly found themselves trapped in a warehouse where the Stingers missiles had been temporarily housed. That had been a very close call. Too close.

Now it was payback time.

Hunn produced a newspaper photograph he'd been saving since the first few days in Washington, D.C. It showed Palm Tree's car, or what was left of it. Blood could be seen splattered all over the burnt upholstery, the windshield and fenders perforated with hundreds of gaping holes.

"See what happened to your friend?" Hunn taunted him.

Ramosa looked at the photo but said nothing.

"Yeah, too bad you didn't get to say good-bye," Hunn went on. "But I think you two will be seeing each other again, real soon."

For emphasis, Hunn forced his boot even deeper onto Ramosa's throat. Bones started cracking.

Now Hunn had a printout of the napkin drawing dangling in front of Ramosa's eyes.

"Recognize this?" he bellowed at the cutout. "That's how we caught you, you dumb shit. You should really eat at better places. That junk food will kill you."

Blood started running out of Ramosa's ears and nose. Hunn just pushed his boot farther into his gullet.

"Now, if you want to explain this little picture here," Hunn said, still in a growl, "then maybe the way you're going out won't be as painful."

Ramosa laughed, and strangely, so did Hunn. He knew there was no way Ramosa was actually going to decipher the drawing for him. But he was interested in how Ramosa reacted to seeing it. What came next, though, threw both ghosts for a loop.

"You Americans are all psychotic," Ramosa gurgled, fixated for a moment on the napkin. He obviously recognized it. "You think you're all so clever that you'll go to any lengths just to prove a point. Whether it's a scribble on a piece of paper or invading an entire country. You people *are* crazy!"

Hunn just leaned his boot onto him a little more. More cartilage snapping.

"You're not making this any easier on yourself, pal," Hunn snarled at him.

"Nor do I intend to," Ramosa shot back in a gasp. "Can't you see the irony, you big lug? I know you people were floating around the Persian Gulf, in that ship that had every new invention in the world able to listen in on people's lives, invade their privacy. All those satellites and spaceships, Stealth bombers, and things that see in the dark. And yet, here we are, with this little scribble—and you don't know what it is. And all your technology and snooping gear and supercomputers and the rest *can't help you*. It's precious!"

Hunn put his full weight on his boot now. "You should have stayed back in Manila, pal," he said through gritted teeth. "With all those ugly women."

But strangely, Ramosa just kept laughing at him, between snorting up rivers of blood.

"Good speech, my fat friend," he spit back at Hunn. "But you wouldn't know how to find your ass with your elbow. You think you can beat them? These Muslims? You're nuts! You'll *never* defeat them. There are more of them born every minute of every hour of every day than you and the almighty U.S. Army can ever hope to find and kill. They are breeding faster than you can eliminate them. Don't you get it? It's in the numbers, man. *That's* why I joined them. They have money. They have great friends, and they paid me well. That's the new reality. Not loyalty—*money*. You and your pretty flags and your movie star heroics. You are the old way. *They* are the future. You're already coughing up blood."

Hunn became infuriated. Finally Ozzi came up next to him, one hand behind his back. Ramosa was grinning like a madman through bloody teeth—a heroin high, maybe, or just the lunacy of a person who knows he's going to die.

"You're both pathetic," Ramosa told them, in one last gasp. "You're too white. You're a dying breed. And when it comes to the little things, you're really, *really* stupid."

But that's when Ozzi revealed what he'd been holding behind his back. It was Ramosa's laptop. He'd found it among the needles under the bed.

"Well, the joke's on you, pal," Ozzi told him. "Before you started crowing, you might have wanted to step on this thing a few times."

Ozzi pushed the laptop's on button, hit the keyboard a few times, and was quickly into Ramosa's files. He lowered the screen to Ramosa's eye level so he could see just what they'd captured: a load of secret documents the Filipino middleman had been keeping, with few, if any, security barriers in place. Just like his long-lost associate Palm Tree, he'd been too clever, too lazy, for his own good.

A look of real horror came across Ramosa's face now. It

was true. He'd started taunting the Crazy Americans while forgetting his laptop was holding a wealth of information.

"Remember that next time," Ozzi said.

Voices approaching in the hallway told them it was time to go. There was nothing else for them here.

Boot still on Ramosa's throat, Hunn took a pillow from the bed, put it over the man's face, and stuck his gun barrel into it.

Then he pulled the trigger three times, sending bloody feathers everywhere.

"Sweet dreams, asshole," Hunn said.

# Chapter 15

*"Coffee is made up of phenolic polymers, polysaccharides, chlorogenic acids, caffeine, organic acids, sugars, and lipids. . . ."*

Li felt her stomach do a flip.

*No wonder the stuff drives people crazy,* she thought. The words scrolling across her computer screen seemed more like a formula for car wax. Definitely *not* something to put in one's body. Good thing she liked tea.

It was nearly four in the morning. Outside, the fog had rolled into her backyard again, arriving like the tide from the reservoir beyond. Li was upstairs, in the old house's master bedroom, the place that had been turned into the *ad hoc* operations center for "ghost team east." Her computer was here, along with two other laptops and a snake pit of wires. Her TV, her DVD player, and her Bose radio were here as well. She had her cell phone close by, too—and her pistol. Neither was very far from her side these days.

She was in this thing deep now. *Very* deep. Harboring federal fugitives. Possession of classified material. Possession of military weapons. Accomplice to murder. . . . She'd wanted Fox to put her in the loop, and in the loop she certainly was. She'd even skipped work all week—not that there was anyone around to notice, not with the way D.C. had been these past few days. It still seemed so crazy, though. She felt like she was at the center of a storm, looking out at everything swirling around her, as if she'd bypassed that iceberg and sailed right into a hurricane. God only knew what kind of a prison sentence awaited her if and when they all got caught. What would her parents think of her then?

But she was cool with it all. Remarkably so. Even when the crap hit the fan and the copter team started showing up on TV and in the newspapers, she was cool because by now she knew the score. She'd viewed both the *"Fast Ball"* and *"Slow Curve"* files many times over. She'd seen what had been found inside Palm Tree's PDA, too—and yes, the French intelligence agent got what he deserved; she was now in total agreement with that. She knew what the ghosts knew, knew what they had done and how General Rushton had pulled them back, at the worst possible moment, thus allowing the Stingers to get into the United States in the first place. She knew it all and was learning more every day.

At the same time, though, she knew that with one phone call she could spill her guts and probably get off on any charges she might be facing. Was it a temptation? Damn straight it was. . . . After Hunn and Ozzi left for New York the first time, she'd sat for an hour with her finger poised over her cell phone, ready to blow the whole thing out of the water. Who would she call exactly? The FBI? Pentagon CID—the Criminal Investigation Division? The NSC itself? At that point any number would do. With all she could tell them, the ghost team members would be rounded up very quickly and shipped back down to Gitmo. Or worse. . . .

Strangely, though, it was Fox giving her pistol back that made her decide not to drop a dime on the ghosts. Fox trusted her. He was counting on her. He believed that like the rest of the team, she was a true patriot. That when she saw irrefutable evidence that something was critically wrong, security-wise, at the very top of the government, she would help those who might be able to save the country anyway.

Yes, it was a heady place to be, in this loop. Historical even. But scary, too.

Very, *very* scary.

Hunn and Ozzi had been gone for nearly nine hours now— longer than their first trip up to the New York–New Jersey area. She missed them. That was another odd thing—and so unlike her. They'd invaded her space just a week ago, but it seemed like they'd been here forever. And yes, at first she'd felt violated, betrayed, a prisoner in her own haunted house, even though these particular ghosts were friendly. But now that they were all gone, the place seemed so empty without them. And she felt so alone. How strange. . . .

She had the TV on in the background. It used to be her only true friend, but it, too, had turned on her lately. Just about every channel she cared about was carrying an unceasing slate of Special Reports, nerve-rattling "Crisis in America" stuff that came across more as reality shows than coverage of a national emergency. At the center of them all, the still-stunning footage of the rogue Coast Guard helicopter, with the three men in the cargo hold waving the old Revolutionary War flag and giving the V for Victory sign. Was this really an unauthorized secret ops team running loose in America? the pundits asked. Or was it a fraud, or a goof, or a stunt? And if they were real, should the government be trying to help them or trying to stop them? That was the debate, along with whether a nuke was going to go off sometime soon inside the homeland.

But Li knew the footage was not a fake. She knew who the masked men were: Fox, Puglisi, and Bates. She recognized their masks. And when the camera pulled back she saw the pilot—or one of them anyway—in the copter's driver's seat, and that was obviously Gallant.

But every time she saw the footage, which was dozens of times by now, she wondered the same thing: why couldn't she see Ryder?

It was creeping up on 4:30 now. The fog in her backyard got thicker.

While she liked the sound of the TV to drown out all the creaks and groans of the old house, the all-night news was bothering her again. She pushed the DVD button to play and her favorite movie came on: Marlene Dietrich's *Blue Angel*. She turned the sound way down, though. It was actually her favorite movie to fall asleep to, but she wanted to stay awake now. She had things to do.

She went back to her coffee analysis page, wondering if it was going anywhere or she was just spinning her wheels. Fox's last request to her was to see if she could somehow clear up the image of the mysterious napkin drawing. No matter what happened with Hunn and Ozzi up in New Jersey, she knew this was a crucial thing to do. All those chemicals were the reason for the stain that was obscuring most of the drawing; it was her job to try to get rid of them, and more than anything, she wanted to come through on this. Then, at least, when they finally caught the ghost team, she would be more than just a casual bystander. She would have contributed. She would be one of them.

She'd been at it for three days now, and by this time the image on the napkin was burned into her brain. The gaggle of arrowlike shapes, all going in one direction. Thousands of people looking up from a city with no buildings below. The bus in the lower corner, the damnable coffee stain clouding up what might be important clues. Once more she called it up on her computer screen.

"'*Ducks*'?" she said to herself now, almost laughing, like when Ozzi first told her what the firefighter from Queens had said. "There's no way those are ducks."

*But what the hell were they?*

It always came back to the coffee stain. *That* was the problem. There seemed to be some kind of writing underneath it; everyone agreed on that. But trying to determine what it said was almost impossible. *It's like the Shroud of Turin,* she'd thought more than once. *You think you know what you're looking at—but then again, maybe you don't.* Was this the most important piece of intelligence of the new century? Or was it simply a piece of trash? She didn't know.

Since midnight she'd been working on a new strategy; she called it the Archimedes principle. The ancient Greek scientist wrote one of the greatest books on mathematics, only to have it lost for centuries after some monk, thinking it was scrap paper, scribbled prayers over it. When Archimedes' book was eventually found again, some brilliant minds used a computer to get rid of the monk's writing on top, finally revealing the great man's words beneath. Li's thought maybe this could be done to the napkin.

She'd spent two hours just downloading different types of software, hoping one could lift one layer off the napkin, that being the coffee stain, and reveal what lay underneath. It was a good idea, but nothing clicked. It was not the fault of the software. The best of them could do many different things to photographs: enhance certain parts, change colors, textures. They could also erase parts of an image or edit new parts in. The problem was, this wasn't a real napkin she was dealing with here. It was only *an image* of one: the original. It was impossible for her to strip away any layers, because it was all one layer.

But how she tried. As long as it took the moon to cross the sky and for her to count 20 different times that fighter jets passed over her house. (She heard them all the time now, almost around-the-clock.)

*Archimedes, hell,* she'd finally thought as the clock struck 4:30. She didn't need a genius from 200 B.C. to solve this problem. She needed Superman—and his X-ray vision.

And that's when it hit her.

Maybe she didn't quite need X-ray vision—but only to flip the image.

She went back to the Net and found a software package that allowed JPEG images to reverse polarity and turn a positive image into a negative of itself. It took her a while, as she had to make copies of the original photo. But when all was set and she pushed the enter button, the napkin drawing flipped and became a bizarro inside-out version of itself. . . .

That's how she found what she was looking for.

"Damn," she whispered. "How about that?"

By turning it to a negative she'd succeeded in dissipating about three-quarters of the coffee stain—and revealing the written scribble below it.

It was a number: *74.* With a circle around it.

"Seventy-four," Li said now, rolling it off her tongue. "What could that mean?"

But there was more. At the same time she could read the number, she realized she could see there was also *more* writing underneath. There was not much, maybe just a shaky line or an ink stain. But she'd never been able to see it before, and even though the image was flipped, it was not clear enough to read now. So by solving one mystery she had created another.

She studied this new problem for a few moments. Maybe if she zoomed in a little and . . .

Suddenly the hairs on the back of her neck stood up. A glare, moving across the glass of her laptop's screen. Someone was behind her. *Oh God.* . . . She whirled around, picking up her pistol and pointing it straight ahead of her in one swift motion.

"Jesus, no!" someone cried out.

Li began to squeeze the trigger. . . .

*"It's us!"* another voice shouted.

She stopped one millimeter from firing.

Hunn and Ozzi standing in the bedroom doorway.

"Christ . . . *don't do that!*" she screamed at them.

But we had to, they said. And they were right. There was no way for them to know if the security of the house had been compromised while they were away. They had to come in quietly and check it out for themselves. That's what people did in these circumstances.

But Li had already forgotten about it. She was so glad to see them, she almost jumped up and hugged them. As crazy as it was, at least she wasn't alone anymore.

"Where have you been!" she yelled at them instead, putting her pistol away. "I was about to go nuts. . . ."

Both of them looked exhausted and dirty and sweaty. But she detected the faintest twinkle in their eyes, especially Ozzi's.

"We had to dump the van, at least for the night," Ozzi said. "We might have been tagged by a couple people, so we left it down in Washington and walked the rest of the way here."

"But what happened up in New Jersey?" she finally asked them.

They both smiled darkly. "We got Ramosa," Ozzi told her wearily.

"Got him good," Hunn added.

And this time she did hug them. Both of them. She was *that* happy. Finally some good news. Ramosa was scum—as bad as Palm Tree. And she knew the prime mission of the team was to eliminate anyone connected with the various Al Qaeda schemes against America. Now they could add one more number to that tally.

But Ozzi couldn't stop smiling. "And better yet," he said, "we got this."

He held up Ramosa's laptop. Li knew what it was right away.

"He was reading that damn thing the whole way home," Hunn said. "And it's a gold mine. Times, dates, people involved. And lots of stuff on the first bus. . . ."

"The *first* bus?" Li asked excitedly. This was unexpected. One other reason for going after Ramosa was that they suspected he had dope on the second bus.

"But we got nothing from him on the napkin," Ozzi said. "He wouldn't give anything up—just laughed at us when we asked."

Now Li smiled and hugged them again.

"Well, then I've got a surprise for you," she said. "Take a look at this . . ."

But no sooner were the words out of her mouth than they all heard a noise outside. A disturbing noise. Tires on gravel. Someone was approaching.

"Damn," she swore softly. "I knew it was too much good news at once."

To her credit, Li knew exactly what to do. As soon as Fox had decided to make her part of the team, the first thing she did was download a document, from a secure CIA site, called "How to Run a Safe House."

And one of the basic principles was if anything happened unexpectedly—like someone coming to the door—the right thing to do was just answer the door normally. Not scramble madly around the house turning off lights. Or try to sneak the "houseguests" out another door. Just act naturally.

So they did not panic. Li got up from her chair, shut off the movie, dimmed the light slightly, then looked out the window. Maybe it was just their imaginations, she thought.

It wasn't.

Two sets of headlights were coming up the reservoir extension road.

In all her time here in the haunted house, never had she seen even one car come up that road, never mind two. *This* was trouble. She could smell it.

"OK, just be cool," Ozzi told her. "We'll be right here. If there's any shooting, just please duck and stay out of the way."

As if to emphasize that, both men checked the ammunition in their weapons. Then Hunn and Ozzi immediately disappeared into the bedroom's shadows.

Li took a deep breath and settled herself. She made her way out of the room, down the stairs, and to the back door. She cracked the door, just a little, but still the fog rolled in. A little more . . . but then she saw something that made no sense. Now there was only one set of headlights, and strangely enough, they were turning around and heading back down the road, away from the house.

Mystified—as if she needed any more mystery in her life at the moment—she opened the back door a bit more and peeked out.

Amazingly, she found herself staring out at a very unexpected sight. She laughed out loud.

It was her car.

Her little beat-up Toyota.

The last she'd seen it, the five ghosts were driving away

in it, heading back down to Cape Lonely. Never did she think she'd see it again. Yet here it was. . . .

Something was odd here, though. It was *her* car; there was no doubt about that. But where was the rust? The bent fender? The cracked windshield?

She came down off the porch carefully, making sure no one was around. Once she was reasonably sure she was alone, she walked out to the car and inspected it thoroughly.

She couldn't believe it. New interior. New radio. Nice, smooth body. Even a new set of tires. It was still warm from being dropped off, and even the engine smelled new.

But how did this happen? How could this be?

She opened the passenger's door and found a baffling explanation. On the seat was a note that read: *We thought you might need this back.*

It was stapled to a bag of doughnuts.

# Chapter 16

It was cold up here.

Wherever here was.

They were in the mountains of . . . well, someplace. Lots
of trees. Lots of ferns and thick vegetation. A falling mist
gave everything a weird sheen. Off in the distance, the sound
of the wind and the cries of animals. Or at least they sounded
like animals.

They were somewhere in the Midwest, maybe on the
western fringes or very close by. But if a million in cash was
put in front of Ryder, he still wouldn't have been able to say
*exactly* what state they were in. Maybe Missouri. Maybe
Arkansas. He just didn't know. And he never bothered to ask.

The stars overhead were shining brilliantly through the
scattered patches of cloud. There was a lake in front of them
and a lush field of tall grass behind. This was where the
copter was now. It seemed in repose, hidden in the shadow
of some gigantic pine trees, its rotor blades drooping, most
of its systems finally shut down. The Sky Horse taking a
well-earned nap.

It was almost a beautiful scene. There was just one problem: they couldn't get a good TV or radio signal up here.
The gadget left for them at the floatplane refueling island
was the electronic equivalent of a Swiss Army knife. It was a

combination radio and TV, flashlight, strobe light, heat lamp, panic buzzer, compass, and clock. But Puglisi had been screwing around with it ever since they'd landed and he'd been unable to pick up anything more than a lot of static.

They'd been encamped here, laying low, for the past 36 hours. This was not so much because they wanted to but more because the mooks had not made any moves, either. Bates had stayed glued to his Eyeball Machine the whole time; he got even less sleep than Ryder. And Bates had become very adept at reading the nuances of the monster he'd built. He routinely listened in on all the U.S. intelligence services, trying to ferret out any information having to do with suspected terrorist teams moving about the country. But truth was, there was actually very little data coming in on that topic. Most of the intell reports bouncing around Washington had to do with the TV coverage concerning rumors that some kind of WMD was going to be detonated soon, possibly within the U.S. capital itself, this and the government's continued denial that a rogue special ops unit was hunting down terrorists inside the United States, despite so much evidence to the contrary.

Bates also continued tapping into the computers of the Greyhound Bus Company itself. He was still looking for anything—a tip, a clue, a strange report from another driver or just people on the U.S. highways, any mention of a Greyhound bus acting unusually. But nothing had come out of this, either. As far as Bates could tell, the company was still blissfully unaware that someone was sneaking around the country in two of its buses.

Most troubling, though, was that the next Al Qaeda missile team had been so quiet. The ghost team knew the general area where the soccer team was supposed to play but also feared that after the five unsuccessful attacks the remaining terrorist cells had readapted themselves and might be operating with even greater autonomy. There was a chance they'd been told not to have any further communication, no more phone rings, nothing. This would be a disaster for the ghost team. There were at least four more missile teams out there, somewhere. How could the ghost team find them if they stopped talking to one another?

Time seemed to be running out, and with it some of the copter team's spirit. It was hard to simply put the brakes on, to let the adrenaline stop pumping. That's when things like sleep and memories and the need to eat properly began to sneak up on you. And the team didn't need any of that right now.

But they were haunted by that one question: what if the mook phones never rang again?

It was now about 4.00 A.M. central time. They were drinking coffee around a fire when Bates finally climbed out of the helicopter, taking a rare break. He had Finch's flag with him. It was no longer pristine and neatly folded. It was now battered, wrinkled, and embedded with dust and grime. They had hung it on the inside of the copter's interior wall, where fumes and oil and all kinds of things were in the air. The flag had got dirty quickly.

Without saying a word, he passed the flag to Fox. He held it briefly in his hands, then began folding and unfolding it, nervous play, almost unconscious. Then he passed it over to Ryder.

Ryder held it to his face and thought of his wife. Then came the vision of *all* those killed on 9/11. The people on the first two planes. All the cops and firefighters who went into the towers and never came out. The people at the Pentagon. The people who fought with the terrorists on the plane that crashed in Pennsylvania. A lump came to his throat—this always happened. His eyes, already tired and bleary, misted up nevertheless. *This* was why they were out here, outlaws in their own country. They were fighting for the memory of Al Qaeda's innocent victims, fulfilling the mission that Bobby Murphy had sent them out on so long ago. *See it to the end,* Ryder thought now. *No matter what happens, just see it to the end.*

"Let's get a little more luck out of this thing," he said softly. The team had come to think of the old Revolutionary War flag as their good-luck piece, responsible for their

not acquiring more than a scratch in their little unde-
clared war.

Puglisi put the TV/radio away and took his time with
the flag. Only Gallant, stretched out nearby and asleep,
missed out.

Uncertain if the little ceremony had raised the spirits of
the ghosts, Bates took the flag back.

But it was strange—because the moment it went back
into his hands, they heard a phone ringing. . . .

It wasn't a mook phone. It was Ozzi. And he couldn't talk
very long because he didn't have any code words with which
to pass on some crucial information.

So Bates just listened very carefully, the rest of the team
gathered round him.

First item, ghost team east had captured and liquidated
Captain Ramosa. This news was greeted with a grim cheer.
*One problem solved, one less hump in the world*, Ryder
thought.

And while the D.C. people were still going through
Ramosa's captured laptop, they were already able to say that
it contained just as much revealing information as Palm
Tree's PDA. Another cheer.

But Ozzi and the others had come across a very special
piece of information for the copter troops. It was a message,
just recently entered into Ramosa's E-mail system, that said
the first bus was going to make contact with a sleeper agent
somewhere along a highway in the Texas panhandle area, 36
hours from now.

This excited the copter team greatly. Hitting the bus itself
would save them from tracking down the rest of the missile
teams one at a time.

But the D.C. crew had come across some more disturbing
intelligence: that another missile team was going to attack
an airplane at Denver International Airport later that very
morning.

This was a problem. Getting a shot at the bus was a huge

opportunity. But the copter squad would have to stop the Denver attack, too.

Trouble was, Denver was at least 400 miles away from their current position, wherever that was.

"Can you do *both* things in time?" Ozzi asked Bates desperately.

Even in the darkness, the others saw Bates's face turn pale.

"I guess we have to try," he finally replied.

# Chapter 17

Abdul Ahmed Ashmani had never been camping before. Though he was from Saudi Arabia and his extended family included much Bedouin blood, he'd never even slept in a tent, never mind tried to live in one.

But that's what he'd been doing, he and three others—two guys named Muhammad Abu and his cousin Azi. They'd been staying in two tents on the edge of the Whispering Falls campgrounds for the past two days.

The tents were very small, made of thin plastic and cord, and though easy to set up, they had a tendency to collapse if the wind blew too hard. And due to the campsite's location, the wind seemed to be blowing hard just about all of the time.

This was not Ashmani's climate, not his pleasure, not his country. He'd gained entry to the United States three years before the 9/11 attacks, paying a French-speaking tour guide to allow him aboard a ferry leaving Quebec for Portland, Maine, without having to show a passport. The bribe was just $100. He worked as a cabdriver in Boston and Providence, Rhode Island, before eventually moving west to Buffalo and finally to the large Arab enclave of Detroit.

Here he lay hiding among a sympathetic population, avoiding U.S. government sweeps following 9/11, working as a busboy, a waiter, and a used-car salesmen. Two weeks ago, he was contacted by an Al Qaeda operative posing as a U.S. correspondent for Al-Jazeera TV. His orders were for Ashmani to move farther west, to this campground, and hook up with his fellow operators. Many rides on many Greyhound buses followed. When he arrived in the nearby town of Horseshoe, he was as surprised as anyone to find his cousin Azi waiting at the bus stop to pick him up.

The two missiles were here, two launchers, too. They had both arrived with the two Muhammads, the soccer players, on schedule, with no problems. There was a reason this particular campsite was so windy. It was practically on the edge of a mountain so high, when winter came thousands of people would go skiing here. But it also presented a clear view of the vast lower Colorado plains. And a few miles away, just slightly to the southeast of them, and about a thousand feet below, was Denver International Airport.

Big airliners took off and landed here all day and night, every hour, every minute, or so it seemed. The afternoon of his first day here, Ashmani sat on the edge of the cliff and counted the planes taking off. In two hours, nearly 50 aircraft of all shapes and sizes took flight—and that did not take into account just as many landings. Ashmani was amazed. He'd spent eight hours once in Mecca Airport waiting for the only flight of the day to land. . . . But 50 takeoffs in two hours? Where the hell were all these Americans going?

One of these planes would be the team's primary target; if they had time and opportunity, they would try for two. Exactly which airplane they would choose to shoot down first had been left to the fates. They had a fresh cell phone hidden in the Muhammads' tent. When it rang, they were to set up the missile and then shoot it at the biggest airplane to take off inside the next 10 minutes.

At least this was the plan. Other teams, like them a combination of sleepers inserted into the United States years before and "soccer players," had not been so lucky in trying to hit their airliners. Ashmani's team had been led to believe, again by their original orders, that by the time they got to shoot at their targets at least five planes would have been shot down already. Yet there had been nothing about anything like that in the American media.

Ashmani knew America was a very screwy place. Its people were also highly unpredictable. For their own security reasons, none of the sleeper/hit teams had had any contact with one another before moving forward. They communicated solely by ringing various cell phones. So neither he nor anyone else in his team had any idea why the previous attempted shoot-downs had failed.

But the rumor that an American special ops team might be knocking off the other cells had been a source of worry. Footage of just such a team had been shown all over American TV for the past three days, along with strident denials by the U.S. government that such a team was on the loose. Of most concern to Ashmani's cell was that these vigilantes, if they existed, might actually be the Crazy Americans, the scourge of every Muslim from Algeria to the Philippines. It was a frightening thought, as no one wanted to deal with *them,* promises of martyrdom or not.

Allah be praised, after all this Ashmani just wanted to shoot the damn missiles and get the hell home.

It was now almost 8:00 A.M., local time.

The four men had just finished their morning tea when Ashmani heard an odd beeping noise, electronic and muffled.

He didn't know what it was at first. He was sitting close to their raging campfire, the crackling wood distorting the sound at first. But then Azi stood up, nearly tripped over the campfire, and scrambled toward his tent. He looked both excited and frightened. That's when it hit Ashmani.

It was the phone. It was ringing.

Their orders . . .

Finally. . . .

"It is the signal," Azi confirmed. "It is time to shoot. . . ."

The two Muhammads went into action. One of them threw Ashmani his watch. Ashmani was the timekeeper. He noted the time on the fake Rolex. Eight-o-five A.M. It was a Saturday.

People traveling early for the weekend. A full airliner. A big airliner.

A fat target.

Ashmani felt his heart start pumping rapidly. Real timing was called for here.

The two Muhammads finally joined them. They were the soccer players and thus the weapons experts. They soon had the first missile married to its launcher. Azi ran down the road to a preappointed spot from which he could see most of the eastern end of the campground and its main road as well. He whistled three times, loud and shrill. Everything was clear.

Ashmani double-checked the missile, another of his duties. The sighting device was turned on. The battery indicator showed a substantial charge. The weapon needed a few minutes to heat up. The two Muhammads took up a position right behind his tent and just 10 feet from the edge of the cliff. A small green steel barrier, similar to a guardrail on a highway, was located here, driven into the rock. It made for a perfect aiming spot.

Once they were set, Ashmani rushed back to his tent and grabbed his laptop. He'd downloaded many regular flight schedules for the airport below. Their orders were to shoot down the biggest plane possible. Only the big airline companies flew the very big planes—except for the odd charter or cargo plane. Ashmani ran his finger down the list for this morning, this date: United. American. Delta. Each had at least one plane departing within the next 15 minutes. Perfect. . . .

He took out his binoculars, returned to the guardrail, and trained them on the airport below. There were five main runways; they crisscrossed one another at fifty-degree angles. Because the wind was always blowing from the west here, those planes taking off left from the runway nearest to them and frequently flew right over the campground itself.

Ashmani trained his binoculars on the northernmost runway. Five airplanes were waiting on a taxiway nearby—a 747 was just pulling into position at the far end. It was a United Airlines plane—Ashmani believed it was heading for Dallas.

*Praise God!* he thought. *We're about to kill a bunch of Texans.*

He scrambled back down to where the Muhammads had the weapon fixed on the guardrail. The weapon was warm, they told him. The sighting device was ready as well. Ashmani was very excited now. He whistled, the signal for Azi. Azi whistled back once. Then returned to the camp site. Everything was all clear.

Ashmani trained the binoculars back on the runway.

The big 747 was beginning to move. . . .

Ashmani whispered another quick prayer, then took the glasses from his eyes. The next thing he saw was a bayonet, reflecting the early-morning sun, coming right at him.

It was strange, in that fraction of a second, when he could see the glint of this very sharp blade so clearly, yet the person behind it still somehow out of focus. He thought it was his cousin Azi, about to stab him, for some long-forgotten incident of their childhood. But then, in the next moment, he realized it could not be Azi, because he was lying on the ground next to the campfire with another bayonet sticking out of his neck, the wound gushing blood like red water from a garden hose.

Only then did Ashmani see the helicopter. It had swooped down from out of nowhere. It was big and white . . . and *very* quiet. Armed men were jumping from it. They were dressed in black combat suits and carrying combat rifles . . . with bayonets.

These men were brutally beating one of the Muhammads. They weren't simply shooting him. They were stabbing him, impaling him, stomping him with their big black boots. The screams were horrible, drowning out the now-departing United 747. It was flying right overhead at that moment, which to Ashmani seemed frozen in time.

The bayonet hit his knee first, then pierced his upper thigh. There was no pain—not right away. He collapsed, though, falling onto the crazy man who was trying very hard not just to kill him but also to make him suffer before doing him in. They tumbled over together, Ashmani rolling out of control and nearly into the raging campfire, winding up in the pool of blood still streaming out of his cousin. All of this was happening in an instant. It was slow-motion terror magnified.

But then something very strange and unexpected happened. The helicopter was still hovering silently right in front of the guardrail. A man was in its pilot's seat, incredibly firing a rifle down at the Muhammad who was still being stabbed by the others. Suddenly the Stinger missile—which the second Muhammad was holding—went off. All fire and smoke, it went right through the helicopter's open cargo door and smashed into the interior fuselage.

There was a violent explosion. The noise was tremendous. The remains of the missile went one way and the helicopter, on fire and spinning out of control, went the other. The copter plummeted to the plains below. In a second, there was nothing left in the air but thousands of sparkling ashes and a cloud of black smoke.

Ashmani found himself laughing—it had all happened so quickly, it almost seemed comical. But then he looked up and saw a gun barrel pointed right between his eyes. And the man behind the gun was not laughing. He looked at Ashmani coldly, almost as if he didn't realize his helicopter had just been blown out of the sky.

Then he mouthed the words: *Remember Nick Berg*. . . .

Then he pulled the trigger—and for Abdul Ahmed Ashmani everything just went to black.

# Chapter 18

It was the worst traffic jam of the week.

Constitution Avenue was shut down; 15th and 17th Streets were like parking lots. And the area around Pennsylvania Avenue? Forget about it. It had been stop-and-go there for the past two hours. And it wasn't even four o'clock yet. That's when D.C.'s real traffic crush usually hit.

Yet here he was again, the same limousine driver, same heavily armored stretch limousine, same arduous circumnavigation of the capital, heading for the White House. Different day. Same gridlock.

And it was the same reason for the traffic snarl: scores of military vehicles, some traveling in groups, some on their own, tying up every intersection, every traffic light, every entrance and exit to the Beltway. Factor in the tourists, the taxis, and cars driven by people who actually lived in D.C., it all added up to a gargantuan mess that no amount of work by the D.C. traffic police could ever hope to solve.

The limo driver was forced to jump a few curbs and run a few red lights, but after a half hour of fighting the jam he was at last within sight of the White House.

It had been a long trip in from Bethesda, and the driver was thankful the limo came equipped with a soundproof glass partition. He really didn't want to hear what was going on in the back of the car today. He was transporting the entire Rushton family once again, this time with the general included. That would make eight times in two days the driver had been on the Rushton hump. Even through the glass barrier, he could still hear the littlest one screaming madly. And maybe a few of the younger ones were crying, too.

The Rushton family had been traveling with the general almost around-the-clock these days. The limo driver had brought them to the photo session at the EOB, to various meetings at the White House and on Capitol Hill, to awards banquets, to more meetings. They were the general's new entourage.

Why the sudden closeness to family? The limo driver had read the blurbs from a few D.C. reporters who'd noticed Rushton's recent unusual behavior. The General knew something bad was coming and wanted to be with his family when the terrorist-induced disaster hit. Or the General almost resigned a month ago because he wasn't spending enough time with his family, so the President gave him permission to take the wife and kids anywhere he wanted. Or the General was home-schooling his kids, infant included, in something called "history firsthand."

The limo driver had his own theories about all this. But he knew, in his business, it was best that he keep them to himself.

He finally reached the south west gate of the White House. Two uniformed guards appeared from their security booth. The limo driver showed his ID; Rushton showed his as well. The limo and its two trailing Suburbans—full of bodyguards from Global Security Inc.—were all waved in.

The driver rolled up to the side entrance of the Executive Mansion, where two more guards were waiting. He'd barely stopped the limo when the doors opened and the Rushton kids started piling out on their own. He could hear Rushton chastising them, telling them to stay together, to bunch up. A White House photographer was also on hand, prepositioned to take a picture of the family. Rushton made his wife and kids say *"cheese,"* but after just a few snaps he waved the photographer away. Taking his littlest kids in hand, he quickly walked into the White House, followed by the guards from the Suburbans.

The limo driver was told to wait.

Once inside, Rushton left his family cold. Accompanied by two plainclothes Secret Service agents, he was whisked down a hallway to a hidden elevator. This brought him down four floors to the White House's subbasement. Here was the National Situation Room, also know as the Bunker. Usually this was where the President and his people would gather in the event of a crisis. But Rushton had appropriated it today, declaring it off-limits to everyone, including people on the White House staff itself.

Rushton had called a very secret meeting down here. This was because, in addition to it being blast-proof, the Bunker was also soundproof and bug-proof. It was automatically swept every hour for listening devices. Plus, it was practically impervious to stand-off electronic eavesdropping. It was, no doubt, one of the most secure places on the planet.

There was another reason Rushton wanted his meeting held here, though. It had to do with a bastardization of a popular tourist slogan: What was said in the Bunker stayed in the Bunker. And what Rushton had to say to the participants here today *had* to be kept quiet. His words would be considered beyond any security clearances, beyond top-secret.

There were 22 people sitting around the elaborate electronics-packed conference table when he walked in. TV screens and communications equipment adorned each of the room's four walls. Blue-tinted recessed lights and the odd shadows they cast gave the room an almost religious feel.

All those in attendance were veterans of special operations. Some were still in the military; others were not. Most had close personal ties to Rushton. He had mentored them, pulled strings for them, put them in for promotions that were all but guaranteed to be approved. About half of them were considered members of Rushton's innermost circle.

The rest were experts in clandestine warfare, cyberstalking, and espionage.

Rushton plopped into his seat at the head of the table. He was sweaty, face puffy, typically out of sorts. He didn't acknowledge those on hand. He simply started talking:

"We have a situation in Denver," he began soberly. "Earlier this morning, an attempt was made to shoot down an airliner taking off from the new airport out there. A missile of some sort was fired at it from a campground nearby. It missed and the plane took off safely.

"Within minutes, park rangers arrived at the campsite where the missile came from. It was close to the edge of a cliff. They discovered the four bodies there, probably the people who tried to fire the weapon. They also found evidence that a struggle had taken place at the edge of this campsite as well as what appeared to be animal parts.

"As you know, in the past week we have heard rumors of . . . well, people who are *suspected* of being terrorists being found murdered at several places around the country. While this is the only instance where it can be *confirmed* these people were trying to shoot down an airliner when they were killed, at this point we'll have to submit that this and those other incidents are probably connected."

Those sitting around the table were more than mildly shocked to hear this. Not that there were terrorist missile teams inside the United States—they all assumed that was true by now. But that Rushton came so close to admitting he'd made a mistake. After so long ignoring any such threat, he'd finally acknowledged that some bad guys were inside the country trying to shoot down airliners.

"The park rangers were quickly relieved at the scene by the local marshal's office," Rushton went on, reading now from a prepared statement. "They ordered the rangers out of their own park, intent on taking over the investigation. But the marshal's men were quickly supplanted by the Colorado State Police. They evicted *all* the campers from the park, and cordoned off a square mile from everyone but their top investigators.

"It was the state police who found the wreckage of a helicopter that seems connected to the incident. It was lodged between two huge boulders at the bottom of this cliff. Its tail section was burned away. Its midsection was in shreds. The flight compartment was splattered with blood.

"The state police investigators weren't sure what happened exactly. But then the FBI arrived. They got rid of the state cops and confiscated all of their evidence, including some photographs and videotape that had been taken at the scene.

"My contacts in the FBI called me immediately. Besides the attempted missile shot, they confirmed what many others have suspected these last few days: that some kind of a rogue special ops team has been roaming around the country. Apparently they showed up at this campground, too. They may have even prevented the airliner from being shot down by getting shot down themselves."

Another surprise for those gathered: Rushton actually admitting that an unauthorized special ops team was operating inside the United States.

"Where are these rogues now?" Rushton went on. "No clues to this were found. There were no bodies in the helicopter wreckage. Even the person who had been at the controls of the helicopter—the person whose blood was all over the pilot's seat—was missing.

"Now news of these events is already spreading coast-to-coast. I asked the FBI to call the state police back in to scour the area for anyone connected to this incident. But it is quickly becoming clear that this is a task too immense for either the state police or the FBI to do alone.

"That's why I have ordered the Colorado National Guard to join in the search. They will be on the streets within the hour.

"That's also why I called you all here. I'm sending you on a special mission."

Rushton cleared his throat, then began again.

"I must tell you my suspicion all along has been that if this renegade unit *was* real, then it must be in league with the terrorist missile teams. We suspect some of these rogues were in on an escape from Guantánamo Bay last week during the course of a very secret prisoner exchange with Iran. These individuals might actually be Americans that were being held at Gitmo for a variety of security reasons."

Here Rushton paused again. An almost painful look came across his bloated face. He suddenly appeared fearful, vulnerable.

"But most of you here know that story," he said.

This was another stunner. Rushton's explanation contradicted what they'd all been led to believe, at least by the media and internal chatter: that these rogues were hardly working *with* the terrorists but just the opposite—they were following them around, somehow staying in step with them, *preventing* them from shooting down any airliners, or at least trying to, and brutally murdering any Muslim terrorists who crossed their path along the way. Indeed, the evidence showed the mysterious team had prevented much loss of life and calamity inside the United States while thumbing their noses at Washington. What's more, they were now regarded as heroes, of mythical proportions, by millions of people across the country. It was virtually impossible for them to be in cahoots with the missile teams.

But this was Rushton's world, and for the moment the people sitting around the table were inside it with him. Most owed their military and professional careers to him; some were very gung-ho to support him. Those on hand who weren't still feared him. No one wanted to become his enemy. There really was no telling what would happen to them if they did.

"Your mission will be simple." Rushton started talking again. "Acting on information I will provide to you when the time is right, you will pick up the trail of these renegades and stop them by whatever means possible."

He let those words sink in.

"You will not be working in concert with other teams being led by the FBI," Rushton continued. "Frankly, they are looking for any more of these alleged terrorists that might be out there. If they happened to come upon these rogues, they would probably grab them up, too. However, in that case, their aim would be to arrest these people and return them to Gitmo. In other words, they're involved in a criminal investigation.

"You people will be involved in a *military* operation. You will have better intelligence, better communications, better weapons. Again, we will let others go after these supposed terrorists. You're going after the rogues. And when you catch up to them, your orders are not to capture and arrest. Your orders are to lose them. Simple as that."

Dead silence in the room.

"You'll go through some training," Rushton went on. "You will get some last-minute details, code words, and security procedures. Then when I give the word, you'll ship out. As of this moment, consider yourselves on call. We're looking at a jump-off point in about seventy-two hours, maybe less."

Still, no one in the room made a sound.

Rushton continued: "We can't worry about rules of engagement. The bottom line is, we have to get rid of these people—quickly and, hopefully, quietly as well. That's what I want. That's what's got to be done."

He looked at the people sitting nearest to him, his closest disciples. "If we are to succeed in other areas," Rushton told them cryptically, "then we must succeed here first."

Thirty long seconds of silence.

Then Rushton asked, "Any questions?"

At first, another uncomfortable silence. But then someone spoke up: "What kind of real-time information do we have on these people? Do we have a general area where we can search for them? Or will we have to look all over the Rockies for them?"

Rushton smiled darkly. "Well, that's the good news," he said. "We don't know where they are at the moment. But we know almost exactly where they will be in about three days' time."

This sounded strange—but no one commented further about it.

Instead another hand went up. "Does the President know about this mission?"

Rushton's reply was quick: "No. . . ."

Again, dead silence in the room.

"Anything else?" he asked.

There was nothing.

"Then, you are all dismissed," Rushton said.

With that he got up and was surrounded by Secret Service men again. They, too, were part of his inner circle. He quickly disappeared into the elevator with them and was gone.

The others on hand began to get up and leave, too, using the more conventional stairs. They left in twos and threes, talking quietly among themselves. One commented that the meeting was like a scene out of a bad movie.

One man stayed behind, though. He was sitting at the far end of the table, and through it all, he had not said a word. He was too astonished, by what he heard, by what was said.

It was Pershing Nash, Li's erstwhile boyfriend.

Looking up at the blue-tinted lights now, he thought, *What the hell am I doing here?*

Rushton's limo left the White House shortly after the meeting broke up.

Reuniting with the two SUVs full of bodyguards, the limo found a hole in the traffic and headed for the Beltway. Traveling at high speed in the passing lane, they turned off at the Bethesda exit. Here they were met by a cruiser from the Bethesda Police Department. With the local cops in the lead, the small parade of vehicles proceeded to the nearby fashionable neighborhood of Blakewood.

Inside the limo, the Rushton clan sat, sullen and silent, exhausted from these frequent excursions they'd been making with their father. They arrived at the driveway of their very tony 12-room house. This was an expensive property, in a very expensive area, what would seem way beyond the means of an Army general, even one as high up the food chain as Rushton. Truth was, the general was deeply in debt, and getting money, quickly and quietly, had been a motivation over the past year or so. But he had other aspirations these days as well.

The limousine turned into the driveway, but any hopes of respite the Rushton kids might have held were dashed at first sight of their front lawn. About fifty people were assembled here. They were contractors and lobbyists for the defense security industry. They were having a late-afternoon catered barbecue at the general's house. As before, attendance for the Rushton family would be mandatory.

The limo pulled up into the house's gravel turnaround. The bodyguards in the Suburbans dismounted and headed for the kitchen in the rear of the house. They hadn't had breakfast yet, never mind lunch. The police car left them here, retreating back down the long driveway and going on its way.

The two policemen inside the cruiser did not think suspicious the white van parked across the street from the bottom of the driveway.

Ozzi was behind the wheel of the van, the same vehicle that had carried them twice up I-95 to the New York–New Jersey area. They'd been dumping it at various spots around D.C., praying each time that it would be there when they returned.

Ozzi was dressed in his Kmart duds now, but his make shift combat suit was folded underneath the front seat. He was trying his best to look like a flower deliveryman, and indeed the van was filled with bouquets, all stolen earlier that day from fresh graves in cemeteries in the area. He had a clipboard in one hand and a cell phone in the other. He was having an imaginary phone conversation; the cell phone wasn't even turned on.

All this was a cover for what Hunn was doing in the back. The Delta soldier was lying atop a bed of dying lilies, facing a hole they'd drilled in the van's rear door. A balancing bar fashioned from an armrest taken from an old chair in Li's house was duct-taped to the floor. A pair of very cheap binoculars was jammed into an indent on the other side of which the van's license was fastened. Two holes had been drilled here as well. Hunn's eyes were pressed up against the binoculars, looking up at Rushton's mansion. The house was painted white, the perfect background for what Hunn was about to do.

They'd been parked here most of the afternoon. No one had questioned them; no one had given them as much as a second look. They knew the always-moving Rushton would have to return home sooner or later; this was better than trying to track him down all over D.C. On first coming here, they'd thought they'd probably have to wait until nightfall, in hopes of catching Rushton then. But when they saw the crowd start to gather on his lawn shortly after they arrived, they felt their luck was staying good.

And good luck was essential for any sniper mission.

It was actually a perfect scenario for them. Rushton's front yard ran 400 feet down to the road. Hunn's hunting rifle was accurate at 2,000 yards. Getting a powerful enough shot would not be a problem. And once the trigger was pulled, Ozzi could have them on the Beltway in less than a minute. Plus the van itself was a great cover. There weren't just thousands of white delivery vans in the D.C. area, driving its streets at any time of day. There were *tens of thousands* of them, as plentiful as yellow cabs in New York City. D.C. was a place that ran on local delivery. It would take months to stop them all or track them all down, as the local law enforcement agencies had discovered several years before.

Even the fact that a large number of people were on the general's lawn was a point in the team's favor. The more witnesses, the greater chance for different accounts to police afterward. More confusion usually resulted.

Eliminating Rushton had always been one of the ghost team's key objectives since leaving Gitmo. They'd suspected his involvement in the Stinger deal all along, and the information they'd found in Palm Tree's PDA and in Ramosa's laptop more than confirmed those suspicions. Just a few months before, Ozzi would have dropped a dime on this whole thing, would have called the cops at very first wind of it, thinking that killing a U.S. general was a very un-American thing to do, not to mention highly illegal. But he'd changed; he did not feel any guilt now. *Rushton* was the one doing un-American things, consorting with terrorists and backstabbing foreign governments. That bullshit *had* to stop. Capping him now was the most efficient and quickest way to that solution. Rushton with a bullet between his eyes might stop the terrorists' operations in their tracks. It might save hundreds of people on a targeted airliner. It might even save *thousands* if what the ghosts feared the second bus was up to—that is, some kind of mass destruction—was true.

Ozzi wasn't proud of the way he felt; he just didn't feel bad about it. That's just the way it was. Plus it was really Hunn doing the dirty work. If it was up to Ozzi to actually pull the trigger, well . . . he wasn't sure he could do it.

They waited for Rushton to come out of the house and onto the lawn. He finally appeared after five minutes or so. Those assembled for the barbecue gave him a hearty round of applause; many of them were privy to his secret agenda, too. Ozzi started the van's engine. If they were going to do this, it was essential they do it quick. They were aligned for a perfect shot. The rear of the van facing slightly uphill, the great background, and no heat distortion in the mild summer air.

"Get ready," Hunn whispered as he inserted the rifle barrel in the hole, the outside of which was further camouflaged by a spare tire.

Ozzi gripped the steering wheel tighter. His own family didn't live very far from here. He'd traveled this street many times growing up. But that was another thing he couldn't start thinking about now.

"I've got a good mark on the fat bastard . . ." Hunn said after a few moments devoted to the aiming process. "Good distance. OK, here we go. Three . . . two . . . one . . . *damn!*"

Ozzi had already braced himself for the sound of the shot. But no such sound came. All he heard was Hunn swearing.

"What's going on?" Ozzi hissed over his shoulder to the Delta soldier.

"His *damn* kids," Hunn hissed back. "They keep getting in the way. . . ."

Ozzi dared to look up on the general's lawn. Hunn was right. Rushton was there, but it was obvious he was going to great lengths to keep his coterie of kids around him.

"What's up with that?" he said. "You think the last place he'd drag his kids to would be something like this. Unless . . ."

Then it hit him.

"*That bastard . . .*" Ozzi whispered. "He *knows* we're on to him. He knows that we know. Palm Tree. Ramosa. Our guys preventing the missile teams from shooting. He knows it all and he figures we'll get around to popping him, too—"

". . . so he's *using his kids as shields,*" Hunn finished the sentence for him. "Can a human being get any lower?"

But it *was* a problem. They stayed in position for a few more agonizing minutes, Rushton moving in and out of range, always keeping at least a handful of his children tightly around him, and frequently holding one in his arms.

Finally, Hunn just gave up.

"Damn, this is no use!" he cursed, pulling the gun in. It was like all the air suddenly went out of him.

"I'm sorry, Lieutenant," he said to Ozzi. "But I just can't take the chance of shooting a kid. . . ."

They drove around Bethesda for the next three hours, keeping an eye on Rushton's house, watching for any new developments. They kept the van's radio turned on the whole time, tuned to the news. They'd heard the first sketchy reports that an airliner was almost shot down out in Denver—it sounded as if their comrades had stopped another Al Qaeda missile team from fulfilling its mission. But then came the rumors that the special ops team might have been killed in the incident. At the very least, their infamous big white copter had gone down somewhere near Denver Airport.

This was a blow; Ozzi felt like he'd been punched in the

stomach. They scoured the radio dial, hoping to learn more, but it was not to be. The FBI had put a news blackout on the entire incident, so all they heard was the same initial report over and over again. Finally, they just turned the radio off. They knew that the first reports from any kind of incident like this were usually wrong. And the copter crew *was* resourceful; they'd been to hell and back several times without getting singed. But even if it was a disaster and the copter team *had* all been killed, Ozzi and Hunn would still have to carry on with their own mission. Not to do so would make the whole enterprise a waste of time.

Rushton's lawn party broke up at around 7:00 P.M.; most guests were gone by half past. Thirty minutes later, Rushton's motorcade began assembling once again. Two more trips around the block and Ozzi was just able to catch sight of the general's limo plus the two Suburbans leaving his home. They were heading for the Beltway. A Bethesda police cruiser met them and provided escort for the short distance to the expressway. When the police car turned away, Ozzi steered the van up onto the Beltway. They fell in behind Rushton's limo.

It led them on a long rambling route around D.C., into Virginia, back to D.C., back into Maryland, and back to D.C. again. This was a security procedure, to lose anyone who might be tailing them, Hunn explained. He'd been trained by Delta in both sniping and stalking techniques, and his patience was longer, more durable, than Ozzi's. On his instructions, Ozzi stayed back in the traffic, at times barely keeping the three target vehicles in sight.

Finally, the limo and its escorts returned to D.C., Ozzi and Hunn still in pursuit. It was now 9:00 P.M. Thunderstorms were sweeping over the area.

Rushton's limousine and its escorts circled the streets close to the White House for another 30 minutes.

The traffic was brutal again, even for this time of night. They went up and down Pennsylvania Avenue no less than a half-dozen times, passing by the security barriers near the executive mansion, zooming by traffic cops trying to sort out the mess, and even traveling on the tail of a small convoy of Army trucks for a few blocks.

All this suddenly changed just about nine-thirty. They were driving along the reflecting pool, the limo, the two Suburbans, and Hunn and Ozzi about ten car lengths behind. Coming up on an intersection, the limo took a sudden right, going through the red light, while the Suburbans went left. Ozzi was at a loss for a moment—what just happened here? Hunn urged him to follow the limo.

Doing so meant Ozzi had to run the red light, too, which he did with ease. They were now right behind the limo.

"Something weird's going on," Hunn said. "Stick to him like glue."

This became a problem, though, as the limo began speeding up. They reached the center of D.C. again. The limo went through a red light on Connecticut Avenue, nearly demolishing a taxi. Ozzi went through the light as well, only to wind up in another traffic jam at the next light. They were right in back of the limo now, Ozzi's apprehension calming a bit when Hunn pointed out that just within this one block alone they could see at least a half-dozen more white delivery vans. They were blending right in. Or so it seemed.

The snarl had started inching forward when suddenly Ozzi heard a tapping noise on his window. He turned to see a D.C. policeman standing next to the van. He was a huge African-American guy his uniform soaked from the recent rain. A bright red ruby stud sparkled from his right ear.

"Just stay cool, Lieutenant," Hunn urged Ozzi, under his breath. "We're delivering flowers here, remember?"

Ozzi lowered the window as calmly as possible.

"Is there a problem?" he asked the cop.

"You boys just ran a red light," the cop replied. "*That's* the problem."

Ozzi was not unprepared for this. He was a resident of D.C., so he had his D.C. license on him. And as the van was a rental, the agreement came attached to the registration. But if the cop ever ran a check on Ozzi's license, God knows what would happen. After all, he was technically an escaped felon. The same was true if, for some reason, the cop wanted to search the van.

But before Ozzi could hand his papers over, the traffic started to move. Hunn saw an opportunity and interceded.

"Look, pal," he said to the cop. "We've been riding around with these flowers all day, fighting this traffic. Everything's dying and we still got a bunch of deliveries to go. The kid just got a little anxious, you know?"

It was not so much what Hunn said but how he said it. He did have a certain amount of charm and he could lay it on thick at times. In this case, the cop fell for it.

"OK," he said. "I'm too wet to write you a ticket anyway. Just watch yourself."

With that, he walked away.

Ozzi felt his shoulders sag in relief. He looked over at the hulking Delta soldier and smiled. Hunn smiled back, a very rare occasion.

"It's called the 'power of persuasion,' Lieutenant," Hunn said. "It comes along with being a bullshit artist."

At that moment, the traffic started to move for real. Ozzi hit the gas and they were back on the limo's tail again.

The slow-motion chase ended five minutes later when the limousine turned back onto Connecticut Avenue and pulled into an alley next to an old redbrick building. This was the Oak House, a very famous, very private club that was a favorite of Washington's elite, or at least those lucky enough to gain membership.

Hunn recognized the place and pumped his fist.

"There's no way his kids are going in there," he said. "I'll bet not even his bodyguards can get in."

And he was right. They rolled past the alley just in time to see Rushton emerge alone from the limo and duck into the club's side door.

Hunn was already looking at the buildings bordering the alleyway.

"Oh yeah," he said, clapping his hands together. "We got plenty of places to pop him up there."

They drove the van to a multilevel parking garage one block away. It was conveniently located, as its roof was adjacent to the roofs of buildings facing one side of the alley.

Parking the van on the top floor of the garage, Ozzi and Hunn quickly changed into their black combat duds, then took the sniper rifle, Ozzi's weapon, the armrest, and the binoculars and walked to the edge of the garage's roof. There was about a six-foot separation between the garage and the top of the building they wanted to get to. Hunn made the leap first, jumping with no more concern than if he were jumping over a puddle in the street. Ozzi, however, made the mistake of looking down between the buildings before he made his move. It was at least 50 feet to the bottom, with nothing but cobblestones and asphalt waiting below.

Ozzi knew he wasn't going to sprout wings in the next few seconds. So he backed up, took a deep breath, then took a running leap. He flew out into space like Batman, arms spread, feet together. He landed, hard, face-first on the gravel and tar roof of the next building over. Hunn just looked down at him.

"You might want to work on your approach, sir," he said drily.

They crept to the opposite side of the roof. It overlooked the alley and the side entrance to the Oak House. It seemed to be the ideal sniper's post. They could set up, get a good aiming point down in the alley, and still remain in the shadows. What's more, the other roofs around them were very dark, too.

"Perfect," Hunn whispered. "We might be able to put two into him from up here."

Ozzi helped him set up the rifle rest. A few loose bricks on the roof's artifice further stabilized the weapon. The thunderstorms had passed over, and even though the roof was wet, the sky above was clear and the stars had come out. Two fighter jets passed over, their engines sounding muted and dim, even though their navigation lights were flashing madly. Somewhere off in the distance, a siren was blaring.

The limousine was still parked in the alley below, its engine running. This led them to believe that Rushton might be in the club for only a short time.

Hunn checked his weapon over and over again. The bolt, the ammo supply, the armrest. He was a hulking individual, big hands, big head, big everything. But he handled the gun like a mother handled a newborn baby. Ozzi thought perhaps all this attention was a way to divert the fact that he was about to take a human life. A repulsive human life, but a life nevertheless. But to get that deep with the big Delta soldier was the last thing Ozzi wanted to do at the moment.

They lay in wait for the next 15 minutes, getting their clothes wet, not speaking, Ozzi counting the number of times the two fighter jets passed overhead.

Then they heard a thump and a slight electrical sound, like a fan had been turned on. Ozzi peeked over the edge of the building and saw the limo driver, only his hands visible through the windshield, adjusting the limo's air conditioner. This convinced them Rushton was about to emerge from the club.

"Can we go over the egress again, Lieutenant?" Hunn asked, never taking his eye from the rifle scope.

They *had* gone over their escape plan already, just after setting up the weapon. Once Hunn took the shot, they would quickly disassemble the rifle and shove the individual parts down the chimneys and water pressure pipes, of which there were many on the roof. Then they would shed their black camos and dispose of them in a similar manner and jump back over to the garage roof. They would retrieve the van and leave, all before the crush of police and security vehicles arrived, they hoped.

Ozzi had begun to recite their escape procedure again when suddenly they heard: *"Hey! What are you guys doing here?"*

They both spun around to see a cop walking toward them, flashlight in one hand, service revolver in the other.

But this was not just some cop. It was the *same cop* who had almost given them a ticket down near Connecticut Avenue about a half hour before. The guy with the ruby stud in his ear.

"I *knew* you guys were kind of queer," the cop said. "Who's delivering flowers this time of night? Dying flowers at that. . . ."

Ozzi was speechless.

But not Hunn.

"Shut your fucking mouth, will you!" Hunn hissed at the cop. Ozzi was stunned.

The cop was, too. So much so, his flashlight started jiggling.

"What did you say?" he demanded of Hunn.

"I said shut the fuck up —and keep your voice down," Hunn replied harshly. "We're part of General Rushton's security team. We weren't about to tell you that back there. But we're up here covering his flank."

The cop lowered his pistol, just a little. He looked like he believed Hunn.

But then he yelled, "Hey . . . everyone . . . are these guys with you?"

At that moment, Ozzi saw about a dozen heads pop up from the roofs of the other buildings surrounding the alley. All of these people were dressed like him and Hunn, in black camo gear. All of them were also holding huge rifles. He couldn't believe it. There were *other* sniper teams up here. Three alone were stationed on top of the Oak House. In fact, there were sniper teams on every roof around them but theirs.

Ozzi smacked himself upside the head. How dumb could they be? There was no way Rushton would have let his security lapse for such a long period of time. He'd just redistributed it to another place.

"They're not with us!" someone across the alley yelled.

"Who the hell are they?" came another voice in the night.

"We're absolutely screwed," Ozzi said under his breath.

But Hunn had other ideas.

Ozzi was amazed at how quick the Delta soldier moved.

One moment his huge sniper rifle was pointing down at the alley below; the next it was pointing right at the cop's head.

"We *can't* get caught," Hunn whispered to Ozzi. "Not now. Not here."

"I'm with you there," Ozzi replied.

"Drop the weapons and put your hands on your heads . . . now!" the cop screamed.

Hunn and Ozzi were frozen in place, but they made no move to lower their weapons.

The cop repeated his warning, shouting even louder now.

Ozzi noticed the cop was armed with a smallish service revolver. A popgun compared to what Hunn was carrying. One shot and the cop would no longer be a problem. Besides, Ozzi and Hunn had been in so many gunfights, so many close calls, in the past few months, they were ready for anything.

Except this. . . .

They could not fire on a fellow American. Especially an innocent guy like this.

"I *will* shoot if you don't lower your weapons now!" the cop yelled again.

"We're on a special operation!" Hunn tried again. But it wasn't working this time.

There were no more warnings. The cop fired his weapon, hitting Hunn right in the chest. The Delta soldier went down instantly, his sniper rifle splitting into pieces as it hit the roof.

Ozzi freaked. He began firing his own weapon, not at the cop but just inches above his head. The cop stumbled backward, falling on his substantial behind.

At the same moment, Ozzi felt the heat of other bullets zinging by him. The snipers on the other roofs were shooting at him!

*Damn.* . . . He had to think at light speed. There would be no copter coming in to pull them out this time. They were on their own. Going back over the roof to the parking garage was no longer an option. But they had to get out of here— and quick.

*Tracers.* . . . He had an ammo magazine on him that was full of them. They were his only ace in the hole.

He went down to his knees and jammed the "hot" clip into his rifle. Then he just started firing.

It was as if a fireworks display had suddenly erupted on top of the roof. Streaks of phosphorus light were flying everywhere, hot burning greenish red, going off in all directions. It was enough of a shock to the other snipers that most of them went heads-down for a few seconds.

When they looked up again, Ozzi and Hunn were gone.

One of the sniper teams atop the Oak House roof was just able to see what happened.

After dropping down to avoid the fusillade, they saw the little guy pull the big guy to the edge of the roof—and then *jump off*.

But Ozzi and Hunn didn't miraculously fly down to the alleyway. Instead, Ozzi somehow managed to drag Hunn, all 260 pounds of him, out of the fire coming from the sniper teams and over the edge of the roof. Twenty feet down was a very rickety fire escape. It was their only chance. Ozzi lowered Hunn down first, or at least tried to, as they both really toppled over together, the rusty iron of the fire escape ladder breaking their fall. Hunn nearly crushed the life out of Ozzi on landing; it was all he could do to get himself out from under the big soldier.

But no sooner had Ozzi done this when he felt himself falling again. It seemed for an instant that he was stationary and the rest of the world was moving. But then he realized what was happening. The fire escape ladder itself was going down, as it was designed to do, five stories to the alleyway below.

He landed hard, again, and then Hunn came down on top of him—again. Once more, he had to crawl out from under the monstrous soldier.

But at least they were on *terra firma*. They'd hit the alleyway not far from the limousine. Ozzi could still hear its air-conditioning cranking at high speed, the silhouette of the driver visible just beyond the windshield.

Ozzi saw the eyes and faces of the sniper teams and the

D.C. cop looking down at him. He let loose another barrage of blinding tracers, almost giddy that he'd made such a dramatic escape.

But then he looked down at Hunn and for the first time realized his chest was covered with blood.

# Chapter 19

Li was eating a doughnut when the sudden barrage of sirens began.

It wasn't like she was in love with the double-filled jelly. Truth was, it was just about the only thing left in the house to eat.

She was up in the master bedroom, as usual. The place was a total mess by now. The old bed had partially collapsed due to the weight of the team's remaining gear. And if anything, there were more wires—electrical, cable, modem—cluttering the floor, a real hazard in the nighttime. Still, the bedroom remained the center of Li's universe. She had even taken to sleeping up here—on the floor curled up in a blanket—not that she was sleeping very much anymore.

She was still praying over the napkin image, trying to find anything else on it besides the mysterious *74* with a circle around it. She'd had no further breakthroughs since the night before, though, when the negative flipflop revealed the number. No amount of polarizing could erase the remainder of the coffee stain; it had also defied any other kind of image-altering, photo-painting software she'd thrown at it.

But at least she was doing *something*. It was the only way she could cope in this very screwy time. The doughnuts had helped, too—their origin wasn't so much of a mystery

anymore, not after Hunn and Ozzi told her they probably
came from friends of Master Chief Finch of Cape Lonely
Air Station. Li tended to get the munchies when she was
anxious or nervous. And she was a lot of both these days.

She'd had the TV turned on all day, this while fraught
again with worry while Ozzi and Hunn were still out there,
somewhere, trying to assassinate the highest-profile general
in the United States. She'd seen the news reports on the
Denver near miss; she'd seen the footage of the horribly
twisted and burned Sky Horse helicopter. Her sense of help-
lessness was nearly overwhelming. She'd tried calling ghost
team west many times. She had three numbers for three secure phones to use for them. But it was no use. Each time, a
recording came back saying the phone was not in working
order.

It would be a disaster if they lost touch with ghost team
west now. The last conversation they'd had was when they
passed on the news about the threat in Denver and the location where the first bus would be two days later. This was the
bombshell information they'd found in Ramosa's laptop: a
detailed map of the first bus's route, the same as contained
on the Mann file, except this one had exact dates and times
and mileage between the spots where the bus was dropping
off its missile teams.

Ghost team west had received this crucial information
and had obviously acted on it in Denver. But what about the
pursuit of the first bus itself, down in Texas? How were they
going to act on that now?

With no copter?

No Eyeball Machine?

No communications?

If they were even still alive. . . .


It went on all day, the same news reports over and over. Now
it was dark, the old house was creaking again, and the fog
was rolling in. Li had her gun beside her, of course, and just
about every light in the house was turned on. But even these
things couldn't do her much good tonight.

Now it was the sirens that got her attention. A discordant symphony off in the distance. From the sounds of it, every police car in D.C. was wailing through the streets. The racket grew so loud, Li set her confection aside, went downstairs and out to her porch for a better look at the city below.

Indeed, it was pulsating with flashing police lights and even more sirens than just seconds before. This city, so quiet just a few days ago, was now alight and obviously in turmoil. Worst of all, Li knew—she *just knew*—that all the ruckus had something to do with Hunn and Ozzi. She could taste the trouble in the air.

She pulled out her cell phone and tried dialing one of the phones Hunn and Ozzi had with them. This was a huge security breach of course. But she wanted to hear one of their voices, just to know they were all right. But there was no joy here, either. A recorded voice just replied that the owner could not be located.

She put the phone away and had started back into the house when she heard the sound of tires coming up the reservoir extension road. She froze on the spot. Was this good or bad? She wanted so much for it to be Hunn and Ozzi, coming home, in one piece. But at the same time she knew they would never so conspicuously drive the van up to the house.

It *had* to be someone else.

She edged her way to the other end of the porch and looked down the road. She saw the outline of a black sports car making its way into her driveway.

She recognized the car right away.

"I don't believe this," she whispered.

It was Nash.

He pulled up in a minor cloud of dust and stepped out of the Viper. He was in full combat uniform and as handsome as a recruiting poster.

"What are you doing here?" were the first words out of her mouth. Not much of a greeting.

He looked self-conscious. And tired. And worried. And just a bit bewildered. He'd never been up to her house before.

It took him a moment to absorb the strange, Addams Family atmosphere.

Finally, he walked up onto the porch and tried to casually lean against the railing. Li didn't know what to do. She couldn't invite him into the house. God knows what he'd see inside.

"Sorry I didn't call first," he said finally. "I just came to say good-bye."

"Good-bye? Where are you going?"

Nash shrugged. "It's top-secret, of course," he began, eyes downcast. "But you know these people out west, these rogue characters? Rushton has put together a team to go get them, if any of them are still alive, that is. For some reason, they put me on this team."

"To bring them back as heroes, I hope," Li said, the words tumbling out of her mouth before she could stop them.

Nash laughed, in an ironic way. "Hardly," he said. "Just the opposite."

Li was stunned. "You mean . . . *kill* them?"

Nash shrugged again. "Those are the orders."

Li just stared back at him, not wanting to believe what he'd just said. This was devastating news to her, but she couldn't let Nash know that. She couldn't let him see it affect her. She had to stay cool—and learn more.

"Very rash procedures," she said. "And where are you going to do this exactly? Does Rushton know where these guys are?"

Nash just shook his head. "Well, it's a bit strange," he replied. "Rushton admitted he doesn't know where they are at this moment—but he seems to know where they are going to be in a few days. He claims he knows the time and location. He thinks we can just swoop down on them and let them have it. No rules of engagement. No chance to surrender."

Li could barely speak; the bad dream had taken another twist. But again, she tried not to let it show. "When?" she asked. "When is all this happening?"

"Sometime in the next seventy-two hours," Nash replied. "We've got to get some equipment together. Some security codes and things. Plus get some kind of transport out there—wherever we are going."

She was on the verge of tears but fought to keep her head. She had to ask him, "Why are you here, then? Telling me this?"

Nash inched a little closer to her. "Because I wanted to give you some free advice," he replied. "There are some very strange things going on, Li, and not just with these rogue characters or the terrorist missile teams. There's something even *deeper* going on. I don't know what it is. I just know there's a very weird buzz going around, and I thought I'd better give you a heads-up."

This was another surprising bit of news. The ghosts had found some files on Rushton at the bottom of Palm Tree's PDA that indicated something even more nefarious might be happening in Washington. But what could it be, beyond what everyone already knew?

At that moment, an aircraft flitted overhead. It wasn't a jet fighter. It was an MD-500 helicopter, a small buglike aircraft used almost exclusively by U.S. military special ops. It was heading for the reservoir and D.C. beyond.

"What is *that* doing up there?" Li asked Nash sternly. "I know only black ops use those kinds of copters. And these jet fighters going overhead all the time? What's going on?"

Nash just shook his head. It was obvious he was a troubled soul at the moment. "I guess that's what I'm talking about," he replied.

They just stood there now, with really nothing else to say. Sad words, something that might have been. Suddenly Li wished she were back at the Wizards basketball game—before everything got so crazy.

Nash looked into her eyes and she into his. He went to kiss her, but she turned it into a hug. Nash got the hint right away. Mission abort.

He stepped down off the porch. The sirens continued to wail in the background.

"I'll send you a postcard," he said, a grim joke. "That is, if they actually deliver the mail way up here. . . ."

He started back to his car, embarrassed now and anxious to leave. He brushed up against her Toyota.

"Hey, at least this thing is looking better," he said. "Did you get a wax job or something?"

She tried to laugh. "Or something, yes," she said.

He opened his car door but then turned back to her one more time.

"You're probably the smartest woman I know, Li," he said, surprising her again. "And definitely the most beautiful. And maybe I'm telling you things you already know. But just be careful—OK? It's important to me."

With that, he jumped into his car and drove away.

Li went inside and collapsed to the floor of her hallway. Nash's words were still echoing in her ears.

*Rushton . . .*

The treasonous general didn't know where ghost team west was at the moment but did know where they were going to be in the next three days. What the hell did that mean? How would he know where they would eventually wind up—assuming they were still alive—if they didn't know themselves?

She sank farther down to the floor. At this point, being hit by an iceberg would have cheered her up. She thought back to all her training, her classes in counterterrorism, psych-ops, deep-issue analysis. All the deductive reasoning that the professors had tried to pour into her head.

First conclusion: this probably had nothing to do with the first bus and its scheduled rendezvous down in Texas. That was happening in less than 36 hours, not 72. Nash and his team would be on their way already, if that were the case.

So if it wasn't the first bus, then what was it?

*Connect the dots,* her instructors used to tell her. *There's always a key piece in every puzzle. . . .*

Then, right out of the blue, it hit her: Rushton knew what the drawing on the napkin meant. It depicted some event that was going to happen. He knew the location and knew what was going to transpire there. But here was the kicker: He must have thought that ghost team west knew, too. And so he was going to send his triggermen to wait for them there, wherever *there* was.

Her friends were walking into a trap. A setup. And at the moment, there wasn't a thing she could do about it.

Suddenly she heard the most horrendous sound. A loud thump, followed by a mighty crash. It was so sharp and so unnerving, her pistol was out of its holster in a flash. What now?

The noise hadn't come from anywhere outside. She was sure of that.

It had come from upstairs.

What Li did next said a lot about her and how she had changed in just the past few days.

It was in this same hallway, on a night not unlike this, just last week, that this whole nutty thing started—this crazy patriotic haunted house story, with seditious overtones. Back then, that night she found her lightbulbs gone, she had walked through the house, gun up, trembling, confused, doing it but scared stiff. And still, she didn't dare go upstairs, weapon or not.

But she'd had enough of this. *All* of it. The spooky crap. This traitorous general. Her country turned upside down. She heard the noise again, but this time, instead of backing off, she went up the stairs in a flash.

Her gun was pointing this way and that, hyper, determined. But she caught herself after reaching the second-floor hallway. She stopped. She listened. The noise was coming not from the master bedroom, as she had first suspected, but from the bedroom down the hall, the place where she'd had that strange conversation with Ryder that night. (She had thought of that more than a few times in the last week.) She began creeping down the hallway, weapon out front, ears open, ready for anything.

The noise came again. A mournful thumping now, followed by the tinkling of broken glass. This end of the hall was particularly dark and gloomy, and this was the first time she'd ventured this way since that night with Ryder. It would have been the perfect time for a flashlight. If only she owned one.

She reached the bedroom door just in time to hear the noise once more. *Thump . . . thump . . .* followed by the sound of broken glass hitting the floor. Li steeled herself, then toed the door open.

Blood on the window . . . that's what she saw first. Smudges of it. Streaks of it. Splatter drops, everywhere. And two hands were reaching for her right through the jagged panes. And behind them the faces of two monsters, right out of hell, in muffled shrieks screaming at her to let them in.

It took her a moment. . . .

Then she realized what was going on. . . .

It was Ozzi. And Hunn.

And both were covered with blood.

She dropped the gun and rushed to the window. The clasps on the sill were rusty and stuck. The two men were hanging off the small roof just outside. This was the back of the house, which was really the front, which meant they had climbed up here, to hide in the shadows, dying, while she was talking with Nash.

She saw their faces now through the dusty, bloody window, hands still reaching for her like a real-life horror movie. Finally she got the clasps to move and the window flew open. Ozzi fell through an instant later. He was as white as a ghost. He was also covered in blood—but Li could not see any wounds.

He could barely speak. "Help him . . ." he was moaning. "Just help him. . . ."

Li leaned out the window to find Hunn halfway propped up against the frame, his legs out from under him. He certainly was covered with blood, and on him she saw a wound. A bad one, right in his chest.

Where she found the strength she would never know. But somehow she was able to grab onto Hunn and, with Ozzi pulling from behind, drag his huge hulk through the window. All three of them landed on the floor with a crash. Li quickly got to her feet, closed the window, and pulled the curtains tight.

Then she turned her attention to Hunn.

With his arms limp, eyes rolled back into his head, she was sure he was dead. And Ozzi, too, for that matter. All the blood had drained from his face. He was shaking, his eyes barely able to stay open. But then she realized it was Hunn's blood smeared all over him, not his own.

"What happened?" she was finally able to gasp.

"He was shot," Ozzi coughed. "Back in the city, while we were trying to get Rushton. He's hurt real bad."

Li looked out the window to the side of the house. "But where's the van?" she asked him as she started to tear away the top of Hunn's combat suit.

"It's back in town," Ozzi told her. "I couldn't get to it. The cops were everywhere looking for us."

Li stopped everything she was doing for a moment. Something didn't make sense here.

"But how then . . . ?" she began stammering. "How did you get him back here? It's at least five miles, uphill. . . ."

Ozzi just looked at her. He was on his knees; they were scraped to the bone. His face was dirty; tears were cutting through the grime. His fingernails were almost gone.

"I carried him," was all he said.

# Chapter 20

## Denver

After the small war at the campground, after the ghosts had killed all four terrorists and destroyed the remaining missile and scattered pig parts everywhere, they climbed down the cliff to the tangled wreckage of the Sky Horse, 200 feet below.

All four were crying as they lifted Gallant out of the pilot's seat. His blood was splattered everywhere, his glasses shattered against the steering column. The rest of the copter was a total loss. All of the cell phones, all of Bates's gadgets, their food, their water, their extra ammo—all of it gone. The only thing they found that was salvageable, strangely enough, was Finch's Revolutionary War flag. It was seared and singed but otherwise unharmed. The team had two of the three big fifties with them, as well as their personal weapons and ammo, but only because this was the armament they'd jumped into the campsite with. It was painful for Fox and Puglisi to relight the fire that had flared up around the copter only to go out following the crash. But they couldn't leave any evidence behind. So burn it they did.

About a half-mile from the bottom of the cliff there was a wide drainage culvert, dug years ago to handle the spring runoff from the Rocky Mountains. This was where the team headed first. Rows of trees and shrubbery lined both sides of the man-made waterway, which was all but dry now. The flora gave them cover from the state police helicopters that quickly appeared overhead.

Once in the culvert, Puglisi went on ahead; there was a housing development a mile south of the crash site. It was the only place they could think to hide, at least until night fell. By the time Puglisi returned, local law enforcement and the FBI were swarming all over the remains of the chopper, or what was left of it anyway. It was a miracle the team wasn't spotted in the ditch, just a few hundred feet away. Puglisi reported that he'd found a shed in the backyard of a house in the development very close to a bend in the culvert. No one seemed to be at home in this house at the moment. The trees were thick on both sides of the ditch all the way down, giving them cover they would need. The team quickly agreed they should try to make for the tiny garage.

Ryder carried Gallant the entire way. He refused to let anyone help him. He had his reasons for this. It should have been him in the copter at the time the missile hit it, not Gallant— this Ryder told the others over and over. He'd been "on the ground" for the last hit before the campground, that being the attack on the terrorists' boat off the water from Milwaukee, so it should have been his turn behind the controls.

But Gallant had never really stuck to the one-two schedule, so when it was time to jump off for the campground attack, as in the past, he told Ryder to go. And Ryder went, but only because he actually *liked* skewering the mooks. He liked shooting them to pieces and stuffing their mouths with bacon. He liked them to see his face, to feel his pain, before he sent them off to hell. But now this was the result. Someone should have been lugging him at that moment, Ryder knew. That's why he insisted on carrying Gallant on his own.

They reached the housing development Puglisi had scoped out with no problems. The law enforcement people, most of them still visible up on the cliff, seemed intent on searching the high areas in and around the campground. The ghosts had to lay low a couple times during this scramble as the state police helicopters roared over. But, luckily for the ghosts, no one spotted them moving on the ground below.

Climbing up the embankment at the bend in the culvert, Fox and Bates carefully cut an opening in the wooden fence at the back of the yard in question. They all managed to slip through this hole and gain entry to the shed, again without being spotted. Bates carefully replaced the wood taken from the fence, making it look as if nothing had been disturbed. Only when they were all inside the shed, among the lawn mowers and the snow shovels and the rakes, did they breathe easy, if just for a moment.

All except Ryder, that is. He laid Gallant down as gently as possible, then collapsed to the floor. Bates gave him some water. Fox lit a cigarette for him. Ryder's combat suit was drenched in blood not his own—it had all flowed out of Gallant. And Ryder's face was grimy, too, and his hands were cut and bruised; his shoulders were at the point of dislocation.

But he had done for Gallant what Ozzi had done for Hunn. He had carried his brother warrior away from the danger.

The only difference: Gallant was dead.

Jack Rucker arrived home from the second shift at the Denver Flats munitions plant to find the door on his backyard shed unlocked and slightly ajar.

He didn't give it a second thought. Parking his car in the garage next to the shed, he was almost too exhausted to think. It had been a long day at work. He was nearly 70 years old. He'd served as a security guard for the plant for almost 40 years. His shifts seemed to get harder to take every day.

He entered his small two-story house by the side door, nearly being mauled by one of his wife's cats eagerly waiting to be let out. Rucker walked quietly into his kitchen. It was past eleven o'clock and his wife had gone to bed long ago. She'd left him a dinner of meat loaf and French fries in the microwave. A note hanging from it instructed him to simply *push the big red button.*

He sat down at the kitchen table and started his coffeepot. The plant had been incredibly busy tonight. Bombs—especially aerial bombs—were a hot commodity these days, and that's what they did at Denver Flats. They made bombs. Rucker had been on the front gate since two that afternoon. Between the parade of government cars going in and trucks carrying bombs going out, it had been nonstop for nine hours.

He clicked on the kitchen's under-the-shelf TV, anticipating some Leno to go along with his meat loaf. But Leno wasn't on. Instead the local news station was in the middle of a Special Report.

It took Rucker a few moments to understand what was happening on the screen, this because when the picture first blinked on, it was showing a replay of the events of 9/11, specifically the second hijacked plane going into the second of the Twin Towers. For a moment, crazily, Rucker thought it had happened again.

But then he realized the station was actually in the middle of a news wrap-up, waiting to go live at the bottom of the hour. They broke for a commercial. That's when Rucker heard two sirens outside. They seemed to be coming from opposite directions; indeed, through his back door window he could see one police car approaching from one end of his quiet suburban street, with another roaring past it in the opposite direction.

*Dumb cops,* he thought.

He turned back to the TV. They were still in commercial break, and this was the only channel the crappy little kitchen set picked up. What was going on? Denver Flats was a national defense plant; the workers were not allowed to carry or listen to radios or watch TV while working. In effect, he'd been sealed off from the outside world for nearly half the day.

Now something seemed to have happened right here in his little community.

He fought the temptation to wake his wife and waited instead for the news to come back on. When it did, at first the news anchors missed their cue and were caught whispering to each other. Finally they snapped to. A graphic popped up in back of them. It showed an airliner going down in flames but also had a huge question mark superimposed on it.

They began speaking. . . .

Rucker sat there openmouthed, his meat loaf getting cold, as he heard for the first time of the events that had taken place up at Whispering Falls campground, not two miles north of him. The missile launch. The dead terrorists. The crashed helicopter. The government's admission—finally—that a kind of rogue antiterrorist group was roaming the country. Various FBI spokesmen were interviewed, urging citizens to be on the lookout for this rogue team, as if they were somehow just as great a threat (if not more so) as the terrorists, who, it was not mentioned in more than passing, might have tried to shoot down as many as five airliners in the past week.

The local news reporter came back on and said, "When asked why it seemed this rogue unit knew more about the terrorists' intentions than the FBI itself, a Bureau spokesman responded simply, 'No Comment. . . .' "

Back to the anchor: "And earlier today, the Governor's office authorized a request from Washington that the Colorado National Guard join in the search."

At that moment, on cue, Rucker heard a rumbling noise outside. He returned to the side window to see a column of military trucks heading in his direction. The image startled him. His quiet street, lit only by the bare street lamps, in what was supposed to be the dead of night—and now three big troop trucks followed by two Humvees, were piercing the darkness. It was the National Guard, looking for the rogue squad.

He returned to the kitchen and picked at his semiwarm meat loaf. But he wasn't hungry anymore. These events disturbed him. He still had memories of life during World War II and Korea, and certainly Vietnam and the first Gulf War. But things had changed so much since then. Terrorists running wild in the country. Rogue hit squads doing the job that the government should be doing. Where was it all going to end?

He wasn't sure why, but at that moment he looked out his back window. The shed door, unlocked and opened a bit when he first came home, was now shut tight. That was strange. . . .

He poured himself a cup of coffee, then went out the side door and into his backyard. Over the wooden stockade fence and across his neighbors' lawn he could see the National Guard trucks driving along the next street over. They had large searchlights turned on now and were directing these bright beams into people's backyards, into their cars, even splashing them all over the homes themselves. Again, this image of the military at night startled him. This just didn't seem like the America he knew.

He walked to the rear of his property—and was surprised again. The shed door was slightly ajar once more. *The hinges?* he thought. Were they getting too old? He usually locked the shed when not using it, if just to keep the raccoons out. And there was no way his wife ever came out here to open it up.

In any case, he was intent on closing his shed door now. A gust of wind might yank the damn thing off, and it would be expensive to replace. One step away from the dark opening, though, he found his feet frozen to the ground. What was wrong? He tried to take another step but couldn't. Helpless, he stared into the shed—and was startled to see a pair of eyes staring back out at him.

It was due to a premonition that he did not step into the shed, and it was a good thing, too. Because the next thing he saw was the barrel of a very large gun pointing right at his chest with a bayonet attached to it by nothing more than a dozen or so large rubber bands.

Just then, he heard the National Guard trucks turn the corner next street over. They were heading back in his direction. Suddenly all the backyards on his block were filled with the harsh searchlights. Rucker thought he was dreaming. This didn't seem real.

He looked deep into the eyes of the person holding the rifle on him and realized now there was more than one person in his shed. And more than one gun pointing out at him. He was still immobile; he was barely breathing. But his mind was clear and in that moment he knew that these people were the rogue team the government was looking for.

Rucker had served in the armed forces during the mid-50s. He voted Republican and considered himself a loyal American. But at that moment, he did something that surprised even him.

Just a half-second before the National Guard truck's searchlight swept through his backyard, he closed the shed door tight, shielding the people inside.

June Rucker woke up to the sound of someone whispering in her ear.

When she opened her eyes, the first thing she saw was a great wash of light pouring in her bedroom window.

"It's OK," she heard the voice whisper again. In the weird shadows cast by the light she saw her husband bending over her. "It will be all right," he was saying to her. "It's OK. . . ."

She looked up at him. She'd never seen him look like this before.

"What is it?" she asked. "Is the house on fire?"

He almost laughed. "No, my dear," he replied. "Something has happened. Were you watching the TV at all tonight?"

"Yes—the news. About the terrorists. And these helicopter people or something. . . ."

"Put your robe on and come down to the kitchen then," he told her. "There's something you've got to see."

Thirty seconds later, June was standing in her kitchen. Four very strange people were there, staring back at her.

They were dressed like soldiers who'd lost their way home. They were bearded, grungy, dirty. One was covered with blood.

June Rucker didn't need any explanation but knew exactly who these people were.

"The people from the helicopter? The ones the government is looking for?"

They all nodded. Jack was standing right next to her. They looked like Ma and Pa Kettle together. He nodded, too.

At that moment, the searchlight swept through their yard again. The fugitives all flinched.

"The whole world is looking for them," Jack said to her, this as June noticed all the weapons the men were carrying.

"I don't think you've exactly captured them, dear," she deadpanned.

"I haven't," he replied. "Nor do I want to."

He took a deep breath.

"I think we should help them," he said.

June stood there for a long moment; it seemed like a part of her life was flashing before her eyes.

Then she said, "I think we should help them, too."

They dug Gallant's grave in shifts.

Fox and Puglisi went out first to carve a hole at the edge of the property, next to the shed, ducking down whenever the searchlights went over. Then Ryder and Bates, Gallant's close colleagues since the beginnings of the team, carried him out and put him in the ground, covering him over and replacing the dug-up strips of grass to hide the spot. There were no prayers. No last words. The constant threat of searchlights prevented any of that.

June Rucker was a retired visiting nurse. She patched their wounds and made them all take some Tylenol. Jack Rucker made them a hot meal. Eggs, ham, and pancakes galore. They took turns using the shower and June taught them how to use her washing machine. While all this was going on, the police and National Guard continued sweeping through the neighborhood but only with their searchlights and not yet door-to-door. The team kept their eyes on the Rucker's living room TV, too, switching between CNN, Fox, and the local all-night news. It was nonstop reportage, but they wound up hearing the same headline over and over again: a terrorist attempt to shoot down a 747 had been foiled, four terrorists had been killed, and authorities were searching the local area for "others connected with the incident."

But each report left the team with more questions than answers, especially about what might be happening back in

D.C. after all this. There was no way they could call anyone back there, though. Even if they had a way to reach their East Coast colleagues, they had no idea what the security situation might be. They would have been crazy to try to make contact, even with a clean cell phone. There would be no way to know who might be listening in.

Whatever the case, the ghosts had to get out of the area, and quick. Not just to escape but to still somehow find their way to West Texas to catch the first bus in the act. They couldn't give up on that now. But how to do it? The bus thing was happening in less than 24 hours and it was more than 600 miles away. The old couple had been almost too good to them, and in return the team had told them everything, including the pending situation with the first bus. But how were they ever going to get there from here? It wasn't like they could steal a car. Or take some hostages. Or shoot their way out.

But as it turned out, June Rucker had the solution. She and her husband would hide them in their car and *drive* them out. They would help them get back into the mountains and eventually on to Texas as well.

And she wouldn't take no for an answer.


But why?

Why were the Ruckers being so helpful?

Psychically bruised and battered though he was, Ryder just had to know. He'd just finished his shower and climbed back into his now-bloodless combat suit when he approached Jack Rucker, sitting at his CB radio setup in the couple's basement.

Ryder excused the interruption and, first off, thanked him for everything he and his wife had done for them. The food. The bandages. Letting them put their comrade to rest, if just temporarily. And most important, for not turning them in.

The ghosts had received help throughout their crusade across America to stop the terrorists. But each time, that help, whether it be food or fuel, had been set up, in advance, by their invisible godfather, Bobby Murphy. Could Murphy's web of friends and influence reach down so far that it would include these two typical home folk?

Ryder asked Rucker right out: "Do you know a guy named Murphy? An intelligence agent type, back in D.C.?"

He was almost surprised when Rucker shook his head no.

Ryder had only one other question to ask then. "Why?" he said. "Why are you helping us?"

Rucker hesitated a long moment, then told Ryder to wait in the basement. He disappeared upstairs for a few minutes. When he returned, June was with him; she was carrying a photograph of a Marine in dress uniform. The frame was ringed with black drapery. She held the photo as if it were the crown jewels.

It was their son. Their only child.

"He was killed, more than twenty years ago," she said. "In Lebanon. When those heartless Muslim bastards blew up the Marine barracks in Beirut."

She started crying; her husband comforted her. The rest of the team had gathered around the couple now. They were absolutely silent.

"The government was wrong back then," she said softly. "Not the soldiers. And not the people supporting the soldiers. But the people in charge. The people in Washington. They had promised to look after my boy, to protect him while he was protecting someone else. But they didn't. And he died for it."

She dabbed her eyes again.

"The problem is, nothing has changed," she went on. "The people still support our country. They support our troops. They support the flag and what it stands for. It's those egomaniacs in Washington that are the problem—the politicians, the lobbyists, and the rest. And for years we've always asked, Why doesn't someone do something about it?"

She ran her finger along the edge of the photo's frame, then looked up at the ghosts.

"Well, maybe now, someone is," she said.

Jack Rucker hugged his wife; she played with a tissue she'd taken from her pocket.

"*That's* why," Jack told Ryder. "That's why we'll get you out of here safely, so you can do what you have to do."

It was a tight fit for the four ghosts, arrayed as they were, in the back of Jack Rucker's 1996 Ford station wagon. Using the sanctity of their attached garage, the four were squeezed into the back bay, a blanket covering them and their weapons, with six plastic bags filled with authentic trash laid on top of the blanket. Then the Ruckers poured about a hundred refundable plastic soda bottles on top of the trash.

June climbed behind the wheel, two plates of freshly baked chocolate chip cookies in hand. Jack had with him an oxygen tank, long unused, that June had left over from her nursing job. It had a thin clear plastic breathing tube, which he put into his nose. A plastic HANDICAPPED DRIVER sign, again from June's visiting nurse days, was hanging from the rearview mirror brace; it completed the scene.

They left at 6:00 A.M. The quiet neighborhood was not quiet any longer. Their development was crawling with state police search teams now indeed going house-to-house, asking for permission to search. It was hard to determine what would happen if a home owner refused.

They drove slowly through the streets, passing by more state police vans, SWAT trucks and cruisers, as well as local sheriff's cars. No one paid them any undue attention. But when they turned the corner leading out of the development, they found a small traffic jam of cars and trucks waiting there. The National Guard had set up a roadblock. Soldiers in full battle gear were giving each car the once-over before allowing it to leave.

They waited for five long minutes, until they were next in line. When it was June's turn to move up, she intentionally gunned the engine, with her left foot planted firmly on the brake. Much screeching and engine smoke resulted; the six Guardsmen manning the checkpoint scattered. June finally brought the old car to a halt some ten feet beyond the stop line. Everyone within took a deep breath.

The Guardsmen recovered and approached the car cautiously. June had her window rolled down as a young corporal walked up beside her.

"You poor boys," she said in her best grandmotherly voice. "How long have you been out here?"

"All night," the corporal said, his men now looking in the windows at the load of trash in the back.

June passed him out a plate full of cookies.

"Take these," she told the soldier. "And don't forget to share them. And if you're still out here at lunchtime, I'll bring you something then, too."

The Guardsmen all broke up. "We'll be here!" one cried happily.

"Anyone bother you last night, ma'am?" the corporal asked her politely, peeking under the foil at the cookies. "I have to ask."

At that moment, on cue, Jack Rucker began rasping.

"Just you and your damn spotlights!" he bellowed at the corporal.

The soldiers were startled and caught off-guard.

"I'm sorry, sir," the corporal said, trying to apologize. "We're just looking for some bad guys and—"

"I don't give a damn who you're looking for!" Rucker complained again, at full volume. "What is this? Nazi Germany? Iraq? I'm handicapped and I'm a veteran. . . . I don't have to take this—"

"Can we go now?" June asked the corporal. "He's always cranky on trash days."

"Sure," the soldier replied, starting to wave her on. "And thanks for the cookies. . . ."

June started to pull away. But suddenly another Guardsman yelled, "Stop!" He was looking in through the passenger window.

"Wait!" this soldier yelled again. "Don't move. . . ."

June froze at the wheel. The soldier indicated that Jack Rucker should roll down his window. He made a big display of it, but finally the window came down.

The Guardsman reached in—and turned up the flow nozzle on the oxygen tank resting on Rucker's lap.

"My dad uses one of these things," the soldier said, noting that the on-off dial had now turned green. "And you've got to turn it on, partner, if you want to be able to breathe."

The Ruckers glanced at each other and shrugged.

"Can we go now?" June asked the young soldier again. A line had formed in back of them.

The corporal hit the roof of the car twice with his hand.

"You bet," he said. "And thanks again for the sweets."

They traveled about an hour down Interstate 55.

The Ruckers had switched places, and now Jack was driving. June was ensconced in the passenger seat working the car's ancient CB radio. While the ghosts were sure their pursuers were monitoring all cell-phone activity, they weren't so sure about CB radio. This was an almost forgotten form of communications these days—but truckers still used them, as did many citizens, especially the housebound, especially out west. Jack and June knew literally hundreds of citizens inhabiting this CB planet.

June must have spoken with a dozen of these people during the 60-mile drive south, this while the team members stayed hidden in the back. They couldn't hear what she was saying exactly, but the tone of the conversations was definitely all business.

They finally reached a truck stop outside the town of Black Hills, Exit 199 off the highway. It was the kind of place that had three gas pumps and a diner that could seat about a hundred. It was called Sky High Diner. Its sign was vintage 1950s.

It was not yet 7:00 A.M. The early-morning rush of truckers had come and gone. The place was empty and would be like that until noon, when it would begin to fill up again. The sky was perfectly clear and really did look high. There was nothing out here but bare mountains and flatlands and highway. It was starting to heat up, the beginning of what would be a very warm day.

Jack Rucker pulled up not to the front of the diner but around the back. Here a huge semi was parked, diesel engine popping, a small cloud of smoke rising from its stacks. June got out and had a quick conversation with the driver. She gave him some cookies, then returned to the car, opening the back of the old Ford.

"Time to move, boys," she said. "And quick. This guy is our friend. He'll bring you to the next place you have to go."

The team rolled out, Jack and the truck driver watching either end of the diner for interlopers. The ghosts climbed up into the back of the semi's very long trailer. It was empty except for a few wooden pallets. The team took the trash bags and empty bottles with them; the Ruckers couldn't very well go home with them. June went into the diner and bought two six-packs of Coke. She handed them up to Ryder. The driver climbed back into the cab and gunned his engine. He was anxious to go.

Ryder looked down at the two oldsters. What do you say to two strangers who just saved your tail at great risk to themselves?

"No thanks needed," June told him. "Just a favor."

She reached into her pocket and came out with a medal. It was a U.S. Marine service decoration; Ryder didn't have to be told who it belonged to.

"Take this, please," she asked him. "And when you get to the last mile on your journey . . . when it might seem like you can't go another stop, take it out. Hold it. Think of my son. His memory. What he died for. I hope it will give you the strength to carry on."

Ryder was speechless. The rest of the team were as well. A helicopter flew over. The truck started to pull away. Ryder had just enough time to snatch the medal from her hand before they were moving very quickly. The two oldsters stood in the empty parking lot, suddenly alone, watching the truck go.

June waved and blew them a kiss.

Jack stood, back straight, shoulders proudly square, and gave them a long, crisp salute.

. . .

Thus began an 14-hour, 400-mile odyssey.

They rode the first semi out of the Black Hills and along the approaches to the Rockies, entering by Interstate 25. The constant grind of gears as the truck climbed the initial peaks was broken only by the thrill of the huge vehicle tearing down the other side of the mountain. The smell of diesel exhaust and burning brakes filled the compartment where the ghosts lay.

Their first stop was at a small town called Pebble Creek. Another diner, this one barely a log cabin, with gas pumps. Another truck was waiting here. This one was hauling wallboard. The team had no conversation with the driver—none was needed. They tried to squeeze themselves in among the huge slabs of hardened plaster, being careful to hide their weapons first. This truck carried them for two more hours, again a cycle of long, smelly climbs, followed by the hairraising joy of barreling down the other side of a mile-long slope.

They changed trucks again midafternoon. This switch was made at another tiny truck stop, this one deep in the forest of the lower Rockies. The transfer was swift, but the team spotted not just one but two helicopters flying over the area. A reason for concern? They were not sure. Copters flew over the Rockies, didn't they?

The third truck was an enclosed lumber hauler. It smelled of thick pine and sap, but because this was expensive wood, it was all wrapped in packing blankets, with plenty of extras for the team to sack out on.

This trip lasted another three hours. The fourth and last transfer took place in a highway rest area in the dead of night. This was another covered semi—no blankets, no expensive wood products. Just an empty trailer. It was the most uncomfortable leg of the journey but was also the shortest. Barely two hours later, the truck stopped and the team piled out.

They were in deep forest with nothing but trees and the

roadway. The driver pointed to a path leading into the thick woods.

"That's the way, boys," he said.

Fox looked at the path and then back at the driver.

"You want us to go where?" he asked, as puzzled as the rest of them.

"You guys need an airplane right?" the trucker said.

"We do," Fox replied for them.

"Then I was told to tell you just walk that way," he said, again pointing to a very narrow path. "And just keep going straight."

With that, he revved up his engine and with no wave, no salute, rumbled away, leaving them alone, in the middle of nowhere.

The first bus carrying the Al Qaeda missile teams would be traveling along Route 27 in West Texas early on the morning of July 3.

It was to stop at a rest area along the highway on the premise of letting its passengers use the bathrooms. At this rest area would be a sleeper agent who'd been living in Texas for seven years, waiting for this day to be activated. He would join the others on the bus, which would then pass through Amarillo, then on to Dallas–Fort Worth, where another missile team would try for another shot at another airliner.

Taken from the cutout Ramosa's laptop, this information was written down in scribbles by Bates during the hasty phone conversation with Ozzi just hours before the campground attack. It was scribbled because it was taken for granted at the time that the two ghost teams would be talking again soon. A very bad assumption, as it turned out.

Why this information was lying inside Ramosa's laptop, virtually unprotected, they had no idea. The laptop contained nothing further on any other sleeper teams. It was the only evidence they'd picked up so far that actually gave the movements of the first bus, where it would be, at a specific time, in a specific place.

Certainly it was a valuable piece of intelligence. But it

couldn't do the west side ghosts much good now. They were hopelessly lost, in the middle of the Rocky Mountains, or at least thought they were. They'd been walking through the woods in the dark for two hours now, not knowing what else to do. The path they'd been told to take was narrow and winding and the forest overhead so thick, it barely let the moonlight through. They were moving in a line, with Bates out front, followed by Fox and Puglisi, and Ryder bringing up the rear. The terrain was so screwy, and with very little light sometimes it was hard for them to tell if they were going uphill or down——a perfect analogy for their lives in the past week.

They must have looked strange, Ryder thought more than once during this trek to nowhere. The four men, heavily armed and armored, right down to their battle helmets and suits, walking through the dense woods. It was almost as if they were in another place, in another time. The Ia Drang Valley? The Huegten Forest?

It just didn't seem like they were still in America.

These and other strange thoughts had been bouncing around Ryder's skull for the past two hours, maybe as a defense mechanism against dwelling on more important things he should have been thinking about, no matter how painful they might be.

Gallant . . . Ryder couldn't count the number of times since the aftermath of the campground attack that when some kind of question came up, he'd turned to ask Gallant what he thought they should do, only to find his comrade was no longer there. The guy had been their rock. Mr. Dependable. A quiet presence that spoke volumes about his professionalism.

*It should have been me . . .*

That was the song going around Ryder's head now, a dreadful tune that wasn't going anywhere else soon . . .

*It should have been me . . .*

Another worry, though, the one he tried to keep *out* of his head, was almost as troubling: Dropped off in the middle of nowhere? Walking through a black forest for two precious hours? With not the faintest idea where they might be or why?

Had they been betrayed? By the Ruckers? By the truckers? By the people on CB planet? It would be a simple deceit if they had. Send them into the woods so deep, that even in summer it got so cold at night, they might not ever come out again. Or just plain get lost. These were the demons nipping at Ryder's heels, when suddenly, he heard Bates cry out . . .

*"What the hell is this?"*

The four of them stopped in their tracks. They were walking in a line with Bates out front. Never had Ryder heard the computer whiz sound so excited. A strange smell came to him just about the same time he heard Bates yell. Burnt wood. Suddenly, it was very thick in the forest air.

Bates had come upon a clearing in the woods. It was what lay beyond that had caught his attention. It was no longer a forest. It was the *remains* of a forest. The landscape for the next mile or so looked more like the surface of the moon than some place in the Rockies.

"What happened here?" Puglisi asked. "A bomb hit this place?"

"Worse," Fox said. "A forest fire. . . ."

They kept walking, though. Strangely, the path itself was still visible. But they were more careful, more aware, than just stumbling along, still not knowing where it would bring them.

It took them a half hour or so, but they finally found themselves back in the woods. Ryder at least was happy to be under trees again; walking through the devastated forest was one of the creepiest things he'd ever done. But they were in for another surprise, because up ahead was another clearing, and this one had not been caused by the scorched earth of a forest fire.

This was a lake.

And floating on that lake, glimmering in the dark, was an airplane.

A firefighting airplane.

Draped in American flags.

# PART FOUR
## The Hunn Solution

# Chapter 21

### Route 27, West Texas

Maria Chunez had never been on a Greyhound bus before.

She'd never had a reason to before today. Growing up in the border town of Mexiras, about forty miles south from Laredo, she'd stayed close to home, never crossing the border or even wondering what Texas was like. But earlier that year, her niece had moved to Oklahoma City, finding a great job right away. As a Christmas present, six months early, she'd sent Maria and her two young sons round-trip tickets to Oklahoma by way of Greyhound.

Maria had spent a lovely week with her niece; now she was heading home. At 35, this had been the biggest event in her life. She loved Oklahoma City; she loved the American people. But most of all, she loved the Greyhound bus.

It was so new and shiny and clean—and *so* pleasantly cool inside. It had a bathroom onboard, which was just astonishing to her, plus TVs, movies, and radios. All of the passengers she'd met on the ride up to Oklahoma had been very nice to her, even when Muneo, her youngest at two years, got fussy. She liked it all so much, she was already dreaming about another trip to Oklahoma City, same time, next year, riding on the big silver Greyhound again.

It was six in the morning now and the bus was heading south on Route 27. Many of the passengers who got on in

Oklahoma City had got off at Amarillo. Since four that morning, it had been just Maria, her two sons, two elderly nuns, and the driver onboard. Maria had slept well in her seat during the night, as had her sons. A rest stop about an hour before had given them a chance to get breakfast, from a vending machine, another novelty Maria had never seen before. Still nearly 20 hours from home, she looked forward to spending the day watching the landscape of West Texas go by.

And Maria was doing just that when she first saw the strange airplane. It was funny that she noticed it at all. She was fascinated by the vast cotton fields, with their red dirt and huge circular watering systems. She was staring out the window, marveling at them, when, off in the distance, she saw the red and yellow airplane. It was very low; that's what caught her attention. It was out to the east, off to her left, flying very fast and coming right at the bus.

Maria had seen airplanes before, of course, but not one quite like this. Its bottom was shaped more like a boat than an airplane. Its wing looked like it was upside down, attached on top of the plane and not on the bottom, as she had always thought airplanes were built. It had two strange things hanging down from the end of this strange wing. They looked like two smaller boats themselves.

*Why would an airplane look like a boat?* Maria thought.

She looked around the bus and wondered if anyone else could see it. But the nuns were asleep and so were her kids. The bus was just about the only vehicle on this part of the highway this early morning. She didn't think it was important enough to bother the driver about it, at least not at the moment.

But when Maria looked out the window again, the airplane had come up on them so fast, suddenly it looked like it was going to crash into them. It was so close now, Maria could see the face of the pilot bearing down on them.

At the very last moment, the plane veered wildly to the right and disappeared over the top of the bus. The noise of its two engines was deafening, though, enough to cause her two sons to wake up crying. Maria blocked her ears. The nuns woke up startled, too.

Just as suddenly, the airplane reappeared. It had turned over and was now riding right alongside the bus, flying so low, it was almost even with them. Planes were supposed to be fast, Maria had always thought. How could this plane go slow enough to match their speed? She had no idea. Its wheels were down now and it looked like parts of its strange wings were lowered and its engines were smoking almost as if they, too, wanted to be moving faster. But the rest of it was a mystery to her.

Maria thought for a moment the plane was trying to land on the highway. Maybe that was it. . . . But then she saw two small doors open on the side of its skin and two men appear behind them. They were dressed in black uniforms and were wearing helmets. They looked like soldiers, except they had beards and long hair and appeared to be disheveled. The plane was so close by now, Maria could clearly see their faces.

She could also see their guns.

This was frightening, because Maria knew about guns. And these were huge. They were hardly hunting rifles but more of the type she thought the military would use.

Again, all of this was happening so fast that just Maria and the bus driver were really seeing what was going on—and he had yet to react. The unreality of it all had overwhelmed him as it had Maria. She sensed he wasn't sure what to do, stop or keep going. The plane started shaking. It wasn't flying fast enough! The men inside crouched behind their weapons as if they were about to fire. She could see them taking aim. . . .

But then something happened, Maria wasn't sure what, but the men behind the guns were suddenly distracted. The plane started shaking again, and with an even louder roar from its engines it was gone. Climbing quickly, it shot off down the highway.

But the strangeness was not over. In fact, it was just beginning.

Barely had Maria caught her breath when she saw the airplane coming again. This time it was heading in the other direction, flying close to another Greyhound bus, this one going north on Route 27.

The weird plane was doing the same thing, somehow matching its speed with that of the bus, the men hanging out of the open doorways now on the other side of the plane, their guns in full view. Maria saw all this in the blink of an eye as the two buses roared by each other, going in opposite directions on the highway.

At that point, the man driving Maria's bus regained his composure. He seemed intent to keep on driving when he looked into his rearview mirror—and suddenly switched lanes. He did this with such speed, everything not tied down on the bus was suddenly airborne. They nearly tipped over, the bus swerved so violently. Maria was just able to grab her kids and hold on, thinking something had just happened to the driver, that maybe he'd been shot. But actually he'd just saved their lives. For not an instant later yet *another* Greyhound bus went by them, traveling in the passing lane as if they were standing still. It was going at least twice as fast as they, driving wildly down the highway. Had it hit them from behind, at that speed, they would have all been killed.

In the split second it took for this bus to go by, Maria could see its windows seemed to be darker than the bus she was on. And it looked like many people were aboard. But she was amazed, too. She didn't know America had so many Greyhound buses. They were everywhere!

Finally her bus driver pulled over to the side of the road. It was now obvious that something was very wrong here. Every vehicle on both sides of the highway had stopped by now, too—except the speeding dark-windowed bus.

Suddenly the weird airplane appeared yet again. It swooped down on top of the speeding bus and, without any hesitation, the gunmen on board started firing at it. Maria's bus driver was on his cell phone now, yelling to someone about the incredible events they were witnessing. The person on the other end must have told the driver to get out of the area as quickly as he could, because he threw the cell phone aside, put the bus back into gear, and started inching forward again.

But now there were many more cars stopped and pulled over on the highway, creating a small traffic jam at the crest of a rare hill. Maria's bus stopped, too, and this allowed them all to look out on the airplane and the speeding bus as they roared down the roadway, the gunners on the plane firing away without mercy.

Suddenly the speeding bus wasn't speeding anymore. It had slowed down so much, the plane had to accelerate or it would have crashed. Finally the plane pulled up and started circling the bus, which by now had swerved onto the median strip and slowed to a crawl.

"They've killed whoever was behind the wheel!" Maria's driver cried out.

Still the plane circled the bus, twin streams of red gunfire tearing up the vehicle in a most methodical fashion. Even with her untrained eye, Maria had to marvel at the person piloting this plane. And the more the men in the plane shot at it, the slower the bus went. Finally it just stopped altogether.

But the airplane dropped even lower now and continued firing into the bus. Suddenly came a huge explosion. Even though they were at least a half-mile away, Maria's bus was rocked by the resultant shock wave. The flash alone was blinding; it looked like a fireworks display was erupting from the back of the bus. Maria could see colors she never knew existed.

Although many people on both sides of the highway were now getting out of their cars to see these events, some even recording it all with their small video cameras, Maria's bus driver resumed driving again. They were about thousand feet away when they saw the airplane climb out of the fireball. It circled the devastated bus once more, then, with a roar of its engines, thundered away, heading west.

Not 30 seconds later, Maria's Greyhound passed the wreckage of the bus. It was totally engulfed in flames. Incredibly, there were some bodies sprawled on the ground outside its front door. Several people onboard had tried to get out at the last moment, but the airplane's gunners had shot them down as well.

As they drove by, Maria got a fairly close look at these bodies. There were four of them; two were still on fire.

All were dressed like soccer players.

# Chapter 22

## Virginia

Dave Hunn was a lucky man.

Not many people could take a bullet practically point-blank to the chest and survive, but Hunn did. Three factors helped him. Factor one: the D.C. policeman had shot him with a small .22-caliber revolver. Essentially a popgun, it was probably the cop's backup weapon, though why he was using it they would never know. Factor two: Hunn was wearing a Kevlar double-weave bulletproof vest given to him when the escapees first landed at Cape Lonely. Thank you, Master Chief Finch. Factor three: Ozzi had somehow stopped the bleeding from Hunn's wound—more of a vicious bloody bruise than a perforation—during his backstreet odyssey of carrying Hunn up to Li's house after the shooting.

Hunn was swathed in bandages now, lying atop the mattress that once made up the huge bed inside Li's master bedroom. His chest was black-and-blue from his collarbone to his navel. He looked like he'd stopped a cannonball and not just a 22. And this was his second wound in the last six months; he'd been shot in almost the same place the day of the Hormuz attack. But he was alive, and at the moment that's all that counted.

"Are sure you'll be OK?" Li was asking him now. "You shouldn't really move around that much."

"I'll be fine," Hunn breathed to her. He really felt that way, though he had no choice, because actually going to a doctor was out of the question. But both Ozzi and Li had received medical training as part of their runup for the DSA, and Hunn knew a little about patching wounds, too. This one would require bed rest and little activity at least for the next couple days.

Trouble was, they didn't have the luxury of 48 hours to just sit around and do nothing. Everything that was in force the night before, when he and Ozzi went looking to pop Rushton, was still in play today. If anything, the situation had grown worse. Rushton's security people had to know by now that someone was authentically out to get the general, to ice him just as Palm Tree had been iced. If anything, this would double the general's security detachment when he was out and about. And if the Rushton kids thought their days of shuttling around with their famous father had come to an end, they had another thing coming.

What's worse, everything the east side ghosts were trying to prevent or solve was still up in the air. An early news bulletin that morning told about a Greyhound bus being shot up on a Texas highway. It was a scant report, but it led them to believe it might have been the west side crew finally nailing the first bus. How they did it the east side had no idea. But this did nothing to solve the bigger mysteries here: What was up with the second bus? Where was it? What were the people onboard planning? What about this theory of Li's, bolstered by Nash's visit, that Rushton not only knew what the second bus was up to but thought the ghosts knew, too?

The walls of the master bedroom were plastered with printout images of the mysterious napkin in all phases of polarities, negatives, false colors, different sizes, and so on. It was such a silly-looking thing, but it was hard to stop thinking about it. Again, if it was inside Palm Tree's PDA, it must have meant something. But they found the more they dwelled on it, the deeper the puzzle became. It was always on their minds, but that didn't make any of it any clearer.

So, if the first bus was indeed destroyed, then the second

bus was now their number-one priority—that and still trying to put a tap shot into Rushton. And that's what Ozzi and Li were out to do tonight. That's why they were contemplating leaving Hunn alone.

"We have no idea when we'll be back, if ever," Ozzi was saying to him now. "And if we don't come back, at some point you'll have to make it out of here on your own."

As he was telling him this, Ozzi gave Hunn one of the clean cell phones he'd stolen from the DSG store in East Newark, this just before Hunn had beaten the owner within an inch of his life.

Hunn took the cell and said, "Don't worry; if it comes to that, I know who to call." Then he winked enigmatically and added, "In fact, I might just call him anyway. . . ."

It was a little before 9:00 P.M. when Ozzi and Li climbed into her "new" Toyota and started down the reservoir road.

They'd left Hunn with little more than the rest of the doughnuts and the TV remote. "Be careful out there," he said as they were leaving. "The mosquitoes are vicious."

Ozzi drove; Li was in charge of their weaponry. It consisted of their remaining M16 clone with about hundred rounds left of ammunition. They had no telescopic sight, no long-range capability, nothing in the way of night vision. They had no edge at all in any attempt they might make on Rushton. But they still had to go out and try, mostly because they didn't know what else to do.

They drove down through the suburban Virginia streets, quickly moving away from the dreariness of the reservoir road. The streets were not as populated as one might have expected on a pleasant summer evening. No doubt the entire D.C. area was still on edge, with so many rumors floating around about massive weapons due to go off, invisible terrorists everywhere, strange doings out west. Ozzi couldn't blame them for wanting to stay inside.

They got on the Parkway, heading into D.C. itself. The traffic was very sparse. In fact, for the last mile before their exit Li's Toyota was just about the only car on the road.

"This is weird," Li said as Ozzi steered onto M street—it, too, was nearly empty of cars. Ozzi and Hunn had told her about the traffic jams that had plagued the district for the last week. But now it seemed as if just the opposite was true.

"This is more of what it was like when all this first started," she went on. "When was it? Last week? Or a year ago? Or ten?"

If possible, the traffic became even sparser the closer they got to the center of D.C., down near the Capitol and the White House. They were heading for the EOB, as it was the likeliest place they thought they would find Rushton. But all they saw now was taxis and panel trucks.

They turned onto Pennsylvania Avenue and started heading inward. At one intersection that came up to a construction detour, Ozzi commented that the public works people had seemed particularly busy digging up the streets of D.C. this summer. Always very bad, it was at least three times the usual volume these days, strange for a place that normally had very little money to spend on itself.

The detour forced them to turn onto Olsen Avenue. All the streetlights were out here; in fact, for the next three blocks it was dark except for the ambient light coming from the few businesses that were still open this time of night. Ozzi knew his way around D.C. Taking a small side street two blocks down would get them back onto Pennsylvania, where they wanted to be.

This particular side street was an anomaly in D.C., as it went on unbroken for three blocks, very rare in a city that was laid out mostly like a wheel with a lot of spokes. Still in the middle of the streetlight blackout, he wheeled onto this odd stretch of road—and immediately hit the brakes. This alley was usually full of nothing but Dumpsters. But something was drastically different here now.

The alley was filled with military vehicles. Not just Humvees and troop trucks, of which there were many, but huge A1 Abrams tanks, too. And Bradley Fighting Vehicles, and LAVs and Stryker APCs.

"What the f—" Ozzi cried.

Li was just as stunned. "What is going on here?" she asked.

Again her thoughts went back to that night when she'd left the parking garage in tears, when she seemed to be the only one on the roads, except that column of Humvees and trucks that had rushed by her. Since then, from what she'd heard from Ozzi, the D.C. streets had been crowded with Humvees and trucks.

But this?

This was different.

Ozzi had pulled about fifteen feet into the alley before hitting the brakes. Now he shifted and started moving forward again.

They passed six massive A1 tanks, their crews lazing at the turrets or sitting on the snouts. With studied indifference the soldiers watched the Toyota go by. Many were smoking. Some were sleeping. One solider flicked his expended cigarette at the Toyota. Whatever the hell was going on here, it didn't seem too disciplined.

They passed more Humvees, more troop trucks, then more tanks. At the end of the three blocks, they saw the most unusual piece of equipment of all in this unusual stationary parade. It was a C2V, a tracked vehicle about two-thirds the size of an Abrams tank that was used for one thing only: battle management, especially coordinating ground forces with air assets. Unarmed but stuffed with all kinds of communications equipment, the C2V was usually found about a mile behind the front lines, coordinating the battle ahead. What was it doing here, with all this armor and personnel, killing time in the shadows?

Ozzi finally steered the Toyota out of the alley and back onto Pennsylvania. At that moment, two F-15s went overhead. The jets were more prevalent in the skies of D.C. lately than pigeons. But suddenly their appearance took on a more ominous meaning. Before, Li and Ozzi and anyone else who bothered to notice had just assumed the overflights were a reaction to the terrorist rumor scare, on duty as part of the heightened terror alert. But what if they were up there for a different reason? The sighting of the C2V command vehicle made both Li and Ozzi think the same thing.

"Could someone inside that thing be talking to those guys up there?" Li wondered out loud.

"But what for?" Ozzi replied.

There was no good answer for that. They continued along in silence.

The streets remained empty all the way to the area surrounding the EOB. Ozzi and Li did spot several Humvees parked in the shadows near some key intersections on the way, only deepening their growing concern that something very strange was happening here. It really didn't make sense. If the troops were in the streets in case of a pending terrorist attack, why were they staying in the dark, so out of sight? Why weren't they blocking or guarding the bridges? Or surrounding the key buildings and facilities? Al Qaeda didn't hit hard targets; they spent much of their time looking for soft, unprotected, unsuspecting targets, leaving the well-guarded stuff alone. So again, why was the Army staying hidden? Why not be visible, be high-profile, and act as a deterrent?

And those jets? What were they going to do if they weren't shooting down hijacked aircraft, an unlikely possibility these days? Were they going to shoot at the terrorists on the ground? One barrage from an F-15 could take out a city block in tightly packed D.C. There had to be a simpler, more efficient way to take out a few mooks should they suddenly be found on the streets of the capital.

And if the rumors of the terrorists exploding a dirty bomb right in the middle of the capital *were* true, again, why were all these troops sticking to the shadows? This wasn't a case of wanting to catch the perpetrators in the act. They had to be caught beforehand, or disaster would result.

None of it made any sense.

They reached the EOB, and by luck Rushton's unmistakable limo was there. Big, long, and black, with several young kids spotted playing on the sidewalk nearby? How could they miss it?

But immediately they both saw the security that had been put in place around the general and groaned. There were plainclothes Secret Service agents lined up in front of the entryway of the building; this Ozzi and Li saw as they drove by as casually as possible. They tried to take in everything they could, because they knew with no other vehicles on the streets except the taxis and delivery vans, all these people watching the EOB would immediately notice the Toyota if they began driving back and forth.

Standing behind this small army of Secret Service agents were at least a couple dozen uniformed White House guards, technically Secret Service as well. Every window on the front side of the building had an armed man in it. Every building on the block had snipers on the roof. Floating above it all were two unmarked Blackhawk helicopters, their huge bulbous noses identifying them as carrying high-tech infrared detection and perhaps eavesdropping equipment onboard.

Ozzi just shook his head. "The President himself doesn't get this much security."

As they didn't want to drive by the EOB again, Ozzi doubled back, returned to the Parkway, and headed for Bethesda. Again the roads were virtually empty nearly the entire way.

"This was the way my father said it was back in 1962, during the Cuban Missile Crisis," he told Li. "Everyone hunkered down in their homes, waiting to get nuked."

They got off at the first Bethesda exit and were soon cruising in front of Rushton's palatial home. But it was more of the same here. Secret Service agents everywhere—surely a violation of the Treasury Department Security Act—plus a battalion of Global Security bodyguards, including two small MH-500 helicopters hovering above the place.

But there was no military in sight. This further convinced Ozzi and Li that the troops in the streets back in D.C.

were there for a different purpose than just protecting Rushton's fat ass.

Dressed in black jeans and a sweater, as close she could get
to a combat suit, Li knew she was a poor substitute for Hunn.
   But even the Delta soldier would have admitted these
were formidable obstacles Rushton had surrounded himself
with. Things had been tight around Rushton before. But after
the attempt the previous night—tellingly not reported in the
newspapers or on TV—the traitorous general had obviously
doubled or even tripled his guard. There was no way Ozzi
and Li would be able to get a shot at him.
   They returned to the Potomac Parkway and started back
toward D.C., feeling very low. Secret Service, Global Security guards, God knows who else? That was a lot of people
watching over just one guy. . . .
   Li almost began to cry again. She thought of her parents
again, especially her father. What would he think of what
she'd been doing this past week? Would he think she was a
hero or a villain? Smart or misled? Patriot or traitor?
   It was really just getting to be too much for her.
   So, right out of the blue, she said to Ozzi, "I *know* how I
can put an end to this. Once and for all. . . ."

Dave Hunn woke up in pain. Strangely, it was not his chest
that was aching—it was his head. He had a massive headache,
the aftereffects of the trauma his body had received just 24
hours before.
   Hunn opened his eyes, taking a moment to remember exactly where he was. It was dark; the clock said 11:00 P.M.
Ozzi and Li had been gone for about two hours. Hunn wondered if they'd been able to get at Rushton or if they were
even still alive.
   Now he realized what Li must have gone through during
the nights he and Ozzi were out trying to turn the world on
its head. It was not easy, living with the anticipation, the
anxiety—and being in the creepy, noisy house certainly didn't

help the situation. At that moment he realized just how brave a person Li was.

Ozzi, too. . . .

But now what Hunn needed most was an aspirin.

He looked around the room, not really wanting to move very much. It was filled with the clutter of computers and their assessories, the walls covered with pictures of the stupid napkin drawing. But no sign of any aspirin.

He lay back on the pillow and thought a moment. Suddenly he was upright again.

There might be not be any aspirin here, but there was something in the room that could help dull his pain. He looked over the mishmash of laptops to a shelf beyond. Sitting there, all alone, a beam of moonlight coming in through the dirty window framing it perfectly, was the bottle of Thunderbird he'd bought during his quick trip up to Queens. Hunn let his eyes focus on it a moment, just to make certain it was real.

When he was sure it was, he finally smiled.

"Come to Poppa," he whispered.

Five minutes and a lot of hobbling later, he and the bottle of Thunderbird were back in the bed together. Hunn twisted off the cap and took a very long gulp. Images of his youth flashed through his mind as it was going down his throat. His first sip of this stuff came at the age of 12, not because he was a bum-in-the-making but because at three dollars a bottle it was in the price range of him and his schoolyard friends. It was the elixir of his early teens.

Now he lay back, his headache fading, his spirits lightening. What a spot he found himself in, he thought in a rare moment of introspection. Everything he'd been through in the past year or so——he couldn't imagine any Arab mook going through what he'd experienced to fight for his cause. Hunn knew someday someone somewhere might accuse him being a terrorist himself. An *American* terrorist. Even he did not like the sound of that.

But at least he could say that he was as fanatical about America and killing mooks as the mooks were about hating America and killing him. In fact, he worked harder at it. This terrorist stuff did not come easy to Americans.

His head was beginning to swim now. Everywhere he looked he saw the pictures of the napkin image Li had draped all over.

"That Dumb-ass thing," he spit again, taking another swig. A kid's drawing that maybe they'd been reading far too much into. Maybe they *were* ducks, he thought with another gulp.

He was feeling good now, but he couldn't just lie here. He needed stimulation to make this day of recovery complete. But what was there to entertain him in this gloomy old place?

The answer was actually right in front of him. Li's TV and its connected DVD player. Hunn's eyes locked on it and went wide at the same time.

What were the chances she had any porn lying around? he thought, the real Dave Hunn now shining through. As soon as the notion came to him, though, he knew there was no way. He wasn't sure Li even knew what porn was.

He leaned forward now and pushed the DVD switch and the tray came out displaying the disk Li had watched last— in fact, her only DVD disk, of her favorite movie. Hunn had no idea who Marlene Dietrich was, but he pushed it to on anyway. The music began, the subtitles popped up, and finally he saw the title: "The Blue Angel."

Nope, no porn here. This was old, scratchy. And German.

*Damn,* Hunn thought. With a title like that, the best he could have hoped for was a documentary of the Navy's Blue Angels aerobatics team.

He took another long swig of Thunderbird.

*If only,* he thought. *If only . . .*

Then he was suddenly sitting straight up again. He felt his body tingling all over. He looked at the bottle in his hand. The dark wine colors, the name so boldly written across the label.

*Thunderbird* . . .

He looked back at the DVD, in freeze-frame on the title of the 1930s movie.

*Blue Angel* . . .

He looked up at Li's napkin images. He tore off the one closest to him and stared at it. *Thunderbird* . . . *Blue Angel* . . . He looked at the napkin drawing. The Thunderbirds performed at air shows. The Blue Angels performed at air shows. Air shows had lots of airplanes in the air at once, going over thousands of people usually right on the tarmac or parking lots at air bases—places with no buildings.

Hunn just shook his head. The words came out of his mouth like someone else was saying them: *"Was this thing a drawing of a fucking air show?"*

He rolled off the bed and landed at Li's laptop. He knew next to nothing about computers or the Internet. But he did know how to get on-line, which he did in an instant, and he knew about Google.

He typed as quickly as he could: "Air Shows July."

The page arrived in a split second. He read the first entry: "Salute to Veterans Air Show." Thunderbirds. Nellis Air Force Base. Las Vegas. Date: July 4.

Hunn thought his head was going to explode. He didn't believe this was happening to him. All the brainpower that had gone into this napkin thing—would it really be a dolt like him who would finally figure it out? He took down another napkin image and held it against the computer's monitor screen. He concentrated not on the drawing but on the number Li had found in the lower corner. It was *74* with a circle around it.

*Could that actually be 7 and a 4?* Hunn thought. *Could the missing splotch of ink she'd been trying to decipher simply be a slash between the numbers, making it a date? Making it the Fourth of July?*

He sat back and slapped himself upside the head.

Just like that he'd figured out where the second bus was going and what it was up to.

• • •

The wind was blowing off the Atlantic.

It wasn't raining, but Ryder felt soaked to the skin. He opened his eyes. The stars above were spinning themselves into strange formations. Constellations he could never have imagined.

He got up on one elbow and looked around. The four old hangars, the dilapidated admin building. The runway with weeds growing all over it.

*Cape Lonely?*

What the hell was he doing back here?

He got to his feet, shaky in the knees. The winds were blowing fiercely. There were no lights anywhere he could see—except over in the Loran building.

He was immediately drawn to it, walking quickly across the cracked runway, the gale working against him. There was indeed a dull light coming from the strangely shaped building. He finally made it to the door and tried to open it. But it seemed as if a hurricane-force wind was keeping the door shut tight.

*Use the key,* a voice from nowhere said.

Ryder reached into his pocket and came out with a key he couldn't remember ever seeing before. He slipped it into the door's lock and turned it. And for the first time in this entire adventure, a key worked the first time. The door popped open.

With some trepidation, Ryder looked in to see there was a person inside, back turned toward him. But this was not Master Finch, doing his lightbulb trick again—or at least Ryder hoped it wasn't, because this person was wearing a red dress. Ryder felt his body freeze up. Since her death on September 11th, during those times that he actually went to sleep his beautiful wife, Maureen, seemed to pop up in his dreams on a regular basis. Always there, somewhere, always in a certain red dress, one that he could never recall seeing her wear before.

Now here it was again. Short, not frilly, plain except that vivid color. He could see an aura of light coming from behind, the lightbulb trick again, no doubt. But then the person slowly turned around . . . and it was not his wife in the red dress at all.

It was someone just as beautiful.

It was Li. . . .

Ryder woke up with a start.

He found himself looking up at the sky. The real sky, with real stars, not as many of them, but all in their proper places.

He was lying on the bank of a river, partially hidden by the branches of a cinnamon tree. An almost ideal setting—except for all that static filling his ears. It was coming from the radio on the firefighting airplane, bobbing on the water of the narrow river nearby. The noise was almost unbearable.

Bates and Puglisi were standing over him.

"Can't you shut that thing off?" Ryder asked them with a yawn, surprised that he'd actually fallen asleep. "Put a bullet into it if you have to."

The day before had been insane. That they'd found the firefighting aircraft, draped in flags as it was, seemed like the real dream. It was an unmistakable sign that the airplane was meant for them, was theirs for the taking.

Once they were able to swim over to the airplane—it was a CL-215, a Canadian-built craft known for its ruggedness—and climb up inside, they found all sorts of provisions waiting for them. Sandwiches, soda, instant coffee, and best of all cigarettes—gifts from the Ruckers' friends, the people on CB planet. There was also a lengthy printout of E-mails sent by these supporters and left behind by whoever had secured the airplane for them. They were messages of encouragement for the team, from people thanking them for what they had done, and urging them to keep on going. Some were so heartfelt, they nearly brought the team members to tears.

It took them about a half hour to get the aircraft in shape for takeoff; turning on and fine-tuning the navigation system took the most time. But the fact that it was an amphibian was another appropriate note in this strange opus. Ryder had certainly flown a seaplane before; during the Philippines misadventure he and Gallant had piloted a huge Japanese-made flying boat called a Kai all around the Filipino islands. While the CL-215 aerofirefighter was about one-fifth the size of the gigantic Kai, it seemed the people who'd arranged for it somehow knew that the team had been operating an amphib just a month or so before. Once again, it left them a little mystified that people out there almost knew more about the team than the team knew about themselves.

And though it might not have seemed so at first, the CL-215 was actually an ideal aerial platform for them. Even better than perhaps the Sky Horse might have been. Because of the nature of its work, the CL-215 had a low-speed capability that just did not exist in other types of planes. About 60 feet long, with a wingspan of 93 feet, the CL also had two huge tanks in the center of its belly, which could scoop up 1,200 gallons of water as it was flying along the surface of a lake, a river, or even the ocean. In practice, that water was then delivered to a forest fire, literally bombing the flames into submission.

This particular capability didn't factor into the ghosts' plans right away, at least not when they set off looking for the first bus. All they cared about then was whether they would have a place to set up their two remaining .50-caliber machine guns. As it turned out, the CL had two perfect locations, two doors, one right behind the flight deck, the other farther along the fuselage on the other side of the wing. By kneeling on the floor and using the safety straps as the temporary stabilizers, Fox and Puglisi were able to fashion two gun stations on both sides of the plane in no time.

So then they had a gunship of sorts. But what were they going to do with it? Luckily, Bates had saved the scribbled notes he'd taken down that night on the mountain. They gave the time and location of the first bus, just as ghost team east had found it on Ramosa's laptop. Once Ryder and Bates were able to discern exactly where they were—by tuning in an ordinary AM radio broadcast on the plane's communication suite they discovered they were in the Spanish Peak section of the lower Rockies—they were able to figure out roughly where they had to go.

The CL-215 had a big fuel capacity, and when they found

the airplane its tanks were full. Getting down to the Texas panhandle area, a few hundred miles away, was not a problem. Nor was finding Route 27. It was just about the only major highway that cut through the upper part of the wide-open West Texas landscape.

It was finding the right Greyhound that proved a bit hairy.

They all knew by now that in any kind of combat the numbers usually worked against you. It was not the ghosts' intention to tear up a section of Texas roadway or harm innocent civilians. On the flight down they discussed just how they would be able to pick out the right Greyhound bus. All they really knew about the terrorists' vehicles came from the Mann report, which said they were just like any other Greyhound, at least on the outside, except that their windows were tinted a little darker than a normal bus, this to mask whatever evil things were going on inside.

But telling the tint of a bus's windows while traveling at 150 knots 2000 feet above a stretch of highway was not an easy thing to do. When the ghosts arrived over the area, just as the sun was coming up, they flew in circles above the cotton fields until spotting a Greyhound going south, the direction in which the Ramosa information said the target bus would be traveling.

They zeroed in on this bus and were ready to open fire on it when Fox and Puglisi, at the gun stations, noticed that not only did the windows not seem so overly blackened but also they could see inside the length of the bus, meaning there was no hidden rear compartment. Ryder pulled the CL-215 away at the last possible instant, averting disaster. Just a few moments after that, they spotted a second Greyhound, this one heading north. Wrong direction, true, but they *had* to check it out. So they got right down on the deck again and flew parallel to it for several frightening seconds before it was determined that this, too, was a normal Greyhound, again because they could see all the way into it, front to back, not to mention the terrified faces of those unsuspecting people onboard, staring out at them.

That's when they spotted the *third* Greyhound—and they

sensed this was the real deal almost immediately. First, it was traveling at a very high rate of speed going south on Route 27. In fact, it nearly forced the first bus they'd buzzed right off the road. Second, when they got down close enough they knew it was the target as indeed the windows did look darker, so much so it was impossible to see into the bus. Plus, why would one Greyhound be traveling right behind another?

The key, though, was when cars and trucks traveling on both sides of Route 27 started pulling over due to the confusion being created by their flying antics—all but this strange third bus. That was enough for the ghosts. They opened fire on the vehicle and kept pouring it on even as the Greyhound tried to flee. When it was over, the four dead soccer players lying on the ground were confirmation they'd hit the right target.

Their nasty work done, a quick retreat was in order. They headed for New Mexico, to a border area known as Las Conchos, which was practically uninhabited yet had many lakes and watering holes where they could land unseen. They set down on a tributary of the Pecos River and stayed here the rest of the day and now into the night, all the time thinking, *Now what?*

Somewhere along the way, Ryder fell into a deep sleep, again a rarity for him. It was the combination of the strange dream and the storm of static that finally woke him up.

Now his teammates were hauling him to his feet.

"You've got to hear this, sir" Bates was telling him. "It's freaking important. . . ."

Fox was sitting on the riverbank nearest the tied-up plane. He'd written notes up and down both his arms. They looked like really bad tattoos. Ryder plopped to the ground beside him.

"What's going on?" he asked the DSA officer with another yawn.

"I'm not sure," Fox replied. "That's the problem . . ."

He explained that just a few minutes before, while he was

up in the plane's cockpit watching over things as the other three slept, the plane's UHF radio suddenly came to life.

"I heard this guy's voice," Fox explained. "It was strange because it sounded so calm. So together. He kept saying the same thing over and over, almost like it was a recording or something. I tried answering him, but it was as if he couldn't hear me. Or didn't want to."

Ryder was still half asleep, still getting his bearings.

"UHF radios can pick up signals from just about anywhere," he told Fox.

But Fox just shook his head. "This wasn't coming from 'just anywhere,'" he said. "And this wasn't just anyone. He knew *a lot* about us."

As proof, Fox displayed the notes on his left arm, using a flashlight to help Ryder see. They contained bits and pieces of information on exactly what the team had been doing in the past week: their missions in Campo, Chicago, and Nebraska. Times and places, all recounted in detail so the person doing the talking would be believed.

Ryder ran his hands over his head, wishing he were still asleep. Was this a hoax? A trick? Who would be using their names on this radio? Who would even know they were here?

He asked Fox, "Did you recognize the voice?"

Fox just shook his head. "No—but I have a good guess who it might have been."

Ryder looked up at Bates and Puglisi. "You guys hear any of it?"

Both said no. Like him, they'd been asleep.

A silence came over them.

Finally Ryder said to Bates and Puglisi, "Do you think it was really *him*?" He careful not to speak the actual name, a superstitious thing more than anything else.

Puglisi said: "Who else could it be? He's got a very long reach."

Fox could only shrug. "I've never heard 'him' before," he said. "So I wouldn't know. But this guy knew everything about us, although judging from his accent, I would have guessed he was just some rancher, calling from nearby."

Ryder looked out at the CL-215. Its radio was still turned on, still turned up in volume, in case the mysterious caller came on again.

"But would he actually know to contact us here?" Ryder wondered. "On this thing?"

Puglisi and Bates just shrugged again. So did Fox.

"No idea," the DSA officer said. "But in any case, this is what he told me . . ."

Fox displayed his left hand now. Ryder looked at the scribbled notes and exclaimed: "Wow, *that's* what the second bus is up to?"

Fox nodded soberly. "That's what he said. And get this: He also said that Hunn was the one who cracked the case."

"Hunn?" Ryder exclaimed. "Really? That's a bit *freaky.*"

"I hear you," Fox replied. "But he was dead certain about it, just like he was dead certain about what we should do next."

Fox displayed the notes on the back of his right hand now. They all read them by flashlight. They included things such as flight paths, times, stops along the way.

"Damn," Ryder swore softly. "When is all this supposed to happen?"

"That's just it," Fox replied. "He said *today.* The Fourth of July . . ."

Ryder was shocked. He looked to the east. The sun was just beginning to come up. "But that means we've got to get going, like right now!"

"Precisely," Fox said.

About 10 seconds of complete silence went by, each man with his own thoughts. Then, suddenly, they were all running. Ryder along the wing and into the CL-215's cockpit, Bates on his heels. At the same time, Fox and Puglisi scrambled back to shore to gather up their stuff.

Once inside the flight compartment, Ryder immediately started the amphib's twin engines. Bates meanwhile slipped into the seat next to him. Ryder had pressed him into service as his co-pilot lately.

"Do you think that was *really* 'you-know-who' talking to Major Fox?" the egghead asked Ryder now.

Ryder just shrugged as he revved the engines to full power.

"I guess we'll know soon enough," he replied.

# Chapter 23

## Las Vegas, Nevada

The Honorable J.C. Hood was running late this morning. He was usually out of his home and on his way to the Las Vegas central courthouse by 7:00 A.M. This was the time his limo driver usually picked him up for the 20-minute trip downtown. Almost 70 years old and a widower, Hood was a so-called day judge. His court handled anything that needed adjudicating during a normal day in Las Vegas—if any day could be called normal in Vegas. Petty thefts, to drunk and disorderly, to murder, the alleged offenders all came before Judge Hood first, who usually set bail, released them with a fine, or had them locked up.

But he was running late today because his driver, Eddie, had called in sick. This was very unusual. In the 10 years he'd been driving Hood, Eddie had never called in sick. True, it was the Fourth of July, but day court in Vegas was open 365 days a year. Still, Eddie would usually tell Hood when he was taking a day off. He hadn't mentioned anything of the sort when he drove Hood home last night.

So now Hood was waiting for a substitute driver to be found and then a car would be sent for him. Justice would have to wait a little while today in Vegas.

It was a pleasant morning; the sky was clear, the weather expected to be typically hot and dry. July Fourth was usually a big time in Vegas, with fireworks and a parade and more than the usual influx of visitors. But there was also the huge air show going on at Nellis Air Force Base, the sprawling military facility just outside town, and this almost guaranteed Hood would have a busier than normal day.

More than 300,000 people were expected to show up at Nellis today, though Hood had heard possibly upward of 400,000 might be on hand, as this was apparently going to be more than a typical air show. Crowds at these sorts of things were usually very well behaved. Still, Hood knew whenever there was a huge number of people put in a confined area, incidents such as drunkenness, assaults, and so on, almost always popped up. And even though the air show was being held on military property, any lawbreakers would be turned over to the local cops and eventually would show up in front of Hood.

Finally a car pulled into Hood's driveway. The judge folded his morning copy of the *Las Vegas Sun* and walked toward the vehicle. It was a Lincoln Continental, the same type of car that Eddie usually picked him up in, but oddly, this one looked more like a rental car than one of the luxury models from the city pool.

And not only did the driver's side door open, but the passenger side door opened, too. A pair of men climbed out.

There was absolutely nothing extraordinary about them except both pulled their suit jackets back to reveal they were carrying handguns in their waistbands.

Hood nearly wet himself on the spot. But the man closest to him said, "Don't worry. We are friends of a friend of yours. He just wants us to entertain you for a few days."

The man sounded so reasonable, Hood was suddenly not so afraid. Before joining the Las Vegas justice system, he'd worked undercover for the CIA for many years. He'd gone through things like this before.

But he was puzzled.

"My 'friend' wants you to 'entertain' me?" he asked. "How? Where?"

The two men smiled. "Out in Dry Springs," one said.

Hood thought a moment. Prostitution was legal in most of Nevada, but not inside Las Vegas itself. Dry Springs was a very small town about forty miles outside of Vegas. It's only claim to fame was that it contained the legal brothel closest to the gambling capital's city limits.

"So, in other words, 'my friend' has asked you to kidnap me?" Hood asked them.

The man who did most of the talking thought a moment and said, "Let's just consider it a short vacation."

"And who is this 'friend' of mine?" Hood finally asked. Throughout his years with the CIA, he'd made many "friends."

One of the men came close and whispered in the judge's ear.

Hood's eyes went wide at first, but then he just smiled and shrugged.

"For that 'friend,' " he said, "I'll do anything. . . ."

## Nellis Air Force Base

It was not even nine-thirty in the morning and already Captain Mark Audette was going crazy. He was an Air Force PAO, as in Public Affairs Officer. His job 364 days a year was to act as a liaison between the local Las Vegas community and sprawling Nellis Air Force Base, which was located just down the street from the famous Las Vegas Strip. He worked with families of personnel assigned here to acclimate them to the new environment. He dealt with neighborhood groups and business leaders close to the base on better ways to handle mutual concerns. He organized softball tournaments, picnics, awards ceremonies. If one of the base's planes went down or there was an accident of some kind, Audette would release the details and handle the media. As far as a military job went, it was easy duty.

It was that 365th day of the year when he really earned his stripes. The annual Fourth of July air show at Nellis usually took months to plan, and for good reason: more than a quarter-million people had attended in each of the last three years. This year, that figure might swell to 400,000 or more because a very special event was being planned: the Salute to Veterans Flyby. In the annals of air show history, it would be one of the largest events ever. "The Super Bowl of Air Shows" was how it was being billed. For this reason, today would be one the busiest days of Audette's military career.

Every year, the stars of the Nellis air show were the USAF Aerial Demonstration Team, much better known as the Thunderbirds. World-famous and admired, the T-Birds' red, white, and blue F-16 Falcons never failed to dazzle with their seemingly impossible aerobatic maneuverings. They would be appearing today, of course. But there was another treat in store for the multitude who would be on hand, something to get everyone's mind off the craziness of the last few weeks. A C-5 Galaxy cargo plane, just about the largest operational aircraft in the world, was heading for Nellis at this very moment. Onboard were no fewer than 500 veterans of both the Iraq and Afghanistan wars. Army personnel, Marines, Air Force, and Navy, many of these people were amputees or men who had suffered other serious wounds in those faraway conflicts. Many were also medal winners, heroes in the sand and mountains. This Independence Day, Nellis would belong to them.

In their honor, a huge flyby was being planned. It was to be made up of the aerial escort for the C-5 bringing these men to the show. The Thunderbirds would be the coleaders of this escort. Other combat aircraft from units all over the country—F-117 Stealths, F-15 Eagles, Marine Harriers, and Navy S-2 Vikings—would also take part. There was even going to be an F-22 Raptor, the mind-boggling sophisticated fighter of the future, on hand, as well as a demonstration model of the even newer F-35 JSF experimental attack plane. Three venerable B-52 Stratofortresses would also be part of the entourage, as well as a trio of B-1 Lancer bombers and three B-2 Stealth bombers.

This was a spectacular gathering of modern aircraft, but there was even more—and this was where the surprise came in: also joining the aerial escort, as a kind of mystery guest, would be the U.S. Navy's aerial demonstration team, the famous Blue Angels. It would be the first time such an air armada, including *both* of the country's air teams, would be flying together.

Coordinating all this aerial activity was a massive job that, thankfully, was being handled by someone else. Audette's role was more earthbound. He was in charge of making sure everything ran smoothly within the gates of Nellis. Getting the civilian spectators onto the base, getting them into the proper viewing areas, and, once the huge event was over, getting them back out the door again.

This wasn't just a case of opening the barriers and letting the throngs in. It had to be done on an orderly basis, the military way, with at least one eye on security. That's why Audette was already going crazy. He'd just come on duty officially—after working until four in the morning—and right away there was a problem at one of the base's four main gates.

It had to do with the large number of motor homes, RVs, and buses the Air Force was allowing onto the base for the day. Most of the spectators for the show would have to walk in from huge designated parking lots surrounding the front of the base, passing by a cursory security check at each gate. But the vehicles lined up at Civilian Access Gate 3—there were nearly 200 of them in all—belonged to handicapped drivers and special needs organizations, such as Indian orphanages and schools for troubled kids, as well as busloads of youth groups. To avoid any kind of discrimination rap or charges of nonaccessible facilities, the Air Force had decided to let these vehicles drive right onto the base.

But now there was a traffic jam of these vehicles at CAG 3. Why? Because the gate itself was not functioning. It was stuck in the down position, and the sentries manning the entrance didn't know what to do.

These were just the kinds of problems Audette did not want but knew he would get today. The good news was, he had a blank check from the base commander to do whatever had to be done to have the show go off flawlessly. And that's exactly what Audette intended to do.

He was now roaring along the flight line in an administration car, local base speed limits be damned, heading for CAG 3. Already thousands of people were streaming in through the walk-up gates; there were two dozen of these. At least 100,000 people were already on-site and hundreds more pouring in every second. Audette checked his watch— it was 0935. The huge assembly of aircraft for the veterans' flyby had been coordinated right down to the last minute. But the majority of the spectators had to be on the base before the show could begin. That was one of the cardinal rules of the show's organizers. Audette couldn't let a bunch of RVs and buses at the side gate screw up the timetable.

He arrived at CAG 3 a minute later, stopping with a screech. The three young airmen who were serving as gatekeepers were in a tizzy. They were attempting to lift the stuck gate manually, this after trying to disconnect the wiring system that made it go up and down. Nothing was working. Behind the jammed barrier, as promised, Audette saw the long line of RVs, motor homes, and buses; they were backed up for almost a half-mile. These vehicles should have been on-site more than an hour ago.

Audette jumped from the car and immediately took action.

"We're going to break it down," he told the three sentries.

They stared back at him, confused. "Break what down exactly, sir?" one asked.

"The gate," Audette replied forcefully. "We're going to break it in two and let these vehicles in."

The sentries looked at each other in puzzlement. Destroying Air Force property of any kind was just not in their vocabulary. The military made you pay for things you broke. But orders were orders. So, at Audette's urging, all four of them took hold of the wooden yellow-striped gate and began pulling on it. It took longer than it would have seemed, but finally the wooden barrier cracked, then broke, nearly sending all four of them on their asses. Audette regained his footing and then looked up at the driver of the first vehicle waiting in line, a huge Winnebago Deluxe. The guy behind the wheel looked about eighty years old. He was displaying both hand-icapped license plates and HANDICAPPED-DRIVER placard on his windshield.

"Welcome to Nellis!" Audette yelled to him. "You may now proceed. . . ."

The old guy got the message. He hit his accelerator and lurched forward, riding over the remains of the broken gate. The drivers behind him saw what was happening and com-menced blowing their horns in triumph. Soon they were pouring through the gate, one every few seconds, urged on by Audette's emphatic arm waving. He would have put an ordinary traffic cop to shame.

It took nearly 15 minutes for them all to go through. Some of the RVs looked the size of battleships. Others were barely bigger than pickup trucks. There were several old converted school buses, even an old moving van that had been converted to a house on wheels. Mixed in were many private luxury coaches, leased buses, and a Trailways coach carrying orphans from LA, as well as a couple Greyhound buses.

Audette waited at the gate until they were all in. Then he instructed the sentries to string some yellow CAUTION tape across the CAG 3 opening.

He would have a repair crew come out and fix the wooden gate later.

John Cahoon was driving the last RV in line.

He'd been waiting outside the Nellis access gate since ten o'clock the night before, queuing up, as many others did, ex-pecting to be let in at the crack of dawn. He was a big air show enthusiast. But this being a military affair, he knew it might not run as smoothly as most. By the time he actually drove onto the base, it was nearly 10:00 A.M., 12 hours after he'd arrived.

That was OK, though, because as it turned out, when he reached the designated parking area for RVs and other large vehicles displaying handicapped or special needs signs, he discovered that in practice the first were being made to go last and the last were going first. Translated: the military personnel in charge of parking the large vehicles made the first to arrive park at the rear of the holding area and then filled in the area from back to front. This resulted in Cahoon getting a front row space, practically right on the flight line itself. From his point of view, it couldn't have worked out better.

Cahoon's wife had asthma; this was how they were able to get a handicap placard, their ticket to this piece of asphalt heaven his motor home now rested on. He was driving a Ford Super Chief, also known as the Godzilla of motor homes. It was 57 feet long and, with its side extension pulled out, 18 wide. It had a living room, a den, a kitchen, two bathrooms, a shower, a washing machine–dryer combo, plus a smoking room where Cahoon stored his scotch and beer. Both he and his wife were retired Boeing workers, out from Chicago to see this show before going on to visit their son's family up in Reno, a few hundred miles to the north. Cahoon's wife liked to sleep late; he, by contrast, was a morning person. So by 10:15, just minutes after reaching this primo parking spot, Cahoon was already outside, with his grill fired up, cooking some midmorning brats and pounding down a beer.

A Winnebago Gold Arrow was parked on one side of him; it was a rowboat compared to Cahoon's rig. He could see the owners still inside, sound asleep in the driving chairs, tuckered out, no doubt, from the long wait in line. Too bad. It was Cahoon's way to make friends no matter where he set down. But the two people in the Gold Winny looked dead to the world. He wasn't going to disturb them. At least not yet.

On the other side, to his left as he was looking at the flight line, was a Greyhound bus. It looked almost brand-new and incredibly shiny, as if it had been sitting in a garage somewhere until today. The tires looked like they had about a hundred miles on them, tops. Even the exhaust system appeared unused. Cahoon's brother once drove for Trailways, the Dog's biggest competitor, so Cahoon had never heard many good words about Greyhound. But he had to admit, this bus was gleaming more than any Trailways rig he'd ever seen, even if its side windows were tinted to the point you could hardly see inside it. *Things must be good at Greyhound,* he would remember thinking.

As Cahoon watched, turning his brats and now working on his second can of Bud, the door opened on the big silver bus and four men stepped out. Three were dressed like soccer players; the fourth was wearing a San Diego Chargers T-shirt with the words I AM CHARGER MAN stenciled across it.

The men set up four chaise lounges, having difficulty getting them to unfold properly. Once they had their seats in place, they retrieved a cooler from the bus. From Cahoon's perspective, just 15 feet away, it looked to contain nothing but water, no beer, no bug juice. Out next came two small video cameras and a box that Cahoon guessed was filled with tortilla chips or Doritos or something.

*Mexicans,* he thought.

He finished his second beer and started on a third. The air grew warmer and the base tarmac more crowded. Thousands of people were pouring onto the base, many walking past the handicap area. Some gazed at Cahoon's smoking grill with envy, staring at his beer. He was wearing a garish T-shirt of his own, one that said on the front: BOEING . . . BOEING . . . GONE! Those people who got the joke laughed and waved. His neighbors next vehicle over just sat in the chaise lounges and talked among themselves. Cahoon could hear parts of their conversation, just bits and pieces, but to him, it didn't sound like Spanish.

After finishing his beer and his first brat sandwich, Cahoon was feeling very neighborly. His wife was still asleep; the PA announcer had just informed everyone they were still an hour away from the beginning of the show. What else did he have to do?

He opened up a fourth beer, even though it was not yet 11:00 A.M., and strolled over to where the four men lay on the chaise lounges.

They were surprised to see him but seemed friendly enough. All four were very dark-skinned, and their hands were rough and oily. Cahoon's eyes were drawn to the box they'd brought out with them. It wasn't filled with snacks as he'd suspected—but cell phones. At least a couple dozen of them.

"Nice set of wheels," Cahoon said, talking to none of them in particular. "Looks brand-new. . . ."

The four men just nodded.

"New . . . new," one said. He was the one wearing the Chargers T-shirt. Charger Man. . . .

"You rent it?" Cahoon asked.

"Long-term deal," was the reply.

"Sweet," Cahoon said, giving the huge vehicle the once-over. He wasn't aware that Greyhound actually leased its buses out to ordinary citizens, and these guys sure didn't look like Greyhound employees. Yet here it was.

"You folks from around here?" Cahoon asked.

"Reno," was Charger Man's reply.

Cahoon brightened considerably. "Hey, that's where my kid lives," he told them. "We're going up to see him after the show. He's a dealer at the Horseshoe Casino."

Charger Man laughed, though the three soccer players didn't seem to be understanding the conversation.

"Yes, we dealers too," Charger Man told Cahoon. "We big-time time wheeler-dealers."

Cahoon laughed. These guys were funny.

"What casino are you at?" he asked them.

Suddenly all four looked frozen. "Horseshoe," one of the soccer players blurted out.

"The Horseshoe?" Cahoon repeated. "Are you saying you work where my kid works? What are the chances?"

They all laughed—it was a helluva coincidence.

"Wheeler-dealers," Charger Man said. "Big-time in Reno."

But now Cahoon was getting confused. Maybe it was the beer, his third—or was it his fourth?—in about thirty minutes.

"You know my kid, then," he said to them. "Larry . . . Larry Cahoon."

The men all laughed. "He's a wheeler-dealer," Charger
Man said again.

At that point, Cahoon thought the Mexicans, or whatever
they were, might be having a bit of fun at his expense. He
drained his beer and threw the can into a nearby trash barrel.
The barrel was empty, so the can made a loud crash when it
hit the bottom. All four men nearly jumped out of their skins.

"Enjoy the show," Cahoon told them.

Then he walked away.

Cahoon checked on his other neighbors, but they were still
asleep. He grabbed another beer and went inside his rig, to
find his wife awake, sucking on her oxygen mask, watching
*The Price Is Right*. He told her about the people from the
Greyhound and how he now disliked them. She was a Christian, a gentle soul who had reined him in, in a positive way,
in the 40 years they'd been married.

"They're just friends you haven't met yet," she told him.

Cahoon drained his beer, thought a bit, then boozily
agreed with her. She was *always* right.

He pulled another pack of meat from the fridge and went
back outside. The four men were still in position, sprawled on
their lounges, but none of them seemed to be too comfortable.

Cahoon threw the meat pack on the grill and started yet
another beer while turning the barbecue. Once he had four
pieces done, he smothered them in Texas hot sauce, put them
on a warming platter, grabbed some paper plates and some
plastic knives and forks. Then once more he walked over to
the four guys in front of the Greyhound.

"Peace," he said. "Peace . . . and barbecue."

And there were smiles all round. Cahoon decided these
guys probably weren't of Mexican extraction. Indians,
maybe—from India, that is. But they all looked a bit undernourished.

Cahoon passed them the extra paper plates and utensils,
then gave each man a serving. They looked at their plates,
the pieces of barbecue drenched in sauce. This seemed
new to them.

"Dig in," Cahoon told them.

And dig in they did. At least the three soccer players did. They went full bore, obviously very hungry.

Charger Man approached his meal a little more cautiously. He carved out a large piece of charred meat, looked at it, sniffed it, then put it in his mouth. He gave it a couple chews—but then suddenly, violently, spit it out.

The next thing Cahoon knew, Charger Man had grabbed him and had a knife up against his throat. And it wasn't a plastic knife, either.

Cahoon screamed, *"Jesuzzz . . . man, what are you doing!"*

"What kind of meat was that?" Charger Man roared at him in near-perfect English.

Cahoon was both frightened and confused. "It's . . . it's barbecue!" he screamed back.

He would have thought this was a huge practical joke if the man's knife weren't beginning to slice into his throat. The three soccer players were suddenly frozen again, unable to move.

"What kind of meat?" the man screamed at Cahoon again.

"It's ribs, man!" Cahoon shouted back as the man started dragging him toward the door of the bus. "Pork ribs! That's all!"

It was only because Charger Man vomited on the spot that Cahoon was able to pull away from him. At that moment two more men came off the bus. They, too, were dark-skinned and wearing Charger Man T-shirts. They grabbed their comrade's knife and literally threw him up the bus stairs, one delivering a mighty kick in his rear end for good measure. Then they turned to Cahoon. They were nervous but trying to smile.

"We're sorry," one said in a thick accent, fighting to stay calm. "He's sick. Sick in the head. Been too far from home. Please forgive him and please keep this between us."

Cahoon felt the slight cut on his neck. He was shaking. It had all happened so fast.

"Yeah, sure," he said to the two Charger men, quickly walking back to his rig. "But get him some help. That guy's dangerous. . . ."

. . .

Captain Audette was finally able to catch a cup of coffee.

It was 10:45—with about an hour to go before the start of the big show. He had his walkie-talkie with him now, but it didn't want to shut up. A battalion of enlisted men, assigned to assist him today, were scattered throughout the huge base. They were calling him nonstop, one every few seconds, updating him on what was going on with the crowd inflows. At the moment, everything was looking good, a troubling note for Audette as he knew when everything appeared to be going good in life that just meant something bad was right down the road. But he'd decided to give himself a moment of relief with a cup of joe. It might be the last chance he'd have for some caffeine in a while.

He was in the Volunteers Tent, right up on the flight line. This was a place where spectators could come should they need information or directions or if they got too much sun or needed any medical assistance. It was a big white shelter with a huge American flag on top, very hard to miss in the sprawl. Audette was also carrying his black briefcase with him, and at the moment he was guarding it with much fervor. Inside was a document he liked to think was almost as secret as the U.S. launch codes of the day. It was the detailed plan for the great rendezvous of escort aircraft for the veterans' plane. Times, locations, altitudes—it was all in there.

Audette sat at an empty table at the back of the tent and dumped his usual five packs of sugar into his extra-black coffee. He'd already handled a dozen minor problems since the incident at CAG 3, but at that moment he was proud of himself because of the big picture. He'd been able to keep this Thunderbirds–Blue Angels surprise hookup thing quiet in the three months it had been percolating, this while it seemed that America and the world were falling apart. The hopes of springing it on the huge crowd would have been dashed if word had leaked out. But so far so good.

Audette had even had a hand in planning exactly how the great flyby would go off, how it would approach the field

and how the crowd would first see it. It was all timed to unfold in such a way that the spectators would immediately
realize what was going on. Usually air show aerobatics were
done parallel to the main runway, starting left to right as
the crowd faced the action. On Audette's suggestion, the
flyby would actually approach the field from the east, meaning it would pass *over* the crowd first. This way the throng
would see the Thunderbirds and the Blue Angels flying together right away. That would certainly get a rise out of the
crowd! Then would come the Harriers, the F-15s and the S-2s,
followed by the Stealth planes, the Raptor, and the F-35 JSF.
Next would be the C-5; the monstrous airplane was due to go
over the crowd at a heart-stoppingly low altitude of 1,000
feet. Following close behind would be the trio of strategic
bombers, the B-52s, the B-1s, and the B-2s.

It would take about forty-five seconds for all these planes
to fly by. Then as one they would go into a wide 180-degree
turn and literally escort the big C-5 down to the main runway, where it would land and taxi and the veterans would
come out to the cheers of thousands. Separate routines by
the Thunderbirds and the Blue Angles would follow. Then
they, too, would land and take their places with the other escort aircraft in static displays set up along the flight line.

It was quite a plan.

Audette drained his coffee and, only because his walkie-
talkie had suddenly fallen silent, got up to refill his cup. After
90 days of hustling, day and night, and with the knowledge
that today itself would be a series of little hells, it was reassuring that he could still manage to sit himself down and enjoy a second cup of sugar-overloaded *café*. For once, things
were under control.

That's when John Cahoon walked into the tent.

He was bleeding from the neck, but just slightly. There
was a medical aid station at the back of the tent, but after
Audette watched the injured man talk to one of the volunteers he was surprised to see the woman direct him over to
Audette's table.

"What the fuck is this?" the young captain groaned.

Cahoon arrived with a thump. "I want to talk to a cop," he told Audette.

Audette put down his coffee and pulled the briefcase back to his lap.

"Why? What's the problem, sir?"

"Some guy just tried to stab me," Cahoon said. "Back where the RVs and things are parked. He's in a big Greyhound bus. He freaked out just because I offered him and his friends some barbecue."

At that moment, Audette's walkie-talkie burst to life. The lull in the communications with his underlings was over. Once again, they were all reporting in, fast and furious. A small fender bender near an auxiliary gate was disrupting flow into the base. There was a power failure in one of the hangars where the Blue Angels' support plane would be housed during the show. The base commander had just been spotted arriving on the scene. Plus there was a small fire in a concession stand by another main gate. Audette gulped the rest of his coffee—then he looked up at Cahoon again. He noted Cahoon smelled of beer, this early in the morning.

"Where did you say this took place?" Audette asked him. His "knife wound" looked no worse than a minor shaving accident. A dab of tissue would have taken care of it.

"Down at the area where the RVs are parked," Cahoon told him. "You know, in the handicapped section. . . ."

Audette's walkie-talkie went nuts again. Porta Potties were overflowing; more electrical outages were happening; the base fire truck was having trouble getting to the cotton candy concession fire.

He looked back at Cahoon. "Sir—I'll pass this on to the police once I have a chance," he said. "My advice to you is to go back to your rig and perhaps move away from these people to another parking space."

Cahoon thought a moment, then turned on his heel and left, without another word.

The volunteer who'd first handled Cahoon and had overheard the conversation approached Audette.

"I'd be glad to go report this to the police," she told the Air Force officer. "If you think it's necessary."

Audette thought a moment—the local Vegas cops on-site were already stretched pretty thin.

"Only when one comes by," he finally told the volunteer, getting up to go. "That guy looks like he cut himself shaving—after having a beer or two. And even if he is right, he said the 'fight' took place in the handicapped section, right? I mean, how bad could it be?"

There was a place on the lower part of the Nevada-Arizona border known as Stinky Valley.

This was a made-up name; it was inscribed on most maps as the West River Wash. The valley was a couple miles wide and 10 miles long. It was surrounded by mountains and high desert, unseen from the nearby AMTRAK tracks. There were no highways within a hundred miles, no houses or towns, either. Few people outside this small county even knew the place existed.

It was called an oil storage plant, but this was a misnomer. In reality it was a depository for oil, gasoline, and other refined petroleum products that for whatever reason were never used, had gone bad, had got old, or were simply not refined enough.

These troublesome liquids would be quietly brought here and dumped, no questions asked. This scar across on the otherwise pristine if barren southeast Nevada landscape was highly polluted and had been for years. Yet due to legislation pushed through by the oil companies every few years, Stinky Valley was heavily subsidized by the federal government.

The centerpiece of the plant was a tributary of the West River, which had been diverted and dammed into a huge pool of water, not unlike the cooling pools used by desert oil field refineries. Thousands of gallons of the toxic petro-fluids were poured into this pool every day to evaporate, thus making at least some of them disappear.

The residue of this process leaked into the West River,

making it one of the most polluted rivers in the country. But in a state that harbored the national radioactive materials repository and legalized prostitution, not to mention border-to-border gambling, a heavily polluted river was no big deal.

The strangeness began here about ten-thirty on this Fourth of July morning. There was just a skeleton crew working the holiday, five plant employees in all, plus a couple security guards who happened to work for Global Security, Inc., the same firm that watched over General Rushton. They'd all just finished their morning coffee break when they spotted a strange airplane circling the plant.

It was a firefighting plane; they could tell by its shape and design. This put a scare into them, as they thought at first maybe a brush fire was heading their way. Stinky Valley was not the place you wanted to be if fire was nearby. If the plant ever caught fire, with all the flammable liquids on-site the resulting explosion would create a new, maybe even deeper Grand Canyon.

But the plant employees were able to quickly check their surroundings via the many video surveillance cameras bordering the place. There was no fire anywhere near them, no smoke, nothing, So why then was a firefighting plane circling above?

The company that ran Stinky Valley was headquartered in Houston. A phone call was immediately made to home base asking if this was a company plane of some sort. The answer came back quickly as no. By that time, though, the airplane was obviously getting lower.

As the people in the plant's high-tower control room watched, the plane came right down onto the evaporation pool and, in an expert maneuver, started skimming along its surface, scooping up hundreds of gallons of the oily water in its underbelly holding tanks.

The plant employees couldn't believe what they were seeing. When one of the security guards made a move to unleash his sidearm, a plant employee made sure the man's gun stayed in his holster.

"Are you nuts?" he reprimanded the guard. "If you hit that thing, it will go up like a bomb and so will we."

It was too late anyway, as the plane had streaked by them and was now starting to climb out, its belly full of a liquid that was more gasoline than water. In fact, it was so flammable, some of the spray that had been kicked up by the scooping technique had gone into the airplane's two engines and now both of them were smoking fiercely.

"I don't know what forest fire that thing is going to fight," one employee said. "But if he drops that stuff on it, the whole state will go up."

As the plane quickly departed, one of the security guards detached himself from the rest, took out a special cell phone, and punched in a secret number.

"Put me through to Rushton's detail," he said harshly. "Something just happened out here that he might want to know about. . . ."

Thirty-five miles north of Nellis Air Force Base, there was a section of desert known as the Nevada Special Weapons Testing Range. It was a highly restricted airspace that included the skies above the top-secret Groom Lake aircraft testing facility better known as Area 51, as well as a number of other secret bases located much deeper in the Nevada desert.

These no-fly skies were the ideal place for the airplanes taking place in the veterans' flyby to assemble. At about 11:20 A.M., a confluence of aircraft began circling in a lower portion of the range.

The big bombers had arrived first: the B-52s from Omaha, the B-1s from Texas, the B-2s from Missouri, then the F-15s, F-117s, the Raptor and the JSF, flying in from Edwards AFB in California. Next came the Navy planes, the S-2 Viking carrier bombers, and then the Marine Harriers. The Thunderbirds showed up absolutely on time, as did the Blue Angels, flying in from Florida. The small air fleet had been loitering over the southern part of the weapons range for a few minutes when finally the huge C-5 Galaxy appeared. It, too, was on time, after picking up veterans in such diverse places as Boston, Maryland, Chicago, and Dallas. It joined the merry-go-round of aircraft at 15,000 feet.

There came now about five minutes of everyone getting on the same radio link. Unencumbered communications were essential if the massive flyby was going to be both safe and successful. Still circling, the various aircraft all switched to a preassigned VHF radio frequency, which had been designated Show Channel One. Each pilot had to check in on this channel and make sure that he could hear every other pilot.

This done, the pilots then did an instrument check with the emphasis on powering down any flight controls that would not be needed during their approach and eventual landing at Nellis. Of course things such as navigation suites, collision avoidance systems, and backup communication sets were kept on. But there was no need for any of the planes to run their air defense radar or electronic countermeasure systems for what they were about to do. The show planes—the T-Birds and the Blue Angels—didn't have these kinds of combat systems onboard their planes anyway, but many of the other entries did. Many of these devices were now shut down.

It was 1135 hours when the C-5's pilot got the call from Nellis. The crowds were in place; the sky above the base was empty. The flyby group was cleared to head in. The pilot confirmed the message with the other escort planes; then looked back into the gigantic cargo hold behind him. There were 504 passengers back there, a huge number even for the mammoth C-5. They were sitting in both seats that lined the inner walls of the huge cabin and special "movie-house" seating that had been installed throughout the big plane.

Most of the veterans were really just young kids—many were barely 20 years old, and few were over 30. They were all wearing their dress uniforms, more Army personnel than anyone else. Many were missing arms or fingers, but many more were missing legs, the telltale signature of a violent wound suffered in wars where the enemy was essentially too cowardly to stand and fight so just left roadside bombs behind instead. The pilot felt a bittersweet tinge in his throat. *These guys are the real heroes,* he thought. *This should be their day.*

As one now, the air armada turned east, where they would fly for just a few minutes before turning around back to the west, lining them up perfectly for their final approach to Nellis.

Back at the air show, the PA announcer was going through a long list of people whom the organizers wanted to thank. This was the last announcement that had to be made before the flyby flight showed up. There were now more than 420,000 people on the base, an incredible number. They were spread along three miles of extended flight line in taped-off designated viewing areas, a pattern of crowd control reminiscent of New Year's Eve in Times Square. Most people brought lawn chairs or cushions on which to sit. Many brought tents and grills and coolers. The crowd really was a cross section of America, too: young, old, black, brown, and white. Lots of retirees, lots of couples. Lots of kids. And there really wasn't a bad seat in the house.

The PA announcer, reading now from a script written in part by Captain Audette, began the run-up to the flyby's arrival. He was doing this from the Nellis main control tower, this while a bevy of Air Force air traffic control personnel were keeping track of the veterans' flight as it approached the base at a leisurely 150 knots. The PA announcer reminded the crowd of the sacrifices made by everyone in the U.S. military these troubling days. He asked that people support the armed services and keep them in their prayers. Then asked for a moment of silence for servicepeople killed in the line of duty over the past few years.

Then, with the soaring voice of a carnival barker, the PA announcer began the buildup for the incoming veterans' flight. Words such as: "never before seen," "historic," and "special surprise" echoed across the base.

Finally, the big moment came. The PA announcer told the crowd to look off to the east, to "that big mountain over there, and be prepared to see something you may never have seen before or ever see again. . . ."

The huge crowd did as instructed; all eyes now were looking east, ready for what they'd been promised would be a vast aeronautical spectacle. But instead of seeing a stately formation of both the latest and venerable U.S. military aircraft, they were shocked to see instead a lone firefighting airplane, painted bright yellow and red, approaching with its two engines smoking badly.

Some in the crowd gasped, but others just laughed. The plane looked like it was out of control, just making it over the top of the mountain. Many on hand thought this was part of the show. Wacky-style private aerobatic acts were not unheard of at events like this.

But there was great panic in the Nellis control tower. This plane had somehow stolen in under their radar net, undoubtedly by flying so low, and no one had any idea how it got where it was and what its intentions were. But it was definitely *not* part of the show.

The first thing the control tower people did was warn the veterans' flight approaching the base, saying they had a "situation unknown" at the moment. But at the same time, the control tower did not tell the flight to disperse. Too much effort and planning had gone into this; plus it was safer to keep the flyby flight together.

So instead, the flight was told to reduce its combined airspeed to just 110 knots, delaying their arrival by just 30 seconds, but keep on coming.

It took just 10 seconds for the firefighting plane to cross the runway and roar over the crowd. It was flying very low, no more than 300 feet off the deck. Its engines were emitting twin trails of inky black smoke and backfiring wildly.

Some people cheered as the plane flew over them; many

believed this was the surprise act promised them, as lame as it might be. Meanwhile military officials on the ground didn't have the slightest idea what to do. There were many unusual civilian planes already on the ground at the base, making up a lot of the static show that would be open to the public once the aerobatics above the base were over. Could this be a late arrival for the civilian part of the show? The Nellis tower crew scrambled for their entry lists, seeing if a firefighting CL-215 plane was among the exhibitors. But even if this was so, why had the plane approached without any contact with the tower?

Meanwhile the red and yellow airplane started a low, ragged circle. It seemed intent on orbiting the area where the RVs and motor homes were parked. It started buzzing this particular area with such ferocity, that some spectators were getting concerned and began hurrying out of the area.

Among them was Captain Audette. He was standing outside the volunteer tent, looking back at the RV holding area, watching the weird plane continuously dive on the motor homes and buses. Its engines now seemed to be on fire; they were trailing so much smoke.

Audette knew this act was definitely *not* part of the show—and now many people around him were getting this message as well. What was moments before just a trickle became a stream of worried spectators, grabbing what they could carry and leaving the area on foot. Not quite a panic yet, but possibly just seconds away from one.

Audette couldn't take his eyes off the screwy airplane. *What was it doing?*

Then suddenly he saw what apparently few others had. The CL-215 was a mess. It was dirty and oily and ragged. But there was something hanging out of its front hatch. What was it? Audette wondered as the plane continued its dangerous antics. Was that a Revolutionary War flag?

Then it suddenly all came together for him.

That flag. The rogue team. . . .

"I thought these guys were dead!" he yelled to no one in particular.

And what the hell were they doing? They continued buzzing the RV section now, and as a result people were running in panic for sure. Suddenly Audette realized this was a good thing. He started barking orders to anyone nearby—airmen, volunteers, Vegas cops—telling them to get as many people out of the RV holding area as possible.

The CL-215 went over once again; now it was barely 50 feet off the ground. That's when Audette realized the fire-fighting plane was actually concentrating on one vehicle in the front row of the holding area. Again something else suddenly made sense.

The people the guy had complained about . . . in the big Greyhound bus. . . .

In a heartbeat, just one word popped into Audette's mind, this just as the veterans' flight was approaching the field again.

*Terrorists. . . .*

The CL-215 was out of control.

Ryder was doing his best to keep the airplane airborne, but he knew it was a losing battle.

It had to do with the toxic substances they'd sucked into the engines during their water-scooping adventure back in Stinky Valley. They'd been directed there by the mysterious radio message, well aware that what they would be taking into their belly tanks was not Perrier water but a highly flammable concoction. That was the whole idea. It was the closest thing resembling a bomb that anyone could think of on such short notice.

It was the first kind of water-scooping maneuver Ryder had ever done of course. He wished more than once that Gallant was there with him; he would have made it look easy. Hitting the top of the evaporation pool, the plane not only sucked up the gas-laden water into its engines; it also took on the 1,200 gallons unevenly. There was more of the combustible water in one tank than the other, making the plane dangerously unbalanced. Combined with the engine problems, it was amazing that they'd made it more than a few miles beyond Stinky Valley, never mind all the way to Vegas.

But here they were, and now they had one last job to do before they crashed.

They could see the Greyhound bus down below them— the same one described by Mann way back when. It was shiny and gleaming and new—and once you were looking for it, it stood out as if it had a spotlight on it. It looked very out of place.

But there was a convergence of events happening now that the ghosts had no control over. The veterans' flight was coming in, and it appeared it was going to do its fly-over no matter what. Of course, this had been the scenario the terrorists had wanted all along. Sneak 18 Stinger missiles into Nellis under the guise of a handicapped placard, launch those missiles at the veterans' flight, hoping to hit anything and everything, from a huge C-5 full of American heroes, to one of the B-52s or a Thunderbird or one of the Blue Angels or the Raptor or the F-35. Eighteen missiles, all fired at once, into such a crowded sky? They were going to hit something—and probably something very big.

And *this* was the most sinister aspect of the terrorists' plan. Low-flying, slow-moving aircraft hit by ground missiles tended to crash immediately—that was a given. But what was worse, they frequently cartwheeled when they hit the ground, this due to factors that had to do with forward airspeed, suddenly interrupted. One fighter alone crashing into this crowd could kill hundreds, if not thousands. If one of the big bombers or even the C-5 was hit and went down anywhere in the throng, the death toll could be in the tens of thousands.

And even in these eternal seconds, with Ryder trying to keep the CL-215 in the air just a few seconds longer, it all became very clear. It had been a typical Al Qaeda move. Do one thing, whether it be setting off car bombs in Europe or spreading germs in Israel or sending teams throughout the United States to shoot down individual American airliners, all to get U.S. intelligence agencies going one way, then do something bigger, deadlier, while you're going the other way. Distraction, disinformation, deflection. It almost worked at Hormuz. Now it was close to working again.

The first bus? Sure, if its crews had been able to shoot down a few American airliners, that would have been a big plus. But in reality Ryder knew now it had been a diversion all along, something to keep them busy and the people of the country on edge, not to mention quadrupling the intrigue in Washington, while all that time laying low with the second bus, planning to do this one big hit by killing thousands of unsuspecting Americans *and* shooting down the cream of the American military's air force. It was the Big Plan approach to terrorism, somehow explained by the scribble on a coffee-stained napkin. And it had gone off nearly flawlessly.

But Al Qaeda had not factored in one thing: the ghosts.

It was the interpretation of that coffee-stained napkin that had brought them here, at this moment, to this place, as the one last hope to avert disaster. There was no time to call the cops, no time to get the air police to converge on the Greyhound bus. It was up to them—and the 1,200 gallons of really bad stuff sloshing around in their holding tanks.

Their wild buzzing was not doing much to improve the condition of their engines; in fact, it was making them worse. But it was necessary. Typically cowardly, the terrorists had parked their vehicle in the midst of many; Ryder knew he'd have to buzz the area below at least a few times to get as many innocent people out of the way as possible.

It was Puglisi who'd come up with the idea of showing the Revolutionary War flag one more time. Jammed between the forward hatch and frame, it was flapping mightily now—this all in hopes that people on the ground would see it, recognize it, and know who they were, and then clear out as quickly as they could.

And this seemed to be happening below them now as Ryder pulled up from a very shallow dive right over the Greyhound to see military people down below hustling people out of the area.

But again this was a timing thing—and it appeared that time was finally running out for the ghosts.

The veterans' flight was now just a few seconds away from arriving over the base. Most of its aircraft were already within range of the Stinger missiles. Ryder could almost feel the disruption in the air around him as the collection of warplanes came in, this as he was pulling out of what had to be their last mock dive.

It was at that moment that they saw the top of the Greyhound bus disappear. It looked like it simply vanished—actually, the roof was cut in two, with each side on hinges, and these doors dropped away. Looking over his shoulder and climbing, Ryder could see the interior of the bus. A chill went through him. There were 18 mooks, some in soccer uniforms, some not, each with a Stinger missile on his shoulder.

Ryder turned the plane over on its wing. Bates was still in the copilot's seat. Fox and Puglisi were holding on for dear life behind them. The plane was in no position to fire the big fifties; most of their ammo was gone anyway.

"Those bastards!" Fox screamed now as he saw what was happening on the bus below. Ryder and Bates were turning the CL-215 as hard as they could, trying to muscle it into one last dive—but again, they were just a few seconds too late.

What happened next happened in slow motion, for Ryder, for all of them. As soon as Fox screamed, they saw six of the terrorists below fire their missiles. They weren't aiming the weapons exactly, just pointing them in the general direction of the veterans' flight, which was flying right over the main runway. In combat terms, it presented a target-rich environment if there ever was one. But at the instant that the team saw the first ignition flash for the first missile to be fired, Ryder hit the water release button on the CL-215's control panel. The problem was, he was still in the act of turning the firefighting plane, not diving as they had intended when this outlandish bombing mission was so hastily planned out.

These simultaneous actions meant that the first barrage of

six missiles actually flew *into* the cloud of combustible water the CL had dropped. Two of the missiles exploded on hitting the liquid; two more went right through it and exploded above. One missile corkscrewed away. The last one went through the rear of the CL plane—and kept on going.

The 1,200 gallons of liquid hit the bus a second later—but not before another handful of missiles were launched. It might have been the fiery exhaust from the missiles that ignited the fire, but whatever the spark, as soon as the load of gas-water hit the bus, it went up in a tremendous explosion. Red, orange, blue, even white flames soared into the sky, climbing into an instantaneous fireball that immediately sought to envelop the CL-215. Ryder saw nothing but fire coming up at them. They'd accomplished what they'd set out to do. But now the CL was about to be cooked. He screamed at Bates to get out of the copilot's seat, something the egghead did very quickly. The great wash of flame hit the plane head-on an instant later. It was like hitting a brick wall.

It was weird what happened next. The windshield evaporated, covering Ryder with a hot shower of broken glass. At the same moment, he started pulling like crazy on the steering column, trying to get them out of the aerial conflagration. And in that heartbeat, he looked over at the empty copilot's seat and it was as if an invisible set of hands was pulling up on that side of the column, too.

*Whose ghost could that be?* he thought crazily, frozen for a moment in time. Was it Gallant? Or "Dirt" Phelan, his wingman who'd died during the Hormuz attack? Or Woody, his old flying buddy who disappeared years ago, not far from here, up around Area 51? Or may be the Ruckers' long-lost son, whose medal Ryder was still carrying with him.

Or maybe he was just imagining the whole thing.

Whatever the case, somehow the CL-215 made it through the fireball. But as a result, it was now nearly covered in flames.

Behind them Ryder could see one of the Harriers had been hit by a Stinger. The pilot was in the process of bailing out, this after steering his jump jet away from the crowd and toward the open part of the main runway. Another missile clipped the S-2 Viking carrier bomber. Its crew was able to put some air under its wings, bringing it up to reasonable altitude. Again pointed away from the crowd, they, too, were in the process of ejecting.

Ryder turned the CL ship over the crowd now. That's when they saw another missile corkscrew its way into a hangar and detonate. Luckily, this was the same hangar that had lost electricity earlier in the day—and had remained unoccupied. Still another missile was on its way toward the Las Vegas Strip itself.

Somehow Ryder nursed the burning plane away from the crowd and now saw nothing but desert and runway ahead. But unlike the military planes around them, those inside the CL-215 didn't have the luxury of ejection seats or even parachutes. They were riding this one in.

The plane dipped so low, it nearly clipped an antenna forest near the Nellis control tower. Fire was working its way up both sides of the airplane. They knew that it was just a matter of time, seconds or less, before the flames would reach the dump buckets. True, they were empty, but just the fumes alone would be enough to obliterate the plane—and everything onboard.

It got to the point where Fox and Bates shook hands with Puglisi. Ryder looked over his shoulder and yelled, "What are you guys doing?"

"Saying good-bye," Fox shouted back darkly.

Ryder almost laughed. "No need to get so dramatic," he said. "Just hang on. . . ."

They were instantly above the runway. Ryder yanked the plane hard left, then hard right, bleeding off what little speed they had remaining. Then he pushed down on the controls; a second later, they hit the runway.

They bounced once, then twice. Ryder was yanking the controls back and forth, trying to get the plane to stop. But all he was doing was causing more sparks and making the fire in the back of the plane even worse.

It was like going through a car accident that lasted 15

long seconds, in ultraslow motion. The four of them were hurled all over the cabin, side windows smashing, metal twisting, the unmistakable screech of an airplane going through a crash.

But then finally, they stopped. About halfway down the runway, the plane's forward wheel just collapsed and they were all thrown forward, smashing against the control panel and the backs of the seats.

But this was where they finally got lucky. The aircraft was so badly damaged, the whole front end simply came off. The four ghosts literally fell out onto the runway. The fire still swirling around them; the others helped Bates, who fell to the tarmac the hardest, dragging him as far away from the burning wreckage as possible.

Ryder finally stopped them about a hundred and fifty feet away. They all looked at one another—their faces were black, their hands and uniforms burnt. But they were alive.

Then they looked back at the flaming wreck; it was going to go up any second. But then suddenly Puglisi jumped to his feet and ran right into the flames.

"What the fuck!" Fox screamed.

But Ryder knew what Puglisi was doing. The Delta soldier had gone back for Finch's flag.

It was dumb, but just as quickly as he was gone they saw him emerge from the flames, running in slow motion just like a movie. An instant later, the CL-215 blew up for good.

Puglisi landed in a heap at their feet, flag ripped and smoldering but, like them all, miraculously in one piece. That was when they looked up and saw a crowd of people and vehicles heading right for them.

"Well, last chapter, man," Ryder said, lying on his back looking up at the smoky Nevada sky.

"We greased them," Fox said with a cough. "The fucking nightmare is complete. They can send me back to Gitmo after this. I can use the peace and quiet."

But, it was not over. . . .

Amid the noise of the veterans flight aircraft, circling the base one more time before landing, the ghosts heard yet another sound. Two huge engines, higher in pitch, not jets, but not from a prop plane, either.

They looked above them to see a V-22 Osprey had appeared out of nowhere and was now hovering overhead. It was a strange craft, half-airplane, half-helicopter, with a wing that tilted, allowing it to land and take off vertically. And this was not one of the all-white experimental-looking V-22s that they were most used to seeing. This one was painted in sinister black and seemed to be bulging with exotic weaponry.

"Something tells me this isn't our ride home," Fox moaned.

Its wing tilted full up, the V-22 landed practically on top of them, and a large group of heavily armed men tumbled out. They were dressed head to toe in black combat suits and were wearing huge Fritz helmets, their faces hidden by opaque blast shields attached to those helmets. Their weapons only faintly resembled M16s; they were lousy with wires and cable attachments and even what appeared to be tiny satellite dishes poking out of the muzzles. Almost two dozen in all, these guys looked like they'd just walked in from a sci-fi movie.

At the same time this was happening, a convoy of base admin cars, Humvees, and ambulances also arrived at the CL-215 crash site. They were followed by four firefighting trucks that immediately began spraying flame-retardant foam everywhere, including all over the four ghosts. Suddenly it looked like it was snowing in the hot Nevada sun. Many civilian spectators were running towards the crash site as well.

The four foam-covered ghosts looked up at all these people with twin expressions of relief and confusion. "We should get paid for this," Fox cracked. "We're the hit of the entire show. . . ."

The armed men from the Osprey immediately sought to take command. Turning their guns on everyone from the base admin people to the firefighters and the civilians, they tried to surround the four ghosts, keeping everyone else away.

"You guys are coming with us!" one of them barked from behind his mask. "Those are the orders from Washington. . . ."

But at that moment, another base admin car arrived with a screech. It was Captain Audette. He'd seen what the ghosts had done back at the RV holding area; he was one of the few people involved who had any idea what had really happened.

"You're not taking these people anywhere!" he yelled at the black-suited gunmen. "They just saved a few thousand lives back there."

One of the men in black got in Audette's face.

"*We* are in charge here!" he insisted.

But instinct told Audette these guys from the Osprey were bad news. "By whose authority?" he demanded.

"Ever hear of General Rushton?" the man in black replied snidely. "We are under his orders to take these people with us."

Audette fired back, "Take them where?"

The man in black was suddenly stumped. He had no good answer for that.

Several hundred civilians had reached the site by this time. They were taking phone-photo images and videos of the bizarre scene, something that made the men from the Osprey very uncomfortable.

Meanwhile, many of the planes from the veterans' flight were still screaming overhead. The earsplitting whine of the C-5 especially made any kind of coherent dialogue impossible; the huge plane went right over, touching down on an auxiliary runway not far from the crash site.

All this time, the four ghosts just stayed where they were, on the ground, still stunned, listening to the two sides argue back and forth. And out on the periphery, one man in a black uniform and helmet stood apart, watching it all, his body language indicating some confusion. It was Captain Pershing Nash. And for what seemed to be the thousandth time in the past few days he muttered again, "What the hell am *I* doing here?"

The man from the Osprey who was doing most of the talking barked out an order above the scream of jet engines. His men started for the four ghosts on the ground. But then Audette yelled a similar order, and his men—air techs and Air Police mostly—closed in on the ghosts as well. A melee broke out as the two sides pushed each other around for about thirty seconds, this while the ghosts continued to watch it all with dark amusement.

"Who knew we were so popular?" Puglisi asked drily.

In the end it was the fact that so many civilians were on hand, with so many recording devices, that caused the men in black to back down. They'd been under strict orders not to be photographed, not to be seen at all, but that aspect of their mission to capture and eliminate the ghosts had gone over-board a long time ago. Audette was still pushing the lead man in black, asking him for papers, IDs, anything that would show he had more authority over the four ghosts than some-one actually based at Nellis.

Finally, Rushton's guy backed down. Their cover was al-ready blown, and he could see there was no way they could do anything with the four rogues, not with such a crowd around. But he was not going quietly.

He barked at Audette, "Well, what the hell are *you* going to do with them?"

Audette had to think a moment. He was just a public af-fairs guy. There were many other officers at Nellis who out-ranked him, and he didn't want to do the wrong thing, not with so many eyes watching him. So, he went by the book.

"I'm going to have them arrested," he pronounced sud-denly. "And put into protective custody."

This seemed to stun everyone, including the men in black.

"Arrested?" the lead gunman said. "For what?"

Audette looked at the four ghosts and then at their smol-dering airplane.

"Trespassing," he said. "And unlawful operation of a civil-ian aircraft above a military installation."

With that, Audette gave a signal to the Air Police. Four of them walked past Rushton's guys, got the rogues to their feet, and led them to one of their waiting Humvees.

As they were passing by, one of the men in black intentionally bumped into Bates.

"You haven't seen the last of us," the man growled.

# Chapter 24

It had not been a good 24 hours for General Rushton. Spooked by the near hit at the Oak House two nights before, he'd quintupled his force of Global Security bodyguards, both near his home and in his traveling entourage. But even his closest friends were indicating now that so many armed men surrounding him were becoming an embarrassment and, even worse, way too visible. Enough was enough. Even the President was taking notice, and *no one* wanted that.

This did little to help Rushton's demeanor. He was paranoid anyway and growing more so by the hour, afraid that he had bitten off more than he could ever chew. Grand plans, counterplans, deceptions, deceit—it was all becoming too much for him. In a strange way, he longed for the "old days" just a few months before, when he was simply the military whip on the NSC, cleaning up messes and barging into the President's office anytime he wanted.

Maybe it was all those trips to the Oval Office that had got to him. Maybe that whiff, so close to power, was what did it. But whatever the cause, he was in very deep now. Too deep to get out. Too deep to turn back. Too deep to do anything but complete the plan.

It was now almost 5:00 P.M. He'd been holed up in his secret office near the top floor of the EOB ever since the assassination attempt. He'd gone to the Oak House club that night to sign up more allies in his plan, a necessary trip, he had believed. But as it turned out, most of the members he'd wanted to speak to were not on hand, scared away that night by all the security Rushton was towing around with him.

This was not good. These people, the *real* power brokers in D.C., knew the score more than the President or anyone else at the top of the Washington political hierarchy. They knew that the rogue team had escaped from Gitmo and that these escapees were crazy and that once they had you in their sights you became crazy, too—whether you were an Al Qaeda operative or a Saudi Prince. Or an *uber*-ambitious general. While they still supported Rushton and his grand scheme—which they secretly referred to as the May 7 Plan—that support could slip away at any moment, should one more wrong move be made.

Which was just one reason Rushton was feeling so low. Things were looking shaky across-the-board. He knew about the events in West Texas, at Stinky Valley, and now at Nellis. He knew that his hit squad had arrived too late to do anything but watch the rogues be carted away by the Air Force. How he wished he'd just killed them all after he rounded them up in the Philippines. They were ghosts all right, and they'd been haunting him ever since he'd first become aware of their existence. And now they were after him—or at least someone was. *That* was the feeling that had got under his skin.

So here he was, just short of arming himself, waiting for the minutes to tick away before the Big Event—the *really* big event—was to happen. The anticipation was killing him. That's why when the telephone on his desk started ringing he nearly flew out of his chair and took cover on the floor. The damn ring was so loud! And as he'd been using mostly cell phones lately, it had been a while since he'd heard this landline come to life.

He recovered somewhat and checked the caller ID. The call was coming from the phone on the secretary's desk right outside his office door.

Rushton hesitated a moment, wondering what new hell this might be. Finally, though, he picked it up only because he wanted the ringing to stop.

"What is it?" he snapped into the phone.

"There's a young lady out here who insists on seeing you," a voice answered. It was one of his bodyguards.

"Who is she?" Rushton wanted to know. "How did she get in?"

"She won't give us her name," the bodyguard said. "But she is showing us an ID badge—security level eight."

Rushton thought a moment. That was the highest security classification he knew of, at least when it came to agencies and departments working with the NSC.

"Well, who is she with?" he asked. "Who does she work for?"

"The DSA," was the reply.

Li walked into the office a few seconds later. She'd been rudely frisked, twice, but that made no difference. She'd left her firearm at home.

She was carrying only her laptop and had dressed in her most attractive business suit, hoping for once her looks would work for her.

Even in his state, Rushton's eyes went wide when he first saw her. He tried to turn on the charm, bowing slightly and shaking her hand. That was his first mistake.

"I don't seem to recall ever meeting you before," he began. "Miss . . . ?"

"Mary Li Cho," she replied, showing him her DSA badge.

He studied it for a moment. "I didn't think there was anyone left down at DSA," he said cautiously, indicating that she should have a seat.

But Li remained standing.

"I'm the last one, at least here in D.C., sir," she replied.

Rushton sat on the edge of his desk. He was taken with her—anyone would be. But any mention of the DSA made him understandably nervous.

"I'm a bit busy," he said. "And these are strange times, as

I'm sure you know. But you were able to get in, past my little army out there, so I assume this must be important. Especially on the Fourth of July."

"It *is* important, General," she told him. "I've uncovered information on the people who are trying to kill you."

Rushton's face dropped a mile. He was stunned, but just for a moment. He recovered quickly and asked, "And how did you do that?"

Li lifted her laptop cover. "It was all on here," she replied. "My job at DSA was traffic coordinator. I saw everything going in and out. I still do, though I've been working at home. I began receiving some very strange e-mails lately. It took me a while to sort them out—but I believe now that I have. And frankly, I'm very disturbed by what I've seen."

Rushton still couldn't take his eyes off her.

"Well, please, then," he said, "show me. . . ."

Li set up her laptop and immediately opened both the "Fast Ball" and "Slow Curve" files. Rushton was shocked upon seeing them. Of course, he was familiar with the information contained in both, but he didn't let her know that. Where the files came from he had no idea. But in a way, he was impressed that she had this sort of bombshell information in her possession.

But there was more. She showed him a file that was almost a minute-by-minute, blow-by-blow account of the ghosts' activities since the day they'd escaped from Cuba: Their landing at Cape Lonely, their sneaking into her house. The split team heading out west to track down the first bus terrorists, the east side crew chasing Ramosa and finally Rushton himself. She told him everything about the night he was almost shot at the Oak House, plus how the west side team knew about Denver, the bus on the Texas highway, and the second bus at the air show.

She gave him names, times, dates, locations. She made clear the connection between Fox and Ozzi and the rest of the team. She essentially told him everything she knew about the rogues—and that was a lot.

Rushton collapsed into his seat after he heard it all. All this running around, with bodyguards, armored limos, his family in the line of fire—and here, before him, in the figure of this beautiful Asian-American girl were all the answers he'd been seeking.

"So you were pretending to be in thick with them?" he asked her. "Gathering information on them all this time?"

She nodded. "That was my job," she said. "That's what I'm paid to do."

Rushton was impressed. "And do you know the location of these assassins?"

"I do," Li replied.

"And you can lead me to them?"

"I can," she answered without hesitation.

Rushton reached for the phone, intent on calling his security detail on the other side of the door. But Li suddenly put her hand on his and stopped him.

"You don't want to do that, General," she said. "Because I have one more file to show you. Something else I intercepted."

She finally sat down and drew her chair closer to him. "Is it wise to be talking here?" she asked him.

Rushton thought a moment and then replied, "Yes—I think so."

Li took a deep breath. "All this goes back to when these people escaped from Guantánamo, do you agree?"

Rushton nodded blankly.

"And I believe it's still a mystery just how they were able to pull it off," she went on. "I mean, it was quite an escape—but obviously they must have had inside help."

"Again, I agree," Rushton said.

She displayed another file on her laptop. "I couldn't get much information on who might have helped them switch themselves for the Iranian prisoners," she told him boldly. "Even my former colleagues were tight-lipped about that. But I did come up with something very interesting concerning the airplane that carried them out."

Rushton's brow furrowed deeply. "The airplane?" he asked. "It came from Iran. It was being piloted by people from the Iranian military. I know that for a fact."

Li nodded and smiled, just a bit.

"This is true," she said. "But I was able to trace it back even further than that."

Rushton shook his head. He wasn't following her.

"Did you know that the airplane in question was actually *leased* to the Iranian military?" she asked him.

Rushton thought a moment and shrugged. "Not an unusual situation," he replied. "Many governments around the world lease aircraft for their military. It's cheaper that way. Even our own Air Force is leasing tanker planes from Boeing. Or at least they're trying to."

"Exactly," Li said. "But I found out just who the Iranians leased this particular airplane from."

She began banging on the laptop again. As Rushton watched intently, she displayed a list of company and corporation names. There were many addresses, contact numbers, and so on, all of them related in some way to the Iranian Transall cargo plane.

Finally she got to the bottom of the list—to the name of the real entity that had leased the plane to the Iranians.

She turned the laptop screen around so Rushton could see it.

It read: "Global Security, Inc."

The same people who'd been serving as his bodyguards for the past month. The same people who were just outside his door.

Rushton froze solid, his face draining of color as he weighed the implications of this.

"My God," he breathed. "Are you sure?"

Li nodded slowly. "It's my job to be . . ." she replied. "I'll stake my life on it. They never mentioned this to you, I assume?"

Rushton numbly shook his head no. He'd gone completely pale. Li said: "General, if they supplied the plane and never told you, I don't think it's too great a leap to assume they were somehow connected to the rogue team's escape. *And,* that there are probably many other things they're not telling you."

In a weird kind of way, it made sense to Rushton. All this security, yet someone gets close enough to almost take a shot at him. All his attempts to stop the rogues, yet they'd beaten him to the punch every time. He remembered that old, worn-out phrase: Just because you're paranoid doesn't mean that they're not out to get you.

Suddenly it seemed meant just for him.

He began to say something, but Li stopped him by pressing her finger against his lips.

She leaned in to him and whispered, "General . . . we've got to get you out of here . . . *now.*"

The door to Rushton's secret office opened a minute later.

The six bodyguards in the outer hallway snapped to— sort of. Most times they saw Rushton only for the time it took to escort him from the office door to the open elevator, where he would disappear, usually in the care of his aides or plainclothes Secret Service men, or their fellow bodyguards.

This time was different. The woman who had gone in to see him a few minutes before now came out with him—on his arm.

Rushton looked weird, or weirder than usual. He was smiling broadly, though his face was very pale. He was carrying his own laptop, too, a first. The woman, however, looked as gorgeous as she did when she first went in.

"Leaving just for a few," the general told them, giving no indication that he wanted them to form a phalanx around him as they had so many times in the past week. "Be right back. . . ."

But the head bodyguard stopped him.

"General?" he said sternly. "If you have no other protection, we *have* to go with you, at least two of us. That's what it says in the contract. . . ."

Rushton looked at the man for a very long time, then glanced at Li.

"Do you really think I need any more protection than this?" he asked with a wink.

The security man did not smile. But it made no difference. The elevator had arrived by this time. Rushton and Li quickly stepped inside it and were gone.

The bodyguard called down to the lobby to pass the word to his men down there that Rushton was on the move.

But the general never reached the lobby. Instead he and Li got off at the second floor and took the stairs down to the basement. A side door led them out to Pennsylvania Avenue. Li's car was parked nearby.

As soon as he walked out into the waning light, Rushton became distraught. He felt very exposed after so long being surrounded by bodyguards. People on the street who recognized him stopped and pointed at him. He tried to turn around and go back, but Li calmed him down, assuring him this was the right thing to do, that he was finally in good hands. At last, they reached her car.

She let him in, locking the door behind him, then went around to the driver's side and got in herself. She turned the key and the Toyota's engine roared to life.

"Where to now?" he asked her, nearly in tears.

Li just looked at him and smiled. "Do you like haunted houses, General?"

Rushton didn't know what to say. That's when he felt a tap on his shoulder. He turned around to see a fist coming right at him.

"Hi, General," Ozzi said, delivering a crushing blow to Rushton's nose. "Remember me?"

When Rushton woke up again, he really did believe he was in a haunted house.

Through barely slits in his eyes he could see he was in a room that was full of cobwebs and covered with dust, with weird light pouring through dirty cracked windows. Even in his first few seconds of hazy consciousness he could hear the old house creaking, the wind running through its rafters, the moaning of spirits just one room away.

Then he heard the telltale sound of someone typing.

He finally opened his eyes fully to see the beautiful Asian woman sitting across the room, at a very messy desk that was covered with wires and cables and pieces of doughnuts. His hands and feet were tied with bedsheets. And on the walls all around him different-sized pictures of the same image, one that he'd seen just once before: the crude drawing of the Nellis attack as depicted on the coffee-stained napkin.

He also saw two dark figures staring down at him. One was the man who'd sucker-punched him in the car, knocking him cold until this moment. He was such a little man in stature, Rushton was almost embarrassed that such a blow from him would put him out. Next to him, covered in bandages, was a huge individual who looked like he ate young children for breakfast. And indeed Rushton slowly recognized both of them. They'd been part of the rogue unit he'd rounded up in the Philippines not two months ago.

And that's when he knew for sure that he'd been had. . . .

Rushton just couldn't believe it. All the planning, all the details attended to, the dreams of power and glory. All gone because, like many aspirants before him, he'd been stupid enough to fall for a story from a beautiful woman.

He reached up and felt blood all over his face, especially on his lips and nose. Then suddenly there was a boot on his stomach.

"You made this job easy for us, General," the large man was saying now. "We were running all over the city trying to find a way to pop you. Now, we can just do it here, all warm and cozy like. . . ."

Rushton could barely speak; he had no doubts these two would kill him, right here, in cold blood.

"You people are crazy, you know," he said suddenly, surprised the words came out of his mouth. "It's people like you that made me do what I did."

The boot felt heavier on his gut. "Save your breath, General. You're going to need it."

Meanwhile, Li was pounding nonstop on the computer—Rushton's computer. Tears were streaming down her cheeks.

"Dear God," she kept saying, over and over. "I just don't believe this. . . ."

It was all in there, everything Rushton had been up to in the last few months, weakly hidden by security walls that Li broke down routinely now. And it was bombshell information, something that could shake the U.S. government to its foundations.

But the strange thing was, it actually had little to do with Al Qaeda, Stinger missiles, or Greyhound buses.

It had *more* to do with Rushton's secret lunches and the traffic jams in Washington for the past week and why the Army was hiding in alleyways and jets were constantly flying overhead.

She read it all, then she got up and spat in Rushton's face.

"What kind of monster are you?" she hissed at him. "Are you just insane or power-hungry? Or both?"

Rushton was almost too dazed to talk.

"I don't know," he finally blurted out, as if all the air had suddenly gone out of him. "I just don't know. . . ."

Ozzi stared at her. He'd never seen her act like this before.

"What is it?" he asked. "We knew he was tied into this thing from the beginning. What else could it be?"

She just pointed to the laptop. "You'll have to read it yourself."

Ozzi and Hunn sat down at the old desk and did just that.

The story that emerged was indeed chilling. It was the last file—the one simply marked "May 1–7"—that proved to be the real smoking gun. It was the same file they'd found in Palm Tree's PDA surrounded by so many security walls, they couldn't bust into it. But here it was now. Notes, memos, letters, e-mails. All of it, in plain English.

Sure, Rushton had been in cahoots with the terrorists, as well as the French intelligence services. He was the one who'd arranged for the Stinger missiles to get into the hands of Al Qaeda; he was the one who'd cleared the way, with an assist from the DGSE, for them to be spirited into the United States via the port of LA without a security search. He'd made sure no one was looking for the Greyhound buses by scaring the hell out of the entire country with false reports about WMD bombs soon to explode somewhere in the United States. He was the one who denied that terrorists were roaming around the country, taking shots at airliners, and that a rogue team of special ops people was chasing after them, trying to prevent disaster.

He did all these things—but it wasn't for money or revenge or some other crazy reason. He did them as a diversion.

For a coup d'état . . .

An overthrow of the American government.

Once again, it was the oldest trick in the book. Get everyone looking in one direction, while you plan something in the other. Cause havoc inside the Beltway and out, then gather together the real power brokers in Washington and basically say to them: See what is happening? The people who attended his secret lunches, the people who smoked fat cigars at the Oak House. Convince them that America had changed way too much since 9/11—or that it hadn't changed enough. Whisper that typical politicians were too weak to deal with a changing world. Portray the President as a misguided intellectual boob. Stir the pot with a few select military commanders who had the same ideas and have them call their troops into the streets for a week, just enough until people in D.C. got used to seeing them—then strike! Tie up every key intersection in the district. Surround the White House and the Capitol with troops. Knock the networks off the air. Then seize power . . . and change the world.

Would it have worked? No way. Rushton's plan read like a bad movie script. But would America be weakened just by the attempt? In the minds of the people? Of the world? Of the financial markets?

*Absolutely.* . . .

"The May 1–7 Plan . . . *Seven Days in May,*" Ozzi said now after reading it through, putting the pieces together,

connecting the dots. A famous novel about a near coup back
in the 1960s. That's why the file was labeled as it was.

"Strictly an amateur," Hunn said now, putting some fresh
ammunition into the team's lone M16 clone. "But dangerous
nevertheless. . . ."

But then Ozzi stepped in.

"Wait a minute," he said. "Putting two into this guy, here,
like this, might not be the way to go. It will only make us
look like the villains once they catch up to us. And at that
point no one will believe any of this is true—no one who
wasn't involved in it, that is. Popping him here and dumping
his body in a ditch is too good for him and bad for us. Somehow we've got to expose this asshole for what he is. . . ."

"I agree," Li said, the blood running ice-cold in her veins
by now. "He's got to go. Just like Palm Tree and Ramosa.
But it has to be to our advantage."

Rushton spit back at them. "Look at this," he said. "A
Chink, a commie, and a moron, trying to put the world back
together again. It's exactly people like you who are ruining
this country. Can you honestly say you think the person in the
White House is capable of dealing with things today? Or
those idiots in Congress? We're on the same side here, in a
way. Power speaks. Power gets respect. . . ."

They let him talk, but they weren't really listening to him.
They were huddled in the corner, trying to think of a way to
prevent Rushton from becoming a martyr and thus encouraging others like him.

In the end it was Ozzi who came up with the perfect solution. No, they wouldn't pop Rushton here. They would do it
someplace that would at least lead people to suspect that the
facade he'd put forward—true-blue, family values type of
guy—was not the real Rushton at all. And once that happened, maybe other people with more juice than they had
would start looking into the whole thing. And maybe it
would get exposed that way.

Ozzi told the others his idea, and they agreed it was worth
a shot.

But they would have to work fast.

. . .

It was around 2:00 A.M. the next day when the Baltimore police got the call. There was an "undisclosed disturbance" at a brothel on the south side of town, a place that was once a playground for the rich and famous but had fallen into disrepair lately.

It was the second time in as many weeks the police had been called to the run-down cathouse. A body had been found there on the first call. Shot in the face, he was still lying in the morgue, unclaimed, listed as "John Doe/Filipino." That case was unsolved of course. No suspects. No motive. Just another skel, found dead in a room full of needles.

The responding unit found pretty much the same thing this night. A dead body. No ID. No motive. Found on the third floor in the same room as the last.

The scene was puzzling even for the seen-it-all cops of South Baltimore. They thought they recognized the dead man's face, but it had already puffed up and was leaking pus. He was stripped of all his clothes, found propped on the filthy bed in the corner of the filthy room. He had a needle still stuck in his arm, his hand still on the plunger.

But he did not look like an ordinary junkie. He was obviously well fed, overweight even, clean, no tracks on his arms, with manicured fingernails, even pedicured feet. They doubted this body would lie unclaimed in the morgue for very long.

No one at the cathouse recalled seeing the man arrive— none of the hired help remembered taking him on. Though this was standard operating procedure in cases of cathouse murders, the cops tended to believe the residents this time. They seemed legitimately shocked that the body was here in the first place.

The cops were also hip enough to know that this was probably a setup, that whoever arranged the scenario had done it to disgrace the victim—a simple homicide not being good enough for him.

The cause of death would eventually be determined as air

being injected into a major artery, causing a bubble to race and then burst in the victim's heart. Painful and not as quick as it might sound. With the dark humor of the police in a tough part of town, they'd almost appreciated the joke. Someone who wasn't really a junkie dying a junkie's death.

But there was one last puzzling piece. Something that didn't quite fit in, at least not yet.

Shortly before the body was discovered in the whore-house, a butcher shop nearby had reported a break-in with some of its goods stolen. That might have solved the how but not the why, for the guy was found dead with an animal in the bed with him.

A tiny pig.

# Chapter 25

Ryder had actually enjoyed his time in the holding cell at Nellis.

He'd spent most of the time playing cards, enjoying the food, and watching TV with the rest of the ghosts.

And he slept, for the first time in what seemed like years. He didn't dream, though. Not about his wife. Not about Li. He just slept, soundly, deeply.

They were incarcerated in name only. Actually, it was more like a stay at a hotel. The bed was soft; the service was great. They were treated like celebrities by the Air Police who were supposed to be guarding them.

And celebrities they were. By now everyone in the country knew who they were, knew what they had done. A large cavalcade of media had descended on Vegas in the last few days reporting on the thwarted attack at the base and hoping to get a shot of the ghosts. Many of these media types were camped right outside the main gate at Nellis, causing many more headaches for Captain Mark Audette than he'd ever dreamed were possible.

Many things had happened in the week they'd been locked up. General Rushton was dead, found in a whorehouse in Baltimore, a needle sticking out of his arm, a pig sitting on his lap. That certainly had Hunn and Ozzi written all over it. The three dozen terrorists who'd been set loose in the United States had all been accounted for and were all dead as well. Good riddance on that note. There was still a smoldering hole next to the flight line at Nellis, but that would soon be repaired as well.

Of course most of the story was still under wraps. Rushton's coup plans, the French government's involvement—all of it was unknown to the public, and to everyone except a handful of power people in D.C. whose business it was to keep such things secret forever, if possible. Rushton had died in a crackhouse brothel. He'd had problems. Pressure of work, and so on. Not the first Washington player to die a strange death and certainly not the last.

The country itself was breathing a little easier. The terrorist threat seemed to pass away with the Fourth of July fireworks. Not gone forever, but at least for a little while. The traffic around Washington returned to its usual slow pace, no more gridlock. No more troops in the streets. No more jets constantly flying overhead. Massive, if secret, court martials were already in the works though.

So it did seem the world was back on-track, again at least for a little while.

But the ghosts couldn't stay at Nellis forever, as much as they would have liked to. They weren't military personnel, not technically anyway, and as their incarceration was being played out and discussed and debated endlessly on the 24-hour news stations, it was becoming quite clear that they probably shouldn't have been in military custody in the first place. And while the four of them appreciated what the Air Force, especially Audette, had done for them, they also knew there were pressures inside and out to have some resolution to their case. Despite their heroics, they were guilty of many, many federal crimes. And while they were the darlings of what people were beginning to call the New Patriotism, even they knew they had to be held accountable for what they'd done. Besides, there were people in Washington who still wanted to exact some revenge on them.

Finally, on their sixth day at Nellis, they were told that

they had to go. But the military was doing them one last favor: Instead of turning them over to the Feds, they were actually handing them off to the city of Las Vegas, where they would be charged with one count each of illegally operating an aircraft, a civil offense. This would give them another breather, at least until reality set in and they were remanded to a federal court in D.C.

That's when the real trouble might begin.

Because of the media swarm encamped around the main gate at Nellis, it was agreed that the ghosts would be transported to the Las Vegas courthouse in a military vehicle, this as opposed to a car from the sheriff's department. A military vehicle would not have to stop to get out of the base, and this would leave the media types waiting there high and dry.

Ryder, Bates, Puglisi, and Fox, now wearing plain, unmarked flight suits, were picked up at their holding cell at 9:00 A.M. They thanked their jailers, up to and including the base commander, profusely apologizing again for tearing up his base. It was clear many people in the military supported them, though; many had already thanked the ghosts for what they had done. Just like those two A-10s they'd encountered over Milwaukee that day, so long ago. The pilots could have easily shot them down and ended all this—but they didn't, because they believed in what the ghosts were doing. It was good to know that many of the people in uniform were behind them all the way.

Leaving Nellis by the main gate went just as they had hoped. The base admin car simply drove off the base, not stopping, leaving the media in the dust.

The problem was, there was another army of reporters waiting at the courthouse, with a forest of satellite dishes accompanying them. Protocol said the military car would have to leave the ghosts at the rear of the courthouse, where they would be turned over to local law enforcement. Six sheriff's deputies were waiting for them here—but they would still have to walk about fifty feet to the rear door of the courthouse itself, and waiting there for them was a gauntlet of media. The four ghosts had agreed beforehand that the less they said publicly the better. But when they drove up and saw the crowd of press, they knew staying by that agreement would almost be impossible.

The deputies took custody of them, and after one last handshake with their military handlers the four of them began their weird perp walk across the parking lot to the back door of the courthouse. They were surrounded immediately by microphones and video cameras, wielded by beautiful newswomen mostly, with a few *GQ*-looking male reporters thrown in. The questions were all stupid and senseless and obvious. "Do you consider yourselves criminals?" "Do you consider yourselves heroes?" "Have you been offered any book deals?" "Movie deals?" "Endorsement deals?"

The deputies did their best, but they were vastly outnumbered. Before they made it halfway across the parking lot, the crush of media just collapsed in on them. More deputies arrived. Pushing and shoving ensued. But it was no use. They were trapped.

*This is how the Beatles must have felt,* Ryder thought, betraying his age.

Finally he just stopped. And everyone else stopped with him.

All cameras turned to him. The others were whispering to him, "If you're going to say something to get us out of here, make it quick."

That's exactly what Ryder intended to do.

Silence came over the courtyard. He looked out on at least a hundred cameras, twice as many microphones, the faces of the media types smiling and accommodating, expecting him to say something great but ready to pounce on him if he didn't.

Finally, he began to speak:

"We did what we did for all the people who died on 9/11," he began. "We did what we did for the families of those who lost loved ones that day. But we're not heroes—not in the way you people in the media might want us to be. We're just

Americans, trying to do what's right. Trying to protect our country."

A short pause. His audience was rapt.

"September Eleventh was an awful day," he began again. "No matter what's happened before or since, it's true, we will never be the same—not until we find every last person who was connected with those attacks and put them in the ground where they belong.

"But something very special also happened on 9/11—or at least I think it did. I heard someone say this once, and so I want to pass it on to you. We know the terrorists spent several years planning the attacks of September Eleventh. We know they got it down to the last-minute detail. The time and effort they put in, the sneaking around, the deceit, all to kill three thousand of our countrymen. Three years, twenty-four hours a day, planning to commit mass murder.

"But what *really* happened? Yes, those three thousand people died, especially in the towers—but *twenty thousand* people were *saved* that day. Twenty thousand people who *didn't* lose their lives . . . because of the bravery of the cops and the firemen and just ordinary people. Like you and me.

"And here's the thing: how much planning went into that? These murderers took three years to plan how to kill three thousand people—but we, we Americans, we saved twenty thousand of our countrymen, and it didn't take any planning at all. The people there just did it. It just happened. Because that's how we are in America.

"And that's why we're different from them."

Five minutes later, the four ghosts were led into the courtroom. It was packed, but not with media types—hardly. Ryder scanned the crowd and was surprised to see some very familiar faces, as well as some not so familiar. Some he would only learn later who they were.

Master Chief Finch and the Doughnut Boys were there. So were Bo Tuttle, his brother Zoomer and cousin Hep, from Campo, Kentucky. And Detective Mike Robinson from the

Chicago Police Department was there. And Donny Eliot, the park ranger from Nebraska. And Dave Hunn's uncle, the priest from Queens, and the NYC firemen Sean O'Flaherty, Mike Santoro and Mark Kelly.

The Ruckers were there, right in the front row. And the truckers who transported the team into the Rockies. And the guys from the company that owned the CL-215 firefighting plane. And the people who owned the seaplane refueling island in Minnesota. Even Captain Audette was in attendance.

They were all here because they *believed*. They had helped the ghosts along the way and now they had made their own way here to show their support, to watch over the ghosts, just as they felt the ghosts had been watching over them for the past few crazy weeks.

But most surprising of all, sitting in the back row was Hunn. And Ozzi.

And Li.

And when she saw Ryder, she blew him a kiss.

The show of support was heartwarming, but it didn't take away the fact that the four rogues were potentially in a lot of trouble.

The infractions that were to be discussed here today were petty compared to what they might be charged with once they were extradited to D.C. If they were found guilty back there, especially on national security violations, they could be locked up forever, in conditions not so different from what they had left back in Gitmo, public opinion be damned.

At that moment, as they were being seated at the defendants' table, Ryder could not shake the feeling that this was the end of the road for them. Their future was very much uncertain.

They all looked at one another, as much to say, *How are we going to get out this?*

Li was thinking the same thing.

They'd been able to slip out of D.C. cleanly to get out here—and even better, no one seemed to know who they were. But she knew that it could very well be her name on the docket next, along with Hunn and Ozzi. Murder? Conspiracy? Numerous violations of the National Secrets Act? They would have been better off leaving the country. But there was no way they were just going to let their comrades hang. Still, their future was uncertain, too.

Finally the court officer came out and asked everyone to rise. A side door opened and the judge walked in. And this was where Li got the biggest surprise of her life.

She recognized him. This day judge from Las Vegas, a place she'd never been before—she took one look at his face and realized that he looked very familiar.

He was a small man, about sixty-three or so. An unimpressive face, with a red nose and huge ears. He seemed almost unsure of himself, his judge's robes appearing to be too big for him by a factor of two.

But that face—it was unforgettable.

He was the little man who'd walked out onto the court of the Wizards basketball game that night so long ago to help the two kids revive their singing of "America the Beautiful." The man who had brought the entire arena to the brink of tears.

But what was he doing here?

The little man took his seat up on the bench and fiddled with his glasses. Meanwhile the court officer called the proceedings to order by saying that the regular day judge, the Honorable J. C. Hood, was on vacation this week and that a substitute jurist would be handling the cases today.

This substitute judge was the Honorable Bobby Murphy.

For information on receiving a
free SUPERHAWKS bumper sticker, log on to:

WWW.SUPERHAWKS.NET

*While supplies last*